GRAPES OF CANAAN:

HAWAII 1820

'Tis not the grapes of Canaan that repay
But the high faith that failed not by the way.

James Russell Lowell
in *Commemoration Ode*

Grapes of Canaan:

HAWAII 1820

ALBERTINE LOOMIS

HAWAIIAN MISSION CHILDREN'S SOCIETY
Honolulu, Hawaii

Cover Design by Pegge Hopper

Published by the Hawaiian Mission Children's Society.
First printing 1966, second printing 1967, third printing 1969,
fourth printing 1972, fifth printing 1979, sixth printing 1984.

Dodd, Mead & Company edition published 1951.

To Betty,
Elisha's Great-Great-Granddaughter

THE BEST DOCUMENTARY NOVEL OF EARLY HAWAII

The First Company of New England missionaries arrived in the Hawaiian Islands in the spring of 1820 to begin their labors in this vineyard of the Lord. Fortunately, the Polynesian people were ready for new beliefs after the death of the conqueror, Kamehameha I, and a revolution that had overthrown the old idols and the old tabus. Still, the work of the American preachers and teachers was far from easy. The dramatic mission story, told before, will be told again. In GRAPES OF CANAAN: HAWAII 1820, it is told by a talented novelist who is also a descendant of one of these missionary families.

On the brig *Thaddeus,* among other members of that history-making group, were a twenty-year-old New Yorker named Elisha Loomis and his bride, Maria. Below decks were a small, second-hand Ramage hand printing press and a few cases of type. This equipment was to serve faithfully in the conversion of these Pacific pagans to the Christian faith, as well as in the education of a generation of inhabitants of the future Fiftieth State. Elisha Loomis, youngest of the First Company, will always be remembered as the first printer to set up shop between the Rocky Mountains and Asia.

Albertine Loomis, great-granddaughter of this Loomis couple, has written the best documentary novel of early Hawaii. This book, GRAPES OF CANAAN: HAWAII 1820, is now happily available in an edition within reach of anyone who wants to know the fascinating and dramatic true story of the earliest missionaries in Hawaii Nei.

The documentary novel is a form practiced by such authors as Irving Stone and Catherine Drinker Bowen. It must stick close to history—and a search through my well-thumbed copy of the first edition of Miss Loomis's book has turned up almost no deviations from what scholarly historians have concluded about this period. The documentary novelist, however, has two advantages over the documentary historian. This storyteller is free to convert into conversation various events and narratives which originally appeared without quotation marks. Again, inferences may reasonably be drawn and deep motives be portrayed and represented without the hedging and footnoting of the scholarly chronicler. The result is a charming narrative which may be read with delight and remembered with profit.

The original intention of Miss Loomis, when her exhaustive research had been completed, was to write the usual novel, inventing incidents and characters to fill out the story and cast. But as she once told me, she discovered that no fictionist could dream up a story more thrilling than the bare truth of the events of those pioneer years of the Hawaiian mission. Nor could he create characters more striking than people like Hiram Bingham and Queen Kaahumanu, or American sea captains more contrasting in personality than "Mad Jack" Percival of the schooner *Dolphin* and Captain Thomas ap Catesby Jones of the sloop *Peacock,* called by the Hawaiians the "kind-eyed chief." Her decision to give a week-to-week narrative that would be authentic but which would read like a novel was wise and the outcome successful, as the many earlier readers of her book will testify.

Other fine novelists have written about the Hawaii of former days. Most prominent among these, of course, is James A. Michener. As the writer of a bio-critical volume on Michener, I can repeat that his giant book *Hawaii* is not history, nor even historical fiction under the usual definition. Mr. Michener told me when he was writing *Hawaii* that he had no intention of including the First Company or any other actual figures, because he wished to be free to tell his story without the trammels of dates and depositions. It is fiction. Indeed, the first words in *Hawaii* are: "This is a novel. It is true to the spirit and history of Hawaii, but the characters, the families, the institutions, and most of the events are imaginary."

This new edition of the documentary novel by Albertine Loomis is strongly recommended, especially to those who, through one or another avenue, have been led to a deeper interest in the true story of Hawaii's first missionary years.

The genesis of GRAPES OF CANAAN: HAWAII 1820 is more romantic than that of most novels. Some years ago, a teacher of literature and creative writing in Detroit inherited a little red trunk that had twice traveled around Cape Horn. In it Albertine Loomis found the journals of her great-grandparents, missionary pioneers in far Hawaii. Through half the night she sat on the floor, avidly reading the trunk's contents, and before morning knew that she must write a book about these adventurous ancestors.

After virtually learning by heart these journals (which unfortunately are still unpublished), Miss Loomis began a long search to illuminate their casual or cryptic references to fellow missionaries, ship captains, traders, American relatives, Hawaiian chiefs, and customs and events in the Hawaii of the 1820's.

.. Her quest took her to many libraries in New York and New England. She spent two chilly days in the Houghton Library of Harvard University, where a friendly librarian sacrificed a New Year's vacation to make the archives available to the visitor. What had been at first a tale of mission endeavor branched out into accounts of adventures in fur trade, the sandalwood-gathering boom, the whaling days, and the fight by a weak Polynesian kingdom to maintain its independence from island-grabbing great powers. In an alcove in the Library of Congress in Washington, D. C., she was thrilled to peruse the hand-written transcript of the inquiry into the conduct of Lieutenant John Percival, captain of the first American vessel of war to enter Hawaiian waters, and his amorous crew.

Finally came the first summer Miss Loomis was able to spend in Hawaii. She sighted the coast glimpsed by the people of the *Thaddeus* in 1820 and viewed the regions where her great-grandparents had dwelt. Much of her material, in fact, was obtained at the Hawaiian Mission Children's Society Library on King Street in Honolulu, in the very complex, still open to visitors, where Elisha Loomis set up his printing office and struck off in battered type in the Hawaiian Language the damp pages of the first books that were to guide the people of a Stone Age kingdom toward membership in the sisterhood of American states.

This research, transmuted by Albertine Loomis's imagination and craft, became the novel now in your hands.

A. GROVE DAY
Senior Professor of English
University of Hawaii

ACKNOWLEDGMENTS

The journals and letters of Elisha and Maria Loomis, treasured in my own family, are the main sources of the story told in *Grapes of Canaan*. To explain and amplify what my great-grandparents recorded between 1819 and 1827 I have read numerous other unpublished documents as well as books and pamphlets long out of print. The quest for this material has taken me to several libraries and historical collections and has indebted me to many persons.

My greatest obligation is to the Hawaiian Mission Children's Society for access to the journals of other members of the first mission company and the rich store of related materials in its Honolulu library.

To the American Board of Commissioners for Foreign Missions I owe the opportunity to read the letters of application and recommendation submitted by the men of the pioneer band and to examine other correspondence for the years 1817–1827.

In the Houghton Library at Harvard University the Josiah Marshall and James Hunnewell papers were opened to me, and in the Baker Library at the Harvard Graduate School of Business Administration the letter-books of Bryant & Sturgis.

The National Archives in Washington, D.C., made available the complete record of the Navy's Court of Inquiry in the case of Lieutenant John Percival. The Spaulding Collection at the University of Michigan provided copies of State Department documents covering the visit to Honolulu of Lieutenant Thomas ap Catesby Jones.

I have received courteous and expert assistance from the Essex Institute of Salem, Massachusetts; the Massachusetts Historical

ACKNOWLEDGMENTS

Society; the Newberry Library of Chicago, Illinois; and the public libraries of Utica and Canandaigua, New York; Pittsfield and Boston, Massachusetts; and Detroit, Michigan.

To all these institutions and their librarians and curators I am heartily grateful. I should like especially to thank Miss Bernice Judd of the Hawaiian Mission Children's Society, whose enthusiasm and resourcefulness knew no bounds, and Miss Carolyn Jakeman of the Houghton Library, who revised her own schedule to accommodate me during a short stay in Cambridge.

I am indebted to the late Dr. W. D. Westervelt for discovering and preserving one volume of Elisha's journal, which apparently was left behind when the Loomises departed from the Islands, and to Miss Ethel Damon of Honolulu for a mimeographed copy of this material. Thanks are due also to Robert Moody of Rushville, New York, for help in reconstructing Elisha's early years and to Mrs. J. Melville Brown of Winnetka, Illinois, for books and reminiscences about her great-grandfather, Hiram Bingham.

Albertine Loomis

Detroit, Michigan
December 1950

CONTENTS

CONTENTS

GRAPES OF CANAAN:

HAWAII 1820

PRELUDE

"A LAND that was found in the ocean" the first voyagers called it, coming upon it from the windward after two thousand miles of arduous travel, "a land . . . that was thrown up from the sea, from the very depths . . ."

And so it was. Volcanoes, bursting through the ocean-floor, had thrust black, jagged peaks above the waters. Rain had etched the valleys and filled them with dancing streams and, from the crumbling rock, had made a soil that nourished great forests.

Then the hardy brown men came from the south, from Tahiti, in their stout canoes and took ashore their gods, their women, their animals, their seeds, their wooden bowls and stone adzes. They named the new land Hawaii—after that fabled and shadowy West, home of their sacred ancestors.

Here in the clustered islands, where there was food enough for all, they lived as brothers. But afterward another horde came from the south; and among these were proud chieftains who could trace their line through twenty generations to Wakea and Papa, as well as humble men who never had heard the names of their forebears. From that day Hawaii knew high and low, feasting and hunger, fawning and treachery, hauteur and cringing—and wars of conquest and rebellion. Chiefs, gaining power, called themselves kings. Courts grew splendid; courtiers indolent and merry. Priests used their arts—tabus, curses, sorcery, human sacrifice—to exalt the nobles and keep the commoners meek and diligent. In the end, the portly chief in his red-and-yellow feather mantle looked so unlike the lean farmer toiling naked in his back-country *taro* patch that some thought him of a different stock, with other ancestors.

Chief fought chief until each island had its king, its *moi*. Then the *moi* of the Big Island, Hawaii, sailed against the islands of Maui and Molokai and Oahu; and blood flowed freely as the young warrior made himself master of all save the most northerly realms. A Pacific Napoleon, white men called him when they heard of his conquests. His name was Kamehameha.

In Kamehameha's day all the land was the king's. To those chiefs who had served him well in war and peace he gave some of it—not forever, but for as long as he lived and found them loyal. Such a holding might be a small island or a series of separate plots. Oftenest it was a fine, fertile valley, widening from a point in the mountains to a broad sweep of beach. Within a great chief's holding were the lands of the petty chiefs; within those lands the *moos,* or fields; within a *moo* the garden patches called *paukus;* and within a *pauku* the tiny *kuleanas* of the commoners. But whatever the size or location of his land, each tenant held it at the will or whim of those above him, and on condition of obedience—and taxes.

Yearly, at tax-time, the overseer of a district called for hogs, dogs, fish nets, canoes, feather clusters, barkcloth, mats, calabashes, cocoanuts and *awa* in whatever amount he thought the king's collector would demand. And what an uproar there was at the place of deposit if the offering was not enough! Meanwhile the king might levy a head tax or a high chief come visiting and call for the fat of the land. Always it was fitting for a fisherman to make presents to his lord from the earliest catch of the season and for a farmer to give the first fruits of his soil. And there was the "Friday" tax; one day each week the peasant tilled the *koele,* a field from which the whole crop was the chief's. Still, if a commoner were thrifty and humble, not wasting what he had nor causing envy by making a show of it, he got along well enough—until the white men came clamoring for the avails of his labor.

The first white man had arrived in a tall, winged ship and seemed a very god. The Hawaiians fed and honored him, eagerly took his iron and offered him their women. But when Captain Cook intervened in a skirmish between his men and their hosts, the Hawaiians struck him down; and his ship, sailing home to England, bore news of his death as well as his discovery.

Afterward many sorts of white men came to Hawaii. They came for provisioning and for escape. They fought for the king, connived at rebellion and sought concessions for far-off business houses; built fortunes, became royal favorites, espoused chiefesses and reared half-caste families; drank, gambled, brawled, rioted, deserted their ships, dallied with brown girls and sired unnumbered "orphans."

Some came only to explore; some to live out their days in Hawaii. But most of them were fur traders, stocking their vessels for tedious months along the Northwest Coast or for the long voyage to China. In "Owhyhee" (so they wrote it in their ships' logs) provisions could be had for a song—"a good hog & two or three barrels of vegetables" for a small piece of iron hoop; six dunghill fowls for "an Iron Chizzle." And when iron hoops and chisels no longer sufficed, the traders broke out rum and wine from their stores or broadcloth and linen or beaver hats and writing desks.

The Island chiefs grew shrewd as the game of commerce went forward. They learned to take more from the farmers and fishermen, to ask more from the eagerly competing foreigners. In time, they refused to bargain for any but the biggest, showiest—and often the deadliest—items the white man could bring: muskets and ammunition, brass fieldpieces or battery guns from ships' decks—and sometimes the ships themselves. In exchange for these, the chiefs had found in their sandalwood forests a product for which the white traders would mortgage their souls, and the gaunt commoner was hounded into the hills to cut, strip and haul the fragrant timber.

Eventually Kamehameha drew all the trade into his own powerful hands. The chiefs could sell only through him; the white men could buy only through him. He adorned his palaces, crammed his storehouses, glutted his treasury with bright Spanish dollars and filled his harbors with foreign-built vessels.

By 1820, then, the Islands were used to white men. But they had not known any like those who came that year in the brig *Thaddeus*. For here were no Yankee traders, no agents from the business houses of Boston, but missionaries—seven men, their wives and children—sent by the American Board of Commissioners for Foreign Missions; fitted out by the gifts of artisans, farmers and shopkeepers; sped by the hopes and prayers of Americans who took their scripture literally: "Go ye into all the world and preach—"

Here were pioneers who came, not to escape a life grown irksome through poverty or persecution, but to transplant a life they had found good. "You are to aim at nothing short of covering those Islands with fruitful fields and pleasant dwellings, and schools and churches," they were charged as they left their native shores, "raising up the whole people . . . a nation to be enlightened and renovated and added to the civilized world . . ."

They brought their damask tablecloths, their long-tailed coats and smartly-cut calicoes, their Bibles and their baptismal fonts, their plows, augers, seeds, medicines—and a printing press.

The press was a secondhand Ramage, built before 1800, with frame of Honduras mahogany and bed and platen of iron. Stout, though small and light for its day, it had already seen much service. But in 1820 the press was not yet worn out. Urged by the long handle, its platen would still make thousands of trips up and down, pressing moist paper hard against inked type, striking off alphabets and spelling books, hymnals, catechisms and scripture tracts full of such strange words as *akua* and *kanaka* and *lani*. In time the screw would loosen and crack, and the American Board would have to replace the gallant little Ramage with a newer instrument.

The printer was probably younger than the press. A farm boy from western New York, he was as full of hesitation and impatience, doubt and assurance, solemnity and nonsense, soul-searching and hero-worship, aches and hungers and gropings as any twenty-year-old. For a long time, since he could not preach and had never kept school, he would be chiefly the Mission's zealous errand boy.

4

But there would come a time when the printing was paramount, when the clamor for books drowned the songs of the dancers, the shouts of the surf-riders and the threats of the sandalwood master. Then the printer would scarcely eat or sleep till an edition was worked off and he could distribute his scanty type and begin anew. And in seven years he, like his press, would wear out.

In those seven years, while the sandalwood business ebbed and Pacific whaling began its great half-century, there were in Hawaii changes so swift that it is hard to match them in history. In those seven years the chiefs turned from idle roving, intemperance and arrogance to sobriety, humility and self-restraint, abandoning tyranny and caprice for responsibility and law. In those seven years commoners, emerging from superstition and cloudy fear, glimpsed the way to earthly dignity and heavenly bliss—through the spelling-book. But between the Americans who came to trade and the Americans who came to teach, those seven years bred a bitterness that outlasted their generation.

This is the story of those first years in the life of the Mission—of Hiram Bingham, leader of the company; of Daniel Chamberlain, Massachusetts farmer and father of five; of Asa Thurston, Samuel Ruggles, and Samuel Whitney, who manned the outlying stations; of the women who shared their husbands' work; of the doctor who turned back; of the reinforcements that came; of the native boys, schooled in New England, who returned to their own people. And it is the story of Elisha Loomis, youngest of that pioneer company, who with his secondhand press and a few fonts of battered type made the first of the books that set a people free.

1820

THE PRINTER AND THE PREACHER

ELISHA heard the thud of running feet on the deck and a shrill Hawaiian voice crying, "Land ho!"

He sat up quickly and reached for his boots. Maria beside him began twisting into garments left ready to hand. Across the shadowy cabin others were turning out. For 158 days they had awaited this moment.

The quarter-deck was bright with moonlight. Under full sail the *Thaddeus* ran before the breeze. As they came from below, the Americans, feeling the hushed mood of the night, spoke quietly. But the native boys chattered, embraced, rubbed noses. They pointed to the western sky and said over and over, "Mauna Kea! Hawaii! Hawaii!"

High over the island of Hawaii a snow-crowned peak gleamed wan and rosy above the clouds, like a sign set in the heavens. Elisha groped for words befitting the moment and found only the homely ones he had used all his life.

Trudging home from a squirrel hunt, leaping the creek and scrambling through the pasture bars, tired to death and famished, thinking of his mother's good stew and dumplings—"Well, we're almost there."

Rattling back from town in the empty wagon, down the long hill by Doc Harkness', over the bridge at John Hobert's, past the tavern and the log schoolhouse, when at last the kitchen lights winked through the trees—"Well, we're almost there."

Now, seeing the dark land loom beneath Mauna Kea's crown, he said, "We're almost there."

9

In the moonlight his hair was as pale as sun-bleached stubble. The breeze ruffled it and made him look more boyish than his twenty years. You could see why the agents of the American Board had not been quite sure Elisha Loomis was the man to establish their mission press.

Of only middling height, he could still look down on Maria's straw bonnet, for she was a tiny person, with slender wrists and ankles, narrow shoulders and a small piquant face. But under her shawl she was big with the child that would be born in July.

"Yes," Maria said. "We're almost there."

It was March the thirtieth. Back in New York State, among the Finger Lakes where Elisha had grown up, that meant springtime— the last snow patches melting from the ravines, the hub-deep mud receding in the wagon track and the school term ending so the boys could get to work on the land.

At J. D. Bemis' printing office in Canandaigua it meant almanacs arriving for a year already a quarter spent, school books (blue-backed Websters and olive-drab "arithmeticks"), richly bound sets of Pope or Dryden or Milton, books of sermons, tales of South Sea voyages. All down the Western Turnpike from Utica to the end of the route at Bemis', the book man jogged each spring, dispensing his wares. Four times Elisha had been there to help him unload. Would the old fellow miss him this spring, ask after him maybe? "Where's that tow-headed, peaked-looking 'prentice gone, J.D.?" Or had they already forgotten him at Bemis'?

Elisha had been barely sixteen when, in company with his father, he had come up from Federal Hollow in Middlesex Township to be bound for five years to Mr. Bemis and learn the trade. At first he was only the "devil." As the greenest 'prentice he must fetch and carry, bear abuse and mockery from his more experienced fellows and tend store at the least convenient hours. But he was content. "Dancing, playing at cards, and the like," he wrote to a cousin at Geneva, "have lost their magic claims upon me. I have given them entirely up, except now and then to exercise myself a little. But to retire with a useful and entertaining book—"

At Bemis' there were shelves of books, elegantly done up with gilt lettering and marbled end papers; and when the long day's work was over, a 'prentice might take one down, if his hands were carefully scrubbed, and lose himself in Campbell's *Voyages,* Ferguson's *Astronomy,* Morse's *Universal Geography* or the majestic *Paradise Lost.*

In the spring of 1819, after more than three years at Bemis', Elisha first heard about the Sandwich Island Mission. Unwrapping new publications from the East, he came upon the *Memoirs of Henry Obookiah.* And when he had read about the boy who ran away from pagan Hawaii, wept from loneliness on the steps of a building at Yale, was tutored and converted and prepared to preach to his own people in the far-off islands, then died of typhus before he could return—when Elisha had read all this, he could not rest until he had gained Mr. Bemis' consent to offer himself as the Mission's printer.

Two months later, on a day in June, he arrived by stage at Cornwall in the Connecticut hills. His master had released him, though his articles had still a year and a half to run; and the American Board, without fully committing itself as to Hawaii, had directed him to join its Foreign Mission School.

There, in the long, gray clapboard building fronting the green, Elisha came to know the Sandwich Islanders Thomas Hopu, William Kanui, John Honolii and George P. (for prince) Tamoree, whose father, it was said, was king of something-or-other. There he explored natural philosophy and Calvinist theology, and worked in the school's farm plot, raising corn and potatoes and beans for the boarders. From the Hawaiians he heard of their homeland, as they remembered it; of how they had sailed as cabin boys or deck hands to the Coast, to China, then around Good Hope to New York or Boston; of how, destitute and bewildered, they had found friends among college boys and preachers and had learned about the spelling-book and the Bible.

Elisha and Hopu walked through the Cornwall cemetery, where Obookiah lay buried close beside the road. Hopu spoke much of his one-time friend—of how keen and quick to learn this boy had been; how good and humble and pious, but merry, too. Then he told of his friend's sudden death: One day Obookiah had talked gaily of going home to burn idols and startle his priest-uncle with the magic of the spelling-book; the next he had been carried off to Rev. Timothy Stone's desperately ill. They had thought, Hopu said, that after Obookiah died no American teachers would be sent to his people; but now God had caused many men to say they would go, taking Hopu and Kanui and Honolii with them as helpers.

Obookiah's memoirs, published in 1819, had given impetus to the Mission, crystallizing a vague, tentative plan into a substantial project and bringing the gifts of self and substance that made it immediately practical. The thin, modest book became a best seller. Peddlers and stationers mentioned it above the year's almanac. Ministers preached on it. Sunday school teachers read aloud from it and young ladies sobbed over it. Alive, Obookiah had been known to a few college boys, tutors and village pastors; dead, he was beloved of the whole Christian public.

At Cornwall Elisha listened carefully when the Islanders spoke in their own tongue, making notes to be used if he ever found himself in Hawaii. But there was still much doubt about sending him with the first mission company. Every wind that blew from Boston brought a new view of the matter. Not until September, when there was barely time to go home and say goodbye, did the gentlemen of the American Board give the word: Mr. Loomis was to sail in the *Thaddeus,* taking with him a female companion and "all necessaries for a printing establishment." And not until October, when he had brought his bride to Boston for the embarkation, did he feel sure that decision would not suddenly be reversed. Then at last the Board's treasurer dispatched him into the city's lanes and lofts to find "a good printing press at reasonable cost," and Elisha knew beyond all doubt that he would sail. The Board would not send out a press without a printer.

UNTIL he was twenty-two, Hiram Bingham had expected to be a farmer all his life. In Vermont he had kept his father's flock, tilled his ground, and repaired his buildings and tools. Now and then he had taught a term in the district school, but in those days nobody made a career of school-keeping. So, feeling the need to strike out for himself, he had about decided to "pursue the business of agriculture . . . in some of the new settlements of the west."

But he could not shake off the urge to preach. Whenever he tried to picture himself clearing and plowing and building in western New York or Ohio, he only became more sure that he wanted a pulpit and a parish.

He resolved to make an experiment—to study a few months and "watch the dealings of providence," to "proceed as far as the way should be open." In December, 1811, under the Reverend Elisha Yale of Johnstown, New York, he began to prepare for college; in 1812 he entered Middlebury; four years later he was graduated. Step by step, through the help of friends and his own persistent effort, the way had been opened.

Middlebury was not Yale. It was a century younger and less pretentious. Until 1815 it shared a building with the Addison County Grammar School, and most of its students were poor boys, working their way. But its founders had been counseled by Yale's Timothy Dwight, and its first president was a Yale graduate. Something of the rugged vigor of the older institution had come to the new one; yet as the young men of Middlebury looked from their hill-top into the neighboring Green Mountains and the Adirondacks stretching into the West, they saw a wider horizon than was visible at New Haven. What there was of the pioneer in Hiram, Middlebury nourished. He heard without fear or reluctance the command, "Go ye into all the world."

Middlebury, too, knew about Obookiah. A student from Torringford had met the Hawaiian in vacation-time and later had had a letter from him. Its respectable English spelling and syntax amazed the college boys and settled for some that much debated question: Could the heathen be educated? Hiram had been sure all along that they could be.

It was with no surprise, then, that he learned in his senior year that the American Board was planning to set up a school at Cornwall for Indians and Pacific Islanders. The surprise came when letters from his brother Amos, then in the councils of the Board, assured him that, if he should apply for the principalship of the new institution, he would be appointed.

Again Hiram faced a hard choice—Andover and ordination three years hence, or immediate service to his fellow-man as a schoolmaster at Cornwall. Again he looked for a sign from heaven and it came. A friend proffered the financial aid that made Andover feasible. He entered the seminary that fall.

But he did not forget the heathen lads. Deep in Hebrew or homiletics, he paused to rejoice that the Foreign Mission School had opened, that an able principal had been secured, and that Cherokees, Stockbridges, Choctaws, Oneidas, Tahitians, Marquesans, and Malays, as well as Hawaiians, were dwelling together in brotherly harmony and learning religion, agriculture, and the *a-b-ab's*. When the news of Obookiah's death reached Andover and set all the young theologians explaining the ways of God to man, Hiram could no longer resist the impulse to go to Cornwall and see for himself. For the trip he chose his last vacation, in the spring of 1819.

And then, once more, a decision confronted him. Amos Bingham let his brother know that he had been favorably mentioned for the headship of the Hawaiian Mission. The plans had grown since the early days of the Cornwall school. No longer did the Board speak of sending out a single American sponsor for the returning natives. Now the talk was of a company of six or seven men with wives and children, that the American home might spread its gentle, wholesome influence in Hawaii. No longer did the Board plan for an indefinite "someday;" it proposed to organize and equip the Mission to sail in October. In October—and Hiram would not finish at Andover until September!

Hiram played for time. He wrote that he was on the point of

accepting a vacation post in Vermont with the understanding that he would return and serve a year after graduation. If, however, the Board had any plans for him—if it wished to make any demands upon his spring holiday— The answer from Boston was clear. Let Mr. Bingham offer himself for the Hawaiian Mission, and the position of leadership would assuredly be his; there were no rivals in the field. Almost on the same day there arrived a letter from Bennington. The rumor had reached there that Mr. Bingham had greater prospects. The Vermont Juvenile Missionary Society had not waited for his refusal; it had already appointed another agent. For the third time, it seemed, the Lord had spoken unto Hiram Bingham that he go forward. He hastened over the mountains to Cornwall.

EXAMINATION DAY at the Foreign Mission School was a proud occasion. Before agents and visitors the dark-skinned boys answered questions and solved problems "with as much propriety as students in college." Hiram noted particularly the creditable performance of Thomas Hopu in theology and of George P. Tamoree in navigation and astronomy. Tamoree had calculated and projected an eclipse of the moon, to be visible in Kauai in September, 1820. By that time, Hiram reflected, if the purpose of the Board held, its mission would be in the Islands.

When the agents had dispersed, Hiram walked up the hill to Goshen. There, on May 11, after earnest conference with the Reverend Joseph Harvey, he wrote: "The Lord . . . must direct. . . . Let him do with me whatsoever seemeth good in his sight." Then, almost as if the matter were settled, he expressed his views on the personnel of the company and on the efforts that had been made at creating a Hawaiian primer. He told, too, of his plans to attend a course of lectures on medicine; to consult the Reverend Thomas Gallaudet of Hartford on the possible uses of sign-language between men of divers tongues; to get acquainted with Daniel Chamberlain, already accepted for the Mission; and, if Dr. Worcester approved, to seek a wife.

Still, he left the door open for the gentlemen of the Board, should they wish to reverse themselves. "I am not conscious," he said, "of shrinking at all from the toils and hardships and privations unavoidably connected with the establishment of a new missionary station among a savage race. But a sense of my unfitness and unworthiness to receive the important trust . . . almost restrains me . . . lest I should . . . seem like assuming that which must be left for wiser men to commit to me or to others abler than myself . . ." Not until July 16 did he unequivocally tender his services to the Board.

Meanwhile he had offered himself elsewhere—as a husband. The files of the American Board do not reveal the lady's name nor tell what town she lived in. But Hiram's crestfallen letter of August 31 shows that, after leaving Goshen, he made a proposal of marriage to a certain Sarah S., daughter of a minister in Berkshire County, that he waited three months for his answer and was in the end rejected. The shadowy Sarah, it seemed, felt deeply the plight of the heathen, but she did not think—nor did her parents—that it was her duty to go to them.

"My son," Hiram admonished himself, when the rebuff reached him at Andover, "despise not thou the chastening of the Lord, nor faint when thou art rebuked of him."

As he packed his belongings and studied for his final examination, he pondered the question: Did God intend him to go out single? His friends did what they could; they mentioned a young lady at Pittsfield, a pious female at Utica, a schoolmistress at Canandaigua zealous for missions. But there was no time to go about interviewing them, and Hiram had no heart for a second attempt. If there were anywhere a wife for him, he remarked with resignation, she would have to come and seek him out.

The ordination was set for September 29; the examination of the candidates, for the previous afternoon. Long before the twenty-eighth, the tide of visitors had overflowed the inn and filled the spare bedrooms of the hospitable people of Goshen. Deacons vied

for the privilege of "putting up" such distinguished guest▓
Honorable John Treadwell from Boston and the Reverend He▓
Humphrey from Pittsfield. The candidates themselves, cause an▓
center of the excitement, were lodged at the parsonage.

When Miss Sybil Moseley, in company with her pastor, the Reverend Mr. Brown, drove in from Hartford-way late in the evening,
the inn-keeper said he doubted there was a bed to be had in the
town, but the minister would know. Leaving Miss Moseley in the
parlor, the Reverend Mr. Brown hastened to the parsonage, where
Hiram Bingham, half-sick with weariness and a raw throat, sat
alone by the fire. All the rest had gone to a meeting at the church;
Hiram offered to step over and ask Mr. Harvey what to do.

"Take them to Deacon Thompson's," the preacher whispered
between items of Bible Society business; and Hiram, wrapping a
handkerchief around his ailing throat, said he would ride along
and show the way. Out from the inn came Miss Moseley; and there,
jogging along together in the Reverend Mr. Brown's chaise, were
Hiram Bingham and the Canandaigua schoolmistress who had
been recommended to him for her missionary zeal.

In the final days of her summer term, Sybil Moseley had shared
in the gift-giving that was making the Mission possible. She had
seen J. D. Bemis' one-time apprentice come home from the Foreign Mission School, on fire with excitement because he was accepted as printer. Dismissing her pupils, she had gone to visit her
sisters at Hartford. From there it was only a step to Goshen. She
easily found means to take that step.

Years later Hiram Bingham wrote of that meeting: "By a hospitable fire in the Thompson home we sat and conversed for a few
minutes. I measured the lines of her face and expression of her
features with more than an artist's carefulness and soon took leave
of her . . . , receiving some very generous cautions from her respecting my cold." The next day he learned that she was the young
lady his friends had suggested.

On Monday, October 18, the Brick Church in Hartford was

sting meeting . . . on the occasion of the de-
ries for the Sandwich Islands." After a psalm
bil Moseley and the Reverend Hiram Bingham
es in the broad aisle" and were married. That
was just six days before the *Thaddeus* sailed.

THE FAMILY

FOR the conveyance of the company to "the Sandwich Islands in the Pacific Ocean (the danger of the seas and other unavoidable evils not preventing)" the American Board had contracted with Hall and Thatcher, principal owners of the brig *Thaddeus,* and with Andrew Blanchard, its captain, in a document "signed, sealed and delivered at Boston on the twenty-third day of October, 1819."

The contract was full of precautions and alternatives: what to do if the passengers' supplies should "unexpectedly become deficient," what to do if "contrary to the expectation and desire of all parties, it should be found impracticable to obtain a permanent establishment," what to do if either of the parties should "complain of having suffered damages, in consequence of a non-compliance with this agreement by the other party." Though they were men of great faith, the agents of the Board knew well what practical measures they must take to safeguard their Pacific "adventure."

The Mission's outfit was the gift of the hundreds who wished them well. Though 1819 was a year of drought, crop failures, bank closings, depression, New England had opened its heart, and the young West along the Mohawk and the Finger Lakes had poured out its substance. For months, by stage and private conveyance, the donations had arrived at the Boston depository from Mite Societies and Fragment Societies and Owhyhee Societies, Male Associations and Female Associations and Juvenile Associations. And whatever these groups gave had been set down in the ledger of Jeremiah Evarts, treasurer. No item was too small to be noted:

19

Westborough, Ms. The Juvenile Straw Soc. A box of straw hats.

Windsor, Ver. . . 1 doz. axes, by Deacon N. Coolidge

Miss M. Forbush's school, 1 Testament and a bundle containing articles of clothing

North Brookfield, Ms. A quantity of cheese for the voyage. . . eight Bibles from five individuals

Concord. A gross of lead pencils from the manufacturer

From "a friend to the mission," 1 box raisins, 1 do. oat meal, 1 do. hulled barley, 1 rocking chair

Another friend (a grocer) 10 lb. souchong tea

Two maps of the stars by Mr. William Croswell, the author

6 reams of printing paper

Mr. Samuel Armstrong, 185 lb. bourgeois type

From a young physician, a set of amputation and trepanning instruments.

The avails of a patch of potatoes devoted to missionary purposes by a poor tenant—$3.63

From three little girls, obtained by abstaining from sugar—50 cents

From a mother . . . a thank offering on the birth of a child—$5

A female friend, 11 children's garments

Several ladies for a heathen child to be named Bethuel Dodd—$18

One smith's vice, carpenter's tools, and 93 lb. of medicines

From Whitesboro, New York. 70 vols. of books. From the students of Yale two hundred. J. D. Bemis of Canandaigua, New York, twenty-one volumes

Articles of stationery, viz. paper, pencils, quills, inkstands, inkpowder, wafers, and blank books

Mr. John Lawrence—for a printing press for the S.I. Mission—$125

These and many more were the belongings that cluttered Boston's Long Wharf as the *Thaddeus* loaded for her voyage. After the big stuff had gone aboard, along with the owners' cargo, lumpy canvas sacks, bursting paper parcels, hampers, satchels and bandboxes still remained to be hauled out to the brig, lying twenty rods off shore. A pile of lumber—a house-frame and the boards for finishing—had been rejected; no room could be found for it anywhere.

By eleven o'clock on the morning of October 23 a crowd had assembled for last words, handclasps, prayers and songs of "melting tenderness;" to hear Hopu speak eloquently in English; to see the handsome but unregenerate George P. Tamoree lift his beaver hat in graceful farewell; to shed sentimental tears as the two young preachers—Thurston, tenor, and Bingham, bass—sang in close harmony "Head of the Church Triumphant."

At one, a fourteen-oared barge, "politely offered by the commanding officer of the *Independence 74*," carried the travelers and their closest friends to the brig. The women, decorously clutching their skirts, were hoisted aboard in a chair. The men went up the rope ladder. The barge stood off as the vessel weighed anchor and caught the breeze. As they dropped down the bay, the voyagers could still see the fluttering handkerchiefs of those who wished them Godspeed.

THEY CALLED themselves a family, but they were still strangers when the *Thaddeus* sailed. Hiram Bingham—stern like the granite of his native Vermont, but genial, too, like its farmlands and homesteads—and Asa Thurston—acclaimed at Yale for athletic and scholarly mettle—had, to be sure, studied theology together at Andover. Samuel Ruggles and Lucia Holman were brother and sister, though as members of an orphaned family they had been parted most of their lives. Schoolkeeping at Cooperstown, Lucia had been wooed by Thomas Holman, medical student, and had engaged to marry him some months before he offered himself to the American Board. Otherwise they knew each other but little, these men and women of the Mission, until Samuel Whitney, sophomore at Yale, tossed up his books to go to the heathen; Daniel Chamberlain, husbandman at Brookfield, Massachusetts, sold his farm; and Elisha Loomis, printer's devil at Canandaigua, asked release from his articles.

Even the husbands and wives, for the most part, were newly acquainted. The Board had early indicated that it wished to send out married couples. It had gladly accepted Daniel Chamberlain, who had not only a wife but five children. Because most of the volunteers had given little thought to marriage, pious friends came promptly to their aid, suggesting suitable mates, arranging introductions and interviews. Asa Thurston's classmates directed him to Lucy Goodale, the deacon's daughter at Marlboro. Zealous go-betweens brought Nancy Welles of East Windsor and Mercy Partridge of Pittsfield the proposals of young men named Ruggles and Whitney. Elisha Loomis, breaking a stagecoach journey at Utica, was led by "divine providence"—so he put it—to Maria Sartwell and found that this auburn-haired, amiable and talented young lady had "long been wishing to engage in a mission."

Some of the girls were pretty and accomplished, some plain and practical. Some were simple and merry as a folk tune, some as sober and comforting as a hymn. But it was not their personal charms that had won them suitors. What had drawn these men and women together was their crusading spirit; their yearning over the poor, the oppressed, the benighted. They shared the same dour tenets, the same strait sense of duty, the same rigid views of right and wrong, the same hope of heaven, the same deep conviction that they were called of God. And they were young and hale and eager.

In joining the Mission they had volunteered for life—life measured breadthwise, as well as by length. All their waking hours, day after day, without surcease or interruption, they had pledged to the cause until they died. And they had tossed their little properties into the Lord's treasury, where moth and rust do not corrupt nor thieves break through and steal.

Some had had nothing to give but their future. Samuel Ruggles, unable to complete his preparation for college, had gone penniless to teach in the Board's Foreign Mission School. Samuel Whitney, struggling through Yale, had long been a ward of the charitable Education Society. Asa Thurston had had to borrow $35 to go to Marlboro about a wife; for Thomas Holman the Board had settled

a $25 debt to the "physicians with whom he had pursued his pro-
fessional studies," because he had "no resources with which to discharge that debt."

But Sybil Moseley, a schoolmistress, had saved $800. On the day
of her marriage to Hiram Bingham she sent it to the Board's
treasurer, saying, "I am leaving my little patrimony in the bank
of the Lord. I do feel that nowhere else . . . could it be so safe."
Her feeling was shared by Daniel Chamberlain, the prosperous
Massachusetts farmer. He had more to give than any of the rest,
but that, he said, was neither here nor there; with his five children,
he would draw more heavily than the others on the Mission's stores.

THE *Thaddeus* proved as skittish and wet and noisome as any brig
in the trade. She was as crowded above as below. Live chickens and
ducks in coops and hogs in makeshift pens, spars, ropes, chains,
barrels and the longboat left scant room on the quarter-deck for
the officers and the "family." In the stuffy staterooms and murky
cabin, chests, trunks and stowed sails were piled almost to the
ceiling. A semicircular table, lighted dimly from the lamp that
swayed and smoked above it, served for meals, meetings and study.
Those whose bunks were in the cabin might have slept in the
market place, for all the peace or privacy they had.

At first, when they were seasick, it seemed more than most of
them, landsmen all their lives, could bear. But they bore it for
five months, keeping their journals cheerful and serene; and in
the end they found their hatred of the brig changing to a homely
affection.

Of the food—beef and rice, dried peas and pudding, day after
day—they could write, "Always good, and better than we deserve."
In rough seas they could joke about the elaborate contraptions of
straps and ropes and boards which some of them rigged up to keep
themselves in their berths. In fine weather, when the men bathed
in the ocean, they could tease the wives who peered out nervously
for sharks. They could smile with pride and sympathy at the
women who sat sewing for the babies that would be born in

Hawaii.

From the outset, they called each other brother and sister, though in some ways Daniel and Jerusha Chamberlain were father and mother to the whole band. To the children—from gangling thirteen-year-old Dexter to Baby Nancy Chamberlain—the grownups were uncles and aunts, always ready to teach the older ones and "mind" the younger.

They held family prayers, kneeling in the cabin while Hiram Bingham or Asa Thurston spoke gravely to heaven what was in all their hearts. On Sunday they had service on deck, winning respectful attention from some of the brig's officers and crew, scornful laughter from others. On week days they studied—the arts and sciences, in which some had explored so much farther than their fellows, and the Hawaiian language, in which all were stumbling beginners.

For five months in calm and storm, in heat and bitter cold, they lived together on board the *Thaddeus;* and long before they sighted Hawaii, they knew each other through and through. In those months on board they came to see, far more clearly than they had seen in October, why saintly Samuel Worcester, giving them the Board's instructions in Boston, had spoken with such earnestness; why he had warned them against "wounds of feeling . . . unkind debates and embittered strifes;" why his voice had trembled a little as he charged them to "maintain brotherly love in its . . . constancy, strength and tenderness" and exhorted them to "much vigilance, much prayer, much crucifixion of self . . ."

But if there were rifts and misunderstandings, sharp words and altercations, repinings and regrets, these were forgotten in the joy of arrival. If any of the company had been found wanting in faithfulness and fervor, their brethren buried that knowledge deep. It did not show in their journals, nor in the radiant faces with which they gazed on Mauna Kea.

IT WAS HOPU who had roused them in the early hours of March 30 to look upon the moonlit mountains. He and the other Hawaiian boys—Kanui, Honolii, and Tamoree—had not slept that night; they had roamed the deck, hung over the bulwarks and climbed to the masthead, knowing that landfall would come before dawn.

Hopu had been away from the Islands almost twelve years. At fourteen, eager to see the world of the white man, he had offered himself as cabin boy, sailed off on Captain Caleb Brintnall's square-rigger and found himself the shipmate of Obookiah. He had changed much in those years. He had gone forth in a *tapa malo* and now he returned in shirt and stock and pantaloons, in leather shoes and worsted coat; and these were but the outward signs of changes within. He had become a New Englander, learned to read and write his adopted tongue, to do farm work and to recite the Westminster Shorter Catechism. He had been baptized and was on his way to becoming a preacher.

He kept saying that his father might still be alive and wondering what the old man would think of this long-absent and greatly al-tered son. Later, when it was daylight, and the vessel had come in close to skirt the north shore of the Big Island, Hopu asked to be excused from his half-eaten breakfast to "go and see where my father lives." Presently with the spyglass he found the place—a valley folded between hills—and eagerly called his American friends to tell them once more how, long ago, he had lived in that valley.

All that morning the *Thaddeus* scudded westward before the "trades." On her port the Big Island, Hawaii, lay green and lush. Below cloud-wrapped peaks, dark forests banded the slopes of the great volcanoes, and from their lower borders scores of streams ran down, watering plantations of *taro* and cane and then cascading over sheer, black cliffs to the sea.

At noon the brig rounded the northern tip of the island and came into its lee, where the rocky beaches were gray and the sunburned hills brown. Then, the breeze failing, the *Thaddeus* lay becalmed. Captain Blanchard readied his guns and sent a boat ashore, manned by James Hunnewell, supercargo, and Hopu and Honolii, to inquire the state of the Islands and the whereabouts of King

Kamehameha. On the brig the rest of the company made shift to pass the time until the boat's return. They could not forget that even now, eighteen thousand miles from Boston, the Mission might be turned back by a simple *no* from the king or by word of native unrest.

They knew—these men and women who had come to "renovate" the Islands—a little of the Hawaiian story. They knew about Captain Cook, his discovery of the group in 1778 and his violent death in 1779. They knew something of Kamehameha—that he had risen from comparative obscurity to conquer and unite the Islands; that he had white men in his service, whose firearms had helped to make his victories. They knew that this king upheld a pagan priesthood, sacrificed captured enemies to his war god and enforced strange, oppressive tabus; yet he had told Vancouver a quarter of a century ago—so the story ran—that he would welcome Christian teachers. They knew that Cook was not the only white man who had met treacherous death on these shores; yet they had heard that the king dealt honestly and peacefully with men of good will. Above all, they knew that Kamehameha was old and that when he died there might be fierce and brutal warfare over the succession.

As they waited through the hot, still afternoon, these things were in their minds.

Then, when the westering sun had cast the shadow of the *Thaddeus* far across the quiet water, they saw the boat detach itself from the blur of the shore and move slowly toward them. A shout went up on deck, and the glass passed from hand to hand.

At last the boat pulled alongside. Hopu, scrambling up the swaying rope ladder, called excited words his brethren could not catch. Once on deck, the Hawaiian boys rubbed noses and gibbered an unintelligible mixture of languages until James Hunnewell interrupted to tell the scarcely believable news.

Kamehameha was dead. For ten months Hawaii had had a new king. The old religion had been swept away, its priesthood dispersed, its temples demolished, its tabus shattered, its cruelties forbidden. There had been rebellion and bloodshed, but now there was peace.

The way lay open for the Mission!

HAWAIIAN CHIEFS

THE new king, Liholiho, son and heir of Kamehameha, was at Kailua, thirty miles down the coast; his "prime minister," the high chief Kalanimoku, lived much nearer. Captain Blanchard advised them to parley first with Kalanimoku.

A light breeze carried the *Thaddeus* into Kawaihae Bay. Early the next morning a fleet of sail-borne outriggers put out from shore, carrying the prime minister's *kanakas* with presents from their chief—cocoanuts, bananas, breadfruit, sweet potatoes and two hogs. Vendors followed with fruit for barter. A few knives, a pair of scissors and some fishhooks bought enough for a feast. The Hawaiians grinned and shouted and gesticulated, while the American passengers tried to conceal a squeamish distaste for their bare tattooed bodies and weird hairdress.

At noon Kalanimoku and his suite came off to the brig in a canopied double canoe. On the quarter-deck the Mission received the chief's party. Portly Kalanimoku, whom foreign traders called Billy Pitt, was dignified in a "white dimity jacket, black silk vest, nankeen pantaloons, white cotton stockings, shoes, a plaid cravat and a top hat." He saluted the American women, and, bowing low, extended his big brown hand to each of the excited young Chamberlains. "Aloha," he said to everyone. "Aloha."

Three Hawaiian chiefesses had come with him—his consort, Likelike, and two dowager queens, Kalakua and Namahana, widows of Kamehameha. Each weighed upward of two hundred fifty pounds and wore, perhaps in deference to the foreign ladies, an underslip of India cotton and over this a *pau,* or native skirt of ten thicknesses of *tapa*, twisted round and round in folds and bafflingly held in place by a tucking-in of ends. But even this was not enough covering for the dowagers. Kalakua wore in addition a bungling overdress of striped calico; Namahana one of black velvet. Their feet were bare.

Attendants flocked after them—corpulent males and females whose lazy office it was to carry spitboxes, wield fly-brushes and light pipes. The deck had never seemed smaller. The queens gingerly tried the benches set for them, then, throwing off their outer dresses, squatted on the floor and called for food. A *kanaka* brought a full calabash, and the royal ladies hunched over it, dipping up the pudding-like contents with their fingers, sucking and smacking with relish. Around another dish the retainers began on their *poi* and raw fish. But Kalanimoku, still in polite conversation with the Mission gentlemen, waited to join the New Englanders at table.

When the dinner bell rang, the queens also went below, though they did not sample the white man's meal. The cabin was hot. Stocks and ruffles wilted; broadcloth coats and whaleboned corsets tormented their wearers. Namahana, too, felt the discomfort. Mounting a sea chest, she had one of her women unwrap her *pau*, divested herself of her cotton underdress, shrugged with relief and waited in nude composure to be swathed again in her *tapa*. "She looked," wrote Lucy Thurston afterwards, "as self-possessed and easy as though sitting in the shades of Eden."

At last Kalanimoku's party climbed down into their canoes and were paddled away. The exhausted Mission family ate a supper of sea bread and tea and pondered what the prime minister had told them. They must go to Kailua, to King Liholiho, Kalanimoku had said in passable English. Only the king could give them permission to live and teach in his realm. But, the premier had added kindly, he himself would come on board again—with his wives and his retinue—and sail with the Mission to Kailua to speak a word for them. The Americans had learned the Hawaiian word of approval. "Maikai," they said smiling, grateful for the proffered support. But they wished that Kalanimoku ever traveled alone.

The crimson had faded from the bare hills of Kawaihae and swift tropic darkness had fallen when the family came on deck after evening prayers. A full moon shone between the peaks, throwing ridges and valleys into sharp relief, flecking the bay with gold. Away toward mid-island stood Mauna Kea, the white mountain, and Mauna Loa, the long. The burned-out volcano Hualalai was closer. Its blunt top and furrowed sides gave it the contours of a fluted cake. Just above them on the slope—empty and ruined—leered the *heiau* where Kamehameha had worshiped his war god.

There came a sudden stir in the rigging. Hiram Bingham was climbing the shrouds with Asa Thurston at his heels. Then, standing aloft at the maintop, Asa, tenor, and Hiram, bass, sang lustily,

> "Head of the church triumphant,
> We joyfully adore thee."

They had sung it in Goshen when they were ordained and again in Boston at the wharf. But never had they sung it with more faith and hope and ardor.

TRUE TO his promise, Kalanimoku brought off his train in canoes the next morning and joined the white passengers on the crowded brig. Though it was Sunday, the *Thaddeus* weighed anchor and stood southward down the coast for Kailua. On the whole, the Mission journals show, the Hawaiians "behaved with decorum." They seemed "pleased particularly with the singing." When the preaching was over, they ate their fish and *poi,* handed round their common pipe and lounged contentedly—talking, talking, talking in shrill, outlandish words. For the Americans that was a strange Sabbath.

Dowager Kalakua had brought on board a bolt of white cambric, demanding that the sisters of the Mission make her a dress like their own. On Monday as they cut and basted, seamed and gathered, the chiefesses sat with them, attempting calico patchwork. There is no record of how the Hawaiians performed, but according to Hiram Bingham the American women fitted out "the rude giantess" with success. The high fashion of the day, a long straight skirt gathered to a very short bodice, was adapted to Kalakua's massive figure. And if color and design failed to make her look slender, she was none the less delighted, for obesity was a mark of beauty among Hawaiians.

On Tuesday morning as the brig came to anchor before Kailua, Kalakua added to her costume an embroidered lace cap and neckerchief from America and made ready to model the first *holoku*. No professional mannequin could have asked a more favorable showing. "Men, women and children, from the highest to the lowest rank, including the king and his mother, were amusing themselves . . . swimming, floating on surfboards, sailing in canoes, sitting, lounging . . . dancing" in the harbor and on the beach. As Kalakua went ashore in her new dress, she was "received by hundreds with a shout."

AT LAST the brethren stood before the young king in his thatch "palace."

"We have got rid of one religion," Liholiho had his interpreter say to them, as he reclined almost naked on a mat. "We shall not be in haste to welcome another."

"These seem good men," Kalanimoku interposed, "and they have useful arts."

"What arts?" asked the king.

"Reading and writing," they told him. "See," said Hiram Bingham, holding out a piece of paper, "that is the king's name, 'Liholiho.' "

The young king examined the written word with care. Then he said scornfully, "It looks not like myself nor any other man." But he listened as his interpreter repeated the contents of the letter addressed to him by the American Board and, putting the documents into the hands of his "secretary," Jean Rives, said he would consider the matter.

Apparently it was the Frenchman, Rives, who suggested that these Americans had come to steal the royal land, that they would carry arms ashore with their goods and that frigates would follow them to seize the Islands.

Liholiho turned in bewilderment to John Young, his venerable English-born adviser. "Do *you* say the Americans have come to make war and take the land?" he asked.

"Would these foreigners bring their women and children if they came to make war?" countered Young.

The king pondered—and agreed that they would not.

Next day Liholiho invited the Americans to a lavish feast in the cocoanut grove near the palace, and the day after that he went on board the *Thaddeus* to dine with the Mission and hear their singing. But still he hesitated. His prime minister, who had come to speak for the Mission, was now half-seas-over with whiskey and *awa*, having deemed this a fitting occasion for a spree. So the king turned to Kamamalu, his half-sister and his favorite among four wives—an Island beauty of twenty summers and two hundred pounds.

"What think you?" he asked her.

"That I should like to learn the writing," she said. "Let them stay and teach us."

"They will take away your surfboard and *awa*," Jean Rives warned. "They frown on pleasures; they forbid ardent spirits; they grant each man but one wife, and she must not be of his kin."

So the king said to Kamamalu, "They will allow me but one wife—and that will not be you."

Kamamalu laughed. She was not afraid of the newcomers' tabus.

Wavering, Liholiho turned again to John Young.

"Have you forgotten," said the Englishman, "that my countryman Vancouver spoke to your father, while he lived, of such people as these; and that he promised Kamehameha to send missionaries from England?"

"Then," said Liholiho cannily, "perhaps the English king will be displeased if I receive these Americans."

Young thought not. But he suggested that a message be sent off to King George; and that, pending approval from that quarter, the Americans be granted temporary residence in Honolulu.

"White men all want to go to Oahu," said Liholiho petulantly. "I think the Americans would like to have that island. Tell them they may land here at Kailua, and when I have heard from the English king, and when I have judged their ways, I will say what more they may do." He indicated a dingy thatched building without floor, partitions, windows or furniture as the lodging he would offer for the Mission family of twenty-two. Water for drinking and cooking would have to be brought four miles on the shoulders of *kanakas*. Kailua's lava-rutted land could not be cultivated.

"Tell the king," said Hiram Bingham firmly, "that Kailua is too small a village and too remote from the center of population to be the site of our main station."

Negotiations had now lasted nine days. Captain Blanchard was chafing to be on his way to Honolulu and the Coast. His contract with the Mission called for "a reasonable time for consultation." A week, he thought, was more than reasonable. He pressed the brethren to debark.

John Young would not predict a definite answer from the king in less than six months. "It is the Hawaiian way," he said.

But Hiram Bingham, too, had his way. It was to answer over and over the same questions and doubts, to reason individually with the king's advisers, to ask again and again to be heard by the chiefs in council. On Monday, April 10, eleven days after the Mission's arrival off the Islands, he told Captain Blanchard he would make a final effort to settle matters.

On Monday Liholiho had a new reason for delay. "I will do nothing," he said, "until Kaahumanu comes."

Here the king was on firm ground, for the dowager Kaahumanu held equal authority with him. Kamehameha, as he lay dying, had named his favorite wife *kuhina nui,* guardian of the realm, because he did not altogether trust his sportive heir, his son by another queen. This, at least, had been Kaahumanu's interpretation of her lord's will. On the day of Liholiho's inauguration she had addressed the young king: "O Celestial One, I report to you what

33

belonged to your father. Here are the chiefs, the men of your father—there are your guns, and this is your land; but *you and I will share the land together.*" Liholiho had not demurred.

Descended on her mother's side from the one-time rulers of Maui and on her father's from a high chief close to Kamehameha, Kaahumanu had been considered in her youth a great beauty. When she was only eight, Kamehameha had taken her into his train and shortly thereafter made her a consort. She became his favorite, singled out for a special jealous devotion. Though he often beat her—once, it was said, for speaking of a young man as "handsome"—and for a short time set her aside when he suspected her of intimacy with another chief, he had high regard for her shrewdness and judgment. Kaahumanu was forty-six when she became *kuhina nui,* wise in the ways of the court and the nation and more than a match for the young king.

So Liholiho had reason to say, "I will do nothing until Kaahumanu comes." But Kaahumanu had gone fishing, and no one could say when she would return. Captain Blanchard grew hourly more restive, and the Mission seemed doomed to residence at Kailua. Then, in the late afternoon of that Monday, Kaahumanu returned from her trip Tall, erect, commanding in her *pau* and mantle, she walked into the village, followed by the straggling company of *kanakas* who bore her accoutrements and her catch.

At sunset the Americans were summoned to the palace once more to lay their business before the court. When they had finished, Liholiho spoke with unwonted decision. "We will allow some of you to go to Honolulu and dwell there one year. If then your ways are not good, you must go. And do not send to your country for more teachers. We do not know yet what to think about this *palapala* and this *pulepule.* But the arts of the doctor are good. The doctor must stay here. The rest may go to Oahu, but he must not go. Hopu and one of the other Hawaiians, too, we will keep with us. They can teach us the *palapala* if we should wish to learn."

Every member of the Mission understood what Liholiho did

not—the need in dividing the company to settle one of the ordained ministers at each station. Should Bingham or Thurston remain?

A ballot was taken. By it, Asa Thurston and Lucy, his wife, were selected to stay at Kailua with the Holmans and the native youths, Hopu and Kanui.

IN THE EARLY dusk after tea Captain Blanchard took the Thurstons and Holmans ashore. Already their personal baggage and a few items drawn hastily from the common stock had been delivered to the thatch cottage near the king's yard.

"You will come to Honolulu with the doctor in July?" Maria whispered to Lucia Holman as they said goodbye. July was when the Loomis baby would be born.

"We'll do your washing at Honolulu, where there is sure to be plenty of water," Sybil Bingham promised Lucy Thurston, "and we'll send the clothes back to you by the king's brig." Lucy looked grateful. They had laundered nothing on the voyage but pocket handkerchiefs.

"The Lord bless you and keep you," said Asa to the Honolulu company. And to Danny Chamberlain, whom he had tutored on the *Thaddeus*, "Be a good boy and get your lessons."

Thomas Holman shook hands with his brethren—Hiram Bingham; the two Samuels, Ruggles and Whitney; Daniel Chamberlain and Elisha. Under their correct, brotherly manner they showed constraint. "Don't forget," the doctor bantered, "that if it had not been for me, none of you would have been allowed to stay."

Captain Blanchard was calling from the boat below. There was barely enough daylight left to get them to the landing and back. The doctor hastened down the ladder. With a flutter of handkerchiefs the little party moved quietly toward shore.

Before midnight the *Thaddeus* would be speeding northward to the island of Oahu.

There was silence on the deck. Were they thinking that this separation might be a scheme of Satan's to hamper their advance? Or a device of the Lord for testing their faith? Or, perhaps, God's solution to the problem that had vexed them on the voyage? For if any of the company could be expected to live at peace with the irascible Thomas and his Lucia, it would be the sunny, tolerant Thurstons.

HONOLULU

IN the Honolulu of 1820 traders talked of salt, oil, hogs, fish, tobacco, hemp, pearls, muskets, spirits and sandalwood. But chiefly of sandalwood. For the last feverish decade of the sandalwood harvest was beginning.

In the ten years before 1820 the fragrant wood had come down from the mountains in an easy abundance that meant rich profits in the China trade for New Englanders; crystal lamps, flowered satins, naval stores, silver dollars and ships for Kamehameha. In those lush years the foreign merchants had known with whom they dealt and that their payment would be full and prompt. But the year that brought the *Thaddeus* marked a turn in the business that foreshadowed its end. Liholiho—young, uncertain, bidding desperately for loyalty—had granted his high chiefs a share in the trade. Thereupon, the brisk commerce grew even brisker; competition and tempers sharpened. Agents of the great American firms—Marshall & Wildes, Bryant & Sturgis, John Jacob Astor's—sent home sanguine letters. In Boston and New York the water fronts hummed and bustled. New vessels were launched, old ones bought and sold, bottoms scraped and coppered, masts reset, rigging renewed, cargoes trans-shipped, bills of lading taken, crews hired, captains instructed. From mid-summer to late autumn of 1820 Boston alone saw nine departures for the Pacific.

Ships, coming faster and faster around the Horn, cut the old six months' voyage to 132 days, 117 days, 112 days. Hard-pressed agents and captains sold their cargoes, their worn-out schooners and their new-built brigs on credit, then schemed and shouted for the payment of old notes, even while they brought in fresh merchandise, showy and overpriced. The voice of the sandalwood master rang harsher as it cried the commoners into the mountains.

Many a morning while it was still gray, a thousand men or more plodded up a wooded valley. They did not know why they must toil in the forests; the hongs at Canton and the wharves on the Boston water front were beyond their ken; but they had seen the king's man with his torch, firing the houses of those who did not turn out fast enough.

They cut down the trees, young and full-grown alike. An overseer pointed to a hollow, as long and as broad as a ship's hold, that they must fill with timber. On the second or third day, when the pit was full, they roped the logs, shorn of limbs and dragged them to the plain. Brush and branches went down in bundles, tied with *ti* leaves to stooping shoulders and smarting backs.

At the beach the wood was dried, filling the land with its waxing fragrance, cleaned—for only the heart was of value—and weighed under the eye of the district's chief and the trader for whom it was destined. If the ship to carry it lay offshore, hundreds of canoes plied back and forth to load her. If the foreign vessel waited at Honolulu, native craft hauled the wood around Oahu or from island to island. If the great ship was still to come, the wood mounted in the agent's storehouse.

Returning unrewarded to his bare hut and wilted *taro* patch, the commoner often felt it hardly worth his while to flood and trample for a new crop when the next summons would come so soon. Old Kamehameha, when he saw the land lying untilled and famine looming, had "ordered the chiefs and commoners not to devote all their time to cutting sandalwood" and commanded the people to farm. But after 1820 there was a new day when no one cared that the people went hungry. No one cared, either, that the hills were being rifled. Kamehameha had once told his overseers to spare the saplings, that there might be wealth for his successors. But Liholiho seemed to think his forests as inexhaustible as the waters of Nuuanu. And the bedeviled agents, captains and supercargoes sought only to get their share—and quickly—not to conserve the trees for an unborn generation.

To the Americans, sandalwood was never an end in itself. Hardly a stick of it ever went to Boston or New York. It was, like furs, a medium of exchange. For teas and silks and dinner sets of blue willow ware, the Chinese merchants preferred their pay in specie, but, lacking that, they would take sleek, black otter pelts and aromatic wood to burn in their joss houses. Thus from the time when Captain Nathan Winship's *Albatross* added Hawaiian sandalwood to her Northwest furs and carried both to Canton, American ships in the Pacific had followed a well-marked course. Outward bound, they called at Honolulu for supplies, dropped off a stock of assorted merchandise and an agent to sell it and signed on *kanakas* for the cruise to the Coast. Returning, they took in their sandalwood, discharged their Hawaiians—paying them in trade and charging well for the cold-weather clothing they had furnished them—and cleared for the Orient.

Past Lintin Island and Macao, they sailed up the river to the anchorage at Whampoa. Then under the patronage of a sharp-eyed fellow, who had assessed "cumshaw duty" and been made happy with gifts, the cargo went upstream in chop-boats to Canton, where merchants named Houqua, Kingqua and Pacqua vied for the trade. But no brash foreign devils could enter the sacred city. All the hongs and go-downs fronted the square at Jackass Point, outside the wall. There the flags of the rival nations flew from tall staffs to show each trader where he might land his goods and seek one of his countrymen to aid him in bargaining. Competition was formidable. Fees, duties, commissions and graft ran high. Only by the shrewdness for which they were famous did the Yankee captains keep the Canton expenses from devouring their profits.

But no amount of shrewdness could prevent the final catastrophe. As the 1820's ran on and cargo after cargo came to Canton, supply far exceeded demand. The price, which had once risen to $13 a picul and had long hovered around $10, wavered and at last sank ruinously.

"Ours is to be stored for a year or two," wrote one harassed captain at the end of the decade, "& God only knows when it will be sold, as there is now at the least calculation 25,000 piculs on the market. Thus I have in a manner thrown away my vessel and cargo & if B & S have not more candor & generosity than falls to the lot of the generality of mankind, I may expect to be kicked out for a d——d fool."

But that is another story.

HONOLULU IN 1820 had everything to sell that you could have found in the crossroad store at Brookfield or Cornwall or on the water front at Boston. There were chandleries, trading posts and grog-shops, where white men dispensed sea stores, pea jackets, cooking pots and rum. Each had its inclosure, fenced with slender poles and tabued against curious or thieving natives, its adobe storehouse, and one or more grass dwellings full of such foreigners' comforts as china tea sets and brass bedsteads.

The grogshops flourished like the green bay tree. They offered not only drinks but gambling, fiddling, singing, hornpipes, wrestling and often downright brawls. Here jack-tars, glad to get their feet on firm earth, could hear the news of the world (six months old) and find robust and ribald comradeship.

But more immediately than any of these wares or pleasures, the crews of incoming vessels wanted women. If the Islands were the Paradise of the Pacific, it was because there every Adam had his Eve.

It had been so when Captain Cook came on his voyage of discovery. At Waimea on Kauai the visitors took women and paid in iron, more dazzling to the stone-age natives than gold. A year later, on Hawaii Island, Kamehameha had tried to keep the women from the ships; but, finding that his tabu only brought the sailors thronging on shore, he had let things take their course. Things had been taking their course ever since.

"Women quite handsome," wrote seventeen-year-old John Boit, fifth mate of the *Columbia* in 1792. "Not many of the . . . Crew proved to be Josephs."

Two decades later Peter Corney's attitude was matter-of-fact. "At sunrise," he recorded, "we fired two muskets and sent the women out of the ship, and at sundown did the same as a signal for them to come on board . . ."

By 1820 these rendezvous had become, at least in part, an organized business. Heads of families might fill their canoes with pretty, laughing girls—daughters, sisters, wives—and paddle off to greet a ship; women lacking conveyance might swim out, unencumbered by apparel; sailors might send their sweethearts ashore with Spanish shawls and lace caps to arouse the envy of the village; but before the fun began, the government must have its fee. A Spanish dollar a head, to the chief on whose land the girl lived, would make things right for as long as the ship stayed. The collector went on board with the pilot.

Captains were more discriminating than their crews. They preferred the half-white daughters of long-time *haole* residents, girls who would not swim out to the ships or take up with any common fellow who came along; girls whose English, American, Spanish or French fathers would see to it that they behaved and did not get a disease. Sometimes a captain took such a girl with him to the Coast, and returned her to the Islands—with child, perhaps—when he called to pick up his sandalwood before going on to China.

So everything was as comfortable and handy in Honolulu as you could ask. There was only one thing the captains did not like about it. Too many men deserted there. Often life on land seemed so good after the harsh months at sea that sailors hid in the village or made off into the back country. When their ships had gone, they left their cover and floated about the district, unshaven, rowdy, feckless—scum on the surface of the foreign community.

It was to this tough, polyglot port that the *Thaddeus* was bringing the earnest Americans named Bingham, Chamberlain, Ruggles, Whitney and Loomis.

LONGNECKS

FROM the deck of the *Thaddeus* in the early morning of April 14, the family watched the gray land of Oahu emerge off the starboard bow, saw jutting promontories take shape and hailed the long-awaited Diamond Hill, guardian of Waikiki Bay.

The sun rose astern to sharpen the features of the island and brighten its colors. There were the cocoanut groves and the curve of sandy beach, where the bathers sported. There was the line of white breakers, marking the reef; there were the steep mountains and the deep-grooved valleys—just as Supercargo James Hunnewell had described them so often.

There, presently, was Honolulu harbor, as fair a haven as the Pacific boasts, shielded seaward by a wall of coral and landward by the Koolau range, though winds still came boisterous through the gap at the Pali. There in the sunlight swirling white mists encircled gray peaks and caressed green hillsides, and streams danced down through a tangle of *kukui, pandanus, koa* and giant ferns.

And there on the treeless flats, amid coarse *pili* grass and gray coral-dust, slouched Honolulu village—some three hundred straw huts, as frowsy as last season's haycock. On the point, the stone-faced mud walls of a fort rose high above the low dwellings. Mounting sixty guns and flaunting the Hawaiian colors—a Union Jack in the upper quarter with a field of horizontal red and white stripes—it seemed to defy foreigners to try any nonsense in this harbor.

Outside the reef the *Thaddeus* dropped anchor and sent its boat ashore to announce that—despite wind, weather and the devil—God had got around Cape Horn.

At the fort Hiram Bingham, abetted by Captain Blanchard, inquired for Boki, the governor of Oahu. But Boki was not at home. He had gone, said the second in command, to another part of the island, and who could tell when he might return? Let the *haoles* talk, if they were in such haste, with Don Marin, the interpreter.

The Spaniard, Don Francisco Paulo di Marin, had been thirty years in the Islands—so long that in 1820 there were few who could remember Honolulu without his luxurious garden and his fine, fat cattle. Before Kamehameha conquered Oahu, Marin had come from Andalusia, bringing animals, seeds and vines. He had introduced the damask rose and the cotton tree, the grape, the tamarind and the prickly pear—which he pruned into hedges. He had imported horses, mules, doves and English hares. He made wine and butter, salted beef to supply the ships and sold his lemons, oranges and pineapples; but he would allow no seeds or roots outside his own garden and no animals beyond his own acres. At his plantation behind the village, in Nuuanu valley, he received the Americans graciously, served them some of his excellent wine and, agreeing that salvation was urgent business, dispatched two messengers on horseback to bring the absent Boki home.

Meanwhile the port master, having collected his fees, sent a fleet of towing canoes to bring the *Thaddeus* into the harbor, for only if wind and tide were exceptionally favorable could a vessel sail through the gap in the reef. Presently ropes tautened, brown paddlers bent to their task, the pilot chanted his orders, and the brig moved through the narrow channel to her berth near the fort.

By his fast-sailing vessel, the *Neo*, the king had sent a message to Governor Boki: "This is my command. Furnish the *haoles* with land and houses and with provisions. Let them dwell in Honolulu for one year, if they do not make any trouble."

The governor was a brother of Kalanimoku, younger and less able than the premier, but as eager to stand well with white men. So when he returned to the fort and heard what the king's messenger had to say, Boki went on board the American vessel to greet the company of teachers. Tall, athletic and tipsy, he grinned like a genial death's head—for, to show his grief when Kamehameha died, he had had his front teeth knocked out with a chisel. He instructed Marin to speak his *aloha,* but he was in no mood, it seemed, to talk of houses.

When, in turn, the brethren called at his palace within the fort, Boki gave them presents of breadfruit and taro. But a residence for their families and a place to store their goods—all that, he said airily, could wait.

Even so, the men of the Mission were not without resources. In Boston the old sandalwood trader Captain Winship had offered the use of his house in Honolulu. He knew how things would be at the Islands, what delays and exasperations the brethren would encounter there, and so he had given Hiram Bingham a note to Don Marin, asking him to unlock the house for the missionaries. When word of Winship's generosity had made the rounds in Honolulu, the American merchant William Navarro offered a small building in his yard. Someone suggested the Lewis place, Captain Isaiah Lewis having gone to the Spanish Main. William Babcock, agent for Marshall & Wildes, said there was room in his storehouse for things not immediately to be unpacked.

About houses, then, Boki could take his own Hawaiian time. But he did send *kanakas* to help set the Mission on shore. They casually hoisted trunks to their skinny shoulders and rolled hogsheads along the beach, paying no heed to Hiram Bingham's orders or Daniel Chamberlain's frantic gestures, treating it all as a merry pastime. A four-wheeled handcart captured their fancy. Two of them seized it by the tongue and capered toward the fort; others dumped their burdens in the sand and followed till a too-sharp turn around a palm tree ended the joy-ride.

Not until all the goods had been landed were the women lowered overside and rowed to the shore. With as much dignity as if to "meeting" they walked beside their husbands through Honolulu village. Past the grogshops and the traders' houses the little procession moved, and in it the first white women to set foot on Oahu. A throng of natives, growing larger each moment, trailed behind, and chattered incessantly. Some bold ones pressed close, plucked at sleeves and peered under bonnets.

"A-i-oe-oe," one laughed, and the rest took it up like a refrain.

"They are saying your faces are small and set far in, and that you have long necks," Honolii explained.

"Long necks. Long necks," the natives kept shouting; but it was not in derision, only in wonder at the strangeness of these newcomers. And Longnecks they were called for many a year.

THE HOUSES smelled of dust and dry grass like a haymow. The windowless walls crawled with vermin. Mice scampered across the dirt floors. In the dark rooms, where capering *kanakas* had deposited them, were the boxed and bundled goods with which the Mission family must now equip their homes, the chaos out of which they must bring a New England order.

They were not dismayed. Though they were teachers and preachers, they had worked with their hands, too, and knew what it meant to rope up bedsteads, to assemble a cookstove, to build a table or a bench out of lumber that had been a crate. The men shed their jackets and pried off lids, brushed walls, repaired thatch, carried in rushes for the floor and wood for the fire. The women put on their oldest dresses and got down on their knees to scrub.

The farm tools had gone into Captain Babcock's storehouse in the governor's yard. Later, if Boki gave the Mission some land and Don Marin was willing to lend his oxen, Daniel Chamberlain would bring out the plow and the harrow. The printing press had gone in, too, and the boxes that held the types and paper, along with most of the books and slates and the maps and globes to be used one day in their schoolroom. In patience they must possess their souls, doing first those simple things that could be done by word of mouth in a tongue they knew but ill. And Elisha, the printer, must be the most patient of all.

By Sunday, four days after they had moved ashore, they were ready to hold public worship in the main room of Captain Lewis' house. Let native nobles or foreign traders come—and some did—

the Mission was ready to receive them in order and peace.

Among the whites were Oliver Holmes, long of Honolulu but once of Plymouth, Massachusetts; Jack Woodland, a refugee from Botany Bay; and mannerly James Hunnewell, supercargo of the *Thaddeus*. Of natives there were Boki, with his fly-brushing, fan-wielding train, and a petty chief or so. After the service began and the word got around that the Longnecks were making a strange *pulepule,* the yard filled up with commoners, who vied for places at the door.

What amazed them most, it seemed, was the hymn singing. Despite the rhythmic accent of Tamoree's bass viol, the staid harmonies were unlike any chant Hawaii knew. When the white men bowed in prayer, covering their faces with their hands, Honolii tiptoed about with finger on lips and whispered, *"Kapu!"* to those who spoke or moved. And when the sermon began, he translated a little at a time.

"Behold I bring you good tidings." On earth let there be peace and good will. It was the command of the one true *Akua* that they live together—brown and white, kings, chiefs and commoners, whether from the windward islands or the leeward—loving one another like brothers. Never again should they take up their spears to kill in behalf of this chief or that, but should use them to cut dead branches from trees, that the bananas and breadfruit might be plentiful for all.

HARSH AND INCONVENIENT as life was in Honolulu, it was not lonely for the Mission family. There was warmth in the welcome of their fellow-*haoles,* of whatever faith or country. White neighbors named Babcock, Elwell, Warren, Navarro, Holmes and Harbottle made gifts of rice, beans, soap and flour from their imported stores, yams and melons from their garden plots. Don Marin sent a woven basket heaped with fruit and a jug of wine. Captain William Pigot and his partner Mr. Green invited the strangers to a "friendly cup of tea" at their establishment; and the next day, having learned that the dishes brought out in the *Thaddeus* had been ground to rubble, they presented the Mission with a full set of brown-and-white china.

But still the native life swirled around them, alien, high-pitched and bizarre. All through the soft, warm nights there came from the fort the hourly clang of an iron bell and the raucous heathen shout that meant "All's well." By day, even after Boki had tabued the yards, native hordes peered through the palings and goggled at the American cookstove. Honolii, listening to their prattle, said they were curious about the women's work. Cooking in Hawaii was a man's job; only cloth-making a wife's. Though they dressed like chiefs—with flowing robes and fancy hairdress—these *haole* women were always busy; they never lounged or fondled pets or played cards.

On the dusty plain the discredited priests of the old religion went about scolding like shrews. If the people had not overthrown the idols and ceased their prayers and offerings, the old men said, there would have been rain. Now it would be dry forever. The streams would fail; the *taro* would die and the people would starve. Then sudden showers fell, and even the children mocked the false prophets, pointing at them with skinny fingers.

One morning a petty chief slipped into the yard, stole four of the precious new plates and made off amid great clamor. When the culprit had been captured, Boki turned him over to the Mission. Usually in Hawaii, the governor explained, one dealt with a thief by going to his house and taking something in return for the stolen goods. If the Longnecks did not want to do that, let them punish the fellow some other way. They could beat him or brand him or shave off his hair—anything so long as they did not kill him with their prayers. The family smiled at that until they saw a former priest and his *wahine* led in irons toward the governor's, accused of praying a woman to death.

In the harbor native brigs and schooners came and went, carrying messages, taxes, sandalwood and roving chiefs. Hundreds of live hogs and dogs were loaded, squealing and yelping, for Kailua, where Liholiho made ready to celebrate the anniversary of his father's death.

47

The Oahu chiefs began to bring foreign cloth to the Mission houses, asking that the Longneck women make them American shirts and coats. As they sat on the floor waiting to be measured or fitted, Hiram Bingham told them about God and the contrite heart. "Maikai," they said politely as Honolii interpreted, but their eyes were fixed on Maria's needle and Sybil's gleaming shears.

ONLY ONE of those who had come in the *Thaddeus* was restless in Honolulu, wanting to be off again. George P. Tamoree, the son of Kaumualii, was afluster to get to his father's house on Kauai. This impatience was no new thing. Boastful, imperious, petulant, yet lovable, the prince had long been a thorn in the side of all the pious folk who had dealt with him. Now his eagerness to move on toward his home was no greater than the brethren's wish to be free of his cocky intransigence. But while Captain Blanchard filled up his water casks, took in fresh supplies and gave his crew leave, there was nothing they could do.

Meanwhile, mingling with his countrymen, the prince enthralled them with his tales of foreign adventure; and in his first days ashore he courted and won Betty, the half-white daughter of Kamehameha's gunner Isaac Davis. Slyly alluding to the biblical instruction he had had in America, Tamoree introduced her to the Mission family as his "rib."

Though he tossed his broad shoulders as if they were already wrapped in a royal cloak, the prince could not have remembered much about his father's kingdom. At the age of seven, he had gone abroad with Captain Rowan—not as a runaway cabin boy like Hopu and Obookiah, but at his father's request, to see the world and be educated in America. For his expenses Kaumualii had entrusted Rowan with "property," though how much and in what form is not known.

Ten years later George wrote to his father about his hardships and adventures. "I was neglected very much," he said, "by the man you send me with; after we came to America, the Capt. . . . became very intemperate & exposed with the property you sent with him

48

. . . and I have to shirk for myself."

The "shirking" took him presently to Boston, where he enlisted "to go and fight with the Englishmen" and be "wounded in my right side with a boarding pike, which it pained me very much."

On the *Guerriere* later he battled "the barbarous turks of Algiers," and visited Tripoli, Naples and Gibraltar. "And now," he concluded, "I am in a good way of getting a good education. But I want to see you very much. . . . You must not expect yet a while, but if God spars my life I shall be there in a few years."

He was at Guilford then, studying with Honolii at the Rev. Herman Vaill's. A few months before, a fellow-Hawaiian had found him at Charlestown, "living with the Pusser of the Navy." The discoverer had written to Obookiah, without benefit of capitals or apostrophes, "i examine him who he was, he answer the king son of attoi, i ask him if he remember his father name, he said his father name tammaahmaah, but he hath forgot his tongue entirely . . . i think this is the very young man been looking for. . . ."

It was indeed the young man, though his father's name was not Kamehameha. For years every trader who had touched at Kauai had heard from Kaumualii the story of his son, lost in America. If, grateful for assistance in a gale, for comforts on shore or for bargains in sandalwood, a captain asked what he could do in return, King Kaumualii had always said, half sad and half hopeful, "You find my boy." That was the only thanks he wanted.

When Tamoree first came under the patronage of the American Board, the agents had been sanguine of his value to the Mission. For three years after he first wrote to his father, the boy, then known as George, remained at school, perfecting his English, picking up some of the Hawaiian he had forgotten, learning to saw the bass viol and distinguishing himself in mathematics and astronomy. But for three years he fumed and champed and fidgeted because his new sponsors did not see fit to escort him home immediately. Whenever a vessel sailed for Hawaii, Tamoree thought he should go in it. Whenever a captain came home from the Pacific, Tamoree thought he should have an interview. Never for one moment could he forget that the blood of chiefs flowed in his veins or that his schoolmates Kanui, Hopu and Honolii were the sons of commoners. That they, being pious, were greater in the sight of God and the American Board than he, a king's son, was something he could never understand.

Now, at last, on May 2 the *Thaddeus* set sail for the Coast, touching first at Kauai to deposit Tamoree and his bride, and the two Samuels (Whitney and Ruggles), whom the Mission had chosen to accompany them. No Yankee would have foregone the chance to deliver the prince to his father and claim the promised rewards. But Captain Blanchard had not for one moment forgotten the fur posts of Oregon nor the importance of reaching them while the season was young. Even if he encountered no delay at Kauai and no trouble on the high seas, he knew he would not be first at Nootka or Keegahnee. Still, he should be able to get his share of the year's skins— from the Russians, if not direct from the Indian hunters. He had a good cargo—blankets, duffel, molasses and rum. Most of his officers had been on the Coast before; he himself knew its every cove and shoal. And furs were high in Canton; prime black otter was bringing $35 the pelt.

James Hunnewell, the twenty-three-year-old supercargo of the *Thaddeus,* did not go with the brig to the Coast. Instead, with five casks of rum and some assorted merchandise, he set up shop in Honolulu. In his spare time, of which there would doubtless be plenty, he was commissioned to supervise the building of a schooner from materials brought out from Boston.

FRIENDS

WHEN the *Thaddeus* had gone, there remained only one foreign vessel in Honolulu harbor—the fine, coppered brig of Boston, the *Clarion,* overhauling after a season on the Coast. But the next dawn revealed new sails off Diamond Hill. Two British whalers came beating up the bay— *L'Aigle,* Captain Starbuck, and the *Princess Mary,* Captain Best.

Old in whaling, Captains Starbuck and Best were new in Hawaiian waters. It was six months since the first whalers ever to visit Hawaii had made a catch off the Big Island, and no American fishers had yet touched at Honolulu. Captain Joseph Allen's *Maro* was even then—May, 1820—at Lahaina on Maui, making her first bold trip north. Not until November did she nose into Honolulu harbor, bringing word of teeming whale-grounds off Japan—word that called ships from New Bedford, New London and Nantucket by dozens, then by scores and at last by hundreds.

But the ships that came in May were from London, the Union Jack flying from their mastheads. The men and women of the Mission could remember well enough when that had been an enemy ensign, when they had heard talk of ruined commerce, of British highhandedness and chicanery, of battles at Put in Bay, Fort McHenry and New Orleans. But it was Red Coats and frigates America had been fighting, not whale-fishers and stubby, sea-battered whaleships. So, without giving thought to a war now five years past, the family invited the new arrivals to tea and, with them, Captain Pigot and his partner Mr. Green, whose gift of brown-and-white dinnerware had made the party possible. It turned out that Captain

51

Best was Irish and that Captain Starbuck was, after all, a New England-er who had transferred his registry from Nantucket to London. Only Dr. Williams, surgeon of *L'Aigle,* was a true Englishman, and he proved a thoroughly amiable person.

"It was pleasant," reads the Mission's journal for May 5, 1820, "to have it in our power so soon after landing to set an American table in humble but decent order . . . and quietly to sit down on these shores in . . . a circle of Ladies and Gentlemen."

Of that evening's talk over the teacups there is no record. The captains doubtless told enough of ocean-borne commerce, of quest-ing for wealth, of danger, disappointment, risks and ruses to engage the brethren long beyond the hour for prayers. But there is evidence that before the party ended, the old-timers had probed with lively curiosity the beliefs and expectations of the newcomers from America.

Did Mr. Bingham really think he could teach the "indians" to read? Couldn't they be converted and baptized without book learn-ing? Did the Mission expect the chiefs, let alone the commoners, to understand doctrines that set smart men quarreling in America? Whom would the gentlemen teach, and how? Would they try to reform the white population?

Hiram Bingham must have answered eagerly. Until now he had not had listeners at once so sympathetic and so skeptical. Yes, he said, the whole nation must be made literate, the humblest as well as the highest. There was an immortal soul in every brown body, however slothful or repulsive the fellow might look. His salvation had been purchased and was freely offered, but he must accept it by an individual act of will. He must experience a change of heart. Bap-tism had no power to save; it was only a ceremonial for recognizing a rebirth, once it had occurred. Preaching and exhortation had their place, but unless each man could read the word of God for himself, how should he tell true preaching from false, how be sure that he had heard aright? So they must start with the alphabet and end with the whole Bible. That was why they had Brother Loomis with them, and the press and types, though they still had much to learn about the language before they could make books.

They would like to begin everywhere at once, Hiram went on, teaching all the chiefs and the common people, old and young. But they were too few for that. So they would tutor the king and the highest nobles as they could, open a day school for the children and wives of white residents who cared to come, and adopt into the family a few of the native and half-caste youngsters one saw running wild through the village, sticking their fingers into whatever calabash they came upon, sleeping under anybody's *tapa*.

As to disputed doctrines, the Mission knew better than to confuse tender minds with hair-splitting. But there were the Lord's Prayer and the Beatitudes and the Ten Commandments. Surely the gentlemen did not regard the Ten Commandments as controversial.

The captains and traders nodded agreement. There in the thickening dusk of May 5, 1820, they did not see these teachers as a threat. They saw them, rather, as men and women from back home, people with whom they shared gentle memories, who had like themselves exchanged comfort and security for danger, harshness and risk. That the prizes they sought were different did not at that moment seem important. No one remembered then that Christianity is really a radical doctrine and education a very yeasty brew. No one foresaw that a people's expanding sense of their own worth could rock a social structure or rend an economic pattern. No one saw any reason to hate or fear or despise the thirty-year-old preacher from Vermont, who knew something of farming, something of carpentering and cabinet-making, a little of doctoring, as well as a great deal about religion.

It was dark when the captains rose to go. Tomorrow, Captain Best was saying, they must all come on board the *Princess Mary* to dinner. But Captain Pigot had his eye on the days beyond, on the Mission's need of comfortable, permanent houses and staunch, outspoken friends. A meeting was what he proposed—a regular, organized affair with chairman and scribe. It would prevent misunderstanding among the white men and prod lazy Boki into action. How about next week on Wednesday?

Next Wednesday, Hiram said, would be quite satisfactory.

In all the lore of the Pacific there is no hardier figure than William J. Pigot, Honolulu trader. And none, it seems, more buffeted by fate and balked of fortune. He came out in 1813, in one of the bold, futile maneuvers of the war era. For John Jacob Astor, when he could no longer send ships from blockaded New York, dispatched to the relief of his fur-post on the Columbia the *Forester*, fitted out in London and sailing under the Union Jack. Pigot was the man who managed the venture.

There was trouble all the way—foul weather, desertions, mutiny. Off Kealakekua the British captain shot the boatswain, jumped overboard, and fled to Kamehameha for protection. Pigot, forced to take command, "got one Alexander Adams to navigate and some islanders to work the ship," and stood for the Coast.

But Astoria had fallen to the British. By the time Pigot, cruising up and down California, had converted his cargo of "fine Irish Linnens" and rum into 70,000 seal skins, his fictitious colors had ceased to protect him. Indeed, he was doubly in danger—from the Yankees because his flag was British; from the British because—thanks, some said, to his own loose tongue—his vessel was known to be American. He decided to sell the brig, skins aboard.

Even that did not come off. The "rough, rugged, hospitable, hard-drinking" Russian Baranov on his rocky promontory at Sitka would have bought the *Forester* for furs. But Pigot, with more furs already than he knew how to market, wanted cash. The deal collapsed, and Pigot moved on to Kamchatka, where he fell in with another American trader named George Clark, stranded there by the war. Even two tireless Yankees could not interest the Russians in the brig; so they got her a new trading cargo and sent her smuggling among the Spanish settlements. In the end she made the Islands, where Kamehameha "conceived a strong passion" for her and bought her for $9,000 cash and 8,000 sticks of sandalwood. A condition of the sale was that the British Adams sever his *haole* connections and enter the royal service as her captain. Thus John Jacob Astor, fur trader, first entered the sandalwood business, and Alexander Adams, born in Forfairshire, Scotland, became at the age of thirty-six a citizen of Honolulu.

Meanwhile Pigot, trying to outwit Baranov and sell his seal skins above market price, found himself in trouble. His furs went to Ochotsk, but the promised roubles never came. After many weeks the Russian American Company repudiated its agent's bargain and informed Pigot, petitioning through the British ambassador to reclaim his pelts, that if wanted them he could go to Ochotsk and get them.

By June, 1818, Pigot had by irksome effort recovered 60,649 of the troublesome skins. With them he embarked in the American schooner *St. Martin* for Hawaii, and there bought the *St. Martin* and dispatched her hopefully toward Canton.

Now, in 1820, he had been out almost eight years—a long absence even for those days. He had sent wood and furs to China, whence the proceeds had gone back to the Astor counting house. But his own prospects of heading home were still poor. He wanted to try something more at Kamchatka. He wanted to sail through Bering Straits and explore the great sea beyond, or to colonize Fanning's Island near the equator, where *bêche-de-mer* could be had for the gathering. Some thought Captain Pigot did not really want to go home, that he had no desire to discuss face-to-face with Mr. Astor the details of his transactions. Perhaps it was only that he had fallen in love with the Pacific and was bound to her by ties he could not break.

AT CAPTAIN PIGOT'S REQUEST Hiram Bingham wrote the circular that announced the meeting. Addressed to "the friends of humanity and truth," it invited "the European and American residents, both temporary and permanent, masters and officers of vessels in port of the different flags, together with the chiefs of the Island" to assemble at the house of Mr. Bingham at five o'clock on the afternoon of May 10 to hear the views of the missionaries and the views of the government with respect to their enterprise; "to devise a plan and take measures to secure immediate and effectual aid" to their object, and "if it should be deemed desirable, to appoint a committee to superintend such a plan."

The hope of the promoters was to build, at once, suitable quarters for the Mission, the cost of the houses to be paid by friendly foreigners, the land to be given by the government. As soon as the Britisher Alexander Adams had been named chairman of the meeting and Elisha Loomis scribe, Captain Pigot made his proposals. But Boki, when Marin had interpreted, said *no*. Nothing of the sort could be permitted. He, Boki, would provide the houses as King Liholiho had ordered. His men would build them as soon as the Longnecks had chosen a site—if his men could then be spared from other business.

A little surprised at the turn of affairs, the *haoles* conferred.

"We know you are friendly to our object," Hiram Bingham began in a moment, "but these gentlemen thought that, since your government has at present many other claims upon it—" He meant the sandalwood; he knew what heavy obligations the chiefs had assumed.

No, Boki said again a little sulkily. He would build the houses just as the king had ordered.

But would he build them soon? Pigot asked sharply. And would they be comfortable? And entirely without expense to the Mission?

Yes, Boki had Marin say. Yes to everything. He murmured reasons why he could not permit them the first site Mr. Bingham had chosen. It belonged to some of his farmers; he did not want to send them away. But if the Longnecks would choose again, toward Waikiki—

The *haoles* appointed a committee to consult with Boki about "the place, the form and the manner of building" and passed on to another matter. Since they could not contribute houses, why not a school fund for what Mr. Bingham was pleased to call "indigent children"? Men and women in America had already made gifts for the support and education of heathen boys and girls to be adopted by the Mission family. About seventy-five cents a day, Daniel Chamberlain estimated, would feed and clothe a young one and provide "the tools of learning."

The plan caught on quickly. There was not a man among them but felt a little stab of conscience now and then at the sight of the wild-eyed children with matted hair and wizened bodies who roamed everywhere and belonged nowhere. Bastards, Captain Pigot called them; but Elisha Loomis, writing his minutes, had a nicer word—"orphans."

In no time the "orphan school fund" had been organized by acclamation, and a committee—Captains Starbuck and Pigot, William Warren and Daniel Chamberlain—had been elected to take subscriptions. Forty-nine dollars was immediately pledged by Captain Starbuck and his officers on *L'Aigle*.

Thus the "first regular meeting ever held on this island" closed in a spirit of generous good will, even though some of the Honolulu *haoles* had refused to attend, grumbling as they went about their business that Pigot, for all they cared, could jump in the bay. Who was Pigot, anyway, they asked, that he should call all hands for the American preachers?

LATE THAT MONTH the Mission began its day school. Ever since the meeting, Hiram and the others had been talking about it among the white residents. Then came the morning when Sybil Bingham rang the little hand bell that had summoned her scholars in America—rang it so lustily that they heard it up at the Jacksons' and down at the Harbottles'. Her Hawaiian scholars came bringing gifts—fresh pork, fish, many kinds of fruit and vegetables, *lauhala* mats and *tapas*.

There were two mellow-eyed Jackson daughters, clinging demurely to their mother's hands; four young Holmeses, sponsored by their pretty sister Hannah; and five or six other boys and girls in their teens—eager, excited, on the threshold of adventure. There were "brown wives," too. Sybil entered their names neatly in the record: Sally Jackson, Poaleme Navarro, Tomaroo Otto, Jennie

Oliver, Mary Green.

The class began. "A-e-i-o-u," the scholars intoned after Sybil, as if this were some wonderful new *hula* chant. "A-b-c-d-e." It would be a long time before Elisha unearthed the slates in Captain Babcock's storehouse so that the pupils could see the *palapala* and write it themselves.

Spelling lessons went slowly, painfully. No one, not even Hiram Bingham, the trained linguist, had learned enough Hawaiian to speak it readily. The torrent of syllables the brown wives poured forth at sight of Webster's woodcuts did not sound like Hopu's carefully enunciated phrases. Honolii was willing, but often baffled. Happily, Hannah Holmes, though she did not speak English, understood it fairly well. From American visitors in her father's home she had heard everything from Yankee curses to tenderest words of love. So she told the others what she thought the Longnecks were saying—about *a*-by-itself-*a*, in-the-beginning-God, and how-doth-the-busy-little-bee. Some of them understood wonderfully well.

But fingers learned faster than tongues. To weave the tiny needle in and out along the matched edges of foreign cloth, pulling the long thread after it, to hold the pieces irrevocably together—this required no words but only the teacher's patient example and the pupil's eager imitation, spurred by the wish to wear a *holoku*.

These were the day pupils. But now that the orphan school fund had grown to $300, the brethren must choose the waifs to be adopted into the family circle and raised as good Christians. They scrutinized the children who flocked up and down the village and questioned this one and that about his home and relatives.

One day, past sunset, when the noisy, curious crowd had scattered, a boy lingered outside the inclosure at Captain Lewis', pressing his bare brown body against the paling, peering wistfully in. Elisha, startled to see the lad there, said, "Hello! Who are you?"

The boy's face brightened, but he did not answer.

Elisha called Hiram Bingham and Honolii. "Would you like to live with us and learn to work and read?" Hiram asked and Honolii interpreted.

"*Ae,*" said the lad, smiling shyly.

"And wear clothes?" Elisha added, for the little fellow had not a *malo* to his loins.

"*Ae.*" The smile grew.

"Then you must tell us your name and where you live," said Hiram.

But they could get nothing out of him.

After a day or two they learned that his father was an American named Beals who had lived at the Islands, gone to sea again and died at Canton. His native mother did not care who adopted her son. To lend out the children among kin or neighbors was an old Hawaiian custom, even before the white men began to come.

They named him William, dressed him in a cotton shirt and nankeen pantaloons, and began teaching him manners and the alphabet. He learned rapidly, outdistancing most of the day scholars. He was the first of the orphans.

"HABITATIONS OF PEACE"

B Y noon on May 11, the day after Captain Pigot's meeting, most of the Honolulu *haoles* were drunk, and all through the afternoon their voices rang shrill and angry along the dusty paths. There were blackened eyes and bruised jaws and wrenched shoulders. If no bones cracked, it was more a matter of luck than caution.

At first they fought for fun, for release from boredom, to settle old grudges or put an upstart in his place; but as the afternoon waned, the notion seeped into the befuddled minds of the Americans that they had a genuine grievance. "Bad-minded" Englishmen, they had heard from natives, were conniving to get the Yankees expelled from the Islands. Their evil talk had reached Jean Rives in Kailua and had gone from him to Liholiho. Soon an order would come to Honolulu and all white men except those who held land would be packed off. At dusk, two Britishers who had not been able to refrain from a bit of boasting, were identified as the chief offenders, and the Americans ganged together to cane them.

"I am neutral," James Hunnewell wrote in his journal, "for I sell Rum."

". . . happily we have had no part in it," Elisha Loomis recorded, "and our dwellings have been the habitations of peace and safety."

As for the Englishmen, they could see well enough how the wind was veering in Honolulu, and they did not like what they saw.

For almost forty years Europeans, and above all Britishers, had won favor and wielded influence in the Islands. Vancouver had pledged his country's friendship and protection; John Young and

60

Isaac Davis had been Kamehameha's faithful aides. An Englishman had been the king's gardener; a Scot had built him vessels and refitted the foreign ones he bought. The Britishers Sumner, Harbottle and Adams had commanded Kamehameha's brigs on voyages and served at the Islands as pilots and harbor masters.

The New Englander Oliver Holmes, who lived the same easeful, pleasant life as the rest of them, was never resented. But when the Winships and William Heath Davis came with their strenuous ways and their sharp bargains, the Englishmen grew annoyed. They seized every chance to tell Kamehameha that these Yankees would cheat him; and all the disappointments and delays that came with the War of 1812, they taught him to charge to the Bostonians. Indeed, the old emperor died convinced that the Winships were deeply in debt to him. And who is to say that they were not?

Yet all this was not enough to keep the American traders away. Since 1815 they had come increasingly, landing their tawdry cargoes; building, without so much as a by-your-leave, their shacks and inclosures along the water front and discharging their good-for-nothing seamen. Kamehameha had craved their goods, and to get them he had sometimes winked at rowdy or brazen behavior. And his son, the new king, did not greatly care what went on in Oahu, so long as he could carouse with his coterie of idlers, white and brown, at Kailua.

Thus the Britishers had their work cut out for them. Despite the mauling they got from their Yankee neighbors on May 11, they continued reporting to windward—truly, that many Americans were canny, aggressive, belligerent and lawless; and falsely, that all Americans, including the newly-arrived missionaries, were in league to possess the Islands.

Mr. Astor's brig *Pedler,* Captain John Meek, 159 days from New York, arrived on May 23. To the missionaries it brought the first word from home—letters written in November and six precious issues of the *Boston Recorder,* October 29 to December 3. They read accounts of their own departure from Long Wharf and of the gala opening on the same day of the Erie Canal from Utica to Rome. They read with full hearts and brimming eyes, because it seemed so long—and yet so short—a time since October, 1819.

To Boki and the Oahu chiefs the *Pedler* offered a market for produce; they stocked her with fruit, vegetables and hogs, and charged Captain Meek a pretty penny. To the Hawaiian women, going out in bevies, the arrival meant a bright, exciting respite from their humdrum poverty. To the grogshop-keepers it meant new customers, for whom to broach new casks. To James Hunnewell it meant unwelcome competition. "Goods are landing," he grumbled, ". . . which will glut the market. Cash very scarce."

But to Captain William Pigot, the *Pedler,* with her black sides and her white bottom and her eight thirty-pound guns, was an old friend that spoke of so many adventures and escapades, of so much smuggling and roistering and barter from Fort Ross to New Archangel, that a man less sturdy would have wept at sight of her.

Pigot had last seen the *Pedler* beneath the giant fort at Sitka, where Baranov had seized her for smuggling powder to the Indians. He had not heard what befell her after that. Yet here she came, direct from New York, with gin, brown sugar and cloth for the Coast and some of Mrs. Pigot's peach preserves for her wandering husband. Captain Meek, one of five sea-going brothers of Marblehead, was doubtless glad to find on the ground so experienced an Astor man as Pigot. He made him agent for the *Pedler* the day she arrived. Next morning, on Pigot's advice, he ordered a barrel of flour from the cabin stores to be delivered at Mr. Bingham's house and in the evening accompanied his agent there to tea. Pigot, who never went empty-handed to the Mission, took this time a jar of Mrs. Pigot's preserves.

To the Englishmen the *Pedler*'s coming meant just one more pesky American captain to watch. And, as if to give them something more to relay to Kailua, Captain Meek's carpenter deserted a week after the brig came to port, and there was the devil to pay in Honolulu.

The carpenter was a good one, and Meek did not intend to lose him. He and Pigot dispatched horsemen to search the valleys and scour the plains, then poked about the village and harbor until they found the fellow's tools aboard the king's brig *Neo*. The *Neo*'s skipper, a young chief whom the white men called Captain Jack, expressed mild surprise at the presence of the carpenter's chest under his berth and high dudgeon at the invasion of his vessel. Brought in presently by one of the riders, the carpenter vowed that Alexander Adams, the British-born harbor master who had once left Pigot's employ for Kamehameha's, had encouraged his flight. Pigot and Meek stomped to Adams' door. Adams denied their angry charge—and the quarrel was on.

The whites took sides, chiefly against Pigot, and drank themselves pot-valiant. Boki and Captain Jack, fortified by rum, let it be known that the government had been insulted. A *haole* crowd milled aimlessly, growing in heat and numbers, then surged toward Pigot's yard as the cry arose to burn the trader's goods and pull down his houses. Attackers with ready fists, flushed faces and torn shirts and pantaloons brushed the Chamberlains' *lanai* and shook the paling at the Binghams' as they converged on the Pigot place; but Mr. Astor's captains had rounded up enough defenders from the *Pedler* to stand them off. Only the craziest would have set a fire there in the midst of a straw village, where every man's property would have gone to ashes in an instant; but to tear down a grass house was another thing. For a while it was touch-and-go whether Pigot's thatch would stay intact.

With darkness, the mob dispersed and the village grew quiet. Daniel Chamberlain wrote to old neighbors in decorous Brookfield an account of the day's affair. "I wonder that they do not drive away every white man from the island," he concluded.

Officially from Boki or by the grapevine—perhaps both—the affray was reported in Kailua; and in a few days the Frenchman, Jean Rives, came down to deliver the king's orders and reprove the peace-breakers. Alexander Adams, as harbor master, was henceforth to have "full power to admit or reject vessels." Messrs. Warren and Navarro, though regarded by the *haoles* as peaceable neighbors, were summoned before Liholiho "to answer charges." A captain about to sail for Kauai was warned "to remove every article from the shore that belonged to him." "All traders," the rumor ran, "must leave as soon as vessels came to take them away."

"We remain undisturbed," wrote James Hunnewell, whose fourth cask of rum had been broached and whose new schooner was nearly ready for the ways. "But we must go," he added, "as soon as we have a vessel." That would be when the *Thaddeus* came back from the Coast.

So it went in Honolulu during the Mission's first summer. Rumor and unrest were as common as sunrise, and the king's will as fitful as the weather. It was conceded that the teachers could stay out the year that Liholiho had granted them. But no one was predicting what would happen after that.

As for Captain Pigot, perhaps he had meant all along to sail in the *Pedler*. At any rate, after the affair of the carpenter he moved on board, cruised among the Islands for a fortnight with his good friend Meek and sailed in mid-June for Kamchatka by way of the Coast. With his departure, the Mission lost its most genial and determined champion, but gained a house—a separate dwelling that afforded Maria and Elisha "a pleasant retreat" from the hurly-burly of the twenty-foot room at Captain Lewis', where so many members of the Mission lodged, received company, sewed for the chiefs, taught school and held public worship.

Though the brethren had chosen a site toward Waikiki and Boki's men had promptly brought timber and begun to set up a frame, work on the promised houses lagged. Sometimes the builders were called to cut sandalwood. Again they must help draw heavy guns from the fort to Punchbowl hill back of the village. It took eight hundred natives all day to get a single twenty-four pounder to the heights, where Boki and Captain Adams had decided they must have a battery. Ordinarily a house could be built in three weeks. Those for the Mission, it seemed, would not be done in three months. Captain Pigot's "pleasant retreat" was, therefore, "particularly welcome at this time," as Maria noted gratefully on July 8. She was expecting her baby within the fortnight.

KING KAUMUALII'S SCHOONER now came to anchor, returning the two Samuels to the Mission family and bringing gifts from a father who rejoiced in the return of a long-absent son. There were thirty-five supple mats, a hundred calabashes of all sizes, spears, fans, brilliant *kahilis,* shells, pineapples, oranges, six chair-frames of sandalwood and three live hogs. They filled the front room at the Binghams' and turned the Chamberlains' house into a veritable country fair.

The Samuels reported. They had seen Kaumualii, only half believing, rise from his royal sofa and clasp George, press his nose to the boy's and weep quietly. For a full thirty minutes the king had gazed on his son without words, and all day he had followed him with fond eyes, as if at a loss to discover in the handsome, confident young man anything of the seven-year-old who had gone away with Captain Rowan. That evening he gave George two chests of fine clothing; on the next day, the stone fort at the river's mouth; on the third, the rich and fertile valley of Wahiawa. Then he named him second in command in the leeward isles, although George's half-brother, Kealiiahonui, had by his mother's high rank a better claim to that title.

For his part in Tamoree's return Captain Blanchard had received fifty large hogs, as much *taro* and sugar cane as he would take and the promise that, when he came back from the Coast, his vessel would be loaded with sandalwood worth a thousand dollars in Canton.

On the representatives of the Mission George's father had bestowed the honorary title *aikane,* and he had offered them women of the nobility for their beds. When the Samuels refused this offer, Kaumualii was sad and puzzled. Other *haoles,* he said, had told him he did well to extend such courtesy.

The king had approved young Tamoree's marriage. He ar-

ranged that the newly-wed couple should live in their own house
and set an American table. And when the missionaries came to
Kauai to settle—as indeed they must—they too should have as
many houses as they could use, Kaumualii said. For the teaching
must not stop at the windward; it must come to his island as well.

Yes, the *palapala* was the thing. The king prized the big Bible
from America and had said he would be willing to study ten years,
if need be, to read it. But the thin, blue spelling-book had gone
straight to his heart. He took it bathing and peeped at its wonderful pages while he splashed in the surf.

Here, then, was a call, loud and clear: Send us teachers, and we
shall do everything they ask; send us teachers and we will learn
with our whole hearts both the *pala* and the *pule*. But the call had
overtones of danger. It came from the two leeward islands—Kauai
and its tiny neighbor, Niihau—that Kamehameha had never conquered, though he had made ready again and again to attack them.
Some catastrophe had always held him back—a violent storm that
shattered his fleet of war canoes, famine and sickness and the death
of many who would have fought for him, threats of rebellion in the
lands he had already vanquished. Time after time Kaumualii had
quaked on Kauai, hoping to repulse the invaders from the windward, but fearing that his puny defenses would fail. At last, in 1810,
white men, who wanted peace for the sake of the trade, had sought
to reconcile the two kings. They had brought Kaumualii under safe
conduct to talk with Kamehameha on Oahu, and there the younger
and weaker king had acknowledged himself vassal to the older
and stronger.

Since 1810 Kaumualii had paid an annual tribute of barkcloth,
fruit, hogs, and calabashes; and Kamehameha had been content
with this. But now that the old Conqueror was gone, no one knew—
least of all Liholiho—how faithful Kaumaulii would remain.
Confused and contradictory reports of his dealings with the Russians, back in 1815, gave color to the suspicion that he could not be
trusted. Then, whether knowingly or in ignorance, he had agreed
with a Russian agent named Scheffer to place "all the wood in the

islands" at his disposal and to make other concessions in return for "five hundred men and some vessels properly armed for the purpose of conquering Kamehameha's islands." Governor Baranov and the Czar had rejected the treaty after sharp orders from Kamehameha had sent the Russians off Kauai in leaky ships. But the affair had left a bad taste.

Old-timers in Honolulu assured the missionaries that Liholiho would resent the settlement of any of their band on Kauai. Traders said frankly they thought there might soon be war between the leeward and the windward kings.

But it was not to seek their own safety that the Mission family had come to the Islands, rather to "preach the gospel to every creature." So they pondered the matter while they waited the birth of the first Mission baby.

"WE, THEREFORE, REMONSTRATE—"

MARIA'S time was at hand, but Dr. Holman had not yet come from Kailua. In the grass houses of the Honolulu station the tension grew. Why had the doctor delayed so long? the family asked each other.

On the morning of July 12, anxiously scanning the bay for an arrival, Elisha saw an "express" canoe—an outrigger manned by six skilled paddlers—enter the harbor. So it was without surprise that the Mission family soon heard a crier going about the village summoning all *haoles* to Boki's house.

It was hot and close there when the door had been shut, for the low one-room palace had no windows. Two *kukui* torches at the far end smoked and sputtered, casting a murky light on the guard with his long spear and on Boki, who stood tall and pompous, his arms folded under his brilliant cloak. Don Marin was at his side. There were perhaps fifty white men present, looking annoyed or amused according to their temperament.

Suddenly Boki strode toward Hiram Bingham and thrust out a packet of letters. They had come from the king, Marin said, with orders that they be read publicly. If these sealed papers that flew back and forth between the American teachers contained words of treachery, the king had said, let their wrongdoing be exposed.

"Read," Boki commanded.

One by one Hiram broke the seals. There were letters to him from Hopu and from Asa Thurston, one from Lucy Thurston to Sybil Bingham and one from Dr. Holman to his brother-in-law Samuel Ruggles. With the eyes of the company upon him, Hiram moved nearer a torch and examined the pages. Above all he wanted to know when the doctor was coming.

He found the answer in his letter from Asa: "Prime minister Kalanimoku will immediately send a boat to Maui with timber to build a house for Dr. H. & his lady . . . Thus it seems that our physician whom we expected to attend us in sickness, is about to take his flight to an island where none of the mission reside."

The doctor's letter to Samuel Ruggles confirmed the unwelcome tidings. He and Lucia were about to move to Lahaina. There was no mention of their visiting Oahu.

Hiram refolded the letters and told Don Marin that they contained only personal matters and that he would rather not trouble the assembled gentlemen to hear them. But the king's messenger insisted. It was His Majesty's order.

The king, said Hiram stoutly, was mistaken about the letters. The Mission was willing, if need be, to submit them to Boki; but he hoped that another, less public occasion might be arranged. Someone in the audience, too stifled and flea-bitten to endure more, told the guard to open up and the *haoles* bubbled forth like lava out of a crater.

But the men of the Mission had scarcely reached their houses when a messenger came from the fort. The Longnecks must read their letters aloud to Boki, he said, lest there be something in them that was important for the king to know. So Hiram Bingham and Samuel Ruggles returned and read the whole packet—all the brotherly salutations and domestic details, all about Brother Thurston's sermons and how Hopu had found his father alive, all about Sister Lucia's frail health and the Holmans' unexpected decision to move to Maui and, with what nonchalance they could muster, the doctor's words about Kalanimoku: "He has more power than any other chief in the Islands, & more than the king himself."

Boki heard the whole, as Marin rendered it, without a flicker on his stolid countenance. Then, with a grunt and a gesture of boredom, he dismissed the brethren.

It was an indignant little company that met next morning to approve and sign the letter Hiram Bingham had been writing far into the night.

"Pause, for a moment," they exhorted Thomas Holman, "& ponder your path, & consider consequences— Read over the instructions of your patrons—look at the fond expectations of the friends of missions, & the readiness of enemies to exult in your downfall . . . & then, if after the most mature deliberation, your love to the heathen should compel you to leave Kailua, you may confidently expect that your representations will receive due consideration. To proceed otherwise, according to your avowed design, is, in our opinion . . . taking an injudicious course . . . We must, therefore . . . remonstrate against this ill advised purpose, & unitedly call on you speedily to desist . . ."

The letter was long and wordy, but to Thomas Holman its meaning would be simply this: "If you change your station now without consultation with and approval from your brethren, you will wreck your own career and endanger the very existence of the Mission." Yet they did not expect him to desist; they had known him too long and too well for that.

They arranged with Boki to dispatch the letter to Kailua by the canoe that had brought the troublesome packet. Then they turned their thoughts to Maria.

Hiram Bingham had had a short course of medical lectures, taken after he had accepted the leadership of the Mission. The course had included midwifery. If need be, he told Elisha when they knew the doctor would not come, he could deliver the child. If a ship with a surgeon did not arrive before the hour of danger, he would know, Hiram said, that the Lord was relying on him. They would trust in the Lord.

That was the thirteenth. On the morning of the fourteenth the whaleship *L'Aigle* appeared in the roads. Half full of oil, she had come back to Honolulu for lime to set a boiler. She did not anchor but stood off and on while Captain Starbuck came ashore. When he was told of the Mission's need for a doctor, the captain readily agreed to lend his surgeon for a few days, and within the hour Dr.

Williams of London was installed in the grass house that had till lately been Captain Pigot's.

For delivering, on July 16, Levi Sartwell Loomis, the first white child born in the Islands, the English doctor would accept no pay. The grateful father urged upon him, however, a token of his appreciation. It was "an elegant edition of Milton's *Paradise Lost.*"

Now, after more than a century, the quarrel of the Mission with Thomas Holman seems unimportant; but in July of 1820, when the brethren were bracing themselves for strife and schism, they believed that their whole enterprise was at stake. The Mission was on trial. It had been grudgingly admitted to the Islands and was still watched from some quarters with suspicion and from others with enmity. Hawaii was less than a year from its latest civil war. Jealousy among chiefs and fear of treachery were strong and real. What the impetuous king approved one day might anger him the next and on the third might look to him like intrigue with an ambitious underling. For a member of the Mission to decide alone on a step in these circumstances was not self-reliant; it was insubordinate and foolhardy. At least that is how the brethren saw it.

What lay behind the doctor's strange conduct?

To answer, it is necessary to go back into the days before the *Thaddeus* voyage and the days of the voyage itself, back to things the Mission family had not put into their journals or their letters, back to things they had hoped they could forget forever.

Thomas Holman had studied medicine at Cherry Valley, New York. When he had completed his courses in materia medica and surgery, he took his diploma and went home to Cooperstown, intending, no doubt, to practice there. A pretty schoolmistress changed his plans.

She was Lucia Ruggles of Brookfield, Connecticut. Cooperstown was a long way for her to have wandered from home, but she was bent on going still farther. Her brother Samuel, who divided his time between studying at the Foreign Mission School and soliciting donations for the American Board, had told her about the company that would sail, probably within the year, for the Sandwich Islands. If Lucia would like to go as a teacher, he said, he would speak on her behalf to influential persons. It would be pleasant, Samuel thought, for a brother and sister who had been apart most of their lives to enter together into this undertaking.

At first Lucia did not consider the proposition seriously; but when she had become engaged to the young doctor, she told him about the Mission and found him much taken with the idea of joining the company. In April of 1819 he secured the necessary credentials and recommendations and sent them with his application to the agents. Early in May he was accepted and directed to enter the Foreign Mission School for training in the Hawaiian language and in the principles of missionary enterprise.

He arrived at Cornwall on May 29, a "young physician of respectable talents," with "very solid testimonials" from his fellow citizens in Cooperstown. But as early as August he had, according to Principal Daggett, "discovered a disposition to complain of his accommodations, & to dictate in the concerns of the Institution." Though they were few and mild in the midst of a long letter, these words proved prophetic. For, as long as he remained with the Mission, Thomas Holman was an unhappy man, displeased with the way things were done and resentful of all regulation.

He had been recommended as "discreet, solid, and pious." Forces of which his Cooperstown sponsors were unaware soon converted discretion into recklessness and solidity into arrogance. Deference and flattery, if applied incessantly, might have kept Thomas Holman amiable. But when his brethren tried to remake him, to bend him toward purposes that were not his own, to press his proud spirit into the mold of Christian humility, he rebelled.

Then there was Lucia. Her comfort was his comfort; her happiness, his happiness; a reproof dealt to her stung him tenfold. Many of his outbursts were on her behalf, for she, too, was out of tune with the sober and devoted Mission family. She was not made for hardship and just too late she knew it. Having decided, not far off Boston, that she was ill fitted for the missionary task, she thought it a virtue to say so, often and insistently, and to warn that she would return home as soon as opportunity offered. And if Lucia wanted to go anywhere, Thomas Holman would take her, though he had to defy hell and Hiram Bingham to do it.

It is needless to recount all the tiffs of the voyage. The sale of some cheese to the seamen, a dose of herb tea for a Chamberlain child, a discussion of the traits desirable in a missionary, a proposal for group study at regular hours—such innocent-seeming items brought on noisy altercations. Eleven bottles of white wine, sent on board at the moment of sailing and handed to Dr. Holman as medical supplies, launched such a fleet of woes that the brethren heartily wished they had left them on Long Wharf.

All the rules by which the family governed its daily affairs on the *Thaddeus* annoyed the doctor. In the ban against eating between meals he saw an odious infringement of personal liberty. If Lucia, who had a private supply of oranges, lemons and peppermints, liked to "piece" at odd hours and offer her little luxuries to others, her right to do so, the doctor thought, was "inalienable." If, when her appetite had failed at dinner, she could wheedle a slice of cold ham from the cook in mid-afternoon, it seemed to the doting Thomas a small enough thing to allow a delicate female.

There must have been times when the doctor, remembering the "discreet, solid" young man he had been in Cooperstown, was appalled at his own strident tones and rash words; but always a moment of yielding was followed by a fresh burst of spleen, in which he despised the humility he had shown and withdrew the concessions he had made.

Ten days before they sighted Hawaii, the men of the Mission met to re-examine the solemn charges given them in Boston and to "fix a few . . . standing rules" for the government of affairs on arrival. But the mere mention of the Board's instructions angered the doctor.

"Property furnished by the Christian public . . . property acquired by the members jointly . . . Should any member persist in violating the regulations of the Prudential Committee . . ."

The new code, he burst out, was being drawn to bear heavily on him alone.

There were heated words between Thomas and his brethren. Voices rasped and nerves jangled. "The instructions under which we embarked—" someone began to remind him.

"I did not understand the instructions when they were given," the doctor snapped, "and I don't believe you did yourselves."

Aghast, his law-loving, code-making brethren admonished him.

"The rule of common stock—"

"Our compact with the board—"

"Maintenance and aid so long as you conform—"

"It was never my plan," the doctor said coldly, "to spend my days in the Sandwich Islands. . . . I may wish to return . . . in case of the ill health of Mrs. H.—or in case I should wish to educate my children in America . . . & I think I ought to make suitable provision. . . ."

So here it was—a declaration of independence before they had even set foot on the Islands. They were not unprepared for it; yet when it came it rather staggered them. They did not see how Thomas Holman could have sat quiet in Park Street Church when the instructions were publicly given and afterward embarked under the patronage of the Board, whose policies were uniform and well known. They did not see how the commissioners, so careful and foresighted in all else, could have accepted for the Mission a man who did not subscribe to its basic principles.

Next day, the doctor had consented to the adoption of the code but warned that he would add as his own private reservation to every item: "so far & so long as I choose."

"The by-laws, of which we transmitted to you a copy," Hiram Bingham wrote to the Board in reviewing the case, "were read & adopted one by one, & we still felt that we could go up to the battle harnessed & prepared for united action, though there was good reason to fear that the Dr. & his wife . . . would break their ranks before the first outpost of the enemy should be fairly possessed."

AT FIRST Thomas Holman pursued his work at Kailua with marked success. Though the old pagan *kahunas* viewed him with jealousy, whispering that he would poison the chiefs, such were his skill and good fortune that all but two of his patients recovered. Because he had warned Liholiho that he could not help the two whose diseases were far advanced, the king did not charge him with their deaths and took pains that others should not. Members of the court, especially the king, rewarded the doctor for his services. Hogs, fruit, cloth, wine and a handsome red-and-yellow feather tippet came his way. If he could have counted them as so much gain for himself, he would doubtless have been happy; but each bit of income reminded him again of the hated rule of common stock. To share with Asa Thurston, the preacher, the avails of the high and specialized art of healing seemed to him illogical and unjust. He hinted now and then that such sharing was a "gratuity from his bounty" rather than a right.

Yet he might have stayed at Kailua much longer, with at least an appearance of content, if it had not been for Lucia. From the day she was set ashore in hot and barren Kona, Lucia was determined to get away. There were privations—painful ones. Water, brought five miles by *kanaka,* was scanty and irregular in supply, often filthy and always so warm as to be almost nauseating to drink. If she washed, she must forego tea or soup. Remembering the bubbling springs and deep cisterns in America, she saw that she should never have left that happy land.

"I verily believe," she wrote in her journal when she had at last got away to Maui, "that great good can be effected among this people with proper means—but I need not tell you never to expect that from me. I only ask your charity to believe that I do not intend to do any harm. I am willing to live forgotten among mankind, if I can live in peace . . . void of offense toward God & man."

Pressed afterward to explain why departure from Kona seemed so urgent, she answered, "I do not know—only I knew it to be my duty to go somewhere from Kailua . . . and I have effected my purpose by the blessing of God."

Thomas and Lucia would gladly have moved to Honolulu, but the king, still sure that all white men on Oahu were up to mischief, was of no mind to let the American physician settle there. Kalanimoku, sorry for the doctor's drooping *wahine,* mentioned Lahaina on Maui—nearer to Kailua and less suspect in the king's eyes than Honolulu, but pleasanter, perhaps, for *haoles* than the Kona coast. He said he would give them some land there and build a house on it if the doctor would agree to come to Kailua whenever he was wanted.

By the Board's instructions Thomas Holman was bound to lay this offer before his colleagues, explaining his concern for Lucia's health, and await a collective decision as to what course he should take. But he was always averse to such deliberate procedure and he knew that his plans stood little chance of being approved. Impulsively he accepted Kalanimoku's offer. Once he had done that, he no longer wanted to go even for a few days to Oahu, where he would have to face Hiram Bingham and hear again about the American Board's instructions.

So the doctor, who had warned that he would follow the by-laws only "so far and so long" as he saw fit, and Lucia, who felt it to be her "duty to go somewhere from Kailua," embarked in the king's brig and took up their residence with a white man at Lahaina while their own house was building.

WORK TO DO

AT Honolulu little Levi Loomis gurgled and wäiled and slept, oblivious of the flurry his birth had caused. Chiefs came to see him; *haole* neighbors sent him presents. The Mission family doted on him. Elisha stood taller and walked firmer now that he had a son. Maria wrote to the friends in Utica, "My sweet babe grows more & more interesting. His presence dispels many a rising sigh."

As for Dr. Holman, time would tell. If he ignored the letter of remonstrance, his brethren would try with a letter of "admonition and suspension" to bring him to repentance. And if he did not repent, they would excommunicate him, cutting him off forever from the Mission and the kingdom of heaven. This was the pattern of church discipline. They were heavy-hearted as they looked into the future, for they knew the doctor would not retreat a single step. Even Samuel Ruggles understood that the end had begun.

Meanwhile there was work to do. The Longnecks did not stay in their tabued inclosures, waiting for sinners to come and hear their gospel. Back of the fort, where Honolulu stretched southeastward among the marshes and fishponds, they sought out the poor and the wretched. Here was the village slum. Into houses but waist-high— dark, filthy, flea-ridden, without so much as a wooden bowl or a woven mat—native families crept at nightfall to sleep, close-packed, on the hard, rush-strewn earth under dusty, tattered *tapas*. Their pigs and dogs and ducks—if they were lucky enough to have any animals—huddled with them; and the places grew foul with excrement.

Daytimes the people lived outside. The strong ones frolicked in the surf or bowled on the plain or hung about the *haole* part of the village to beg or steal. But there were some so ill or indolent that they only lounged in the shade of their shacks—fly-nipped and scabby with an itch that was too common to be noticed. If there was food, they ate whenever hunger impelled, plunging their dirty fingers into the sour, fermenting contents of the common calabash. But there was never an abundance, and often nothing at all. No wonder, then, that their skins hung on their protruding bones like drying fish nets on the rocks.

For the blind and the aged, the sick and the insane, the Hawaiians showed no pity; they taunted them and drove them away, left them to starve or buried them alive in pit or stone-pile. They mated so casually, killed so calmly their unwanted infants, gave away so readily their children to other households that those who had come from America to "save" them thought at first they had no hearts at all.

But the men and women of the Mission held certain truths to be self-evident. And their creed, so annoying to many both here and in their own land, taught that the vilest and the humblest had the right to know and to choose. To these, as well as to overfed princes and dowagers they must reveal the eternal truth. So they followed the paths that wound intricately among the fishponds—royal ponds, from which a hungry commoner could draw a single mullet only at risk of his miserable life or his shrunken limb—and talked with the people, or tried to.

They were misunderstood—these Longnecks. Their prayers terrified; their clothes aroused envy; their homilies stirred resentment. But they persisted. One of the sisters took a dropsical, sore-covered orphan home to nurse it. Hiram Bingham dressed an ulcerated lip or gave a fellow some salve for his blistering rash.

All of them, as they came and went, spoke softly and smiled. They did not rub noses in the Hawaiian manner but held out their white, unblemished hands to grasp the scaly ones of their brown neighbors in *aloha*. Gradually, though they made little of the spoken words, the people began to see meaning in the quiet, trustful friendliness of the newcomers. And those of the Mission discovered hearts in the commoners.

Down in the harbor the *Levant* had taken the *Pedler*'s place, so close to the land that at night when the gibbering natives had gone indoors for fear of ghosts and the foreigners had drunk themselves to sleep, the Chamberlains in the Winship house could hear the voices on her deck. She was the annual Boston ship which, by agreement between the Perkins firm and the British Northwest Company, brought supplies to the post on the Columbia River and freighted furs to Canton. She was loaded now, the record shows, with 13,414 beaver skins, 860 otters, 266 beaver coatings, 6,770 muskrats, 259 minks, 104 foxes, 116 fishers and 37 sea otters. Before proceeding to Canton, she had stopped at the Islands to complete her cargo with sandalwood on her owners' account.

Directly on her route to China lay the island of Kauai, where Kaumualii, his queen and Prince Tamoree waited for the teachers they had begged the Longnecks to send them. The *Levant* would provide free passage to Waimea, Kaumualii's capital, if any of the Mission wished to go. The question that had persisted since the two Samuels returned from the leeward had to be answered now.

The brethren sat long in conference. Could they say *yes* to Kaumualii, who promised land, dwellings, a meeting-house, oxen for plowing and a strict keeping of the Sabbath throughout his realm? Could they say *yes,* also, to Kalanimoku, who had sent urgently for someone to instruct his favorite youths at Kawaihae on Hawaii? Dare they leave the Thurstons unassisted at Kailua? How safe was a lone white woman in a heathen village if her husband's duties summoned him elsewhere?

In the end they willed a further partition of their small company. When the *Levant* sailed, Samuel and Nancy Ruggles, Samuel and Mercy Whitney and Nathan Chamberlain would go in her to live and work on Kauai. In a fortnight or so, when Maria was better able to get along without him, Elisha would go in the *Neo* to

Hawaii Island to live at Kawaihae under Kalanimoku's patronage and teach the premier's favorites. Chubby Daniel Chamberlain, self-reliant at seven, would be sent to Kailua to relieve the loneliness of the Thurstons.

On their last Sabbath together they met in Maria's room in Captain Pigot's house to break the bread and sip the wine of communion, poignantly aware of the partings to come.

Resolutely they forced their minds from qualms and failures to promises and duties and hopes. They sang; and, though the thatch dulled and muted their voices, to Daniel Chamberlain it was "sweet indeed." "I thought," he wrote afterward, "I never heard music more heavenly."

"LITTLE TEACHER"

AT Kawaihae Elisha's grass house faced the sparkling bay where the *Thaddeus* had waited on the first day of April for Kalanimoku to come aboard. His back, or landward, door looked toward Puukohola, the great ruined temple where Kamehameha had once honored his war god. Scattered bones and dried cocoanut husks now littered its fire-scarred stone platform; but only a year ago its thick lava walls had enclosed one of the finest *heiaus* in the land—a central idol hall, surrounded by a drumhouse, a fire-making house and a house for stretching *aha* cord.

Here at Puukohola human bodies had trembled on the altar and human blood had gushed beneath the sacrificial knife. This, like the other *heiaus,* leeward and windward, had been the center of that dark magic which had propitiated a thousand gods and kept a hundred thousand mortals abject and cowering.

No temple in Hawaii had been raised with more priestly advice or consecrated with more ceremony. *Kahunas* had scrutinized its design, approved its vast measurements and performed the rituals that had kept it tabu. Chiefs had come far to carry stones for it; and multitudes of commoners had camped like an army while serving out their work tax on the shrine. Even Kamehameha himself had labored at Puukohola. A soothsayer had told him that only by raising this *heiau* would he become master of all Hawaii; so Kamehameha had built and dedicated, and then he had carried forth his god to subdue four islands in bloody warfare and frighten a fifth into vassalage.

Only a year ago the new king Liholiho had spent the summer in the shadow of this temple, uncertain whether his dead father's nobles would support him or raise rebellion in favor of some other contender. And here in August rumors had come of "free-eating" at Kailua, where some of the most powerful ones were trifling with the ancient tabus. A chiefess, the whispers ran, had eaten a banana—and lived. Men and women had dined together in secret; and so long as the priests had not learned of the act, all had been well. Here, then, at Kawaihae, while some pled with the new king to uphold the old ways and enforce the tabus with rigor, Liholiho had made his choice—to go to Kailua and throw in his lot with the free-eaters and the iconoclasts.

In a little while, the frightening word came from Kailua that the king himself had broken the eating bans and cried out to burn the gods and demolish the temples. More terrible, Hewahewa, highest priest in the kingdom, had applied the torch to a *heiau*. From Kawaihae, even while Puukohola flamed, an army marched southward in fierce but vain defense of the old religion. It was then that Kalanimoku, friend and confidant of Kamehameha, had proved brave and wise in the cause of his son. He marshaled loyal warriors and, when the forces clashed at Kuamoo near Kailua, triumphed for Liholiho and the new ways.

These were the events that had shaken Hawaii while the *Thaddeus* made its way toward the Horn in the final weeks of 1819.

Now in the summer of 1820 Kalanimoku divided his time between Kawaihae, where he kept his own household, and Kailua, where the king lived. With wise counsel he tried to curb the influence of the giddy young courtiers who drank with Liholiho from dawn to midnight. True, Kalanimoku loved the bottle himself. But he could see with half an eye what happened when designing *haoles* traded on the king's weakness.

At Kawaihae, where his grass houses dotted the shore and straggled up the rocky slope beneath the ravaged *heiau*, Kalanimoku had gathered ten promising youths, adopting them according to Hawaiian custom from *alii* families. Some he had had with him a long time; some had come lately. But he loved them all and sought to train them for the duties and burdens of chiefhood. It was for them that he coveted the book learning that had come in the *Thaddeus;* he did not wish to neglect any good thing, either native or foreign, that would make the boys able and steady.

A week after he was installed at Kawaihae, Elisha was reaping a teacher's reward. "I am contented and happy," he wrote, "persuaded that my labors will be productive of good . . . gratified with the attention, diligence, and good conduct of my pupils."

Along with the premier's bright-eyed protégés, the school enrolled Likelike, Kalanimoku's favorite wife (formerly Boki's). Kalanimoku himself came when he was not busy drinking or attending to business. Mornings from nine to twelve and afternoons from two to five, six days a week, the scholars sat before their young instructor, conning their spellers or writing English words on their slates.

Kalanimoku was a liberal patron. He provided a schoolhouse, with neat mats and a table and chair. He furnished Elisha's dwelling with a hammock-bed, slung from the roof, a writing stand, a lamp and a bookshelf. He assigned a *kanaka* to prepare the teacher's meals in the *haole* manner and serve the "fat of the land and the sea . . . well cooked."

Every hour of the day Elisha turned to some good purpose—his classes, devotion, reading, letter-writing, study of the language, self-examination or exercise. At 5:30 in the morning he jumped down from his swinging cot as the dawn crept over Kawaihae bay. At ten in the evening he said his solitary prayers, extinguished his light and climbed aloft to fall into untroubled sleep.

But peace and routine were not the Hawaiian way. The earthquake that one day shook Elisha's grass house and toppled his books was as nothing compared to the unheralded arrival of the king with a hundred attendants. Relinquishing his seaside house for a smaller one inland, Elisha tried to go on with the school. But the tipsy and demanding Liholiho soon put an end to that. Because a council of his chiefs had decided early that month that the court should move permanently to Honolulu, the young ruler was having a last fling on this island—a fling in which Bible reading and the study of Longneck words were to have no part.

"I hope he will shortly be off," Elisha wrote on September 25. And next morning he saw with delight that "His Majesty's fleet . . . 50 sail—mostly canoes" was bound outward. School resumed within the hour.

Kalanimoku was not at any time the most faithful of scholars. A white man had once told him, "You are too old to learn." At fifty-odd, the premier was inclined to agree. When he tried, along with the young chiefs and Likelike, he went ahead as fast as any of them; but he could not hold himself steadily to his teacher's exacting demands. He had to fish, and he had to drink. There were days at a time when he was stupid with rum and so touchy that the natives kept out of his way. Elisha found him on the beach one morning, naked and wallowing. He tried to rouse him, to coax him indoors, to stir in him a sense of shame. "Go away, Little Teacher," the prime minister said crossly. "Old Billy Pitt too old to learn. Go away."

Afterward Kalanimoku was ashamed of himself and came back to school for a while to sit cross-legged on the mat and squint at his book with none-too-sharp eyes. He came sometimes, too, when the cook was setting out Elisha's supper and talked—now gravely, now lightly—about affairs of state. Soon, he said, the king would be settled on Oahu. Houses were already building at Waikiki for all the court—queens, dowagers, the little prince and princess (Liholiho's brother and sister) and the chiefs, great and small. At the recent council, Kalanimoku boasted, he himself had made a strong speech in favor of the move. Kaahumanu, guardian of the realm, was also for it. It would help control the foreigners who had been getting out of hand at Honolulu. And perhaps the king would not get drunk so often there. Kalanimoku broke into a sheepish laugh, knowing, perhaps, what Lumiki, his Little Teacher, thought of others who got drunk.

84

"LITTLE TEACHER"

A STONE'S THROW from Kalanimoku's establishment at Kawaihae was the adobe hut of John Young, the weathered old Englishman who back in April had influenced the king to give the Mission a year's trial. Olohana the natives called him, because in the early years he had rallied them with the seaman's cry, "All hands!" He had come out in 1790 as boatswain of the *Eleanora*. Trapped on shore by a sudden tabu against the launching of small craft, he had seen his vessel sail from the Islands without him. Afterward he and Isaac Davis, a fellow Englishman, had entered the service of Kamehameha, who rewarded them with titles, lands and *alii* wives.

On Sunday afternoons Young visited Elisha and spun long, rambling tales of the Islands under the Conqueror. He told of the part he had played when Kamehameha attacked Oahu, routed its defenders from the beach and the foothills and drove them relentlessly up the rugged, narrowing gorge until they plunged to their death over the Pali. Elisha had heard that story; everyone who visited Honolulu heard about the battle of Nuuanu, but Young told it as an eyewitness, and the horror and hopelessness of the retreat became real for Elisha as never before. Young told, too, how he had stood, grief-bowed among the native chiefs as they tried to catch Kamehameha's dying words and how in the days of mourning, when all Hawaii went mad with passion, he barred the doors of his houses and kept his family within so that his half-grown boys and girls should not see sorrow turned to saturnalia.

Even in his youth Young had not gone much to school or to chapel, but he was quick to see worth in the new learning and to recognize the sincerity of the American teachers. Sitting quiet, his eyes half-closed, his gray hair shaggy above a deep-creased face almost as brown as a native's, he heard Elisha read from the Bible and sing a favorite hymn. The two of them knelt, then, and prayed—the one with his life before him, all untried and full of hope; the other with a strange, eventful career behind him.

THE DAYS at Kawaihae were in some ways Elisha's happiest in the Islands. At Honolulu he had felt futile and ineffectual. Now he was doing an important work. But more than that, from this backwater he saw the past story and present ways of the Hawaiians with a depth and clarity impossible in the turmoil of Honolulu. He knew the time would come when Hiram Bingham would ask him about these things and listen to his answers with respect. For the youngest and least schooled member of the Mission that was a satisfaction indeed.

He missed Maria, of course. But in living apart from her he saw how much he had come to love her, how sweet their comradeship had grown. He remembered a dozen gestures and intonations that he had scarcely noticed in her presence. He saw now as never before how gracious a providence had led him to her in September of 1819.

The twenty-seventh was their first wedding anniversary. "The experience I have had," Elisha wrote in his journal at Kawaihae, "convinces me that marriage is one of the greatest blessings of life, where there is a union of hearts, and I can truly say this happiness is my own."

Maria's letter must have reached him about that time. From it Elisha learned that his son thrived, that the work of the Mission went forward, that—this briefly and without explanation—Dr. Holman and Lucia had come to Honolulu and that the family had moved at last into the new houses on the plain toward Waikiki. "They are not completed yet by a considerable," Maria wrote of the houses. "Last night I slept . . . without either door or window and alone with the exception of two little native girls on the mats & my infant in my arms."

That was not the way they had planned it when they married in Utica a year ago. Elisha wondered impatiently how long it would be before Liholiho grew tired of carousing and took his train and his prime minister to Oahu.

MISSIONARY ROW

THE schooner *St. Martin,* owned by the absent Pigot, arrived in Honolulu in distress. Her whole crew was stricken with scurvy and her captain was in critical agony. Pigot's partner, Mr. Green, thought the Mission's doctor might be sent for and called on Mr. Bingham to discuss that possibility. Hiram did not hesitate. He would have done as much for any neighbor, and to the house of Pigot and Green he was under special obligation. So he wrote Dr. Holman a note, urging him to come and treat the crew. The *St. Martin* then sailed for Maui and returned in a few days with the Holmans.

"They were received with welcome by the Mission family," Hiram Bingham wrote some months afterward.

". . . we were treated by our brethren of the Mission with manifest indifference," is how the doctor saw it.

Maria said only, "They eat at our table but take their lodgings in a house a few rods distant."

At meal times the family now felt again the old fear that a chance word, spoken in innocence, would touch off a painful argument. When the new houses were ready and the Mission moved from the village, the Holmans went to board at Mr. Green's. After that, they held themselves aloof from the Mission, mingling more and more with the captains and traders. Though they came to Sunday services and attended the quarterly examination of Sybil's school, they withdrew afterward like strangers. Hiram Bingham and the doctor exchanged curt notes about medicines and wrapping paper and longer letters about the quarrel that lay between them. There was little in their intercourse to suggest that they were brothers, pledged to a lifetime of love and loyalty; nothing in their conduct to remind the little world of Honolulu that they had come out together to serve a common cause.

At Lahaina Kalanimoku's men finished the fine house they had been building for the American doctor, that he and his *wahine* might live beside a running brook; but Thomas and Lucia, happy now in Honolulu, had no wish to isolate themselves again on Maui.

THE NEW Mission dwellings stood side by side just seaward of the Waikiki path, some three quarters of a mile from the village. Though they did not equal the frame house the Mission had reluctantly left behind in Boston, they were good by Island standards. Boki let the Longnecks know that nothing had been slighted or skimped and that the best of workers had been employed.

House-building in Hawaii was an art. A man of special skill, the *kuenehale,* had to be found and appointed to watch over the whole undertaking. He knew which timbers should be brought from the mountains for the posts—whether of *uhuihi* or *kauila* or *mamane*. In such a house as Boki had ordered for Mr. Bingham there were six on each side and three more at each end between the corner posts. They were tall, for the *kuenehale* was informed that the Longnecks must not be forced to stoop in their doorways.

Set firmly in the earth and notched at the top, the side posts held the horizontal wallplates. A ridgepole joined the loftiest gable posts; and paired rafters met each other at the peak, each bracing its forked lower end firmly against an upright timber.

Great balls of cord, braided from *ukiuki,* were used in lashing part to part. A workman needed strong, muscular hands to wind and knot the sennit and pull it tight about each joint. When the frames were ready, the *aho*—small poles, each the size of a walking stick—were tied horizontally from post to post and from rafter to rafter until the houses looked for all the world like wicker birdcages or loose-woven baskets turned bottom-side-up. At least Sybil

Bingham said so when she strolled out one moonlit evening with her husband.

Finally thatchers set to work to cover the skeleton. Beginning at a corner, a worker placed with his left hand a thick bunch of *pili* grass against the *aho,* roots upward, tops spreading along the ground. His right hand brought the cord snugly around it as his left, now free, reached for the next tuft. Slap, twist, reach; slap, twist, reach—squatting on the earth or standing on a scaffold to thatch the roof-peak, he kept his measured, moderate rhythm until he finished his stint.

Three of the houses, though they stood some ten feet apart, were connected on the seaward side by a shed, into which each dwelling opened its gable end. The shed in turn had two doors toward the beach and one eastward toward Waikiki and Diamond Hill. This was not the native builder's notion of a good *lanai.* Nor did he like to puncture his trim thatch walls with gaping window-holes, which he must cover with hinged wooden shutters. He saw no need, moreover, to plaster a thick coating of mud on both the large, separate storehouse and the small cookhouse adjoining the *lanai.* Yet all these things the *haoles* asked, and Boki had ordered that their wishes be heeded.

In the old days when the tabus held, only no-accounts would have occupied their houses without the ceremony of *ka oki ana o ka piko ka hale,* the cutting of the navel string of the house. No, the owner and his friends first gathered round outside, and a *kahuna pule* came who knew the proper prayer. The priest stood, ax in hand, before the door where the thatch still hung long over the opening, and in set phrases asked the owner whether all was ready. If it was, he held a block of wood under the tuft to be cut, chanted the prayer called *kuwa* and cut the thatch to the rhythm of his chant:

Orderly and harmonious is the prayer of the multitude to God.
Kuwa cuts now the *piko* of the house of Mea.

He stands! He cuts! The thatch is cut!
It is cut! Lo it is cut!

The Longnecks had no such ceremonies. They only moved with their handcart and settled their books and bedsteads into place. Then when Sunday came, they held their dedication service, for the Bingham house was church and schoolroom as well as dwelling. "Except the Lord build the house, they labor in vain that build it," was Hiram's text. "Except the Lord keep the city, the watchman walketh but in vain."

Missionary Row smelled sweet and clean after the sodden old houses in the village. Morning sun slanted through the eighteen-inch window slits and the tall doorways, and sea breezes stirred the white curtains and the copperplate valances. Ceilings of yellow *tapa* and wall-coverings of fine-woven, patterned matting lightened the rooms; high-post beds from America, toilette stands and settees contrived from oddments, walnut writing cases, mahogany medicine chests and rows of leather-bound books gave comfort and charm to the apartments.

The schoolroom at the Binghams' had long plank benches on three sides. The *lanai* held the common dining table, and the mud-plastered hut nearby housed the cookstove. Honolii's one-room house stood separate a few feet from the Row.

Girl boarders—by this time there were several of them—had the landward room of the middle, or Loomis, house. The boys, fewer in number, lodged with the Chamberlains at the *waikiki* end of the Row, or with the Binghams, where they slept in the schoolroom. Already the place seemed crowded. Yet, then and always, a Mission house was a hostel for those who needed shelter.

A sunken-eyed native of Calcutta, left stranded by a ship; a consumptive sailor; a half-caste infant, deserted by its native mother; an "ingenious mechanic" from New England, looking for a pious boarding place; a discharged Negro seaman, his chest on his back, taunted and pelted by his shipmates—such they welcomed, for an hour, a few days or many months, according to the need.

WORKMEN WERE still thatching Honolii's cottage when they took the wounded gunner there from *L'Aigle*.

Aboard that familiar British whaler there had occurred what the journals called "a melancholy accident." As, homeward bound, *L'Aigle* had fired her farewell salute, a gun had exploded and a sailor named Keyes had lost an arm and been horribly burned. Captain Starbuck had come promptly ashore to raise a fund for Keyes (heading the subscription with his own gift of $200) and find him a place in the village to recover—or die.

To receive the luckless fellow, with Dr. Williams in attendance, seemed to the family at Missionary Row a small return for all the captain's kindness—so small, indeed, that they added fifty dollars to the fund for Keyes.

But this would never do, Captain Starbuck blustered, knowing well that the Mission was poor. If Mr. Bingham insisted, here was twenty of the fifty back as *L'Aigle*'s parting gift to the orphan fund. So they strove to outdo each other in generosity. But the captain had the last word. In a day or two he returned with a plate of butter and a wooden washtub full of crockery. Putting their hands into "Captain Starbuck's tub" was rated thereafter a high privilege by the sisters who had washed their clothes in Nuuanu stream.

A light burned all night in Honolii's house, for as often as Keyes groaned in his pain, Dr. Williams went to him with a potion. In the early hours of October 20 the lamp's flame, fanned perhaps by a sudden puff, caught at the thatch wall and raced up the seaward gable. There were shouts of "Fire!" and a great running about. The Mission family turned out in night clothes, looking in the rising glare like so many tousled ghosts.

They had been told by natives that when fire seized the straw, it laid all in ashes. But they refused to believe it. The wind was light and blowing away from the Row. There was a chance. They prayed as they ran.

They moved Keyes to the Chamberlain house; Dr. Williams' trunk and books, their own bed clothes and wearing apparel they tossed into a heap at the other end of the yard. They knew that

Hawaiian custom sanctioned stealing at a fire, but in their panic they forgot to place a guard. Native men scuttled up to help put out the flames, and their *wahines,* tagging behind, took good care of the pilfering.

There was a water pail in every house, and Captain Starbuck's washtub served as a reservoir. It was two hundred feet to the spring that Daniel Chamberlain had cleared out as a temporary well. How they got enough bucketfuls back to the fire they could hardly tell afterward. Daniel Chamberlain had shouted the orders, and even the Hawaiians had obeyed. But he had not told Hiram Bingham to climb to the roof and beat out the flames that were licking along the ridgepole. That rash and successful operation was Hiram's own idea.

An hour later, amid the acrid smell of wet ashes and lingering smoke, they appraised the damage and loss. The house-frame was unharmed. Less than half the thatch would have to be renewed. Some pantaloons, shirts and towels had been stolen.

WHEN CAPTAIN STARBUCK came to take Keyes and the doctor away, Hiram Bingham asked him, with a glance toward Sybil's swollen figure, whether he could see any way to leave Dr. Williams a little longer. Dr. Holman had gone to Kauai on the eleventh, he explained. There both Mercy Whitney and Nancy Ruggles were soon to be confined. But *L'Aigle* was full of oil and overdue to start for London. Captain Starbuck said he would keep a sharp eye out for whales as he departed. If he took any near the Islands, he would come back, set his surgeon on shore and cruise around a little longer. Otherwise . . .

Certainly, Hiram said. They would leave the matter to God.

On the ninth of November, his small skill supported by his great faith and resourcefulness, Hiram Bingham delivered his own firstborn, a daughter who was named Sophia.

REUNION

IN early November Kalanimoku said to Elisha, "Take my young chiefs to Oahu, to the house of Boki, my brother. Teach them there, and when the king goes to Oahu I will go with him." He added that he would then build two fine houses for the Longnecks—as fine and large as the doctor's empty house at Lahaina. He did not say whether he would resume the *palapala*.

The premier's household, including the young teacher, then embarked for Kailua and afterward with Liholiho and his train for Lahaina on Maui, arriving on the sixth. When would there be a conveyance to Oahu? Elisha immediately asked. Nobody could tell. But at sunset a strange vessel anchored in Lahaina roads, and Elisha learned that she was the *Cleopatra's Barge,* Captain John Suter, 141 days from Boston, Honolulu bound.

Though he had fat packets of mail for the missionaries at the Islands, Captain Suter was thrown on his beam-ends, so to speak, when a member of the company, looking young enough to be a cabin boy, came on board at Lahaina, seeking passage for himself and a parcel of natives. Elisha eagerly explained that he had been away from Honolulu three months, that he had a wife there, and a baby son—

"Come along with your injuns," the captain said heartily. Elisha had a stateroom to himself; and on the floor of the great cabin, where the elite of New England had once made merry, Kalanimoku's protégés spread their mats and slept as they were carried to Oahu.

The *Barge* was a famous vessel. Built for Salem's rich East India merchant, George Crowninshield, by Salem's noted shipwright, Retire Becket, she became the first American pleasure yacht and the show-piece of the decade. Before she sailed on her first cruise in the spring of 1817, sight-seers had gone aboard her by the thousands. In one day nineteen hundred women and nine hundred men had viewed her spacious and glittering cabin, her five fine staterooms and her forecastle. She had cost $50,000, and that was without her furnishings—the silver mugs, lacquer trays, crystal decanters, lyre-backed sofas and pier glasses.

When Crowninshield died, the brig and all her trappings had gone on the auction block. Now in 1820, having changed hands three times, she belonged to Bryant & Sturgis, who had bought her with an eye to the sandalwood trade. She was just the sort of vessel to catch the fancy of a king or chief.

Her master, Captain Suter, was as shrewd as they come and as pious as he was shrewd. Oftenest told as proof of the piety was the story of how Suter kept his big Bible on the cabin table and read it daily, working straight through from Genesis to Revelation with never a change of course. A scapegrace clerk named Preble used to move back the bookmark and cause the good Baptist to read the same passage many times, wondering why he did not get on any faster. But that was years before. In November 1820, young Charles Preble was no longer playing tricks on captains. He was himself commanding the B & S brig *Becket,* three weeks out of Boston on her way to the Islands.

Instructions for the *Cleopatra's* voyage had filled many pages. Two Bryant & Sturgis ships would be coming off the Coast that fall, bound home by way of Canton. To replace them in the Pacific, B & S were sending out, under Captain Suter's general direction, four vessels, three of them newly added to the company's fleet. The *Barge* was to be sold if possible to the king. The *Lascar* would go to the Coast for furs. The *Tartar,* a large new ship, would carry to Canton the sandalwood received for the *Barge.* The *Becket* was almost an afterthought. She had cost Bryant & Sturgis only $5,500, and a small vessel was always useful as a tender.

As to letters, the *Barge* carried sixty-one for the Mission. They had been accepted in America on condition that the captain either hold them until he left the Islands or have them opened and read in his presence. That was to prevent word about prices or sailings from leaking out to the firm's detriment in dealing with the chiefs. But after one look at the honest, news-hungry faces of Hiram Bingham and Daniel Chamberlain, Captain Suter told them to take the letters—and if there was anything in them about the trade, just not to blab it to Blanchard or Boki.

Captain Suter got back to Lahaina from Honolulu on November 11. He invited the king and his suite to dinner on the *Barge*. Three days later the bargain was made. For the brig and her cargo Liholiho had promised to pay eight thousand piculs of sandalwood. If prices held in Canton, that would be $80,000.

Contract in pocket and the first part of his mission speedily accomplished, Captain Suter brought his sea chest—and doubtless his Bible—ashore at Honolulu to await the next Bryant & Sturgis arrival from America.

ONCE HE had bought himself an elegant vessel, Liholiho plunged again into his revels at Lahaina. That he must soon go to Oahu, that he must as king adopt a firm policy toward the Honolulu foreigners, that he must decide whether the Longneck teachers should stay beyond a year—all this he remembered only too well. But for a little while longer he wanted to forget it. So with his queens and his shameless favorites and his hundreds of *kanakas* he made off to the other side of Maui on a spree.

Hopu and the Thurstons and Danny Chamberlain, who had followed his majesty from Kailua, waited impatiently at Lahaina for his permission to go on to Honolulu. But the king said *no*. After the fun there would come, perhaps, a day for repentance and prayer, and he wanted his "tabu minister" to stay close at hand in case he was needed. Let Mr. Thurston remain on Maui and not go to Oahu—at least not yet.

The Americans acquiesced miserably. They dared not unpack

lest a sudden move find them unready. And in that they were wise, for in the middle of December, the king abruptly sent word that the Longnecks might embark for the leeward. Only Hopu remained behind; he thought it his duty to stay with Liholiho. The rest a native brig delivered at Honolulu—bedraggled and weary—in time to keep Christmas with the family.

On Christmas day, 1820, there were sails off Diamond Hill. Bryant & Sturgis' brig *Lascar,* Captain Harris, and their ship *Tartar,* Captain Turner, though they had left Boston a month apart, came up the bay like racers straining for the finish line. These were the vessels Captain Suter had been expecting. Their timely arrival filled him with holiday cheer.

The B & S ships carried cheer for the Mission, too. There were letters from home, and the captains, because it was Christmas, gave them at once to the waiting brethren. There were supplies from the Board—wheat flour, rye flour, Indian meal, wine, cider—things impossible to get in the Islands, things that tasted of home.

But what, above all, made this Christmas day memorable in the Mission was the news that the *Tartar* had brought out their houseframe.

"Say to the missionaries," Bryant & Sturgis directed Captain Suter by letter, "that we shall bring the frame of their House in the Tartar free of freight, and as we do so much for them they must aid you if they can."

1821

BITTER THINGS

THE two and a half acres that lay about Missionary Row were bare indeed. In building the houses Boki's men had trampled the sparse wild grass until the last spear had died. This was *kula* land—land that could not be watered from the streams. And because there were neither horses nor oxen to be had, it could not be plowed. Boki had told the brethren to get their beasts from Marin, and Marin had refused. All the animals were tabu, he said; he was keeping them for the king. So Daniel Chamberlain had sent the plow to Kauai, where Kaumualii had lent the Mission a horse to draw it.

In the end the brethren turned to and spaded a garden plot by hand. Their backs ached, and even though it was the "cool" season, their clothes were soaked with sweat.

Then they planted, enriching the soil first in the native manner with a mulch of leaves. One acre they put to Indian corn; the other to sweet potatoes, squash, cabbages, beans and melons. Daniel Chamberlain was happy. Next to harvest, seedtime is the best season to a farmer.

This was *Hoo-ilo,* the natives said. The *kona* wind would soon bring rain.

The *kona* blew, but it did not bring much rain to Honolulu. "It is *kona-ku* which carries rain," a chief explained. "This that comes now is *kona-mae,* the withering wind."

Dry though it was, the seeds sprouted. Daniel gave each green blade tenderest care. All through December he worked in the garden every hour of daylight. He and his boys carried water a bucket at a time from the well to the growing plants.

The natives made more dire predictions. January was the month, they said, for the *enuhe,* a worm that ate all green things.

One morning Daniel, on his knees in the corn patch, held one of the tender shoots in his hand and looked at it. Then he scratched the earth around another. "No *enuhe* did this," he said grimly. "It's cut worms." He poked at the dry soil around a third hill and uncovered a wrinkled, dull-brown worm an inch long. When he turned it over, it was pale underneath. "Cut worm, all right," he said, and tossed away the shoot he had held.

The soil had never before been cultivated; the weather was cool; everything was right for cut worms. Only a spell of hot days would put a stop to them. But vigorous hoeing, Daniel thought, might help. So all day long the hoes grated an even rhythm in the sandy soil.

A few mornings later the clouds lay smooth over the mountains. This, the natives said was *papole* and foretokened rain. They were right. A downpour soaked the inclosure and flooded the grass houses. What was left of the garden and the corn began to flourish.

Rains continued fairly frequent, and many days were warm. Soon the corn was high enough so that the leaves gave out a silken rustle, a sound that surpasses all other music to a farmer's ear.

Then, when January was almost at an end, Daniel appeared one morning just after dawn at the Loomises' door.

"I wish you'd step out here," he said to Elisha. "I want you to look at something." Daniel led Elisha to the cornfield and pointed to one of the leaves. It was infested with worms perhaps an inch and a quarter long, and so were all the others as far as they could see. The *enuhe* had come, according to prediction, in the month of January.

In a few days not a leaf of corn was left, and many other plants had been destroyed. Only the melons and potatoes survived and ripened to supplement the scant diet of the family. It was small return for their labor.

Since the day when he volunteered for the Mission Daniel

Chamberlain had envisioned vast stretches of Hawaiian lowland furrowed and planted, acres of ripe wheat ruffled by the trade winds, maize bursting with ears, mills turning beside the rivers, flour and meal and cow's milk for every heathen child. Now he knew it would not be so in his time.

The Hawaiians did not want wheat bread and cow's milk. For them there was nothing to equal fish and *poi.*

Taro, from which *poi* was made, flourished the year round, if planted a little at a time. Broad, thick green leaves showed that the roots were ready for pulling at one end of a garden patch as the ground was trodden at the other for the setting of new crowns. A good farmer worked all day until sunset, weeding and watering his *taro* until, after twelve months, it was ripe.

Once pulled from the ground, the *taro* roots were dried in earth ovens, then pounded. When there was not too much going after sandalwood, the *poi* pestle thumped early and late, and the calabashes of the people were filled.

As for the fish, they abounded in Hawaiian waters, and a skilled fisherman knew many ways of catching them: casting with nets of *olona* cord, fishing with hooks of bone or ivory, hurling sharp-tipped wooden spears and luring the octopus with cowrie shells. They fished at night with flares along the reefs or by day beneath the rocks. They bartered part of their catch for yams or *taro,* and ate some of it raw, blood dripping down their chins.

What did such a people want with wheat bread or cow's milk?

But Daniel did not altogether despair. In a clear, firm hand he wrote: "Here are thousands of acres of land that would produce wealth and comfort for a people who know hunger. Though at present no waving cornfields nor whitening wheat fields are to be seen, and it may be long before a comfortable supply of bread can be produced here, yet in the day to come, this may be as handsome a place as the world will afford."

Six months had passed since the brethren at Honolulu first wrote to Thomas Holman in stern remonstrance against his moving to

Maui. When he ignored their protest, they suspended him from the church and admonished him to repentance. If he had then said, "I was wrong; forgive me," they would have joyfully restored him to good standing. But if he had said that, he would not have been the Thomas Holman they knew so well. A hundred times, it seemed, he had announced his fierce independence, his proud self-sufficiency, his scorn for their rules, his belief that his first duty was to Lucia and his first concern to insure his own future. So he had said instead, "I am glad I went to Lahaina."

He had said a great deal more, too—most of it in writing, for on the *Thaddeus* the family had learned how painful and how futile it was to talk. So even while he was at Honolulu, the doctor had received Hiram Bingham's solemnly worded inquiries and answered them with pert and quibbling letters that would have been amusing if they had not dealt with matters so grave.

Then the doctor had gone to Kauai to attend Mercy Whitney and Nancy Ruggles in childbirth, and the brethren at Honolulu could not but wonder how successfully he was pleading his case with those at the northerly station.

They need not have been concerned. Samuel Ruggles, in whom affection for Lucia warred with his duty to the Mission, joined with Samuel Whitney in advising those at Honolulu to do what must be done about the doctor. That meant excommunication.

Finally on the sixteenth of January at a meeting duly called for "consultation and prayer" the main body of the Mission reviewed all that had passed since Thomas Holman of Cooperstown, New York, first offered himself to the American Board.

At Cornwall: ". . . a disposition to complain . . . and to dictate . . ."

In Boston: ". . . censuring . . . the very kind and polite attention of the Treasurer in locating the family in the different apartments of the *Thaddeus*."

On board: ". . . rudely censured Capt. Chamberlain & his wife . . . for proposing . . . to sell to the seamen a little cheese, which must otherwise be lost."

Later: ". . . a habit of . . . putting a grossly erroneous construction on the language of others."

In March: ". . . he considered the medicines as his own & his art as his own, by means of which he intended to make himself able to return to his native land."

March 20: ". . . only so far & so long as he chose."

At Kailua: "Had it not been for me, none of the mission would ever have landed on these islands."

Still at Kailua: ". . . the Dr. declares that he will never come under the superintendence of Br. B. no, *never.*"

At Lahaina: "I am glad that I came to Lahaina."

From Kauai: "In *all* my conduct I feel that I have studied the welfare of the Mission."

Hiram Bingham stood before the solemn little company in Missionary Row and read from the doctor's letters and from memorandums about his conduct. Daniel and Jerusha, Lucy and Asa, Elisha and Maria and Sybil listened with set faces and full, angry hearts, as memories came flooding back.

Then Hiram turned to the Bible: "Now we command you, brethren, in the name of our Lord Jesus Christ, that ye withdraw yourselves from every brother that walketh disorderly, and not after the tradition which he received of us."

They cast their votes on bits of paper. Without dissent they excommunicated Thomas Holman and suspended Lucia, his wife. But it was a bitter thing to do. Next day Maria wrote in her journal, "None of us slept much last night."

Letters carried the somber word to the Holmans at Kauai and reminded the doctor that the medical outfit belonged to the Mission. Though the family had thought that Thomas and Lucia might immediately take passage for America, the Holmans stayed on at Kauai for many weeks. Then, in the spring, after their baby, Lucia Kamamalu, had been born, the doctor came alone to Honolulu and lived in the traders' colony. He was cold and correct when he met his former brethren, and delivered up, on written request, a good part of the medicines, though he retained the books and instruments. In June he brought Lucia and the baby to Oahu and took lodging in a house belonging to James Hunnewell. It was October before there was a sailing for home.

The doctor found enough to do. Among the *haoles* there was always someone to be bled or bandaged or physicked. As long as he could hang on to the outfit, Thomas Holman could do very well for himself. But he knew that one day there would come a call, too peremptory to be denied, for the last item of Mission property. The withdrawal of his means of making an independent living was, as he saw it, but the final injustice in a long series. Well, he would tell his story in America. Since the Board had broken its contract with him and ruined his prospects in the Islands, let it pay him for the months of service he had given. Let it pay him well.

But Thomas Holman could not wait until he reached home to state his case. He would have been more than human if he had not talked that summer to men so ready to listen. In the tight little foreign community, where free-lancing and enterprise were valued highly, where newcomers met the doctor early and often, the legend began to grow: The whole thing had been about some oranges and lemons; Mr. Bingham had charged the doctor—or was it his wife?—with stealing oranges on shipboard; the Mission had expelled the doctor all on account of a few paltry oranges.

Sometimes the men who said these things were drunk; sometimes they were angry with the missionaries for their own reasons. Other threads, coarser and gaudier, dominated the anti-Mission pattern when it was fully woven, but the thread of the Holmans' spinning was clearly discernible.

HULAHULA

BOKI, like his brother and the king, had thought it would be good to learn English if he did not have to apply himself too steadily. His first teacher, a stammering resident, had soon given up his task, because, "Bo—bo—Boki, you know sir, is ve—ve—very te—te—jus—you know, sir." Afterward Boki let Hiram Bingham visit him each day for a little lesson—often a very little one. But before he had made any marked advance, the governor found himself too busy for books.

For one thing, he had to arrange for the *hulahula*. There had not been much dancing on Oahu since Kamehameha's death. When the old religion was shattered, the idols destroyed and the priesthood abolished, the hula master hid away his god, the *akua hulahula*, dispersed his musicians and his dancers and then fell ill and died. After that the chants were heard only when a group gathered of their own accord, perhaps to hail the birth of a child.

But when Boki learned that Liholiho's court would soon move to Oahu and that Kalanimoku's wife, Likelike, was expecting an heir, he determined to revive the *hula* in splendor. So he called on those who had danced for the old master. Many responded; a new master was found and musicians appointed. Soon the sound of calabash drums and the repetitive chanting of voices drifted toward Missionary Row.

The Mission's scholars grew restless.

"We must go," said one and another. "It is for the king. The governor bids us dance."

"We must not," said Hannah Holmes. "Boki has no right to call us from the *palapala*. There are enough empty-heads who cannot learn to read. Let them dance."

HANNAH HOLMES was Hawaii's child. She had gay, pliant ways and a quick smile. She loved sunshine on waterfalls, the shadow-patterns of breadfruit and *kukui* leaves, the gentle, ceaseless motion of cocoanut fronds in the trade winds. She took joy in the changeless mountains that hemmed her little world, in the streams that poured endlessly seaward, in the sudden gusty rain that swept down the valley to "knock at the house" and in the rainbow that came after. And she was stirred by the ancient *meles* that extolled the gods and hero-chiefs and by the rhythms of the *hula*.

But Hannah was New England's daughter, too. From her father, Oliver Holmes of Plymouth, Massachusetts, she had her zest for inquiry, her eagerness to know the truth behind the things she saw and the far consequences of the things she did. From him she came by her love of order, propriety, decorum and a brooding sense of duty that turned easily to one of guilt.

Therefore, though the *hula* drums set her blood tingling, Hannah said, "We must not go."

Hannah was past twenty when the missionaries came to Honolulu and had known man's love and motherhood; but the beauty and wonder of the *pala* and the *pule* compelled her strangely. There were the little texts in Hawaiian that the Longnecks taught the scholars on Sundays—familiar words in new poignant patterns. They spoke them together, and Hannah liked to call the first word a breath ahead of the others as the leader did in a *hula*.

> In the beginning God created the heavens and the earth.
> God is in heaven, and he is everywhere.
> God loves good men, and good men love God.
> We must pray to God and love him.

These first, and then, as the weeks went by, longer, more thought-stirring ones:

Look unto me and be saved, all ye ends of the earth.
Thou shalt love the Lord thy God with all thy heart, and thy neigh-
    bor as thyself.

Here, then, were the answers to her questions about the world,
the rules to guide her life. Hannah spoke haltingly with her
teachers about these things—with Sybil Bingham, when the other
scholars had gone and the two women sat together, sewing. Or
with Maria Loomis, when little Levi lay quiet in Hannah's arms.

She did not tell them about her own baby, perhaps because that
was something that belonged to the past, to the "time of dark
hearts." She told them only that now she was joyful, that now she
must learn and learn and learn.

For a Mission scholar it was not enough, of course, to know
some gospel in Hawaiian, repeating by rote what the teacher said
slowly and stiffly. The goal was to read the Bible itself—in English.
To do that, you began with the spelling-book—with the *a-b-c*'s and
the *a-b-ab*'s and after that the columned words of one and two and
three syllables with their varied accents. You read, presently, little
pieces in which words were joined together in stories about rude
boys and apples, cats and rats, foxes and brambles. And then one
day you looked into the great book itself, where the teacher had
opened it, and saw: "Thou-shalt-have-no-other-gods-before-me"—
and you had read the first Commandment.

Hannah sped through the lessons in Webster and by the end of
the second quarter was reading in the Bible. She was not alone in
her triumph, for William Beals, the little orphan boarder, had kept
with her all the way. The two received, at the public examination,
small Bibles of their own as rewards for their achievement.

Most foreigners who came to the school exhibition that first
year said they were "amazed" and "highly gratified" at the progress made by native scholars. But portly, graying Oliver Holmes
was just plain proud. Besides his Hannah, there were his George, his
Mary, his Polly, his Jennie and his Charlotte, and they all "made
good proficiency." Even Polly, who at fourteen had gone, unwill-

ing, with a Northwest captain on his cruise and had borne his
child in bitterness, seemed happy now.

Hannah's father had come out in the *Margaret* in '93, and, finding the Islands more to his liking than the forecastle, had asked
for a discharge. He still prized the paper on which his captain had
written that Oliver Holmes had "ever behaved with great propriety, as an honest and active man towards his duty while on
board" and was discharged "by his own desire to tarry on
shore . . ."

From the first he prospered. Kamehameha had given him land,
a title and an *alii* wife. Holmes built himself a great establishment
at the edge of Honolulu—houses for himself and his growing
family, houses for his one hundred and eighty tenants and *kanakas,*
and houses for white visitors, though they came rarely in those
days. "Pa Homa" the natives called the place, because of the *pa,*
or paling, which encircled it.

But it was not only the king's gifts that had enriched the
Plymouth sailor. By 1810 the ships of his countrymen had begun
to stop at Honolulu for fresh provisions and to winter there when
they came off the Coast. From selling them vegetables and goats,
Oliver Holmes drifted into a kind of partnership with the Boston
captains, whereby he served them as host while they were on
Oahu and as agent when they were away. Thus he shared in the
profits of the early sandalwood era and furnished his grass houses
with comforts from America and luxuries from China.

In the first days of the Mission, Hannah had invited the Longnecks for special Sabbath evening meetings at Pa Homa. It seemed
then that she could not get enough of talking with God in prayer.
Timidly she told Mr. Bingham that if he would make *pulepule*
there, she would bring together some who had not been bold
enough to go to the Mission houses. Let Binamu speak in English,
she said, and she would put the words into Hawaiian as she did
at the day school.

She arranged a stand for the Bible and a lamp to light its pages,
and then she sat at Hiram Bingham's feet to tell her assembled

friends and neighbors what the reading meant. There was prayer, too, and a hymn; and Oliver Holmes, loving the old tunes that spoke of his boyhood, let the tears come as they would.

Now AS Boki's messenger roved about the village, summoning this one and that to join the dancers, there were rumors that the Longneck school would be dissolved by state order. Hannah and the other scholars were distressed. They wanted to do right, they said. But what was right? There had never been such a dilemma before.

On Sunday Hiram Bingham read from the Bible: "Let every soul be in subjection to the higher powers. . . ." That meant that they should obey their rulers in all things that were consistent with the law of God. But on Monday Hiram went to Boki to seek a compromise, so that the school need not be closed.

Boki said, "It is well to have both the *hula* and the *pala*. The people of your school may dance in the morning and in the evening; they may read their books in the afternoon."

But they were not to dance at all on Sunday, Hiram insisted.

Very well, Boki agreed a little sullenly. Not on the Longnecks' tabu day. But when the king came, it might be otherwise. It would then be as the king said.

Hour after hour in the days that followed, the drums beat in the governor's yard, and the dancers practiced their steps. Musicians thumped their calabashes ecstatically, while the long rows of agile dancers moved in rhythm, feet stepping lightly, hips swinging, arms flowing, faces aglow.

Then, one day, word came from the windward that Kalanimoku was sending Likelike down to Honolulu, so that his heir might be born where the splendid *hula* flourished. Boki was delighted and urged the dance master to whip up the zeal of his performers and bring their work to perfection. For that, the master said, he really must have an *akua hulahula,* a god of sandalwood. The wood was brought, the figure carved out, draped, and placed in its corner. Honolulu throbbed with the dance from dawn to dark, and, when the moon was full, on into the evening. Likelike, her hour approaching, could rejoice that full honor would be done her off-spring.

Early one morning the cannon began to boom, and the news spread through the village that a man-child had been born. Close to the door of the house where the mother and child lay, the guns continued to crash till two hundred pounds of powder had been expended to hail the noble birth.

Up and down the village natives drank rum and embraced each other in an orgy of rejoicing. White men toasted the little chief, first in one grogshop and then in another, picked quarrels about him and sang wild ditties in his honor. At mid-day it was announced at the fort that any person who wished to see the child might do so by paying a Spanish dollar; and the curious and the worshipful thronged the house till nightfall, almost suffocating the mother as they elbowed forward to see the wizened bit of brown flesh that was their new-born chief.

All morning the *hula* continued with fine frenzy, but shortly after noon a heavy rain fell. The dancers scurried to cover and the *hula* master, irate at this rout, beat his god with a cudgel and berated him with curses.

Before the next dawn a solitary gun had announced the death of the child. Villagers groaned and sobbed and continued to drink. The skies wept, and the *hula* was canceled indefinitely.

Likelike, burning with fever, lay on drenched, sodden mats and called for *kanakas* to bear her to the governor's pond and immerse her in the soothing waters. Eight or ten times in the course of a night she cried out that she must be cooled again.

Boki asked Don Marin what he thought of this, and Marin shook his head. It would be better, he said, if Likelike could bear the pain, lying quietly on her bed. But she pleaded that she could not. So the *kanakas* lifted her great body and laid it once more in the shallow pond.

For five tortured days the chiefess survived her infant son. Then on the Sabbath, while Asa Thurston preached in the Mission's schoolroom, a concerted groan from two hundred native throats told that Likelike was dead. Cannon sounded from the fort and then were still, but the piteous wailing of the people went on and on. Commoners shaved off locks of hair from the sides of their heads; some knocked out teeth; others, with smoldering bark, burned markings on their faces, arms and necks. Thus mutilated, they milled about and, between gourds of *awa* and bottles of rum, kept up a ceaseless lament.

At evening, when Kalanimoku had come from the windward with his friend and father-in-law Kaikioewa, the Longneck men went down to express the sympathy of the Mission family. Though not averse to a funeral sermon, the premier said he would in other respects follow the customs of his country. Likelike's bones would be preserved, her flesh torn from them and cast into the sea. The sermon, Kalanimoku said, pausing in the pebble game with which he sought to forget his grief, might be preached at any time the missionaries desired. Seeing Elisha with the others, he cried suddenly, "Lumiki! Little Teacher!" He took Elisha's hands in both of his and held them to his bosom, then touched his nose to Elisha's. But he returned at once to his game, pointing out with a sly smile the very *tapa* under which his opponent had hid the pebble.

PALAPALA

THERE were flashes in the gathering darkness, and a deafening roar from the bay. The earth trembled as the sound rolled up Nuuanu valley and around Punchbowl. It was a twelve-gun salute, soon answered from the fort, to honor His Majesty's arrival in Honolulu harbor.

At once a crier made his rounds, calling for fresh rushes for the governor's yard and for hogs, dogs, *taro* and *poi,* that the king might be fed. In the morning the dancers, whose duty it was to bring the ground-covering, walked single file in stately parade from the marshes to the fort with bundles of rushes on their backs. *Kanakas* and farmers, marshaled by overseers, carried huge calabashes or, two-and-two, supported between them the poles to which live animals were tied. Presently a fleet of canoes put out to tow in the *Cleopatra's Barge,* becalmed in the bay. There was another heavy discharge of cannon as Liholiho landed and staggered into Boki's house.

He had not come to stay, it turned out. He had only run away from his queens and counselors. Putting Jean Rives in command of his new brig, he had taken his favorite wife and boon companions aboard and sailed abruptly and riotously from Lahaina. That was the way he liked to do things.

Four times in the king's brief stay in Honolulu the men of the Mission tried to lay before him the matter of their frame house, stored since Christmas day in Boki's yard. No man could build in Hawaii so much as a grass shack without royal leave. Certainly the Longnecks would need the king's most explicit permission if they were to erect so strange and permanent a thing as a house of wood. So they called at the fort.

The first time, stupid with rum, Liholiho said nothing. Indeed, he scarcely knew that Hiram and Asa were there. His favorite wife Kamamalu, sitting near her lord, took his listless hand and, smiling her apology, presented it to the gentlemen in *aloha*.

The second time, still a little groggy, the king heard the proposal out. "No," he said at once and with decision. "You must not build a wooden house. My father never allowed a foreigner to build except for him."

On the third day the men took their wives and their infants to the fort.

"King Liholiho sleeps," said Boki, as he ushered the callers into his palace. At the far end of the room lay His Majesty, in a *malo* of bright green silk, a half-empty bottle in his hand. With Kamamalu on the mat were Boki's wife, Liliha, and some other Oahu chiefs, male and female. The women fondled lap dogs and ate with unmistakable relish the fleas they picked from them. One cuddled a young pig.

They pushed their pets aside, reached with plump arms for the Mission babies and passed the little ones around, inspecting their fine apparel, poking fingers into dimples, wiggling tiny toes, cooing Hawaiian syllables. Sophia Bingham cried a little, and then snuggled happily against the big, soft bosom of a chiefess. Levi Loomis reveled in it all.

Next the *haole* ladies had to take down their hair and let the *alii* women stroke and braid it. Few women in Hawaii had long hair. They cropped theirs all around with shark's teeth, then whitened and stiffened the foretop until it stood up like bristles. Now and then they took out their bottles and brushes and looking glasses—for these things they had always at hand—and swabbed on fresh whitewash. It was all very cozy and intimate, and, as the Hawaiians said over and over, *maikai*. But Liholiho slept on. There was no chance to speak of the wooden house.

Once more before the king sailed back to Maui the brethren

sounded him out. They told him that when it rained, the wet ground and dampened thatch of Missionary Row made the women ill, gave them lung trouble so that they coughed and grew thin like Binamu's wife.

Liholiho, almost sober for once, said impatiently, "Yes, build. But when you go, take everything away with you."

When you go? Barely two months remained of the twelve the king had granted them at Kailua in April, 1820. Did he mean, then, to send them away at the year's end? There was embarrassed silence.

"I am going to Maui. Do not build your house until I come again," he said suddenly and waved the Longnecks away.

THEY KNEW the seaports—Kailua, Lahaina, Waimea, Honolulu— where vessels came and went, white men mingled with natives, and chiefs held colorful sway. But they did not know the back country. Now in this second spring of the Mission, they were beginning to explore—over the Pali into Koolau, westward to Pearl River and southeastward beyond Diamond Hill.

Elisha, taking the orphan William Beals as interpreter, set out in mid-March to tour the rim of Oahu. They traveled five days, crossing hills and grasslands, fording streams, skirting fishponds, climbing rocky ledges, walking the fine, bright sand of the windward beaches. Everywhere nature smiled, benign and sparkling; everywhere humans were gaunt, wizened, desolate.

They went to lonely fishermen's huts, to farmers' hovels, to a little community clustered around an *awa* still, to a village where a choice kind of *tapa* was in the making. Standing in the midst of a crowd or sitting in the shade of a house, Elisha drew out his testament and read, while William interpreted or recited in Hawaiian the simple precepts used in the Mission school.

"In the beginning God created the heavens and the earth."

"We must pray to God and love his word."

"Images and idols we ought not to make or worship." (Elisha had seen two on a hillside—wooden sticks draped in *tapa*, with offerings of grass and leaves before them.)

Fear, wonder, unbelief, ridicule played over the brown faces before him, but the listeners liked the resounding words, the spacious promises. It was a better thing, they seemed to say, than the message of the sandalwood crier or the tax collector. Soon they began to speak the phrases after William and sometimes chanted them far into the night. Once, as in the deepening dusk Elisha laid his Bible aside, a lanky fellow brought a *kukui* torch and stood holding it to light the page, so that he need not stop reading.

Again as Elisha recited, "In the beginning—" a *maloed* youth lifted up his voice and joined him.

"How do you know these things?" Elisha asked him.

"I have been at Honolulu," the young man said. "I have stood by the house of the Longnecks and I have heard these words. I have heard many saying them together as one voice. So I have told my people, 'One day the Longneck *haoles* will come to us with their good words'—and now you have come."

It was hard to tell him that they could not stay, and that it would be long before teachers would live in this village as they did at Honolulu.

Four nights Elisha shared the stench of the houses, the lice and fleas that made sleep almost impossible, the common *tapa* under which men, women, children and pet hogs lay down together. Usually there were potatoes or *poi* in the family dish, but sometimes a house was bare of food and the host wept because he had nothing to offer his visitors.

On the fifth morning they were in northwest Oahu at the foot of the sandalwood mountains. They cut across the great rocky point that stretched westward and made straight for Pearl River through the grassy uplands and the wooded gulches. Elisha had thought they might be at home by eight o'clock, but it was eleven when they came into the Row. They had traveled a good three hours by the stars.

The next day Elisha set down what he had seen and what he felt it meant to the Mission.

Four thousand houses. He had counted, inquired, estimated. Twenty thousand persons, then, allowing five to a house. Those who had placed the island's population at sixty thousand he thought had exaggerated; but no one had exaggerated, or could exaggerate, the misery. "Twenty thousand human beings," he wrote, "wretched and ignorant . . . oppressed by their rulers and without God and without hope. . . . Though inhabiting one of the most fertile countries in the World, they are often ready to starve for want of the necessary sustenance of life . . . have no encouragement to work or acquire property, as everything they possess lies at the disposal of the chiefs and is liable to be taken away by them at their pleasure. To rouse such a people from their degraded state, to give them the light of science and revelation, and all the blessings of civilization and christianity is . . . our appointed work. But who is sufficient for these things?"

It was a long time before he could lie down in his soft, clean-smelling bed and not be haunted by the memory of filth and vermin at Kaneohe, or eat of good salt beef and sea bread without seeing the gaunt faces at Kahana.

LIHOLIHO HAD SAID in the beginning, "Do not teach the people. Let the *palapala* be for the chiefs." But that was not the great obstacle in reaching the commoners. It was the want of books. It was the want of teachers. It was the language.

All their planning in America, all their language study on the voyage had given them little they could use in Hawaii. It had given them much, indeed, to unlearn. In the rush of syllables that made a native's sentence seem a single long word, they heard relatively few different sounds. There were no sibilants and no *th*'s or *ng*'s. There were many vowels, but only five distinct vowel qualities and only a few consonants. Laying their ground work in America, they had thought they might have to add new symbols to the alphabet. Now they saw that fewer than twenty-six would be enough. A letter for each sound and but one sound to a letter— this was their principle. And in their primer they would limit the sounds to those the natives actually used and could distinguish.

They managed the vowels readily enough with the help of their Latin. But no other language, ancient or modern, gave aid when it came to the interchangeable consonants. For years ship captains and traders had written the place-names—Owhyhee, Woahoo, Atooi, Hanaroorah—and the names of chiefs—Tamaahmaah, Krymokoo, Tamoree, Carhoomanoo—just as they thought they heard them. Whether the quick-moving tongue of a native formed a *t* or a *k*, an *l* or an *r*, a *v* or a *w*, these hard-pressed men of business did not know nor care.

But men who would make books, who dared not squander a small and costly paper stock by printing with a bad orthography, must listen and ask, ask and listen, until they were sure.

"Is the dance called *hulahula?*"

"*Ae.*"

"Is it *hudahuda?*"

"*Ae.*"

"Or *hurahura?*"

"*Ae.*" The native wondered why he must answer the question over and over. He did not hear the changed consonant.

"Is the crescent moon *hido, hilo* or *hiro?*"

"*Ae.*"

But which? "Hi'o," the natives seemed to say, with a quick tongue-flourish that quite obscured the troublesome sound.

Was the governor Boki or Poki? The natives saw no difference. Were clothes made of *tapa* or *kapa?* One answered distinctly with a *k*, another with a *t*. But when they listened to the Longnecks they could not tell one sound from the other.

To arrive at utter confusion, then, it was only necessary to name the Islands' chief vegetable. *Taro* could as well become *talo* or *kalo* or *karo* or perhaps *tado* or *kado*.

So the men of the Mission wrestled with the letters, arguing earnestly among themselves. Dare they drop *r* and *d* and *b?* Would *k* serve all the purposes of *t?* Could *u* be confined to the sound of *oo?* If the alphabet were cut to twelve letters, how could foreign words—Bible names, cities, names like Loomis and Bingham and Thurston—be kept recognizable?

To Elisha the delay in printing was endurable only because he had a share in readying the language. Though he was not college trained, he had a quick ear and a passion for perfection, and he threw himself into the business of listening and recording with the same zeal that had made him a good printer at nineteen.

As SOON AS he had moved to his new houses at Waikiki, the unpredictable Liholiho called at Missionary Row with a train of queens and servants.

In the Thurstons' cottage, once Honolii's, he fingered the bedspread and valances, tried out the homemade rocking chair—a dangerous venture for one so portly—touched Asa's books lightly and respectfully on their spines and squinted at himself in Lucy's small mirror.

At the Chamberlains' he tried the American beds, rolling with noisy glee on Jerusha's feather tick. But he was not tipsy this day—only in high spirits. Everything was *maikai*.

Kamamalu, who had been to inspect the Bingham apartment, met her lord in the *lanai* and held up to his view little Sophia, most fascinatingly dressed in layer on layer of white. Together they entered the schoolroom and heard the boarding scholars in a lesson. That, too, was *maikai*.

And *maikai* were the well with its sweep and bucket and the cookhouse with its stovepipe and teakettle. And above all the handcart. Catching sight of it as he came from the houses, Liholiho sprang in and cried to his *kanakas* that he must be drawn to Waikiki. They grasped the tongue and started. The king in his *malo* and helmet sat tailor-wise, facing the rear, rocking as the cart jolted. Queens, chiefs, fly-brushers and pipe- and spitbox-bearers straggled behind or ran to keep up with him.

That was the first of many visits. Whenever he passed on his way to or from Honolulu—and for one of Liholiho's habits that was bound to be often—he dropped in to salute his new friends, the

Longnecks. Whatever they were doing, whether praying or eating or keeping school or laboring over their alphabet, they invited him to join. Sometimes he had drunk a little, sometimes not, but now he was always jovial and friendly.

Time was running out. The year he had granted the Mission was expiring. The brethren sought to know the verdict. The American house, still stored in Boki's yard waiting for the king's decision, was disappearing board by board as natives took what they fancied. So one and another spoke a word in Liholiho's ear or dropped a hint before a queen or counselor.

About the middle of April Liholiho and several chiefs, having come in at dinner time, sat with the family and its boarders at a long table in the *lanai*. On the red-checked cloth was set out the everyday fare—salt beef, sea bread, *taro,* coffee, tea, goat's milk, molasses. The king ate with relish, then beamed on them all and told them: "You are my good people. You shall stay in my islands and teach. You may build the wooden house."

Next day they began digging the cellar.

In the village rumors were still going round that the Longnecks had come to seize the Islands. Little bands of natives peered into the excavation and whispered about the guns and powder the *haoles* would store there. But the king no longer gave ear to such nonsense. When the frame was up and an Englishman begged, "Let me tear down this house, or you will lose your land," Liholiho looked at him with such scorn that no words were needed. When another told him of reading in an American newspaper that frigates would come in five months' time to help conquer the Islands, Liholiho said, "I will wait five months. Then if the frigates have not come, I will send *you* away." That ended most of the gossip.

In Missionary Row the king looked at the writing of one of his favorite young chiefs and saw that it was fair and black on the page so that its meaning would be clear to any who had learned. "I was foolish," he said, "to give up my own study. I would begin a second time, but I am ashamed. My friends would laugh at me." He wished, he said, there were forty teachers and that all the people could have the *palapala* at once. He would be glad to help the missionaries speak better in Hawaiian; let them ask him about the words they did not know.

And the half-finished wooden house was indeed *maikai*. He would like such a one himself, three stories high. In the top story he would pray to the foreign god. But he was afraid he would have trouble about the cost. The brethren half promised him one as a gift from the good people of America. Surely, they told themselves, the Board would find such an expense justified. They did not know that the latest Marshall & Wildes cargo included two frame buildings, designed to be sold to the chiefs for sandalwood.

IN SICKNESS AND HEALTH

THEY were loath to concede anything to the flesh, but one day in June Daniel Chamberlain, working on the frame house, complained of the heat, laid down his mallet and went wretchedly to bed. It was the dysentery. By morning there was no doubt of that. Jerusha struggled through one day of nursing, gave up and took to bed herself. Mary Chamberlain and William Beals sickened, and after that almost the whole family, one by one, went down with the fever.

Hiram Bingham mixed purges of calomel, senna and tartar emetic, and prescribed for those not yet stricken "Salt dissolved in Vinegar, stirred into Mint Tea and taken at intervals of 2 to 4 Hours." Despite this dose, Hopu fell ill; and a day later Hiram himself was seized, leaving only Elisha and Asa Thurston to share the duties of physician, nurse, steward, cook, carpenter, minister and teacher. School was dismissed; the frame house was forgotten; for the first time in fourteen months the gospel was not preached on the Sabbath. Elisha and Asa slept scarcely at all. Unshaven and haggard, they hastened from house to house, doing what they could for the ailing.

By the end of the week Daniel Chamberlain was on the mend. Sybil, Lucy, Dexter, Danny, Maria and William Beals looked brighter and less feverish. Only Hopu still lay limp on his mat. Above his white nightshirt his face looked ashen-gray rather than brown. He did not open his eyes but merely stirred now and then, and mumbled between blistered lips. In panic, they sent to the village for Dr. Holman.

Within a fortnight they were all up and around. Hopu, once the fever left him, regained strength and good spirits faster than any other. His soft speech and ready laugh again spread cheer and comfort in the houses. The long table was set once more "in decent order" for the family and orphans. Sermons and spelling lessons resumed. The house-building went forward.

The Mission had survived the dysentery. But as its members looked at each other's gray faces, they saw that they were not the hearty, blooming company that had debarked from the *Thaddeus*. They had spent themselves too lavishly already.

The women especially. Unable to get native help worth its salt, they had baked and washed, ironed and sewed, scrubbed and swept, fetched and carried, trying to make life in Missionary Row resemble life in Brookfield or Bennington. As partners in the great work, they had taught half-castes, disciplined orphans, made ruffled shirts for chiefs and silk dresses for dowagers, kept meticulous journals, struggled to learn the language and served tea to visiting captains.

These things they had done while carrying their unborn babies and afterwards while nursing their infants. Before sun-up they had dragged themselves, heavy-bodied and aching, out of bed. They had weakened their eyes and strained their nerves, mending and patching by candlelight.

And though they had done all this, they had failed. They had not given their husbands the kind of homes they had thought to provide. Their houses were filled with the sulking and cackling and quarreling of a score of heathen orphans, the whimpers and cries of teething or colicky young ones and sometimes, no doubt, the sharp words of grownups, though not a breath of that ever got into the record. There was no time for tenderness, for talking things out together, for consoling and inspiring, no time for the soft encouragement men need to do their work.

As for the tasty and nourishing dishes the women would like to have set forth to tempt appetites and renew vigor—those, too, were out of the question. For as the whalers came—more than a score of them that first year after Captain Allen's discovery off Japan—and poured out their dollars for fresh fruits and vegetables, meat, fish and fowl, the chiefs grasped excitedly at the booming profits. Prices soared beyond the Mission's reach. Sweet potatoes were $3 a barrel; so was *taro*. New-cured pork was $26.

The Mission had come out in 1820 with $500 in cash (Spanish dollars secured at a total premium of $10 in Boston) and $317.87 in "stores for use after arrival." That had seemed a liberal allowance. And just at first there had been so many gifts of food and supplies and of money for the support of orphans that Daniel Chamberlain had managed to keep the Mission well provided. By the second year, it was supposed, there would be vegetables from the Mission's own plot. But that dream had died when the first planting withered and the *enuhe*-worm came.

So in 1821, though they dwelt in the garden of the Pacific, the family ate salt beef and sea bread and were often put to it to get enough of even such depressing fare. *Haole* merchants of the village would sell their beef ($20 a barrel), their flour (at $15), their rice (at $10), their bread (at $10 the hundredweight), or their molasses (at $1 a gallon) only for cash. When its cash was gone, the Mission must buy from shipmasters who would take bills on the Board's treasury in Boston—take them at an advance of 25 to 30 per cent. But whalers and China traders, however good-natured, did not like to deplete their own stores.

In the end, the Board bought beef, pork, bread, flour and molasses in America and paid freight to send them round the Horn. Usually the flour caked so hard it had to be pulverized with hatchet or hammer; sometimes it was full of weevils. When a vessel was slow in coming and the Mission storehouse grew bare, the family had to choose between hunger and debt. Once they borrowed $200 in cash, giving a draft on Boston for $240. But they did not like to deal in this way with a Board that administered the gifts of the public.

It was not strange, then, that they were all prey to disease, that letters home spoke of sisters "confined to their couches," of "symptoms of an impaired constitution," of "extreme prostration and debility." It was not strange that Maria, after viewing herself for a fleeting moment in a small square of mirror, wrote, "I think you would find me greatly altered"; that Samuel Ruggles grew so thin, sallow, nervous and dyspeptic that the whole company worried about him; or that the second and third Bingham children were born with too little vitality to stay alive.

YANKEE ENTERPRISE

IN Hawaii in 1821 it was almost as easy to sell a brig as a bolt of
dungaree. The ships Kamehameha had bought in his heyday—
the *Forester,* the *Albatross,* the *Bordeaux Packet* and the rest—
were falling into ruin. Left rotting at some harbor's edge, these
vessels might be used for storage or broken up for salvage by the
very *haoles* who had sold them to the Conqueror and no Hawaiian
would object or even notice. In 1821 the Islanders wanted fresh
paint, bright brass, clean yellow rope, spotless canvas, hardwood
panels, full-length cabin mirrors and gewgaws. They wanted their
ships to be fleet and stout and lasting, too, but these qualities were
harder to judge, and the chiefs were disposed to take the white
man's say-so about them.

The *Cleopatra's Barge* was perfect for Liholiho's taste. It had
seemed good, when Captain Suter pressed him, to promise eight
thousand piculs of his uncut wood for such a vessel. And if that was
not too much to pay, then surely Captain Blanchard's offer of the
Thaddeus was a bargain. For this brig—fine enough to have carried the Longnecks from America—and his Hawaiian-built
schooner, the *Young Thaddeus*—as pretty a toy as ever a skipper
handled—Blanchard asked only four thousand piculs. The king
quickly agreed to the purchase, but he did not like to be bothered
about the papers. Boki, he said, would take care of all that. So Boki
signed. And shortly, with a salute of three guns, the *Thaddeus'*
American flag was lowered and the flag of the Islands hoisted in its
place. Not a stick of wood had been paid; but the old crew moved
ashore, and the *Thaddeus* belonged to the king.

In Kamehameha's time, after terms were settled, the foreign crew stayed aboard, and foreign colors remained at the masthead while the vessel went among the islands to collect her own price in sandalwood. Only when the final picul had been cleaned, weighed and consigned as freight to Canton, had the seller relinquished the property. But by 1821 a new day had begun. The Hawaiians bought on credit now.

It was easy to sell a vessel in Hawaii that spring, but you had to have the vessel there for the chiefs to see. Marshall & Wildes of Boston seemed not to know that. Their two new brigs, built especially for Kaahumanu, guardian of the realm, and Kaumualii, king of Kauai, were already a month overdue when Captain Blanchard closed the sale of the *Thaddeus*. Dixey Wildes himself had taken the orders, in the fall of 1819, when Liholiho first gave his chiefs freedom to purchase on their own. Wildes had promised that the *Inore* and the *Tamahourelani* would surpass in swiftness and elegance anything that had till then been seen in the Islands.

Departing, Wildes had charged his agent, William Babcock, to remind the buyers early and late of their agreement about the brigs and the need for keeping it. With each passing day Babcock's task grew harder. A year and a half may not be long for the building of a superfine brig and passage half way around the globe, but to the Hawaiians it seemed forever.

Where were the *Inore* and the *Tamahourelani?* William Babcock asked angrily of every comer in the spring of '21. Where were those brigs about whose imminent departure from Boston Josiah Marshall had long since written him?

He asked this of Captain Cole, arriving in February in the *Eagle,* an M & W schooner intended for the Coast.

He asked it of his B & S rival, Captain Preble, whose tiny brig *Becket* came briskly to port in March.

But chiefly he asked it of himself, as, fuming and disconsolate, he turned his spyglass down the bay and saw nothing that pleased him.

Then, on an April morning, he caught in his glass a stir aboard the *Becket* as she swung at her mooring, and the next instant glimpsed Captain Preble going aboard, accompanied by—heaven help M & W!—Captain John Suter. Babcock summoned Cole. But long before the *Eagle* could be made ready for the pursuit, the Marshall agent saw what he had feared to see—the *Becket* slipping out of the harbor. He knew—for he was no greenhorn—that she stood for Kauai. He knew—for he was himself a Yankee—that Preble and Suter would sell her there if they could.

How Captain Cole, with help from a fellow-captain, got his schooner under way in fifteen minutes was something for the traders' journals. And for Mission journals, too, since Hiram Bingham, who had spoken for a passage to leeward in the *Eagle* whenever she went, was left, astonished, to get there as best he could. But, though Cole reached Kaumualii's court only a breath behind the B & S men, he could not block the *Becket's* sale. Artful Suter and personable young Preble so charmed Kaumualii's queen that she declared the brig was exactly what she must have. As for Kaumualii, he had not, he said, forgotten his bargain with Captain Wildes. But that was long ago, and Captain Wildes had not sent the brig. Surely Captain Wildes did not expect him to wait forever with no brig.

"The king of Kauai has purchased a very inferior Brig & Cargo of Captain Suter, for 3500 piculs of Wood," Cole wrote, breaking the news to Josiah Marshall. The price at $10 a picul was more than six times the brig's cost in America. Whatever the expense of the cargo and voyage, Bryant & Sturgis had made a neat profit.

It was May 22 when the Marshall brigs came in together. To explain their slow passage (198 days for the *Inore*, 231 for the *Tamahourelani*) their captains told of headwinds, gales, leaking casks that necessitated stopping for fresh water and a prolonged visit to the Marquesas for sandalwood that proved not worth the gathering.

It took months after that to persuade Kaahumanu and Kaumualii that they must accept the vessels they had ordered. Content with his *Becket*, the king of Kauai could not see that he needed another brig; and Kaahumanu did not find the *Inore,* even with an oil portrait of Kamehameha adorning its cabin, quite up to the expectations roused by the *Cleopatra's Barge.* Eventually both king and *kuhina nui* yielded to *haole* insistence and took the vessels. But they could not pay in "cash"—that is, wood delivered. They could only promise so many piculs still to be brought down from the mountains, and in 1821 nobody knew how many times a particular tract of forest had been mortgaged.

Ships were not, of course, the only items bought that year on credit. All sorts of goods poured into the market. The *Paragon,* Mr. Marshall's biggest ship; the *Arab,* in an independent "adventure" by two long-time Pacific traders; and Mr. Astor's capacious *William and John* arrived in quick succession to unload full cargoes. Rum, fine cloths, guns, hollow ware, an old cannon and a 71-ton schooner, framed in New York and taken down for shipping to the Islands, figure in the accounts. It was not, in 1821, a matter of selling off odds and ends left over from a fur voyage. It was a matter of getting all you could while the boom lasted—while the chiefs still wrote their names (having learned from the Longnecks) nonchalantly on notes; while Liholiho remained in that jolly, bacchanalian state where you could have sold him the moon for sandalwood if only you promised immediate delivery; while no one doubted that there was wood enough in the hills to settle every account as soon as the common people could be put to work harvesting it.

As a matter of fact, more sandalwood was shipped to Canton in that season (1821–22) than ever before—above 21,000 piculs according to one reckoning, fully 30,000 by another. In 1822–23 another twenty thousand went to market. But it was not enough—not nearly enough. In one year had been created the great Hawaiian debt that was to cause acrimony and bitterness for a long time to come.

The traders were not wholly blind to what they were doing that year. A Marshall man wrote home to Boston: ". . . we have been obliged to trust them and now we have got to fight for our pay." Bryant & Sturgis had warned Captain Suter: "There are so many expeditions gone and going . . . that we fear there may be some difficulty in keeping the chiefs to their contracts and the only safe way is to keep the property in your own possession till payment is received." That Suter departed from "the only safe way" is not surprising; the conditions of 1820 and 1821 called, not for safety, but for risk. Suter took the risk.

Afterward, too, the traders saw clearly enough what they were doing, when each arriving supercargo competed with his own firm's perspiring agent, taking, for cloth or crockery, wood his colleagues had earmarked for debt payments. Every agent knew that as long as a fresh supply of goods came to market, it would be next to impossible to collect the old accounts. But every Yankee wanted his share of the cream while the skimming was good.

A strident, critical note crept into the traders' letters after 1821. Somebody had to be blamed when the wood came slowly or was small and crooked; when the price dropped to $6.50; when the fire of 1822 wiped out the Canton warehouses and sent thousands of American piculs up in fragrant smoke; when the chiefs questioned the prices of new goods or met insistent dunning with shrugs; when reading and law-making, church-building and teaching pilgrimages began to replace spending in Hawaiian affections.

Sometimes it was their own associates in the trade whom they berated. This one was "slack," that one "a rascal," or an agent found himself "thwarted" by the "miscalculations" of a superior. Often it was the rival firm they blamed. Those fellows underbid, selling their goods "at almost the prices in America." They were "trying to injure." They were crafty, lying, two-faced scoundrels.

Always, of course, it was the natives—"such faithless people as all the Islanders . . . appear to be." "You might as well calculate on the wind."

And increasingly it was the missionaries.

Any Sunday at Missionary Row the traders could hear things said that were no help to business, no comfort to a frantic agent who must get wood for his firm or be swept from the scene by a new broom from Boston. They could, if they went to "meeting," hear the chiefs reminded that the common people were their brothers, whose souls ranked in heaven's eyes with the souls of the *alii*. They could hear earthly pleasures disparaged and fleshly indulgences condemned, and the rulers of Hawaii exhorted to sobriety and admonished to be the guardians of their people. They could hear talk of books and schools enough to teach the whole population. And they could see Kalanimoku or the king's mother, Keopuolani, or now and then the king himself, listening with quizzical, earnest faces, trying to fit this new gospel into their scheme of living.

These were not pleasant things to hear and see if you were in Hawaii to collect old debts or to sell new goods for ten times their worth.

HONOLULU HAOLES

IN some ways the summer of 1821 was a great season in Honolulu. There were more Americans than ever before and more New England rum and flag-waving. The Englishmen, who the year before had thought to get the Yankees sent off for good, had subsided, admitting defeat. The United States government had taken official note of far-off Hawaii and commissioned one of the traders to represent it as consul. The Fourth of July that year was observed with fitting hilarity. Old-timers gave birthday parties. The schooner *Astor* was launched with patriotic fanfare and a double grog allowance all around. Yes, it was a great season.

But the life of an agent ashore was not always so spirited. After the flurry that marked each new arrival, after contracts had been signed, brigs and schooners had gone to the Coast, merchant ships had sailed away to Canton and whalers to their fishing grounds, there came the doldrums, when a man could sit all day in his grass trading hut and not sell an ounce of rice or an inch of broadcloth. To pass the weary mornings he could drink and quarrel and gamble at cards, and in the tropic afternoon he could drink and drink and drink again, until he had blotted out the nagging memory of home, drowned his righteous wrath at the debtor-chiefs and dissolved his lurking fear of a bad season on the Coast or a ruinous slump at Canton. In the cool, spicy evenings he could make love, and then fall asleep, dream and wake to another day of boredom.

It took a tough moral fibre to live otherwise in Honolulu. Even James Hunnewell, who "had the courage to live here as he would live at home," suffered ennui and complained that he could not bring his mind "to the study of anything to improve it." This was something of an admission from one who had driven himself to master Bowditch on navigation at fifteen.

The same tedium that led men to drink and dally sent them calling at the Mission, where linen tablecloths, cups of steaming tea, modest and soft-spoken females and plump, prattling infants offered diversion. For indolence and carnal sins the family had only tight-lipped disapproval, but they did not publicly censure established *haole* ways nor turn any trader from their circle because he tippled or had a brown wife. Like an apple sound and sleek of skin but spoiling at the core, relations between the village and Missionary Row still seemed cordial in 1821. Actually, annoyance, dislike, anger and corroding bitterness were rising and someday, like the debts of the chiefs, they would have to be reckoned with.

It did not help matters that bluff, hearty Captain Pigot was gone. After his cruise with Captain Meek in the *Pedler,* Pigot had taken out the creaking *St. Martin* on what proved to be her last voyage. Somewhere between Hawaii and Fanning's Island she must have foundered; by the summer of 1821 the family had given up hope of seeing Pigot again—of watching him come up their path, hampered by his "rheumatiz," or hearing him call all hands to meet another Bostoner or New Yorker just arrived.

Into Pigot's place as village host and master of ceremonies Captain William Heath Davis had stepped willingly enough. Davis had been in the Pacific trade since 1810 and did not mind saying that he considered himself the boss of Honolulu. To meet the missionaries he brought Ebbets of the *William and John* (brother-in-law to the lamented Pigot), Masters of the *Tamahourelani,* Grimes of the *Inore,* Tom Meek of the *Arab,* Porter of the *Mentor* and young John Coffin Jones, at Honolulu in the dual role of Marshall agent and United States consul.

Davis' talk was sprightly, glib and continuous. He would be the Mission's greatest friend, he assured the family. Now that they had almost finished building the frame house, they must let him know when they needed anything to equip it. Captain Brown had given them Chinese wallpaper to cover the unplastered walls; Captain Porter had brought them some lumber. Now what could an old stand-by like Davis get them?

Daniel Chamberlain spoke up. They had dug a new well close to the kitchen and lined it with stones; the water was pure, but it rose and fell with the tide. They needed a pump. Did Davis know where they could get one?

Davis did. He said he would raise one from the old *Albatross,* lying abandoned and dismantled in the harbor. Let Mr. Chamberlain and Mr. Loomis come with him and Captain Ebbets and they would have the Mission a pump in no time.

What memories those two captains must have had as they went aboard the rotting hulk! She had carried furs and sandalwood for the Winships; wives, warriors and taxes for Kamehameha. Davis, in his *Isabella,* had been in company with her when she poached all up and down the California coast for sea otter and took so many that her crew broke up water casks to make room for skins in the hold. She was a "dull sailor," and Nathan Winship had been glad to sell her in 1816 for $2,000. It was Ebbets, now blackening his hands and smudging his face as he loosened the pump, who had bought her then. In less than a month he had sold her to Kamehameha for four hundred piculs of sandalwood, immediately delivered. That (about $4,000 in money) was considered a good price in those days.

But the talk was not only of bygone days. The captains brought up the subject of brown wives. You couldn't expect a man, they said, to do without women for two-three-four years—maybe more, now could you? It wasn't nature, was it? Otherwise why had the men of the Mission been so careful to bring out their own wives?— which, of course, the traders couldn't do. And what difference did it make, anyway? If a man had a brown girl that made him happy as long as he stayed in the Islands, wasn't that all right? What a wife at home didn't know wouldn't hurt her. And the brown girl had never heard of marriage or monogamy—that is, unless the missionaries had taken the trouble to tell her.

Daniel and Elisha carefully turned the talk back to the *Albatross'* colorful story. They had learned not to be drawn into arguments about the foreigners' custom of taking temporary wives.

DAVIS CAME again to help install the pump in the well. But this time he was drunk and belligerent. Mr. Bingham, he said, thickly, barging into the room where Elisha was hanging wallpaper, had tried to separate man and wife, father and child. Mr. Bingham had expelled a good man from the Mission, all on account of some oranges, but that wasn't the worst Mr. Bingham had done. He had tried to separate man and wife. Man and wife, that was it. He had tried to separate them. Mr. Bingham was a bad man. In the Thurstons' room, where Asa sat developing a text for his Sunday sermon, Captain Davis repeated his maudlin accusations. Hiram Bingham, absent just then from Honolulu on a pastoral visit to the Kauai station, would have been as puzzled as any of them if he had heard the hiccuped charges.

A few days later Davis collared Elisha in the village and asked him, with the sly chumminess of a drunken man, whether Mr. Bingham hadn't tried to force Hannah Holmes to marry Hopu. Hadn't he, now?

No, said Elisha indignantly. But the family was beginning to guess why, a little while ago, Hannah had stopped coming to the Mission. At first they had groped for the reason in a kind of hurt bewilderment. They had asked the other Holmeses, who had smiled blandly and said they didn't know. They had asked Sally Jackson and William Beals. Had Hannah ever been displeased with what was done at school? Had Hopu or Honolii said anything to make her angry? Was she tired of sewing and of wearing a *holoku?* Sally and William had no idea.

When at last they knew with certainty that Hannah had been William Heath Davis' brown wife in the days before the *Thaddeus* came, that she had borne him one child and would presently bear him another, they could not bring themselves for a long time to write of it in their journals. For months her name, which had crowned every reference to the day school and epitomized their hope and their success, was absent from all the accounts. Then Elisha mentioned her, in connection with Davis, as one would mention a stranger: ". . . the girl by whom he has one child and with whom he now lives."

Though Captain Davis and his cronies still came to the Mission and were often helpful, they grew more critical and snarling. Meeting them in the village, where Davis kept open house and the liquor flowed freely, Elisha or Asa or Daniel could now expect a tongue-lashing from one of the crowd. A trader would shake his cane and declare for the fiftieth time that the Mission had "rendered itself eternally miserable" by its low-down treatment of Dr. Holman, asserting that there were a dozen men in Honolulu who would take their oath that the doctor had never stolen an orange in his life. Another would grumble that the missionaries had given the chiefs a false notion of prices in America—prices of framed houses in particular. Or what was this rumor that King Kaumualii of Kauai would send his brig *Becket* to Tahiti at the missionaries' behest? Didn't Bingham know he could bring on a war by intriguing with Kaumualii, of whom Liholiho was so jealous?

As for Davis himself, the family gave up hope of seeing him sober. He came three sheets in the wind and called for brandy from the stock he had given them as a present. He cursed until the sisters were almost as red-faced as he. Over and over he told his grievances against Mr. Bingham—who, being still at Kauai, could not defend himself.

Elisha hid the brandy and held his tongue, knowing how little good—indeed, how much harm—noisy altercation would do to the cause of truth. He saw the captain's friends, who were far from straight-laced, shake their heads at his growing childishness and endless repetitions, heard them try to wheedle him out of his senseless rage or to coax him home when he grew offensive. Elisha thought compassionately of Hannah.

THEY BUILT the church that summer. By June the orphan school fund, started the year before, had received, all told, pledges of $707. Of this $527 had already been paid in cash or goods, and the amount was ample for the needs of the moment. Some of the traders, pleased with this report, asked if there were anything else they could do for the Mission. Build a church, perhaps? They had seen the schoolroom at Missionary Row so crowded on Sunday that late comers had to listen at the windows.

You could get a sizable fund in Honolulu in those days for almost any cause—the relief of a wounded sailor or of a foreigner whose houses had burned down, the proper burial of a penniless consumptive or the celebration of Independence Day. The church project was announced late in June, and in a few weeks enough had been subscribed by chiefs and *haoles* to assure its success. Some of the gifts were doubtless conscience money, some easy openhandedness; some bespoke a kind of civic pride, some a nostalgia for village churches in America. Little, it is certain, was given that a gospel of self-restraint might be more widely preached.

In August the native house-builder and his workmen began to raise a frail thatched structure, fifty-four feet by twenty-one. Captain Brown of the *Paragon* gave mahogany for a pulpit; a ship's carpenter shaped and finished it. Another planed and hung the double doors and set glass in the "pulpit window."

On September 15, a Saturday, Asa Thurston conducted the dedication service for a goodly crowd dressed in everything from working "blues" to feather war capes and helmets. Afterward a few of the Mission's most helpful friends partook of something which Elisha termed "a refreshment" and Maria called "a dinner." But Captain Davis was not of the company. Before this cheerful occasion he had stopped coming to the frame house. The brethren could no longer call him friend.

Another who could not be called friend was John Coffin Jones, Jr. This dapper Bostonian of twenty-three had come out in the *Tamahourelani* charged with a double responsibility. As Josiah Marshall's agent he would join William Babcock and others in serving his firm's interests. As United States consul he faced the Augean task of ridding Honolulu of its human rubbish—the runaway or discharged seamen whom one Yankee captain had described as "the off-scourings of the earth."

Bryant & Sturgis were not pleased with the choice of a business rival for the consular post. "Mr. Marshall has got young Mr. Jones appointed *Consul* for the Sandwich Islands," William Sturgis wrote to Captain Porter of the *Mentor* when the selection was news in Boston. "You will treat him civilly and show him your *ships* papers if he comes on board. . . ." At the same time, foreseeing a drastic clean-up, Sturgis advised the *Tartar's* Captain Turner, "If called on to take men on board whom you do not want, say you are not bound home and cannot take them. Treat Mr. Jones civilly, but avoid having anything to do with him if possible." Whether the new official failed to clean up Honolulu because his competitors would not help him, or because he was himself busier with commerce than with cleansing, the fact remains that things got no better that season.

The young consul's reform assignment might have been expected to draw him close to the missionaries. But Jones was a Unitarian, and he could no more see eye-to-eye with the Calvinists than he could accept crooked, spindling sandalwood as prime quality. All that the Mission stood for—religion by revelation, man's essential depravity, salvation through vicarious sacrifice, God in trinity— John Coffin Jones scorned and detested. To him, not scripture but "common sense" was man's guide. To him, the natives were not souls to be rescued from ignorance and sin; they were "simple children of nature," and simple they ought to remain—though not so simple as to ignore their business contracts or to live without American luxuries.

"KING OF THE WINDWARD ISLES"

THE news went like wildfire through Honolulu that Liholiho had sailed in an open boat for Kauai. A few days before, he had gone some forty miles on horseback to see about the sandalwood cutting. Then one morning he had coaxed the chiefs who were with him—Boki and about thirty others—into a little sailboat, and without chart, compass or provisions had ordered the helmsman to steer northwest across the wide, choppy channel.

No one at Honolulu thought the tiny, Hawaiian-built boat would make its port. Not Kaahumanu and Kalanimoku, who ordered the *Barge* to cruise between the islands keeping a sharp lookout for wreckage or survivors. Not Liholiho's five wives who set out rescue-bound in the *Inore*. Nor the Mission family who filled their journals with foreboding and exclamation points. Nor even Boki's spouse Liliha who, while the *Inore* was loosing her canvas, embarked in a single canoe with a little white sail and four paddlers.

But the king's boat lived in the turbulent sea and came at dawn into Waimea roads. All night the desperate party had sailed with the fresh trades abeam and the waves breaking over them. *"E hoi kakou—o make!"* the frightened ones had cried. "Let us return before we perish." But the king, half-drunk and fearless, refused. If the boat hove about and returned, he said, he would jump out and swim across. Everybody—*haoles* and Hawaiians—had thought he should not go to Kauai to talk with Kaumualii about their proper relationship. But now he was going. He would have it settled whether he was lord of all the islands as his father had been, or only "King of the Windward Isles" as George (Prince) Tamoree had called him lately in a letter. Windward Isles, indeed!

Undismayed at the lack of a compass, he spread his hand wide and named his index finger "nor'west," the direction in which Kauai lay. His fellows dashed out the water with calabashes and peered into the dark ahead for the land they sought. They almost overran it; but as the blackness yielded to gray, they discovered Kauai, far off under their lee bow, and came about quickly to stand in toward it.

So, utterly defenseless, Liholiho reached the northerly island against which his father had thought to sail in overwhelming force. Whether rashness impelled him or far-seeing guile, it is hard to say.

Kaumualii, dressed in his Christian clothes, with three unarmed servants, went off at once to the boat, rubbed noses with Liholiho, gave his *aloha* to the company and bade them come ashore. On the beach the two kings stood facing each other. Behind Kaumualii were his household; the Kauai Mission family, including Hiram Bingham; John Coffin Jones, who chanced to be at the leeward; and a handful of other foreigners. With Liholiho were his bedraggled comrades of the voyage. Kaumualii spoke gravely.

"King Liholiho, hear! When your father, Kamehameha, was alive, I acknowledged him as my superior. Since his death I have considered you his rightful successor and, according to his appointment, king. I have many muskets and men and much powder; these with my vessels, the fort and its guns and the island are all yours. Do with them as you please. Send me where you will. Place what chief you please as governor here."

There was a moment's silence. Then Liholiho spoke.

"I did not come," he said, "to dispossess you. Keep your country and take care of it as before, and do what you please with your vessels. You are the king; I am the emperor. But I shall not take away anything that is yours."

A shout rose from both parties, as Kaumualii led Liholiho to a house in his yard near the fort.

Afterward the two kings, in a surfeit of brotherly love, traveled forty days about Kauai. With their hundreds of retainers they visited all the seacoast villages, west, north and east. When they returned, Liholiho still made no move to go home; he went on enjoying Kaumualii's hospitality at Waimea. On a September Sunday the two kings, spurning the preaching, sported all the morning in the surf and sailed all the afternoon, each in his own American brig. At evening, as they came to anchor side by side, Liholiho said to Kaumualii, "You must come on board my *Pride of Hawaii*." This was his new name for the *Barge*. Cleopatra was nothing to him.

Kaumualii demurred, then yielded. Perhaps he had not yet seen the polished mahogany panels, the bird's-eye maple inlays and the rich velvet upholstery. Perhaps he had seen them but had not praised them enough to satisfy his overlord.

As the two kings walked toward the grand saloon, Liholiho quietly gave orders to his sailing-master. And so deftly did the men put the vessel to sea that when Kaumualii became aware of the brig's motion and ran on deck, the mountains of his country lay dark and distant against the twilit sky.

"Where do we sail?" he asked fearfully.

"To Oahu," answered Liholiho, "and you shall visit me as I have visited you here."

Kaumualii looked again at the fading outline of his island.

"Farewell, beautiful, beloved Kauai," he sighed.

IN THE HAWAIIAN MANNER—by the spreading of a black *tapa* over them as they lay on a low platform of mats—Kaumualii, king of the leeward isles, and Kaahumanu, guardian of the windward realm, were joined as consorts.

By this act, Kalanimoku explained to the shocked Longnecks, the fear of war was ended. He found this union better than a dozen promises of loyalty made by Kaumualii at Kauai. Kalanimoku would not say that Liholiho had done well to carry Kaumualii away in his brig and bring him captive to Honolulu. But now that he had done so, Kaumualii and all his household must stay on Oahu. On that the principal chiefs were agreed. They would send young Kahalaia or someone else of their number to govern at the North.

As for Kaumualii, was he not alive? Was he not free to come and go over the whole of this island with his retinue of chiefs and servants who had now arrived from Kauai? Was he not still called king? And was he not honored by this union with the high-born and powerful Kaahumanu, once a queen of Kamehameha?

Kapule, Kaumualii's former queen, would not be greatly disturbed by the loss of her husband, Kalanimoku said. In the easygoing fashion of the Islands, she had been wife to her stepson, Kealiiahonui, as well as to Kaumualii. Indeed, some said that she preferred the younger man to the older. So now, having lost the father, she could console herself with the son.

But Kapule, it soon appeared, was to lose both of her husbands. Within a week the windward chiefs had decreed that the marriage *tapa* must again rest on Kaahumanu, this time binding to her the prince Kealiiahonui.

Now the fate of Kauai was doubly sealed.

CHANGES

WHEN the Holmans sailed for home in October, the foreign colony at Honolulu outdid itself to give them a send-off. The traders showered Lucia and the baby with presents and heaped such praise on the doctor that, in spite of the Mission, he went away in a glow of satisfaction. Captain Porter, whose *Mentor* was to carry them, promised Lucia she should have anything she wanted from Canton. She had only to make out her list before the ship went up-river from Macao and he would fill her order to the last pound of souchong and the last yard of silk brocade.

"Please to accept of my unfeigned thanks for your kindness to us since we have been with you," Thomas Holman wrote to James Hunnewell, whose house he had occupied for four months. "May God reward you tenfold. . . ."

Yet Hunnewell had not, like so many of the others, become a partisan in the cleavage between the doctor and the Mission. While extending courtesy and kindness to the Holmans, he had remained, and would remain, the Mission's friend. He was, in fact, on friendly terms with everybody—a difficult feat in the Honolulu of 1821.

Some of Hunnewell's colleagues in the trade, as they grew more touchy toward the Mission, centered their resentment on Hiram Bingham. They regarded him as a stern despot who imposed bigotry and bias on a company of naturally mild, easy-going men and women. They rejoiced extravagantly when he left Oahu to visit the station on Kauai and implied that his co-workers in Honolulu must feel equally happy at his departure.

But here and there in the missionary journals are bits that show how much the family loved and leaned on its leader—bits that, pieced together, reveal him, for all his firmness and idealism, as considerate and understanding. His code was strict, but no stricter than that of Elisha or Daniel Chamberlain or Asa Thurston; he was uncompromisingly righteous, but so were Sybil and Maria and Lucy. Despite Thomas Holman's claims to the contrary, the unity of the group was real, not seeming, and its loyalty to Hiram Bingham was spontaneous, not enforced.

As soon as Asa Thurston's return from Kailua had given the Honolulu station two pastors, the Whitneys and Ruggleses had written from Kauai that they wanted a visit from Brother Bingham. They needed him to baptize their babies, they said, and to advise them on a dozen different problems. In mid-summer Hiram had gone to the leeward for a stay of several months. And it was just as well, perhaps, that he and Thomas Holman had not had to meet in the village during the doctor's last weeks in the Islands.

RETURNING TO Honolulu in November, Hiram Bingham found changes, some good, some bad. For one thing, the family, settled in the frame house, had protection and comfort far beyond anything Missionary Row had offered. Though there were no clapboards to finish the outside and no gleaming white paint to cover it, there was stout, rough sheathing to turn back storms of dust and rain, and there were pine floors and a shingled roof, glass windows and board partitions and stairways.

Downstairs the Thurstons, Loomises and Chamberlains each had a room; in front at the right of the central hall was the schoolroom. The Binghams would have the chamber above. Part of the cellar had been partitioned off to hold the long dining table, another part as a kitchen. In the dooryard toward the Waikiki path were shade trees, brought from the mountains, still uncertain whether to live or die in their new surroundings. A neat wooden fence bounded the inclosure.

The grass church, too, greatly improved the Mission property and facilitated the work. Prospects for a garden had brightened when Kalanimoku had given the Longnecks some land at a little distance that could be irrigated in the native manner. Whaleship captains, of whom there were a good many that fall, had been generous.

But there had been some falling off in both the school and the Sunday congregations; boarders had misbehaved or deserted; the language study had progressed but slowly; Don Marin had again refused to let the Mission have oxen; and the family were plagued to distraction by the antics of Captain Davis and his fellows. Persis Thurston, born two days before Dr. Holman's departure, was a bouncing child, but Lucy's persistent cough had them worried; they feared she would go into quick consumption.

It was wonderful how Hiram's presence put new heart into them. Asa, relieved of preaching, became his wife's assiduous nurse. A new scheme of personal invitations to the chiefs on Saturdays, followed by Sunday-morning reminders, brought some increase in the church attendance. Flighty and obstreperous orphans quieted down, now that Binamu was in the house. Though he taught no classes, his occasional visits to the schoolroom stiffened the day scholars' will to learn. The whole Mission felt a surge of faith and confidence.

After a week Hiram sought Captain Davis at his house in the village. Quietly enough, for Davis was sober, they thrashed things out—the Holman affair and the question of Hannah. Davis retracted much and laid much blame on Dr. Holman, who, he said, had misrepresented the Mission's doings. Two days later, he returned Hiram's call. He brought the Mission a bolt of seersucker and stayed to tea. But he did not consent to Hannah's coming back to school.

1822

SPELLING-BOOK

THE printing press was still in Captain Babcock's storehouse. It would have been foolish to go to press with an imperfect orthography, more than foolish to print Bible passages so badly rendered that they promised earthly riches when they meant to proffer heavenly. So the printing waited, and the only schoolbooks at the Mission were Webster's speller and the English Bible.

The brethren had once hoped Providence would open a way for them to confer with the British missionaries in the Society Islands, where the work of reducing Polynesian speech to writing had been in progress for many years. When Kaumualii, about to send his brig *Becket* to Tahiti on a trading voyage, had offered free passage to two Longnecks, it had looked for a little while as if Hiram Bingham and one of his colleagues would talk face to face with the Englishmen, hear their advice and get samples of their publications. But when Kaumualii was carried captive to Oahu that fine prospect faded. By the end of 1821 the men of the Mission knew they must work things out alone.

Though there were still sharp differences among them about the interchangeable consonants, they settled tentatively on a Hawaiian alphabet of seventeen English letters and agreed that the time had come to start printing.

Elisha hired four natives to haul the press to the Mission yard in the handcart. Steadying the precious "engine" as he walked alongside, he thought of Uzzah, stricken because he touched the Ark of the Covenant "when the oxen shook it." He could not blame Uzzah; he knew how the young Israelite must have felt.

The thatched house in Missionary Row where the Chamberlains had lived was to be the printing office. There the press and the boxes of accessories and parcels of type were deposited. Elisha unwrapped and distributed his two fonts into the cases. It was good to know that his fingers still found their way unerringly to the compartments. A wonderful thing, this memory of muscles and nerves, so tenacious that, once fixed, a skill was scarcely diminished by the lapse of time. It was two and a half years since he had done such a job at Bemis'.

On a Saturday early in the new year, he began to set type for page one of the Elementary Lessons, afterward called the *pi-a-pa*. On Monday, January 7, when he was ready to strike off the first copies, he summoned the family to share the great event.

The high chief Keeaumoku, brother of Kaahumanu, was in Honolulu that day. "Have you called on the Longnecks since they have lived in a wooden house?" Kalanimoku asked him. Keeaumoku had not, but the idea of such a visit pleased him. So the governor of Maui joined the group that had assembled to watch the first printing in Hawaii.

Elisha locked up the form and lifted it into place. Then he swabbed on the ink and pressed the paper over the besmeared type. A gentle push and the frisket rolled under the platen. Now all was in readiness for the final triumphant act—a pull of the lever and the impression indelibly made.

Elisha looked at Keeaumoku, whose eyes had followed every move. "You pull?" he asked, indicating the lever.

"Me pull," Keeaumoku agreed, all smiles. He seemed afraid to release the handle once he had swung it, but at last he retreated a step and watched Elisha strip off the sheet, wondrously speckled with *a*'s and *k*'s and *l*'s and *o*'s.

"*Maikai*," said Keeaumoku.

STEADILY NOW, though slowly, Elisha turned out the spelling sheets. And the scholars, old and young, who had learned to recognize the

Hawaiian words when written on slates entered eagerly into the new game of reading print.

They quickly mastered the simple lessons and at once became teachers of their fellows. In a month's time, Hiram estimated, there were not less than five hundred scholars among the petty chiefs and half-whites of Honolulu and Waikiki.

Then Kuakini, Keeaumoku's brother who was governor of Hawaii, came down to Oahu. A young chief of his household had been in Honolulu and had seen with his own eyes the thing that made a book with a single mighty stroke. Kuakini had embarked forthwith. The governor beamed when Elisha showed him how the press worked; how the large printed sheet, when folded and cut, became a little book. But when Elisha began to teach him the letters, he yawned.

Something, however, moved him next day to attend church. Liholiho had sent regrets. "I am tipsy," he said, "and it is not right to go to church drunk." But the two governors, Keeaumoku and Kuakini, came with the lesser natives and were by Hopu's translation enjoined: "Be wise now, therefore, O ye kings, and be instructed, ye judges of the earth."

Kuakini's messenger was at the Mission early the next morning demanding "all the *palapala*." Elisha made the sheets ready. Before the week was out, Kuakini had mastered the whole series and with the help of a Tahitian composed a letter in Hawaiian to convey his pleasure in the lessons and his desire for more.

Keeaumoku, meanwhile, was loath to return to Maui, where there were none of the excitements that Oahu provided. He showed the book he had printed (Elisha had folded and cut it for him) to all who came to his house in Liholiho's inclosure at Waikiki. But he did not learn to read it. A little lazy and a little miffed that his brother, Kuakini, who had not made a book, had learned in a week to read one, Keeaumoku spent his hours in the surf and at games of chance.

Then one night he dreamed. He saw all Hawaii burning, as if the molten lava from Kilauea's crater had deluged the islands from windward to leeward, kindling the forests and searing the plains. Even the channels flamed, and there was no place where chief or commoner might flee.

When he awoke, Keeaumoku saw the white surf still breaking over the reef and the green cocoanut fronds still moving in the breeze. But he could not shake off his terror.

He went to the Longnecks. "I will come under your instruction," he said. "Send me books and a teacher. My household will attend to the *palapala*. I will go no more to Maui until I have read the word of God and gained a new heart."

At first he sought to turn his sister Kaahumanu from her pleasures, saying that together they should build a schoolhouse for the people. She only fondled her pet pig and pretended not to hear. So Keeaumoku opened his own Waikiki house as a teaching center.

Soon Liholiho, though desultory in his own studies, requested a hundred copies of the Hawaiian spelling-book for his friends and attendants. Elisha went to the king with the books.

"Look," said Liholiho, "I have written a letter to the English King George. I do not want him to be angry with me on account of the American missionaries."

"It is a good letter," said Elisha when he had read it. "Liholiho does well in his studies."

"The *palapala* is useful in sending communications afar," the king went on. "But it is not good for the common people. If you teach the common people, they will grow lazy."

"Our gospel is for everyone, whether high or low," Elisha said. "That is why we print—that there may be thousands of books, enough for all."

Liholiho shrugged. "The *palapala* takes all day. No time to cut sandalwood. The people must cut sandalwood."

TROUBLE-MAKERS

GEORGE P. TAMOREE, once the crown prince of Kauai, was now scarcely better than a commoner. Even before Liholiho abducted his father, George had sunk from the high position accorded him when he first came from America.

A fire, starting in his own cookhouse, had burned all his buildings and with them his books, some of his fine clothes and his elegant furniture. After that he had not lived as a *haole*. He had consorted more and more with petty and disgruntled chiefs. He had drunk and idled and written letters that embarrassed his father and inflamed Liholiho.

Kaumualii, growing in grace and in command of the spelling-book, had seen the mistake he had made in setting George—for all his foreign glamor—above Kealiiahonui as "second in command." Before a year was out, he had regretted the action that raised the son of a common woman to such a height. Gradually he had withdrawn his favor, leaving Tamoree to dwell without rank or influence in his own valley.

Now, of course, it mattered little which son called himself heir-apparent. Never again would one of the house of Kaeo reign in Kauai. And George, seeing all of his splendid dreams vanish, grew surly and perverse.

At the Waimea station on Kauai the missionaries, sorely missing Kaumualii's patronage, had little time to think of the young man they had called Prince. But when his grand establishment went up in flames, menacing their own houses, they blamed him for his carelessness. And when he wrecked the *Young Thaddeus,* they were righteously indignant.

Hiram Bingham had chartered the *Young Thaddeus* from the chiefs, placed Hopu in command, and hastened to Kauai for the birth of the second Whitney child. His ability as a midwife, twice tested at Honolulu, was almost as much in demand these days as his pastoral services.

Tamoree, with no vessel to his name—though his father had purchased several—grew green-eyed to see Hopu confidently handling the neat little craft. One day while Hopu was on shore, George rushed on board the *Young Thaddeus* and ordered the crew to weigh anchor. The Oahuans refused, but George had brought enough of his own men to do the job. Taking possession of the yards and ropes, they soon had the schooner skimming toward the land, Tamoree at the helm, a wild joy in his eyes.

They skirted the reef and came about again into the roads. Then Tamoree ordered the maneuver repeated. This time the wind was too light to carry the schooner off, and the surf drove her against the rocks. The prince and his crew jumped and swam ashore, leaving the *Young Thaddeus* to go to pieces in the waves.

Tamoree said he was sorry. Indeed, he *was* sorry that he could not repeat that glorious moment when they had brought her past the reef, escaping the jagged coral by inches. How to mollify the windward chiefs, who still owed James Hunnewell and his partners a large sum for the *Young Thaddeus,* Tamoree did not know or care. Perhaps he thought his father's captors owed him a schooner ride. Perhaps they did.

But there were white men at Honolulu who used the incident against the Mission. This George, they said, was a protégé of the preachers. This schooner, they said, had been chartered by Mr. Bingham, and he was responsible for it. The chiefs, they said, would seize upon the wreck as another excuse to welsh on their contracts. And the missionaries would encourage their defaulting. This affair of the schooner was but a sample of their disregard for property rights. It only proved again that it was a bad day for business when these preachers set foot in the Islands.

So the merchants fretted. And indeed their woes accumulated. The old *Thaddeus* after one trading voyage lay dismantled on the shore below the fort. William Sumner, commanding her for the chiefs, had found her quite unseaworthy. "Had not Providence protected us," he reported on his return, ". . . the whole of us must have perished." And even the magnificent *Barge* was suspect. Beneath the mahogany panels some of her big timbers had been found rotten. The king's carpenters were dubious about renewing them.

It galled the chiefs to owe thousands of piculs for such vessels. They felt tricked and cheated. They slowed down in their sandal-wood deliveries. Let the men who had sold them such "useless tools" wait, they said, a good long time for their pay. The agents waited, morose and testy, and wrote home to America that the preachers were to blame.

PERHAPS IT WAS only coincidence, but three days after the Binghams had sailed for Kauai in the *Young Thaddeus* Captain William Heath Davis paid the Mission his first visit in months. He was in an ugly mood.

Elisha could guess what angered the captain. The Loomises, a few days since, had been making calls in the village and had visited Davis' house in his absence. Hannah had received them eagerly, asked about everyone at the Mission, invited them to try out the splendid hand organ the captain had lately bought, clung to Maria's hand and wept a little when they left.

Captain Davis did not openly refer to this visit. His accusations were vague and his threats veiled. He harped again on last year's theme—that the Mission had meddled in his private affairs, had tried to take Hannah away from him. He thought it only proper to warn them that they must mind their own business or be sent off. The king, he said, had promised him that no more missionaries would be allowed to land, however many came around the Horn. The American consul had promised him justice and protection in his rights.

Next Sunday Davis came again. The church was filled. Liholiho was there, and many chiefs, captains, sailors and native commoners—as many as five hundred. Asa was glad. He would not have liked a falling-off as soon as Brother Bingham left. "Look unto me, all ye ends of the earth," he exhorted them. The king fixed his eyes unswervingly on the preacher's round, earnest face. Yesterday Liholiho had for the first time examined the Longnecks' printing "engine" and had struck off a sheet with his own hand. Lately he had grown to love his spelling-book and had scarcely touched his bottle at all. Now he wore the pious air of one who had forsaken old and evil ways and set his feet, rejoicing, on the paths of virtue.

As Asa began his sermon, Captain Davis came in at the rear, sauntered to where the royal party sat and squatted on the ground at the king's feet. Lounging against Liholiho's knees, he looked up into his face with a waggish grin and addressed him in low but audible tones. If the king heard any of Hopu's carefully prepared translation, it was not Captain Davis' fault.

At the Amen the captain was on his feet inviting first Liholiho and then other chiefs to dine with him. But there were few who said *yes*. They had heard the king answer boldly, "This is the Sabbath; I shall dine at my own table." They took their cue from him, and Captain Davis' party was ill attended, this time at least.

It was clear that the truce was over. Davis would now do everything he could to hamper and defeat the work of the missionaries. This opposition he thought he owed them for Hannah's sake. He could not forgive them for poisoning his Eden.

He declared that all of the Holmes children would be withdrawn from the school. But Oliver Holmes thought otherwise. George and three of the girls still came as day pupils, and little Charlotte remained as a boarder and special helper to Maria. A little later when Maria scolded the child for a bit of naughtiness and mildly punished her, the *alii* Mrs. Holmes made her first visit to the Longnecks and led away her daughter in anger. But Oliver Holmes came at once to place a chastened Charlotte again under missionary discipline. It was hard, he said, for his wife to understand that the children must learn American ways as well as Hawaiian. Nevertheless, Charlotte was to stay with the family and behave herself. Charlotte, curtseying prettily as Maria had taught her to do, promised perfection.

After her seventh child was born, Mrs. Holmes grew ill and full of pain; she sighed and whimpered, and neither native nor *haole* medicine could help her. When she died, the Mission took George and the ten-months infant into the family.

Oliver Holmes was touchingly grateful. He was uneasy about the young ones, he said. Pa Homa was no longer the quiet, sheltered place it once had been. So many foreigners came now to see the girls. He wanted his daughters to marry white men, of course, but respectable ones, agents and shipmasters. He did not want them running off here and there without his knowledge, getting themselves bad names. And he didn't want George to be a loose fellow. Going to school at the Mission would keep him straight till he was old enough to know what was good for him. Later he would take an *alii* wife and raise a fine family. As for the baby, it was so sickly that perhaps the missionaries could do better for it than anyone at Pa Homa.

Oliver Holmes' faded blue eyes were sad as he sat in the Mission schoolroom, giving up his baby, planning for his son. You could see that his ideas were not the strait-laced ones of the missionaries, that he resented the family's unspoken criticism of his dealings with Hannah and Polly. But where else could he turn in his perplexity?

GOOD WIND, ILL WIND

VANCOUVER had once promised Kamehameha a vessel from the English king. Vancouver was long dead and so were Kamehameha and the English king in whose name the gift had been offered. But when he was regent before his mad old father died, the king who now ruled as George IV had ordered a vessel to be built at New South Wales and delivered to the Hawaiian king. In April, 1822, the schooner *Prince Regent,* armed with "six smart little guns," came sailing into Honolulu harbor, and the British, whose influence had somewhat waned in the Islands, stood again in Liholiho's eyes a wonderful people.

To make the presentation, Captain Kent followed in his sloop *Mermaid.* He had touched at Tahiti and taken there some passengers for the Marquesas—some Tahitian Christians designated to open a mission, a deputation of two gentlemen from the London Missionary Society on a tour of inspection in the South Seas and William Ellis, preacher-printer, whose work in the Society Islands the brethren had heard so much about.

Adverse winds had caused Captain Kent to change his course and stand first for the Hawaiian Islands. He would stay at Honolulu about two weeks, he said, before proceeding to the Marquesas.

Hiram Bingham hurried home from Kauai. Conferences and hymn-sings were held, excursions undertaken. Hospitality burned bright in the Mission family. The sisters, baking wheat bread, steaming puddings, stewing dozens of mountain apples into sauce, were so encumbered with household tasks as to miss some of the wise words of their guests. But it was happiness to serve these

fellow-workers, to make them as comfortable as the simple appoint-
ments of the Mission house would permit, to introduce them to
alii friends, to demonstrate for them the Mission's first accomplish-
ments.

Awed by the strange chance that had brought this help to their
doorstep and grateful for even the little time allowed them by the
impatient captain, the brethren spread their publications and their
tentative translations before William Ellis and bombarded him
with their questions. They could see how alike the two tongues
were—the Hawaiian and the Tahitian—when on his first Sunday
with them William Ellis preached to a native congregation without
an interpreter.

The nine Tahitians stayed in houses set apart for them in the
households of Kaahumanu and Kalanimoku, but they came often
to the Mission—the women in white dresses, shawls and straw
bonnets—to sing or pray or just to talk. Auna and Aunawahine,
having discovered a relative in Kaahumanu's train, were received
with special interest by the dowager and her two husbands. There
and elsewhere on Oahu, all up and down the plain from Ewa to
Waikiki, Auna proclaimed that God was good and the new learning profitable for all men.

The natives listened to this handsome, strapping orator and
thought how good it would be to have him preach to them in place
of the earnest but halting missionaries. "Why do you go to the
Marquesans?" Kaahumanu asked Auna. "Here we would give you
food and a good house and let you help the Longnecks from morning till night." She reminded him that her husband Kaumualii
was a true follower of the new religion, though she was not, and
that he would be a patron to anyone who taught of the white man's
God.

Kaahumanu had another thought: Let the maker of Tahitian
books, Mr. Ellis, also stay in Honolulu; for Auna had said that at
the Mission house they were exceedingly sad when they thought
of his leaving them.

There were consultations about the unprecedented proposal—

that a missionary of the London society should serve for a time under a Boston board. All three of the visitors held the view that was later officially stated by their sponsors: "It is not of the slightest consequence who does the work . . . if it be done seasonably." They saw no reason why Mr. Ellis should not bring his family with all speed from Tahiti and dwell with the Americans as long as they needed his help. The case of Auna was different. It was hard to justify his withdrawal from the Marquesan project, however much the Hawaiian chiefs admired his talents.

The Englishmen had almost decided not to change Auna's assignment when something happened that put a new face on the matter. Captain Kent announced that he had contracted with Captain Davis for a trip to Fanning's Island, to take provisions to a hardy few who gathered *bêche-de-mer* on that bleak, rock-ridden shore.

Only a week earlier, taking tea at the Mission house, Captain Kent had said regretfully that nothing must keep him more than two weeks in Hawaii. Business of importance, he implied, pressed him to be gone—to the Marquesas, to Tahiti, back to New South Wales. But somehow Captain Davis had changed all that, and the missionary visit that had seemed about to end was suddenly extended.

For four months, until late August, the Englishmen lived and worked in the American Mission; and in that time great things were accomplished in the schoolroom, in the chapel, on preaching tours and in the printing office. To Elisha it was like the creek as he had seen it back home in a dozen springtimes—gushing free and fast down the valley, tossing to bits the ice that had all winter held it in check. That was how the Hawaiian Mission went forward in 1822.

THE FIRST Christian marriage in Hawaii was Hopu's. He had waited many months while the gentle, bright-eyed girl of his choice was trained by the Mission in the lore of homemaking and the duties of a wife.

Hopu's days were crowded with teaching and translating and

with the menial tasks—from hauling wood to washing windows—that he shared with his white brethren. Only at meals and family worship could he gaze at his Delia and watch how modestly she bore herself.

"Fairest flower that grew between the snow-capped mountains and the sounding sea" she had seemed to him when, traveling with the king on Maui, he had seen her in the back country. He said: "As the Almighty has excited in my heart such strong yearnings for her, I think it is His will that I marry her." The brethren agreed.

When Hopu found her, Delia could already weave a mat and sing a *mele* with much grace. After a year in the Mission family she could sew, cook in the American way, bathe and "change" babies and read a little in the Hawaiian primer. And she had given her heart to God. In August, while the English and Tahitian visitors were still with them, the wedding was held in the grass church.

To honor the marriage, the king came and several of the principal chiefs, some in their finest feather capes, some in their European best. Hopu wore his "gentlemanly black suit," Delia a trimmed straw bonnet and the white dress she had made herself.

"*Aloha,*" said the chiefs, taking the little bride by the hand. "*Maikai,*" they beamed on the proud Hopu. They especially admired Delia's bonnet. Like her vows of eternal faithfulness, it was a new thing for a native woman.

IT TOOK the *Mermaid* several weeks to refit and load for the voyage to Fanning's Island—weeks in which Captains Davis and Kent went about like old cronies, voluble and happy in their enterprise. Then, reminded that there were no native women on Fanning's, Captain Kent sought a companion for the voyage. Whether the winsome Mattatorewahine, Christian convert and missionary-elect to the Marquesans, had already granted him her favors it is hard to say. If during the trip from Tahiti to Honolulu her sultry beauty had kindled desire in him, neither Mattatore, her husband, nor William Ellis, her pastor, had noticed anything amiss. In any case, the captain now wanted Mattatorewahine and meant to have her.

One evening in May, Mattatore burst into a quiet conversation at the Mission house and told his almost unbelievable story. Captain Kent, he said, had come at dusk to the grass house in Kaahumanu's yard with a dozen or more of his sailors and carried off Mattatorewahine to the *Mermaid*. He had tried to protect her, but he had been powerless among so many strong-armed fellows. Mattatore wailed in anguish and called on the Christian God to return his wife unsullied or to rain evil on the man who had coveted her.

Stern and angry, William Ellis went aboard the sloop next morning. He was told that the woman might go ashore if she wished. But when he spoke to Mattatorewahine, she cast down her eyes and murmured, "The captain will not let me."

In the old days a man had only to choose a native woman who pleased him and she came to him in all the ready innocence of Eve before the fall. Now, alas, this bliss had been blighted; if the girl had been taught by the missionaries she would be less willing, though she might be more desirable. So with Mattatorewahine; she brooded, accused herself, berated her seducer. It was, Captain Kent soon decided, "no go." Before he sailed for Fanning's Island, he "graciously" restored her to her husband.

"She will only walk on the plain," Mattatore told William Ellis sadly. "She is not right in her mind. She will not wear her decent dress, but wraps herself, naked, in a square of cloth and walks on the plain. All night she walks, with her head hung down in shame. She will not come to me in bed. Despair has taken fast hold of her soul. We cannot go now and teach the Marquesans."

On August 22, Captain Kent, having returned from his voyage to Fanning's Island, summoned on board his passengers for Tahiti. Auna and his wife remained in Hawaii. William Ellis was departing, but with the promise soon to return. Daniel Tyerman and Rev. George Bennet bulged with notes for the London Missionary Society's files. Mattatorewahine was forced on board, protesting piteously. For a few days she roamed the decks as she had the Honolulu plain, bewildered, haunted; then she lay quiet in her berth and died. The captain, who knew more of such things than the rest of them, directed her burial at sea.

GUARDIAN OF THE REALM

FIRE leaped high in the inclosure before the house of Kaahumanu. The *kanakas* who had gathered the fuel and fanned the first slender tongues of flame stood guard now with wet fly-brushes and full calabashes to quench stray brands and sparks. Kaahumanu was burning idols.

On Hawaii, where she had lately traveled with her retinue, she had seized and destroyed images by the hundreds. From caves and dens and the thatch of commoners' houses her men brought them forth, some mere painted sticks or bunches of knotted straw, some carved of wood or stone. Together with the tall, fierce poison god that had belonged to Kamehameha, they were flung down in the royal inclosure at Kailua and kindled.

Here at Honolulu the pyre was small compared with the windward burnings, but it proclaimed, nonetheless, the dowager's zeal. And watching the smoke puff upward, Kaahumanu saw completed the work of destruction begun in 1819 when she had encouraged Liholiho to break with idolatry.

Kaahumanu had known then that the tabus, bearing so heavily on women, were a curb to her power. She had seen how the overthrow of superstition would strengthen her. She had hinted to Liholiho that the old ways were foolish and pointed out that prayers and sacrifices to the gods had not saved Kamehameha from death.

Liholiho, irked by the ceremonial restraints and priestly bans on his indulgences, had wavered, then consented. A feast was made ready, of tabu food as well as free. Long tables were set up in the cocoanut grove, one for men and one for women. Kaahumanu instructed the king in his role. When the guests were in their places, he rose and said to Chief John Young, "Cut up these fowls and this pig;" and when the foreigner had carved, Liholiho strode abruptly to the women's table, seated himself by the queens and ate, asking them to eat with him. The natives watched in horror. Each moment they expected to see their monarch struck down by the fury of the gods. When nothing happened, a petty chief cried in awe, "The tabu is broken!"

Then Liholiho gave his commands: "Throw down the idols. Destroy the *heiaus* and temples. Abolish the priesthood." Kaahumanu had triumphed. Now, three years later, she had set out to destroy the lurking roots and remnants of idolatry; and so the relics burned.

But hers was an atheistic fervor. She gave no allegiance to the God of the missionaries. True, when she saw Kaumualii kneeling in devotions or spelling out verses in his English Bible, she no longer hurled a plate at him, as she had once done. She had even, when she was sick, allowed Mr. Bingham to visit her and pray for her recovery. She had commanded her noisy household to be silent while he spoke and had gratefully let the Longneck women bathe her temples with sweet-smelling water. When she was well again, she had called at the Mission house with presents, and on state occasions she now offered the brethren her right hand instead of her little finger. But she loved her Sabbath amusements—bathing and gambling and feasting—too well to go to church. And as to the *palapala,* she spurned it altogether. Written characters on a red-bound slate and printed ones, black against white paper, left her unmoved.

But there was another thing from abroad that greatly diverted her. Years before the *Thaddeus* people came, foreigners had given her bits of cardboard that bore the likenesses of European kings and queens, together with other amusing designs. They had taught her to name them and to use them in games that were as full of suspense and chance as the old Hawaiian gambling sports. So she became a devotee of cards. With Namahana, her sister, and the other chiefesses, she lounged by the hour on her mat and played whist or backgammon.

"If she can learn the devil's game," fumed Elisha, "why can't she learn to read?"

"She can," said Hiram Bingham. "There is no question of her mental endowment. But until God touches her cold, proud heart, she will not."

Without the approval of Kaahumanu, guardian of the realm, even the king's fitful interest and the premier's growing devotion, even the acclaim of Keeaumoku and Kuakini, were not enough to speed the *palapala* through the land. Therefore the men of the Mission worked untiringly to win her to their cause.

One Saturday afternoon Hiram and Elisha, calling at her new American house near the harbor, found Kaahumanu at whist. She and three other dowagers lay on their stomachs, facing each other, their bosoms resting on cylindrical pillows. The Longnecks, entering, had to step over their bare feet and ponderous limbs.

Kaahumanu did not speak or even look at her visitors. Propped on her blue satin cushion, she went on dealing the cards to Namahana, Kinau and Kalakua. Hiram and Elisha sat on mats and waited—waited almost an hour. The queens dealt and played; there was no sound but the snapping and shuffling, the swish of fly-brushes and an occasional Hawaiian syllable of pleasure or disappointment.

Finally Kaahumanu threw down her hand, rolled over, sat up and spoke imperiously. "Let the two Longnecks come and sit beside me, one on this side and one on that, and let us talk."

Hiram Bingham had a present for her, a spelling book which Elisha had bound in dark red tapa. It bore her name on the flyleaf. Kaahumanu was greatly taken with it.

"*Maikai,*" she beamed, holding it aloft for her familiars. "*Palapala.*"

Hiram took the book again and opened it. "Here are the five important letters," he said. "No word can be made without them."

Kaahumanu gave a bored glance, but when Hiram began to point and to say, "Ah-A-E-O-Oo," she hunched closer. Soon she was chanting the magic sounds with him. "Ah-A-E-O-Oo." She motioned Elisha to join in.

"Ah-A-E-O-Oo," they said, over and over. Then Hiram's voice dropped out; Elisha finished the round and stopped. "Ah-A-E-O-Oo," read Kaahumanu quite by herself.

"Maikai," said Hiram. Then, pointing, "Again."

"Ah-A-E-O-Oo." It was perfect! The guardian of the realm had mastered the first lesson. Exulting, she addressed the three women who still reclined on the mat. "I have got it! There will be no more cards today. No, nor any other day. I will have as my sport the *palapala.*"

As Elisha and Hiram made ready to leave, Kaahumanu asked, "What time do you hold the *palapala* at the home of my brother? I will attend."

They told her tomorrow was the Sabbath. Would she not come to church? When the sun was well up in the heavens, at ten?

Kaahumanu did not promise. But she came, rattling over the plain in her American-built wagon, drawn by six *kanakas.*

"I will have forty of the books," she told the brethren who grasped her hand in fellowship after the service. "All my people shall study with me and my two husbands. Send us the books and a teacher. We begin tomorrow."

They sent her the little orphan, William Beals.

CONCLUSIVE VENTURES

ALL his days William Heath Davis played the game boldly. Years before, smuggling along California, he had lost the *Cossack* by capture. Now in 1822 word came by the *Eagle* that his one-time brig had been seen in coastwise trade at Monterey and Santa Barbara. He had hardly landed from Fanning's Island before he began sounding out John Coffin Jones on a plan to recapture the *Cossack*.

There was nothing for Jones and the Marshall firm to lose, it seemed. Davis would charter the *Eagle* for $2,000, send her under Captain Rogers to outwit the Spaniards and bring back the *Cossack*. Even if the *Eagle* failed, she would at least have the charter money and the profit on her voyage. If she succeeded, her owners would get half-rights in the *Cossack*, still presumably a good vessel.

The bargain was sealed and the *Eagle* sailed. On October 3 Captain Rogers returned with a small cargo of wheat, a depleted crew and a strange story. In taking the *Cossack*, he had lost the *Eagle*. Mr. Marshall's schooner, loaded with Monterey beef, had fallen to the Spaniards at Santa Barbara.

Honolulu buzzed. Had it been only the wind failing the *Eagle* when, short-handed, she had tried to follow the *Cossack* to sea? Or folly on Rogers' part, stripping the *Eagle* to man the *Cossack* after his ruse had got her from her Spanish crew? And who now owned the *Cossack*? Who would pay for the *Eagle*? Had John Coffin Jones, thinking he could not go wrong, made a bad bargain? How much did Davis stand to lose on his last earthly venture?

That it would be his final venture there was no doubt; for months he had been "drinking himself to death," and from the day of the *Cossack*'s arrival till November he drowned his worries in increasing drafts. Then he died; and the Honolulu traders, thronging the *haole* burying ground to hear the young American consul read the Episcopal service, paid tribute to one of their most intrepid colleagues.

"Ashes to ashes and dust to dust," read John Coffin Jones, and was doubtless sad at the death of this man who had owned, commanded and sold a dozen vessels, who had helped found the sandalwood business, had caroused and traded with the Russian Baranov, made money and lost money with equal nonchalance. But Jones was only twenty-four. Perhaps, as he read, he was already thinking how he would unsnarl the financial affairs of his dead friend and avoid Mr. Marshall's censure. Perhaps he thought, too, of Hannah Holmes, the beautiful *hapahaole* wife whom Davis had guarded so jealously. At any rate, it was not long before he took Hannah and her two little boys into his establishment.

The Mission family had hoped that Hannah would come back to school, but she sighed and said no, the *palapala* was not for her.

DANIEL CHAMBERLAIN had never thought he would be one to put his hand to the plow and then look back. But by 1822 he was forced to admit that his children were a problem to the Mission. Jerusha was the first to see the difficulty and put it into words.

The day she came upon her sixteen-year-old Dexter teaching a girl orphan tick-tack-toe, their heads almost touching over the slate and their laughter ringing through the schoolroom, Jerusha had caught her breath. What was happening, she had asked herself fearfully, to this son who had grown like a weed and taken on the voice and look of a man? What would happen to that other son, not much younger, at far-off Kauai? Must they send the older ones away, back to America, at least until they had married? For a while she kept the worry to herself; then presently she shared it with Daniel.

By this time Jerusha was full of concern about her Mary, romp-

ing with the orphan boys. Hawaiian youngsters matured early and
felt no shame about their bodies. Girl boarders no older than Mary
ran off from the Mission to sleep with sailors. To keep her little
daughter of eleven "nice," Jerusha withdrew her from her brown
and half-white comrades and doomed her to lonely, humdrum days.
Mary recited her lessons alone to Mrs. Thurston, not in the schoolroom with the orphan scholars. She sewed patchwork for tedious
hours at her mother's side. For a little while this served, but it would
not give the answer for long.

When the Mission laid the Chamberlains' problem before William Ellis, the British Missionary answered quickly, "Let them take
their young family home and rear them in a Christian land. No
service they might give here is worth the ruin of their children." In
Tahiti, now that Christian ways had triumphed there, he said, he
would be willing to bring up his own four to adulthood. But in
Hawaii he would not risk keeping them beyond the age of six.

The brethren discussed the question earnestly. They must do
more than solve the dilemma of one family. They must set a pattern
for the time when Levi Loomis, Sophia Bingham and Sarah
Ruggles were six, a pattern to be followed down the years until
Christianity had conquered and changed the Islands. They saw
clearly enough that in separating their sons and daughters from
the native children they would deny in part their own creed—that
all were brothers, equal in God's sight. This denial they regretted.
But they were afraid.

In the Chamberlains' case there were other considerations. Daniel
was crippled with rheumatism; that was one factor that could not
be ignored. The farm program had failed; that was another. And a
letter from Boston told of reinforcements on their way. A second
company, including five preachers, a doctor and a secular agent, had
embarked in the New Haven whaler *Thames,* hoping to reach
Hawaii in March or April of 1823. If Daniel's duty to his family
called him home, he could be spared now better than at any earlier
time.

To give up the work for which he had come out was for Daniel a heavy disappointment; to turn back, as the doctor had done, a bitter humiliation. To pull together again the threads of the old life in America would be painful almost beyond endurance. But there seemed no other way. Late in 1822 the Chamberlains with the full approval of their colleagues began to look for a passage home.

1823

OUTRAGE

THE *haoles* in Honolulu were outraged. Not since 1812 had America's fur trade been so threatened. Not in a decade had there been such bravado and bombast, such ranting and bluster, so much pounding of tables and war talk.

A Russian decree had forbidden vessels of other flags to buy and sell north of 51°; and a Russian sloop of war, delivering written orders, had driven the Yankee brig *Pearl* from the Coast after only twenty days of trading. With a paltry 373 skins she had slunk back to the Islands, where her captain's story soon had the hotheaded traders in a frenzy.

Would all the skin-ships be forced out of business? they asked each other. Would the United States government protect its merchants? Would there be war?

"Should war take place with the Russians," Eliab Grimes wrote to Josiah Marshall, "I wish you would send me a [privateer's] commission. . . . I should delight . . . to be revenged of those people as they have taken such a high stand."

War did not come, and Grimes did not need his letter-of-marque. But the events of 1823 foreshadowed the end of the maritime fur trade as far as the Yankees were concerned. Already they had turned their eyes toward California; and commerce there, though illicit, increased apace. Marshall's little *Eagle* had made two good voyages before she was captured by the Spaniards. The *Owhyhee,* the *Rover* and the *Convoy* from Boston, and the *Washington* and the *Waverly,* built in the Islands, plied jauntily between Honolulu and the mainland ports. Beef, hides and tallow, horses and cattle began to figure larger than furs in the account books of Boston. Only the sandalwood, long overdue and coming slowly to market, kept ships in the China trade.

Now the luckless *Pearl* was making ready to go down to Canton, where Captain Chandler hoped to save his voyage from utter ruin, by getting a freight to Europe or America. His unsold cargo he left with James Hunnewell. If anyone could wring a profit from those boxes of buttons and bales of blankets, Hunnewell could. But the captain was not sanguine. Under the circumstances he was glad enough for passage money from the Chamberlains. He notified Daniel when to come aboard with his family and effects.

ON THE AFTERNOON of March 20 a little procession straggled from the Mission yard toward the village. Daniel limped alongside the handcart which carried the luggage. Under his sober eyes the boy orphans pulled it carefully, indulging in no capers. Dexter walked with his mother, who held her baby born in Hawaii. Nathan and Mary, hand in hand, scuffed the dust of the path with their Sunday shoes. Danny trudged along with Elisha, and Nancy with Sybil Bingham. The young ones were not sure how to feel about this departure. It was exciting to be going somewhere, especially to America; but Hawaii had been in many ways a jolly place to live, and they were fond of their uncles and aunts of the Mission.

Jerusha was flushed from the effort of getting all her family togged out at one time. She had worked half the night and was numb with weariness. Daniel's face was the color of clay, and he pressed his lips together to keep them from trembling.

The chiefs had gathered at Kaahumanu's new house in the village to make their *aloha*. Kaumualii wept. Liholiho asked that his greetings be delivered to the American Board. He would welcome, he said, the new teachers now on their way and provide for them as he had done for the first Longneck company. Kaahumanu said she was sorry they had never persuaded Don Marin to give Mr. Chamberlain oxen for the plowing. Kalanimoku took Danny on his knee and let the little fellow quiz him one last time from the speller.

The sun was almost down behind the mountains when the Mission family rowed out to the *Pearl* and, at Captain Chandler's suggestion, held a farewell service. Asa prayed. Hiram spoke feelingly of their work together and of the Lord's will, which must be done. They all sang, choking on the tender words. Then there were brisk goodbyes and a host of messages to be delivered in America. Before sunrise next morning the *Pearl* was out of the harbor.

FEAST TIME

I T was feast time again. To observe the fourth anniversary of his father's death, Liholiho had ordered lavish and splendid ceremonies which would last a fortnight.

"Will you acknowledge, as you celebrate, the one great God who presides over the destinies of men?" Hiram Bingham had asked the king.

And Liholiho, considering a moment, had exclaimed, "Indeed! On the first day let us have a grand *pulepule* and also a grand *luau*. I will go to the church with my chiefs; and afterwards the American missionaries shall come to my *lanai* to eat and drink."

From the grass church to Liholiho's bower at Waikiki—a long and lofty *lanai* of slender poles and green branches reared for the occasion—a motley train proceeded. There were the king and his armed guards, the men of the Mission, a score of ship captains and white residents and more than a hundred retainers of rank. By royal edict black was the court color for the day, whether one wore European clothes, or a tapa *malo* and mantle.

The banquet table, stretching a hundred feet under the leaf-canopy, held every sort of Hawaiian delicacy—*poi* in calabashes, pineapples, melons, bananas, papayas, *opakapaka* and mullet wrapped in *ti* leaves and great wooden platters of hog and dog and fowl, roasted underground. From foreign stores there were rich yellow cheeses and bottles of wine and brandy.

The king mounted an improvised throne at the head of the board. His wives—the favorite Kamamalu, then Kinau, Auhea, Pauahi and Kekauonohi—were placed on his right; his little brother

Kauikeauoli, Kalanimoku and Kaahumanu on his left. With a sweeping gesture he signalled the rest of the company to be seated.

At this moment the princess Nahienaena arrived. Straight through the western doorway attendants drew her four-wheeled carriage, decorated with foreign flags and festoons of silk. Liholiho sprang up to lift the slender girl from her cart and bear her on his shoulder to a chair next to the young prince. "This," said Liholiho with pomp, "is my sister, the daughter of Kamehameha." And as the skirmish for places resumed, servants pulled away Nahienaena's vehicle.

Even without this dramatic interlude the seating of the company would have been a turbulent affair. For the hundred or more Hawaiians it was still a novel thing to occupy a bench or chair while eating; native feasts were spread on the ground. Here, by Liholiho's orders, the customs of the *haoles* and the *alii* mingled in a new, perplexing pattern. Yet after the elbowing and the altercation, the uproar fell away, and the king's voice could be heard commanding the appointed ones to cut and pull the roasts into portions for distribution.

The commoners who had fringed the procession from the church now surrounded the *lanai*. Their gaunt, disease-marred bodies jostled each other; their wistful brown eyes peered through the lattice at their king and the bounty of his feast. But they were not noisy like the usual native crowd; they gazed in silence or spoke in whispers, awed, perhaps, by Liholiho's armed guard and the great warriors, promenading in their feathered war cloaks and tippets.

Kamamalu was a gracious hostess. Her Hawaiian guests required little attention as they gnawed roast meat from the bones and sucked the juice from dripping sections of melon. But the queen summoned and dispatched *kanakas* here and there to put her foreign friends at ease, to carve the giant cheese and distribute the servings. And all the while her dark eyes sparkled like the spangles that trimmed her black dress.

Again there was commotion at the west end of the bower. But instead of natives *haole* sailors now peered in at the openings. On this day the grogshops would be deserted while jack-tars on liberty sought a rarer diversion. Almost at once Kamamalu spied the new-comers and ordered that they be fed. They laughed, good-natured and rowdy, as the *kanakas* passed in and out of the hall carrying them refreshments.

When at last the company had eaten and drunk to sluggishness, two musicians—one with a calabash drum and one with a nose flute—began their rhythmic noises. But there were no dancers. In-stead, a company of taxpayers entered through the western door. In *paus* or *malos* of white *tapa,* they walked in single file to place their tribute at the king's feet, then went out at the eastern end. This was but the vanguard of those who, while the feast days lasted, would bring their produce from the farthest parts of the island. In some districts the collectors might roam the villages and farm plots to gather the dues and forward them to the king. But the people liked to make a great ceremony of the payment—a ceremony in which the chief, calling the name of each scrawny fellow who knelt to deposit his tax, became, briefly, a proud man and his district a place of note in the kingdom.

More than an hour the procession continued, until four hundred commoners had passed through the crowded *lanai.* Some of the visitors slipped away; but the men of the Mission made no move to go. For them the spectacle had meaning, both hopeful and sobering. In such a society a few converted chiefs might turn their subjects by hundreds toward salvation. But therein lay the problem. The Mission's task was not to raise the banner of Christ over a surrendered nation, but to enlighten thousands of darkened minds, one by one.

On Sunday, April 27, while village and plain still rang with Liholiho's festival, the whaler *Thames* dropped anchor in the roads. She had brought the long-awaited second Mission company. To "reinforce" the diminished pioneer group, the Board had sent three ordained ministers, two licensed preachers, a physician, the wives of all of these, a secular agent, a Negro girl and three Hawaiian boys who had been at school in Cornwall.

Hearts nearly burst with rejoicing. It was almost too good to be true, they kept saying over and over—pioneers to late arrivals, Hawaiians to Longnecks, Lucy Thurston to her girlhood friend Elizabeth Bishop, everybody to the serious young bachelor who bore the loved name of Chamberlain.

At sunrise on Monday twenty well-manned whaleboats towed the *Thames* into the harbor and brought her to anchor within a stone's throw of the fort. A quay had been built there since the arrival of 1820, but the new company could not use it to step ashore from their boats. It was tabu for as long as the feast days lasted, the more because the king's new house, even now being "warmed," stood at its landward end.

As he had done a month earlier when the *Active* brought Mr. Ellis back from Tahiti, Liholiho remitted the harbor dues, which would have amounted to $80. "Captain Clasby," the king wrote. "Love to you. This is my communication to you. You have done well in bringing hither the new teachers. You shall pay nothing on account of the harbor—nothing at all. Grateful affection to you. Liholiho Iolani."

So those who had vowed to turn back the "reinforcements" were set at nought. Captain Davis had once claimed to have the king's promise that no more preachers should land, but he was five months in his grave, his threats forgotten. Jean Rives had bragged that the new Longnecks would not put ashore so much as a satchel; but the king's *kanakas* were now carrying their trunks and barrels into Boki's storehouse.

Still, talk was cheap, and Captain Clasby heard plenty of it. The nation, white residents told him hotly, was "already nearly ruined by the worthless set of fellows" his passengers had come to join.

THE GREAT FESTIVAL throbbed on toward its climax. In dancing and sports, tabus and tax ceremonies, calabash drums, *kahilis* and gorgeous feather capes, the spirit of old Hawaii renewed itself. In guns and orations, gin and brandy, gold braid and epaulettes, velvet and broadcloth, the new *haole* ways were conspicuous. Ten thousand words from their seasoned colleagues could not have told the new missionaries more clearly that in 1823 Hawaiian culture was a fluid blend of the native and the foreign, and that the foreign component was itself a mixture of the best and the worst that the white man could offer.

As for Liholiho, he was a battleground for the old and the new. In the first day's observance he had saluted his pagan father's memory with Christian prayer and toasted that wise old *awa*-drinker with heady foreign drafts. His new palace, finished just in time for the celebration, was of grass like the palaces of his forebears, but it was lofty (thirty feet at the peak) and had wooden doors and shuttered windows. Indoors there was one great room, its floor covered with patterned mats of native manufacture; but three glittering cut-glass chandeliers swung from the ridgepole, mirrors and steel engravings decorated the walls, crimson-upholstered Chinese sofas and mahogany tables furnished the place with European grandeur.

To pay for his palace the king had taxed his people as tradition dictated. A great chief had contributed $40 or even $60, a petty chief perhaps $10. Foreign merchants, as tenants, were assessed from $5 to $20, though what they sold to fit and furnish the place must have been many times their tax. *Kanakas* in the royal household, from cook to pipe-lighter, had paid their little fees. It was also traditional to tabu a new house and require all who entered it to make presents to the owner. But when the criers shouted far and wide that the king's house was tabu, they proclaimed that anyone who wished to see its splendid interior must pay, not some bit of produce or handicraft, but a Spanish dollar.

When the seven new Mission brethren, with Elisha and William Ellis, called at the palace to present their commission from the American Board and their certificates of American citizenship, they found Queen Kamamalu seated on one side of the hall collecting taxes. Here again the old and new ways met. As on the day of the feast, bands of the king's subjects were coming from outlying districts to march in single file past the place of deposit. That was Hawaiian custom. But whereas the chiefs and overseers had long kept their tax accounts by tying knots in cords, the queen used the *palapala*. She sat at a long table with a writing case before her and a native secretary on either hand, making neat entries in the roll-books.

She rose quickly when she saw the Longnecks enter and came over to them with words of *aloha*. Elisha, steward for the company, began to count out dollars for the admission fee. "No," Kamamalu said firmly. "The Longnecks shall not pay."

Elisha explained that his friends had letters to deliver from the chiefs of the Mission in America. When could they read them to the king? he asked.

Another day, Kamamalu advised. Certainly not at the moment, for the king had drunk too freely and would not know who was speaking to him nor what words were said. Let the Americans return tomorrow. Then she herself would have time to talk with them. She hurried back to her table, sat down, arranged the folds of her loose pink silk dress and resumed her accounts.

Other chiefs were not so busy. Farther down the long room, Kaahumanu, Kalanimoku, Boki and many more of the *alii* welcomed the strangers and plied them with questions. The conference lasted an hour, while the king in a chintz *malo* slept on a velvet couch, fanned by faithful attendants.

On the way out the men of the Mission examined the pictures that hung on the grass walls between the hand-hewn side posts— steel engravings of naval engagements and land battles and one of Buonaparte, whom Liholiho admired because of his father, the Pacific Napoleon. Two full-length paintings of the king himself were side by side in gilt frames. In one he wore his yellow-and-crimson cloak and a helmet; in the other, a British-looking uniform with epaulettes and a sword.

Near the door, in frames like the rest, were two crayon sketches, crudely drawn and flagrantly obscene. A jesting *haole* had presented them.

ON THE LAST DAY the festival reached fever pitch. This was the day of processions. This was the day of scarlet and gilt. *Kahilis,* thirty feet tall, nodded their scarlet plumes above the crowd. Scarlet-clad royalty was borne aloft in whaleboats or double canoes mounted on bamboo platforms or on Chinese bedsteads lashed together into great cars of state. The *alii* bearers, massed in solid phalanx, wore feather cloaks of red and yellow and tall crested helmets.

Kamamalu wore a *pau* of scarlet silk; the huge Chinese umbrella that shaded her was of scarlet damask fringed with gold. Scarlet, too, were the *malos* of Kalanimoku and Naihe, who stood, arms folded, on the right and left quarters of her whaleboat chariot. Scarlet and gold were the trappings of Kinau's and Kekauonohi's cars, and scarlet and orange the seventy-two-yard kerseymere *pau* of dowager Namahana. Wrapped round and round, it held her arms straight out from her body and trailed in a long train carried by retainers.

The canopies and draperies that adorned the bedstead-coach of Prince Kauikeaouli and Princess Nahienaena were of yellow figured moreen; their youthful *alii* attendants wore scarlet. Hoapili, their step-father, and Kaikoewa, their guardian, followed them as servants, the one bearing raw fish and *poi,* the other a dish of baked dog for the refreshment of their charges.

Everywhere there was glitter and brilliance, and the strong tropic sun enhanced it all. Out from the fort, along the shore, in and out among the village houses, back and forth along the Waikiki path that one day would be called King Street, the pageant moved, sometimes in a single long, splendid queue and again broken into segments that countermarched or serpentined or passed each other in opposite directions. There was order but not restraint. Imagination and playfulness prevailed. At Kamamalu's caprice her seventy porters, moving as one, whisked her cart from this line into that. Pauahi, in mid-afternoon, leaped down from her couch and, seizing a torch, set fire to its costly covering. As the flames mounted, she stripped off her *pau* and, reserving only a small square of handkerchief for a fig leaf, tossed in her dress. Her attendants followed her example. Who knows the yards of broadcloth and *tapa* that burned that day to commemorate Pauahi's childhood escape from the fire that had destroyed her grass home?

All day singers and dancers by the hundreds moved across the plain, meeting the parade here and there, encircling the highest chiefs, shouting praise and affection, beating calabash drums, chanting *olis* and *meles,* choruses and responses.

Only Liholiho was not splendid. He had been too drunk to trouble about costume or conveyance. In *malos* as scanty as any a poor farmer wore in his taro patch the king and his intimates rode horseback, hardly sober enough to keep their seats. A bodyguard of fifty or so in old, shabby uniforms followed on the run as the party scampered from place to place. Commoners, too lowly to join in the dance, tagged along, hooting and shouting—perhaps in acclaim of their monarch, perhaps in ridicule.

Of this day's revels Rev. Charles Stewart, just arrived, wrote solemnly in his journal, ". . . highly interesting as an exhibition of ancient customs, which, it is probable, will soon be lost forever. . . . There is much reason to believe, that a taste for these ceremonies . . . will be so far lost—even before the lapse of another year—that they will never be repeated . . ."

They never were.

REINFORCEMENT

ONCE more there was use for Missionary Row, where the grass cottages, though shabby, were still intact. But even with these to take the overflow from the frame house, it was hard to make so large a family comfortable. The men fell to and did what they could. They moved a partition, completed a stone cookhouse begun weeks before and shunted luggage and bedsteads until their backs were lame and full of cricks. The sisters stretched the long dining table to its full extent and engaged a man to help with the cooking.

Meal time became language time. Turn about, each brother or sister recited a single Hawaiian sentence, committed to memory. Two a day and one on Sunday gave them thirteen new sentences each week. After dinner the brethren spread their crude maps on the table and discussed how to distribute the new teachers. The natives, had they been allowed to decide, would have settled them here and there on the instant. Every chief who had made progress in the *palapala* now thought to have a Longneck in his domain, to build a private schoolhouse and to gain prestige thereby. But the men of the Mission saw other points to consider. They must reach the great masses of the people as soon as possible. So they sat, weighing and arguing by the hour.

At length in May the Richards and Stewart families and Betsy Stockton, the Negro girl, departed for Lahaina. And a little later the Thurstons, joined by the Bishops and by Hopu and his Delia, went willingly to their old stand at Kailua. But it took three quarters of a year to complete a survey of the field and assign the others, for the needs and opportunities of the Big Island had been, till now, little studied. The "deputation" that left Honolulu late in June and returned early in September made a tour of Hawaii, "preached at every village . . . suffered with hunger and thirst with heat and cold . . . visited . . . volcanoes and collected . . . curiosities." Wherever they went they found a desire to hear the new word and receive instruction. Their report, presented finally on October 15 at the Mission house in Honolulu, called for immediate development of two more stations on the island of Hawaii, one at Waiakea in Hilo district and one at Kaawaloa on Kealakekua Bay.

When all the assignments had been made, and the last detachment had gone to its outpost, there remained at Honolulu Hiram Bingham, the Mission's leader; Elisha Loomis, maker of books; Abraham Blatchley, the new physician; William Ellis—preacher, linguist, printer and expert on native ways; and Levi Chamberlain, secular agent.

Levi Chamberlain was no raw youth. He was past thirty and had tasted business success. First apprenticed to his uncle, a prosperous Boston merchant, and afterwards in a partnership with a young friend, Chamberlain had bought and sold with profit the goods of East India and China. Those whose opinion counted in such matters were saying in 1818 that the Chamberlain firm was assured of a brilliant future. But in that year Levi joined Park Street Church and at once lost his wish to lay up earthly treasure.

He did not act hastily, however. It was 1821 before he sold his shares to his partner and entered Andover Seminary. In the meantime he had seen the Hawaiian Mission sail and had heard the exciting news of its arrival and of the Islands' changed regime. Apparently he then intended to follow Hiram Bingham and Asa Thurston into the field as a preacher, but he soon abandoned the study of theology and took a post under Jeremiah Evarts, the American Board's treasurer.

Now his friends said he was in training to succeed Evarts at some future day, but again they were wrong. Levi Chamberlain was far from robust; the work in the treasury office was confining. A sea voyage and a change of climate, he was advised, might put him on his feet. And both at the Islands and in Boston the belief prevailed that the Hawaiian Mission stood in urgent need of a good business agent. He sailed without a female companion—on the Board's advice, though contrary to its previous policy.

Elisha, who even before Daniel Chamberlain's departure had fallen heir to the Mission's accounts, surrendered his scrubby notebooks and dubious inventories to the newcomer, breathed deep with relief and turned his thoughts to the printing.

WHILE THE PRESS stood in a frail, inflammable grass shack, Elisha could not rest. He had seen the natives dig and hew the gray coral blocks along the shore and heap them into walls and fences, and the brethren had used such stones to build the cookhouse. Elisha had long ago decided that a coral printing office, safe from fire, rain and dust, was a prime need.

Levi Chamberlain agreed, and they raised the frame on August 21. Nine days later they had put up the walls "snug and firm . . . of old coral, dug in the plain." So far the cost had been two hundred and fifty dollars; another fifty dollars, they estimated, would see it finished, and it would be well worth the price. They sent to Canton for tile and, until that came, made a temporary roof of boards, hauled from the village in the handcart.

By December 4 the building was roofed, the inner walls lined with *tapa,* the type cases moved in and the press leveled and secured. On the twentieth Elisha began to set type for the hymnbook.

"The Hawaiian hymns: for praise to Jehovah, the eternal God . . . printed . . . by the missionary people." So read the title of the first hymnal. Its sixty small pages held forty-seven poems, composed to the rhythm of beloved old tunes—Newton, Tisbury, Calvary, New Fiftieth and Uxbridge.

A few were translations, conveying in clipped, vowel-filled syllables the thought of Pope's "The Dying Christian to His Soul," of Watts' "Fiftieth Psalm," of a chorus from Handel's "Messiah" or of Tappan's ode in honor of the first reinforcement, "Wake Isles of the South."

But most of them were original. Ever since his return, William Ellis had been making these *olis* with neat rhymes, well-wrought stanzas and now and then a refrain. He submitted each new piece to native criticism. If the words he had composed drew *"Maikai!"* from a chief, the hymn was preserved for the book that was to come. Meanwhile it could be sung in meeting, lined off by one of the Longnecks, attempted a verse at a time by native voices that reached for the high notes—and flatted, that strove for the brisk tempo—and came off tardily.

Hiram Bingham had been the next to try his hand at composing. Then everybody caught the fever. When Elisha asked his old pupil Kalanimoku to turn teacher and fit him for *oli*-making, Kalanimoku proposed that they collect a little school. At the Mission house they summoned the whole family, and the old chief sat proudly in front and taught them what to write on their slates. It made him chuckle to see the Little Teacher so hard at work, his head bent and his pencil stumbling slowly through a word like *hoomalama-lama.*

IN THE SUMMER of 1823 the *Rover,* Captain Cooper, brought a cargo of horses from the California coast. Hoofbeats became a commonplace on the Honolulu plain, and a cavalcade of foreigners or a single native, bareback, with hair streaming in the breeze ceased to frighten the Mission children.

Soon there was racing. The course ran from the village toward Waikiki, extending almost to the Mission house. Day after day the whole populace, native and white, thronged beside the road, shrieking and cheering. Games of chance like *puhenehene* and *kukini* were forgotten as men bet and won or lost on the new sport.

It became the style to own a horse. Captain Cooper gave the young chiefs lessons in riding; Kalanimoku, though he would never mount a horse, had a stable built. Captain Rogers offered to break Kaahumanu's stallion to the harness. All day he worked him, hitched to a light wagon. At sunset the horse dropped in the shafts and died. So Kaahumanu had no beast to draw the splendid coach that Dixey Wildes brought out presently and sold to her. But that did not greatly trouble her. Her *kanakas*—half a dozen or so at a time—could seize the tongue and drag her briskly to meeting or to Waikiki. She preferred to ride alone in the driver's seat, while Kaumualii lolled in the plushy interior and Kealiiahonui sat high in the footman's post behind.

When Kalanimoku gave the Longnecks a piece of good land in Manoa, Levi Chamberlain threw caution to the winds and bought a horse for the Mission. As Elisha broke the rich soil for planting, he thought how it would please Daniel Chamberlain to hear that they could at last till a plot properly.

Cattle, too, came from California that summer, and no longer did the Mission have to do with goats' milk for its children. But keeping animals in the inclosure brought its difficulties. Levi Chamberlain nearly lost his life at the horns of an angry bovine; and once, when some "evil disposed person" let down the bars and the Mission cow with her calf "eloped" up Punchbowl, the busy brethren had to lay aside their printing and translating, their teaching and sermon-writing, and, armed with clubs, go in a body to bring her back.

QUEEN MOTHER

KEOPUOLANI, the king's mother, studied earnestly, for she felt that life was slipping past her.

"I must learn," she said, "or I shall die before I obtain the good thing that I desire." So her book was always at hand, and she read it early and late.

Liholiho was not pleased. "You study too much," he objected. "It is not good. It is well for you to study a little if you like, but not always, all day long." His own time was still divided between the mild pleasures of the *palapala* and the more potent joys of rum and revelry.

"You will die and go to the fire!" warned his mother. "Why do you not listen to our teachers?"

"The missionaries are not good," retorted Liholiho.

"In former times," the queen reminded him, "you told me the teachers were good."

"I have discovered," said Liholiho, "the part that is good. If we learn the speech of foreigners we will be better able to do our business with the merchants; but there is no good in the praying and the preaching and the Sabbaths."

But the queen was not persuaded. She listened eagerly to the sermons and held prayers in her household both morning and evening. She sent away all of her husbands except Hoapili, with whom she had lived the longest.

Sometimes she sorrowed for the ones who had died too soon—her grandfather Kalaniopuu, her father Kauikeaouli and her husband Kamehameha. They had not lived to see these good times.

They had trusted false gods. They would burn in the fire. The thought stabbed her.

One day she said to Liholiho, "I will go to Maui, the island of my ancestors, and there I will reside the rest of my days, where it is quiet and I can give thought to the teachings of the Longnecks. I will take with me the prince Kauikeaouli and the princess Nahienaena. They too must learn the good ways. The Longnecks will give us a teacher, or perhaps two, for they now have many in their company. And you, my son—why do you not come and dwell with us?"

"No," said Liholiho. "I came here from Kailua. All the chiefs said, 'Go, live at Honolulu, where the foreign ships are coming all the time.' It would be very foolish to go away now and live on another island."

So the queen mother moved to Maui, but the king stayed on Oahu. He was not ready to turn to the new learning. He was drinking again, as heavily as in the first days of the Mission, and the urge to wander and rove was upon him as never before. With a great party of comrades and retainers he went to Puuloa near Pearl River. Reluctantly he accepted Hiram Bingham's offer to join his train so that the *palapala* might be at hand whenever His Majesty felt inclined toward it.

The Puuloa encampment was dark and comfortless. In the king's house—one of those requisitioned without warning from the villagers—Hiram was allotted a space six feet by three, partitioned with mats from the royal apartment. "The occupancy of every inch . . ." Hiram wrote afterward, "was stoutly disputed by the *uku-lele*" (a term which meant lice, long before it was applied to a musical instrument).

At Puuloa, near the great lagoon that today is Pearl Harbor, revelry went on hour after hour. But sometimes Liholiho grew thoughtful at night and sat with lamp burning, idly turning the pages of his spelling-book or his Bible. On such nights Hiram talked with him, pleading with him to change his ways, to save his own soul and lead his people toward the light. For as they had traveled and talked with the common people—behind Diamond Hill, up the valleys, along Pearl River or over the Pali in Koolau—the brethren had heard one thing oftener than any other: We are waiting for the king to turn and take up this *pala* and this *pule*. Let him send out the crier to say that it is good; then will we harken.

But Liholiho, both sad and annoyed, said, "I cannot repent now. In five years I will turn and forsake sin. I have given my word to the Lord that I will repent in five years."

No sooner had the king returned from Puuloa than he induced his hilarious friends to sail with him to visit his mother on Maui. Five guns, fired in rapid succession, proclaimed their arrival off Lahaina. Liholiho landed alone in a small boat and hurried up the beach.

Keopuolani had gathered her household for evening prayers. The king burst into the circle, knelt before his mother and gazed silently into her face for a moment. Then, placing his hands on her cheeks, he kissed her twice. The queen's eyes shone with love and pride.

"I have brought my comrades," Liholiho announced presently. "They will soon be ashore. Where shall they sleep?"

In her new dwelling, the queen mother said. She would withdraw to one of the smaller houses in the grove. But the light went out of her eyes. She did not like her son's bibulous companions.

Jean Rives came ashore in the dusk, and the bottles clinked as the *kanakas* unloaded the boat. All night there was a wild singing and pounding of drums; only at sunrise did the noises cease. In the open space before Keopuolani's door, the spent merrymakers sprawled as quiet as if death had struck them down in the midst of their orgy. Torchbearers and musicians slept among their burned-out *kukui* branches and calabash drums. Empty bottles were scattered everywhere.

Seeing them thus, the queen mother cried, "Shameful! Shameful!" and hid her face in her shawl.

The Longneck William Richards chided the king.

"Do not be uneasy," Liholiho said suavely. "I cannot repent at once. My wickedness is too great. But I have already told Binamu that in five years I will turn and forsake sin. I have spoken to Jehovah that in five years I would turn and be a good man, and that then He might look at me, and if I am good preserve me, and if not, send me to the place of punishment."

Thus Liholiho repeated his promises. Then he sailed with his party back to Oahu, where every empty bottle could be replaced with a full one. But he did not stay away long. In the fall his mother fell ill; and express messengers were dispatched to all the islands, both leeward and windward, to summon the *alii* to Maui: "Keopoulani, the chief of the highest blood, is ailing."

Soon the brigs and schooners arrived, their decks crowded and even their chains, bowsprits and tops filled with natives. Kaahumanu and Kaumualii came, Kalanimoku and his suite, Naihi and Kapiolani, Laanui and Namehana, Boki and Liliha, Keeaumoku and Kuakini.

Kalanimoku spoke to William Richards. The queen mother was far more ill, he said, than anyone thought. The chiefs would like to send a vessel immediately for Binamu and the new American doctor. If there was anything the doctor could do with his medicines and his instruments, let it be done; but if not, then let Binamu come and wash her with water in the name of the Lord, that she might go to heaven.

A pilot boat sailed and in three days returned with Hiram Bingham, Dr. Blatchley and the American consul, John Coffin Jones. When the doctor said that Keopuolani was dying, Hoapili asked again that she be baptized.

The brethren conferred. Had her probation been long enough, her conduct sufficiently correct? They must be sure, for she would be their first recognized convert. At length, they decided in her favor.

The house was filled with weeping chiefs. Keopuolani lay, barely breathing. She did not feel the touch of Binamu's hand on her brow nor hear the words that made her one of the elect.

"It is well," said Hoapili. "This morning she told me, 'It is not dark now. My thought is that Jesus Christ will receive me to his right hand.' That is how she spoke when last she spoke to me. She was not afraid."

When the queen died, Kalanimoku moved swiftly to safeguard the peace. Official orders went everywhere with the king's proclamation that no man should mutilate himself nor injure another nor seize any property nor perform the abominations of the days of dark hearts. If any were found to do so, it was said, they should be put at once in irons. But all who wished to wail might wail.

The sound of lamentation was heard throughout the district. *"Auwe! Auwe!"* the people moaned, prolonging the last syllable with a trembling of the voice. Around the house of death a multitude of commoners assembled. Some stood upright, casting their arms toward heaven; some bent their faces to the ground; others clutched their hair as if to pull it out. Tears fell in torrents. Vessels in the harbor canted their yards and set their colors at half mast.

Under a cluster of *kou* trees a platform was raised for the bier. Pallbearers and mourners—chiefs in European dress, missionaries, and other whites—gathered close. More than three thousand natives squatted or stood in a wider circle, and, as they had been bidden, ceased their wailing when the service began. They sat, almost too awed to breathe, as Hiram Bingham spoke in Hawaiian, "Blessed are the dead which die in the Lord."

In a few days the missionaries and John Coffin Jones sailed for Oahu. But the chiefs did not return to their homes. Their *kanakas* threw up temporary houses, all near the place of burial; and here for some weeks the *alii* dwelt to honor Keopuolani. They thought it right to build a wall around the queen's tomb, taking the stones from a crumbling heathen altar. So all the chiefs toiled together, lifting and dragging the heavy blocks while their *kanakas* walked alongside with feather *kahilis*.

"I WILL SEE THIS KING GEORGE"

AT Lahaina, where the chiefs had been assembled since Keopuolani's funeral, Liholiho announced that he was going to England: "I will see this King George; I will see what he wears, the kind of houses he has, how he rules. I will study his laws, and I will have an understanding with him that each of us will treat the other fairly and respect his country forever."

Some of the chiefs demurred. It was an unknown thing for a king to travel in a foreign ship over thousands of miles of ocean. Let Liholiho send a message to the English king—a written message, which he could now prepare, with help from his teachers, in his own hand.

"No," said Liholiho. "I will see King George. I will go."

A ship was at hand. Captain Starbuck's *L'Aigle,* ready once more to sail home with a cargo of sperm oil, would carry the royal party.

But to Kaahumanu, to Kalanimoku, to Hoapili and to Namahana the voyage remained dubious. Seeking time perhaps to alter the king's views, Kaahumanu proposed making ready the *Cleopatra's Barge.* "Let the English whaler go its way," she said. "If our king is to take this voyage, why does he not go in our own ship?" But she reckoned without Liholiho's impatience.

"I will sail on *L'Aigle,*" he said.

Of his five wives he would take only Kamamalu; of other companions Boki and his wife, Liliha; Manuia and three other young chiefs; and, as his interpreter, Kanehoa, the son of John Young. He would carry well-filled treasure chests for expenses and gifts; he would settle the succession upon his young brother, Kauikeauoli, and commit the government in his absence to Kaahumanu, regent, and Kalanimoku, premier.

At once Kamamalu sent four pieces of brocaded satin—black, scarlet, yellow and pink—to Honolulu, to be cut into dresses by her friends at the Mission. Her women would do the sewing, though she herself was not incapable of lending a hand if the time grew short.

As preparations went forward, Kalanimoku expressed foreboding. "My eyes grow dark," he said sadly to Elisha. And this was true, for the premier was fast going blind. "No more see Liholiho." Elisha knew that, though the old chief was often tried by the irresponsible young king, he loved him dearly.

In a few days Kamamalu came to the Mission house to receive her gowns and to bid her friends goodbye. "For myself," she said, "I do not desire to leave Hawaii; I would not go to visit those countries that lie across the sea; but I must heed the charge of our father, Kamehameha, and follow the king where he chooses to sail." She departed, barefooted, with the unaffected dignity and grace that befitted a queen.

"She will walk the streets of London, I suppose, with that same air," said Maria.

"HE LEFT the islands and went to a foreign land in a triangular canoe, called Paimalau." So ran the ancient story of the god Lono, and though his subjects long expected him, he never returned. Now, like Lono, Liholiho was about to commit himself to a long voyage, from which the return was uncertain. His weeping people—chiefs and commoners—crowded the beach near the stone quay on the morning of November 27, 1823. The king said to them, "Attend to our good friends the missionaries."

Kamamalu, standing near him, spoke a tender and plaintive farewell to her homeland:

"O skies, O plains, O mountains and oceans,
  O guardians and people, kind affection for you all.

Farewell to thee, the soil,
O country, for which my father suffered; alas for thee!"

"They passed from the shore amidst the wailing of the people," wrote Elisha in his journal, "saluted by the guns of the forts, both from the beach and the hill. The vessel continued lying off and on until about three o'clock, when she put out to sea."

1824

SCHOLARS

FOR Elisha, much of 1824 was remote and shadowy. Only the business of printing seemed real—only the tall piles of tough, white foolscap or demy, waiting for the impression; only the small pica types, their faces wearing gradually away; only the great screw, playing looser and looser in the nut; only the finished jobs—seven thousand alphabet books, four thousand catechisms, two thousand hymnals. With the ink scarcely dry, and for the most part without binding or even stitching, the folded sheets were snatched from his work table and sent where the cry was loudest at the moment.

Earlier the common people had said, "We are waiting for the king to tell us about the *pala*—whether it is good or bad." But Liholiho had never quite decided whether the nation would gain if all the farmers and fishermen and artisans learned to read. Would it not be ruined, instead, he asked himself, because once educated, the commoners would not willingly go to cut sandalwood? So he had wavered and given his heart to merrier matters.

But now Kaahumanu, the regent, and Kalanimoku, the prime minister, ruling the Islands in the king's absence, had made up their minds about the learning. They were for it. In April they called a council in Honolulu. A hundred chiefs and head men came together in a grass schoolhouse. The Longnecks, too, were present, unsure what this meeting portended until Kalanimoku stated its object.

"Are we not here," he asked, turning to Kaahumanu, "to make public our resolution respecting the learning and the law of the Lord?"

She replied, for all to hear, "We are."

Then Kalanimoku, who was the orator of the day, set forth in ringing phrases the contrast between the old ways and the new. "Let us," he cried, "have a general attention to instruction." And when he asked the chiefs whether they agreed with him, a hundred voices shouted, *"Ae!"*

Excitement spread through Honolulu and out into the districts, both windward and leeward. Everywhere new scholars joined the schools that had been opened. Everywhere there was clamor for more schools to be established. From morning to night you could hear the droning of Hawaiian voices as they conned the *pi-a-pa*. The rulers had spoken. The *palapala* was good.

The call for books resounded through the Islands. It might be from Kailua: "Send us books. We have not one on hand, and half the applications from distant places we have not been able to answer." Or from Lahaina: "Our books are gone. There are but two schools where the number of books equals half the number of scholars. If we had the books, we could establish many more schools." Or from Kaawaloa: "The great cry is for books and teachers. Those who were once . . . opposed are now soliciting instruction." Or from Kauai, where Kaahumanu traveled with a great company, inquiring how the people, bereft of their king, made out with the *palapala*. ". . . tell the posse of Longnecks to send some more books down here. Many are the people—few are the books. I want . . . 800 Hawaiian books to be sent hither . . . By and by, perhaps, we shall be wise."

Books for Oahu were issued at the Mission house, but sometimes, when the supply ran out, the disappointed ones besieged Elisha in the printing office.

"Who is your teacher?" he asked such a fellow, hoping to put him off.

"My desire to learn," cried the brown youth with passion, "my ear to hear, my eye to see, my hands to handle. From the sole of my foot to the crown of my head I love the *palapala!*"

Elisha patiently lifted from the press the form of a broadside on port regulations and, replacing it with that of the *pi-a-pa*, struck off a copy for the delighted lad. But he regretted his impulsive act, when, an hour later, more natives came demanding that books be made for them, too.

"You must see Mr. Chamberlain," Elisha shouted, waving them away. "He alone gives out books." They pouted and wheedled, for they knew one who had got his straight from the press. At last they went off, disappointed.

Printing had become the most expensive department of the Mission. The meticulous reports to Jeremiah Evarts, treasurer, showed that plainly. Yet the men of the Mission were loath to sell the books or even barter them for produce. In the end, they asked the chiefs to help provide the means of learning for their own people, to buy the paper themselves, if the merchants had any to sell. Then there could be books for all who sought them.

Before he left for England, Boki had donated a quantity of cartridge paper—enough for 1,500 copies of the primer. It was strong and durable and served well. Namahana sent some white *tapa,* and as an experiment Elisha printed two or three hymnals on it. But it was not suited to the *palapala.* "I will get paper from Canton," Kalanimoku declared. But he found no captain who would accept his commission. None of those who were China-bound were sure of returning to Honolulu within a year. Kaahumanu was able to buy a little from the foreigners. With a supply that had come out from Boston in the *Parthian,* this sufficed for the hymnal and the first edition of the alphabet book. But still there was not nearly enough paper for the Mission's needs.

Every book, then, must serve many persons; and the first in any household to master his primer was sent out with it to teach. Many a school had but one book for a score of learners, and some, crowding in as best they could, saw the letters so often inverted or askew that they read them better that way.

FIVE HUNDRED SCHOLARS took part in the quarterly examination that spring of 1824, and Kaahumanu was among them. More humble than the brethren had thought ever to see her, she came into the meeting-house, preceded by her youthful teacher William Beals and followed by the thirty members of her immediate household who had studied with her. She carried a slate on which she had written her composition. "This is my word and hand," it began in handsome round letters. "I am making myself strong." Another sentence followed, more pious and not so boastful, then the signature, KAAHUMANU. Her class was the first called, and she the first in it to spell aloud twenty Hawaiian words. Afterward she stood with her people on one side while the next band came forward in single file.

Namahana and Kinau were there with their households to be examined. Kalanimoku, called away to Maui on business of state, had sent in his composition. Kaumualii, far advanced in his studies, was a proud spectator. But Keeaumoku, who had dreamed of the Islands aflame, was not there. A month ago, amid the wailing of his people, he had laid down his books forever. How he had fared at his examination no one could tell.

A group at a time the scholars chanted in unison the passages they had committed to memory. Each class, as the examination went on, seemed bound to outdo its predecessors in the zest and perfection of its exercises. As Kaahumanu listened, she grew more and more excited. *"Hoolea ia Iehova,"* the voices shouted in chorus. "Praise the Lord," the queen exclaimed, then spontaneously addressing the company, urged all to walk in the new and the right way.

When the examination was over, she sent her two husbands away with the crowd and went quietly into the Mission house. "I am ready now to be sprinkled with water in the name of the Lord," she told Hiram Bingham when he came in. For a fleeting moment the Mission's leader looked nonplussed. Then he began to explain to the proud dowager that not yet—not until after many months of probation and exemplary conduct—could she take her baptismal vows.

Kaahumanu was angry as she left and bore herself with the old arrogance, offering her little finger instead of the "right hand of fellowship."

OF ALL THE boarding scholars William Beals had proved the most faithful. Other boys had been sent away for thieving or dirty talk or had run off, resentful of discipline. Girls, one day demurely lisping bedtime petitions, had turned brazen hussies when a ship came in. Usually they wore their American clothes when they left. Sometimes they came back after a night or a week or a month; for, once they were used to it, they liked the Longnecks' food, even though its price in prayers and study was high. But when a girl had run off to sleep with a white man, she was not welcome in the Mission family. Even if she escaped disease and pregnancy, she was a disturbing element, poisoning the minds of the other scholars against the Longneck discipline and filling her comrades with restlessness and romantic longings.

The boarding of adolescent natives, then, had proved worrisome and profitless. Once spent, the orphan fund of 1820 and 1821 was not renewed. Departing boarders were not replaced. By 1824 the Mission was exerting itself almost wholly toward the instruction of grownups. The children's hope, as they now saw it, lay in widespread reform, new convictions and customs for the whole nation. That meant more books, more adult schools, more native teachers, more sermons that struck home in wayward hearts, more noble examples in *alii* leadership, more laws.

William Beals was the proud exception among the boarders. The first of the orphans, winner with Hannah Holmes of the earliest rewards for scholarship, Elisha's companion and interpreter in his first tour to the back country, teacher of Kaahumanu and her household, he had never caused them a moment's uneasiness. Not, at least, until the day he fell strangely ill.

Dr. Blatchley gave him a course of salivation, and he improved. Then one morning he said that his relatives in the village wanted him to come and live with them. They had been coaxing him a long time, he confessed, to leave the Mission. Now that he was sick, they insisted. Hiram Bingham tried in vain to dissuade him from going. In his trig suit of worsted, his ruffled white shirt, his polished leather shoes, and his *haole* hat, the boy who had come to them without even a *malo* said goodbye. His brown eyes were sad as he told them he meant to come Sundays to the church and, when he was rid of his sickness, help them once more with the school for native teachers.

But when William came again to the Mission, he was unconscious, carried by two frightened natives. In the night, his relatives said, the boy had begun to shriek and beg for medicine. Later he had fallen into a fit and could neither speak nor hear. Yesterday he had cried and said he would die and not go to heaven. The American doctor and the American preacher, they hoped, would mend all that. But the doctor could not save William's life and Hiram Bingham could offer no promise of heaven.

William died before midnight. They made him a plain wooden coffin and gave him a Christian burial. Six native teachers bore his body from the Mission house to the church. In the procession marched "a few foreign residents," Kaumualii, Kaahumanu, and other chiefs, a number of natives, including William's relatives, and the Mission family. Mr. Ellis preached. "All flesh is as grass," he read from St. Peter, "and all the glory of man as the flower of grass. The grass withereth, and the flower thereof falleth away: But the word of the Lord endureth forever."

NO SANDALWOOD

AT sunset on a June day there was singing on the plain just beyond the village. A small, bright-eyed girl who had won her lover from a rival was, with a dozen or so loyal friends, rejoicing in her feat. Over and over the little group chanted the ditties of triumph and the *meles* of love's pleasures, taking their cue for each new phrase from their leader, the victorious minx.

Newcomers joined them until there were scores of them there in the dusk. Then, all in a moment, their sway was disputed. The jilted one came forth with her partisans, singing of faithlessness and jealousy, of broken hearts and spiteful jests. For a long time the voices clashed or mingled in dissonance or rude counterpoint until it was fully dark. Then they fell silent, and the rivals went their ways—one to enjoy her conquest; the other to mope deserted under the family *tapa*.

Next afternoon the parties came together again, with crowds of spectators. When the song-battle had raged for two hours, the singers suddenly lined up at the water's edge and one after another, following their leaders, plunged in for a twilight swim. As they splashed and giggled in the surf, you could not have told one faction from the other. Still, this was only a truce; and for two more days the contest went on with increasing verve. Volunteer marshals kept the crowds back, while in the open space the two principals advanced and retreated by turns, singing and pantomiming, until it grew dark or "some evil-minded person" threw stones into the crowd.

On the last day each party began with a collation in the home of

its "she-captain," then formed its ranks to flaunt its new songs and
routines. Praises of the heroines rang out extravagantly, and the
leaders shone as never before. On and on they danced, till suddenly the girl who had first boasted her success in love gained the
victory "by a very bold stroke." Taking up a *pala-oa,* a stalk of
sacred fern, she struck it on the ground "with every possible mark
of contempt," broke it with a stone and threw the pieces at her
opponents—"a thing never done before . . ."

Some of the shocked watchers cheered; some, disapproving,
threw stones. The whole company dispersed. The next evening the
plain was empty and quiet save for the sound of the *tapa* mallet,
the *poi* pestle and the *pi-a-pa.*

Almost any afternoon, though, the people might be out again,
old and young, for a stone-rolling or a javelin hurling or a kite-
flying or a horse race. Or a chief might open his ponds to the
commoners for a fishing frolic. All night, in that case, the people
would gather, till there were thousands of them waiting for the
signal. Nets would have been strung to keep the mullet and *nehu,*
the *akeke* and *opule* from escaping seaward, and at dawn native
feet would churn the shallow water and native hands grasp the
bright, squirming creatures, as much for the sport as for the food.

There was time, it seemed, for fun and for the *palapala* too. But
none for cutting sandalwood. In 1824 nobody was cutting sandalwood.

By 1824 the American traders had grown grim about the debts. In
January John Coffin Jones turned over his contract and his consular
duties to Thomas Crocker, who had come out in the *Paragon.* Then
Jones headed home, leaving conflicting reports of his plans for
the future. In a year of residence Crocker collected for Marshall &
Wildes only a hundred piculs.

The Bryant & Sturgis men did not do much better. The *Lascar,*
Captain Harris, forbidden the fur ports by the Russians, lay twelve
months at the Islands and loaded only four hundred piculs. The
Champion, Captain Preble, took eleven months to garner six hun-

dred, less than half a cargo. The *Sultan,* Captain Clark, had, in September of 1824, "done nothing for the last year." John Ebbets had "suffered by leaving someone from a rival firm to collect his wood." Dixey Wildes, on the scene since March, wrote Marshall in September, "Captain Blanchard is still here; he has his ship nearly full, principally very bad wood." Still it was wood, and in larger quantity than any competitor could boast.

James Hunnewell was the ablest of them all. By the beginning of '24 he had 1,026 piculs, which he hoped to ship in Captain Blanchard's *Octavia* and then go home himself. But six months later he wrote his brother, "I can only say you need not expect me home until you see me . . . My hope of realizing something handsome from the *Thaddeus* concern has vanished."

Yet at Canton in 1824 the price of sandalwood was rising—rising from a ruinous low of $6 a picul to $10, $12, $14. Any merchant who now collected his old debts would be paid for his years of waiting. It is no wonder that two plaintive, wishful themes ran increasingly through the talk and the letters. "When Liholiho comes back . . ." the merchants said over and over, growing steadily angrier with the regent and the prime minister. "When the United States sends a gunboat here . . ." they began to add. For word out of Boston told them their government was aware of their plight.

As early as the preceding fall, a Bryant & Sturgis partner, admitting that the firm's prospects looked "wretchedly bad," saw hope in the "intended visit of one of our Ships." The sloop-of-war *Peacock,* the writer reported, had sailed for the Pacific. "When she joins Commodore Hull," he went on, "either she or the Frigate will visit the Islands . . . and we know that Comm^e Hull will be disposed to afford all the aid he can for the security & recovery of Property."

From Honolulu, Dixey Wildes put it more briefly and confidently to his partner: "We are expecting Capt. Hull or one of his sloops of war—should they come here the natives would soon pay all their debts."

Yes, when Liholiho came home—sobered, no doubt—and when the United States naval vessel visited the Islands and its commander talked sternly to the chiefs about their obligations, then, the traders told each other, some of the spelling-book nonsense would cease. There would be a burst of activity in the dwindling forests, and once for all they would balance their accounts.

But the time was not yet. The Pacific squadron was busy surveying harbors along California. And the king was half a world away, debarking at Portsmouth, being welcomed and escorted to London by a British peer, unpacking at the Adelphi, depositing his funds—such as had not been pilfered on the voyage—in the Bank of England, gracing a box at Covent Garden, anticipating an audience with King George and catching a virulent form of the measles.

No, the time was not yet.

PELE VANQUISHED

ON Maui and on Hawaii, where the old ways survived and
the old beliefs lingered, there were many who feared and
threatened and ridiculed the *palapala*. There was still
talk of vengeance from the ancient gods for the rifling of their
altars; of dire calamity in the making for those who followed the
Longnecks' Jehovah. Held in particular dread was Pele, the god-
dess of volcanoes, who dwelt, according to legend, within smoking
Kilauea on the Big Island and, when angered, hurled ashes into
the air and lava down the mountainside till it hissed into the sea.
Offerings of hogs or fruit could still be had by one who posed as
Pele's priest, and a self-styled priestess could spread terror in the
land.

On an August day in 1824 natives brought to the Mission house
at Lahaina word that such a priestess had come to Maui and was
telling the chiefs that they must cast off the *palapala* and send
away the missionaries; that if they did not do so, a volcano would
burst forth in Lahaina and destroy all who favored the new learning. To avert this doom, the priestess said, the Lahainans must not
only change their ways but must sacrifice to Pele "a man, a dog, a
white fowl and a fish."

Let the foolish ones tremble if they would, the Christian chiefs
said scornfully when they heard this story. They themselves were
strong in the Lord; they would meet this impostor and show her
what was what. They named as their spokesman Kalakua, once
consort of the Conqueror, now wife to Hoapili. She was as firm in
the faith as any chief in the kingdom.

In the morning when the cry rose, "Pele is coming! All powerful is the Pele!" they stood in a circle to receive the false priestess. Around them on all sides were those who waited in hope, fear or curiosity for the outcome.

She came along the beach from the south, moving slowly and silently among hundreds of watchers, her countenance fierce, her black hair long and disheveled. Before her she held a two-pointed spear and her fly-brushes, one white, pointing upward, and one black, pointing down. Two little girls, walking beside her as her ensign-bearers, each carried a pole with a sheet of old *tapa* waving from its top.

"I have arrived," the old crone croaked, looking round the circle.

"We are all here," said Kalakua.

"Love to you all."

"Yes," said Kalakua guardedly, "love, perhaps."

"I now present myself to speak to you. . . . I have come from . . . England whither I have been to attend your king . . . but I have returned into your presence."

Kalakua spoke with scorn. "Don't you come here to tell us your lies. What have you there in your hands?"

"I have the spear of Pele and her *kahilis*."

"Lay them down," said Kalakua. "Lay them down, I say. Do not come here to tell us you are Pele. There are volcanoes in other parts of the world besides Hawaii. The great God of heaven, He governs them all, and you are a woman like us . . . Light is now shining upon us, and we have cast off all our false gods. You, therefore . . . go back to Hawaii, plant potatoes, make *tapa*, catch fish, fatten hogs and then eat. Do not go about saying to the people, give this thing or give that to Pele. Go to school and learn the *palapala* . . . and send also your little daughters." Then Kalakua held up the speller and the hymnbook. "Here," she said, "is our foundation."

The priestess kept silent.

"Now," Kalakua went on, "I will ask you a question. Answer me honestly and tell me no lies. My question to you is this: Have you always been lying to the people, or have you not? Tell us that we may all hear."

"I have been lying," said the woman quietly, "but I will lie no more."

A chief said, "It is now a proper time to pray to Jehovah, for there are many people present, and He is our God."

After the prayer, as the people began to shout, "All powerful is the *palapala!*" Pele threw the old *tapas* that were her ensigns into a fire. She would have burned the two-pointed spear as well, but someone cried out, "Stop! I want that to dig the ground with." And so Pele's spear became an agricultural implement.

PELE WAS now vanquished on Maui, but in the interior of Hawaii, where there were no schools or preaching, she had her followers still. And this seemed wrong to Kapiolani, the wife of Naihe, who lived at Kaawaloa.

In the days before the *Thaddeus,* Kapiolani had loved her liquor. She could outdrink Liholiho and had almost never been sober. But after she had lived at Honolulu a few years under the missionaries' sway, she found a new heart. At Kaawaloa, where Rev. James Ely had been assigned, she built a church and a schoolhouse, supplied the preacher and his family with everything for their comfort and became a notable patron of learning.

Still, she was not content. When she and Naihe went to Kau to try to collect a little sandalwood, she saw village after village of poor, untaught commoners, and the sight troubled her. Since there were not enough Longnecks to go to the interior, Kapiolani decided to go herself, on foot, straight across Hawaii through superstition's stronghold, then down the eastern slope to where her Christian friends, Mr. Ruggles and Mr. Goodrich, preached in Hilo. When news came of Kapiolani's mission, Joseph Goodrich set out to join her, but Samuel Ruggles did not go, because he had no shoes.

As Kapiolani came up the southwest slope, multitudes entreated her not to go on to the volcano. She had preached against Pele, they warned, and Pele would have her revenge.

"If I am destroyed, then you may all believe in Pele," Kapiolani answered. "If I am not, then you must all turn to the *palapala*."

At Kilauea, the great smouldering volcano in the center of the island, the preaching chiefess met the missionary from Hilo. As they walked together along the rim of the crater, they encountered Pele's priestess, doubtless the same who had visited Lahaina.

"Who are you?" asked Kapiolani.

"One in whom the god dwells." The woman showed a piece of *tapa,* saying that here was a *palapala* from Pele. But she was reluctant to read it, muttering, when challenged, a "medley of nonsense."

Out of a calabash, Kapiolani drew her spelling-book and hymnal. "I, too, have a *palapala*," she said.

The priestess shuffled off, her head down, still mumbling.

"Let us visit *Halemaumau*," said Kapiolani. "Let us look without fear into the lake of fire and watch the work of Jehovah."

At the brink of the fiery pit stood the man whose duty it was to feed Pele. Every day he picked red *ohelo* berries and threw them into the orifice. "Go no farther," he cried as Kapiolani and her Longneck friend approached.

"And what will be the harm?"

"You will die by Pele."

"I shall not . . ." said Kapiolani. "That fire was kindled by my God." She took a few berries and ate them, then tossed some stones to Pele. "Now," she said, "let us pray." She designated one of her train to lead the *pule,* in which the whole of her company should unite.

Then, triumphant, the little band started down the fern-fringed path into Hilo.

DEATH AND REBELLION

KAUMUALII, once king of Kauai, lay dying in the house of Kaahumanu. Pleurisy and a diarrhea had quickly taken his strength, and the ministrations of the Mission's doctor had given way to those of its pastor.

In his last hours Kaumualii made a will. He called for paper and ink, but, being too weak to write anything, he instructed Kalanimoku to put down his words. All his possessions must be held in trust for Liholiho. The premier and the regent must see to this. But there was another thing that they must do: they must pay his debts to the foreign merchants—especially for the ships he had bought. For that, they must gather more sandalwood on the leeward isles. They must see to it in his stead, for he was about to leave this life.

Kaumualii spoke painfully; but he made his wish clear. Kalanimoku wrote the words with a quill so that they stood fine and large on a white sheet. Then he held the writing case close while the king, supported by two *kanakas* and by Kaahumanu, subscribed a wavering "Kaumualii."

If his younger son Kealiiahonui, sitting apart in the shadows, felt defrauded, he gave no sign. No mention was made of the son who had been called Prince in America. George would do well to hold his little valley under whatever monarch and governor ruled Kauai. When, next morning, the chiefs from Kauai, George among them, arrived in the *Becket,* Kaumualii did not open his eyes nor speak to them.

About noon, at a sign from Dr. Blatchley, Kaahumanu ordered

the door fastened and the window curtains dropped. Then the people, knowing that death had come, raised their voices to wail. Some beat on the door, others on the shrouded windows. In a little while the curtains were opened, and the people could see the dead king, lying on a mantle of green velvet, his legs and abdomen wrapped in yellow silk, his chest and head bare, except for "a wreath of feathers across his eyes." His war cloak draped the head of the couch, his feather tippet the foot. So Kaumualii lay in state in the land of his captivity.

Afterward they took him to Maui that he might be buried near Keopuolani. It had been his wish. For were they not brother and sister in Christ?

GEORGE, WHEN HE CALLED at the Mission, had his own theory about his father's death.

"The old woman gave me some food," he muttered, "and I had the same sickness that my father had."

He did indeed look sick. But Elisha charged the bloodshot eyes and bloated face to long-continued dissipation. He suggested that Dr. Blatchley look him over.

George swore violently, with a swaggering air. "The old gentleman," he said, "was poisoned with the help of your doctor. As for me, three days ago I ate with Kaahumanu, and I have been up every night since, vomiting. But I have survived. I would be a fool to get into the power of this doctor. You sent away the only good doctor—"

Sharply Elisha told him to stop talking nonsense.

"I shall never see Kauai again," the prince whimpered. "I am as good as dead now."

But despite his forebodings George P. Tamoree lived to return to Kauai. Not many days after his father's funeral he sailed with Kapule, the deposed queen, and Kahalaia, a nephew of Kalanimoku, who was Kauai's new governor.

There were plenty to connive with the prince against Kaahumanu and her government. Up and down the valleys that summer resentment and disaffection ran rife, and every vessel that came from the leeward to Honolulu brought ominous rumors.

It was not the issue of the island's independence that seemed most likely to throw Kauai into open rebellion. The distribution of land, Kahalaia warned his uncle, was the question which would bring war, if war came. By Kaumualii's will, all who held land on Kauai were confirmed in their holdings, whether great or small. But those who had little or none at all, led by the crafty old chief Kiaimakani, were calling loudly for a new division. And Tamoree was their man.

Property rights, these malcontents said, had always been settled by battle. Whenever a new king rose to power he threw all the land together and divided it again among his aides. A good custom, the rebels declared. This thing of settling regency and title by the *palapala* rather than by force of arms was bad. Let Oahu and the windward isles abide by the missionaries' foolishness if they would; Kauai would keep to the old method.

ALARMED BY RUMORS of war, Kalanimoku hastened to the leeward in his little schooner, the *New York,* using as his pretext the need to look after the *Cleopatra's Barge,* wrecked on the rocks at Hanalei.

But the prime minister was too late to prevent rebellion. His arrival at Waimea seemed, rather, the signal to attack, and before dawn on an August Sunday, a handful of insurgents armed with bayonets forced their way into the fort. They killed some of the garrison and wounded others. Six of the rebels fell mortally hurt; the rest soon fled in disorder. In the midst of this confusion Kalanimoku took charge and sent to Honolulu for reinforcements. But first he sought out Samuel Whitney and, asking his prayers, advised the missionaries to hurry to his schooner while it was still in the roads and go in it to Oahu.

When the *New York* came to anchor in the early morning, all Honolulu rang with the cry of war, and grew noisy with the roll of drums and the crack of muskets. The accoutrements of battle—

caps, cartridge boxes, feathers, swords—came out of hiding. By Namahana's order, it was said, a thousand men would embark at sunrise tomorrow for the relief of Kalanimoku; and Kaahumanu had sent an express to Hoapili at Lahaina, commanding him to add his forces to those from Oahu. The criers, having shouted "It is war!" till their message grew stale, now ran here and there saying, "Well nigh slain is Kalanimoku by George Tamoree and his party."

Kaikioewa stood near the landing and proclaimed with spirit, "I am old like Kalanimoku. We fought together beside our king, Kamehameha. Shall I desert him now, when the rebels of Kauai rise against him? No, I myself will go; and here are my men also."

But amidst all the fervor and excitement, some men had sober thoughts. Even before the missionaries from Kauai had been welcomed and refreshed at the frame house, the native teachers began to appear, asking Hiram Bingham, "What now? Are we to go and fight against the Kauaians or continue with our books and our schools? And what shall we say to the men in our schools when they ask us, 'Shall we kill for the sake of Kalanimoku?'"

At mid-morning the chief Laanui came. He had on a hussar's uniform and looked very handsome. He asked earnestly whether he did right to lead the thousand men his wife Namahana was dispatching to Waimea.

Hiram Bingham told him that the war—if, indeed, "a strife commenced without preamble, manifesto or any declaration of cause or purpose," could be called a war—was not of Kalanimoku's making nor of Kahalaia's nor Kapule's. It was George and Kiaimakani who had "taken up the sword."

"It is stated in God's law," said Hiram, "that such as take up the sword shall perish by it"—he showed Laanui the passage in the English Bible—"but remember also that the Lord bids us to love our enemies. If, then, you take any man captive, be merciful to him and let him live."

Laanui understood and was comforted. "We do not go to kill the men of Kauai," he said. "We go to put an end to fighting. We will take the rebels and bring them to the windward and put them to farming."

The rebellion was soon quenched. Kiaimakini was slain, and George, who had fled with Betty and their baby into the hills, was captured, hungry and destitute.

Establishing his old friend Kaikioewa as governor, Kalanimoku returned to Honolulu, where the people shouted and wept to see him come ashore, and hailed him as "the iron cable of Hawaii."

When Elisha heard that George had been brought, a prisoner, to Oahu, he sought him out at the fort, where a grass hut in the back part of the grounds had been assigned him and his family.

"I have been wronged like my father before me," George lamented, straddling a backless chair and shaking a finger at Elisha. He was slovenly in a crumpled shirt, soiled pantaloons and bare feet. "The missionaries were once my good friends in America, but now they have joined with my enemies to undo me and rob me of my lands. Kaahumanu I despise, and Kalanimoku and all his warriors, and Bingham, too, for he is with them in all they do. But you, Lumiki," he began to fawn, "I do not hate. You are my good friend since the days of the Foreign Mission School. Do you not think I have been treated badly?"

Back at his press, Elisha could not forget the haunted eyes and whining voice of the Kauaian pretender. Remembering the debonair prince of the *Thaddeus* company, he grieved that all the boy's promise had come to nothing.

A GOOD HALE PULE

THEY never knew who fired the grass church on the Sunday after Kaumualii's funeral. Some said it was a drunken white man whom Hiram Bingham had reproved for disturbing morning service. Others declared it was a native who blamed the Longnecks for the death of Kaumualii.

But at the Mission house they knew only that in the midst of evening family worship the bell clanged, and they scrambled up from their knees and ran out to see the end of the meeting-house in full blaze. Though there were buckets at hand, no one attempted to form a brigade. It would have been useless. Instead, white men and natives joined in rescuing the furniture. They carried out the seats and the mahogany pulpit and tore loose the window and door frames just in time to save them.

Then suddenly the whole building was burning, and the salvagers withdrew, some to remove articles of value to the Mission yard, some to weep silently, and some to cry aloud, *"Auwe! Auwe!"* as the *hale pule,* frame as well as thatch, fell to ashes. But there was no thieving as in the olden days.

Shortly after sunrise the next morning Namahana and her husband Laanui, with a small retinue, were at the Mission house to sympathize with the Longnecks in the loss of the chapel.

"We will punish the dark-hearted fellow if we can find him," said Laanui.

"I have already given orders that a new house of prayer be built," said Namahana. "It shall be larger than the one that was burned, for many have stood outside on the Sabbath who would gladly

218

have gone in to hear the good word. Timber I have collected to build myself a new house, but I shall use it now for the Lord's house, and later I will attend to the matter of my own."

Kalanimoku came not much later. He said he would support Namahana's orders. Moreover, he would take the workmen off his own half-finished stone house and employ them to build the new chapel.

On an appointed day, the principal timbers having been brought to the spot, scores of natives came to raise the *hale pule*. Some had bundles of slender poles to be lashed horizontally across the posts and rafters. Others carried on their shoulders enormous packs of long grass for the thatching or rushes to cover the earth floor. Kalanimoku's chief builder directed them, and his carpenters fitted in the door frames and windows, made new seats to supplement the old, and set up a paling around the yard. Chiefs and commoners bent together to the task, and none was exalted to a special post save by his skill.

Seventy feet long and twenty-five wide, the church could seat six hundred.

"It will serve for now," Kalanimoku said. "Soon we must build of stone and have a good *hale pule* that will not burn, with room in it for more than a thousand people."

If THERE WAS anything the Longnecks wanted, Kalanimoku had told them again and again, they must send and let him supply it at once, free of charge. He had built a stone house for the Ellises; and when, because of Mrs. Ellis' illness, the British missionary returned to England, the chief gave the house to the Mission and it became the home of the Binghams. The land in Manoa was his gift. And often he sent a hog, some fish, or a bundle of *taro* just as a reminder of friendship. In return, when he needed a hammer or file or other tool or trifle, he would send a man to the frame house to borrow it from his good friends.

The great stone house he was building stood beside the Waikiki path, opposite the Mission yard and church, so that he might live out his days near his beloved Longnecks. He planned to shape it in the main like the Wooden House in the village—the one Consul Jones had brought out to sell to Kaahumanu. It should be of two stories and there would be a fine veranda across the front, reached by a broad flight of steps, surrounded by an ornate balustrade and flanked by the tall glassed windows of his upper hall. Indoors there would be a spacious room where the chiefs might gather in council, or Binamu conduct a meeting for prayer. And it would be furnished more splendidly than the house of Liholiho, now standing empty on the quay.

He had his people dig the cellar, hew the coral blocks from the reef and burn the lime for mortar. Two by two the *kanakas* brought stones up from the shore, slinging them with cords to the poles they bore on their shoulders. When the house was ready for the interior finishing, Kalanimoku bought boards and hardware from the *haoles* in the village and finally bargained with the Marshall men to complete his mansion in sumptuous style. All in all, it cost him a pretty penny, especially as the walls crumbled in the rainy season and had to be renewed at great expense.

Once finished, it became the show place of Honolulu and the center of government activity. Beneath the cocoanut trees in its spacious grounds thousands of the people could assemble to hear the word of the chiefs or the word of the Lord. As the men of the Mission spoke more freely in Hawaiian and their native congregations ran to three, four or even five thousand, Kalanimoku's yard became the place for preaching in the native tongue.

The first service each Sunday was held in the church, with a sermon and hymns in English. The wooden pews were filled with sailors, merchants, *hapahaole* residents, great and petty chiefs— each with a modicum of American finery—and chiefesses in *holokus* and straw bonnets. Later in the premier's yard the commoners heard preaching in Hawaiian. Bareheaded, in *malos* and *paus,* hordes of them sat on the ground, filling the area to the last inch, and a few stood at the rear, the better to see the face of the speaker. There were always some who had come from the faraway villages of Koolau or Waianae, traveling on foot all day Saturday to hear the words of Jehovah spoken with the resounding confidence of those who knew and understood them well.

Though he gladly gave his yard for the preaching, Kalanimoku said again and again, and his words were echoed by Kaahumanu, that a huge church of stone must be built, where all who sought new hearts could gather to hear the truth.

But Kalanimoku had forgotten the unpaid notes lying in the cashboxes of the merchants. After the quiet of 1824 and '25 the call for sandalwood would come again, as loud and insistent as ever. The chiefs would have to defer their church-building for a long, long time. So long, in fact, that neither Kalanimoku nor Kaahumanu would live to see the stone church, called Kawaiahao.

1825

TEN WONDERFUL LAWS

THE common people loved the gospel because it held that they were brothers to the *alii,* brothers even to the *haole* traders and the learned Longnecks, descendants, like them, of two wonderful (though sinful) forbears who had lived in a garden. So they greatly fancied the "begat" passages, those that started: "Now these are the generations of Esau, who is Edom," and ran on through resounding name-lists, as when a great chief reckoned his ancestry from Wakea and Papa.

And they loved the "blesseds." For, though a man were lowly, he could hear Binamu read, "Blessed are the poor . . . for theirs is the kingdom . . . Blessed are the humble . . . for they shall be given much land . . . Blessed are the hungry . . . for they shall have food."

The chiefs, too, loved the beatitudes—loved them for their cadences and repetition, and for their fine, full words about comfort and mercy and peace-making.

And the chiefs loved "In the beginning . . ." loved to hear how God said Let there be light; how God divided the light from the darkness; how the waters were gathered together, and the dry land appeared; how herbs and trees, sun and stars, fowl and fishes and beasts came forth; and how at last God took dust of the ground and breathed into it—and there was man.

In their heathen days, they had heard in the chants of the priests and the bards another story of creation.

> O Kane, O Ku-ka-Pao
> And the great Lono, dwelling on the water,

Brought forth are Heaven and Earth
Quickened, increasing, moving,
Raised up into Continents,
   The great Ocean of Kane,
   The Ocean with dotted seas,
   The Ocean with the large fishes,
   And the small fishes,
   Sharks and Niuhi,
   Whales,
   And the large Hihimanu of Kane
   The rows of stars of Kane,
   The stars in the firmament . . .
   The large stars,
   The little stars,
   The red stars of Kane. O infinite space,
      The great Moon of Kane,
      The great Sun of Kane,
      Moving, floating,
      Set moving about in the great space of Kane,
   The great earth of Kane . . .

In the old days, too, the poets had sung of how Kane and Ku and Lono "formed a man out of the red earth and breathed into his nose, and he became a living being"; "mixed earth with the spittle of the gods and formed the head of man out of white clay." While Kane and Ku and Lono were creating the man from the earth, the legend ran, Kanaloa, the spirit of darkness, tried to make one of his own. When the clay was molded, he called it to come alive, but no life came to it. Then Kanaloa, very angry, said to the others, "I will take your man, and he shall die." And so it happened. The man was called Kumuuli, the fallen chief.

All this was declared false after Liholiho had triumphed over the old religion, and its telling was forbidden. But when the chiefs learned the Bible story of Creation, the words were pleasantly familiar—the darkness, the light, the heavens, the earth, the air, the ocean, the stars, the whales—and then man, the fallen one. It was as if they had formerly listened outside the house where these things were told and had heard them dimly; now they had come inside and heard plainly and positively how the world was made and how man fell. So they greatly loved "In the beginning . . ."

But most deeply stirring were the "thou shalt nots," tabus that were not the whim of some earthly chief or priest, bearing down cruelly on women or the common people, but the *Kanawai* of Jehovah, Commandments designed for man's good, both here and hereafter. It became the aim of the ruling chiefs that the whole kingdom should live according to these ten wonderful laws.

From time to time since Liholiho's departure, they had sent out criers on Oahu to pronounce the new decrees; and Kaahumanu had gone to Maui and later to Kona on Hawaii and recited the laws to throngs of people, instructing the head men of all the districts to publish them by herald throughout their realm.

"There shall be no murder."

"There shall be no theft of any description."

"There shall be no boxing or fighting among the people."

"There shall be no work or play on the Sabbath, but this day shall be regarded as the sacred day of Jehovah."

"When schools are established all the people shall learn the *palapala.*"

Now, in 1825, the chiefs searched their hearts as never before. The war on Kauai had made them especially thoughtful about their duties as rulers; and the sermons of Binamu, each devoted to a separate Commandment, opened new vistas of quiet, orderly, dignified behavior. But as they pondered these matters, the chiefs saw also that the *haoles* in the village—the men of the trade—and those who came in the whaleships often ignored the Commandments and gave a somewhat different picture of life in the Christian countries beyond the oceans.

When Liholiho and Boki come home, the chiefs said, they would know.

The Hawaiians had long obeyed some of the *Kanawai*. They had always honored fathers and mothers, and their days had been long upon the land. They had utterly abolished idols before the Long-

227

necks came.

Theft they had dealt with in a way that had served well enough, though it could scarcely have been pleasing to Jehovah. In the old days if a man took something from one below him in the social scale, it was not stealing; for that which was taken had in reality belonged by virtue of rank to the taker. And if a commoner made off with the calabash or the weapon of a superior, the injured man could go to the thief's house and take back his possession, along with anything else he saw that he wanted.

But when the *haoles* came with their bean pots and silver spoons, their monkey wrenches and linen towels, their sawed lumber and their keen-edged axes, this method no longer served. Complaints from foreigners rang unceasingly in the governor's ears. White men did not want to go poking into native huts to find their lost articles. They wanted Boki to haul up the thief and arrange for restitution and punishment.

Gradually the enlightened chiefs saw what they must do. Some of them put their men in irons for proven theft or set them free only to work and pay for what they had stolen. The boy prince Kauikeaouli, when his beloved *kahu* was found accessory to a theft, consented quickly to the man's dismissal. "My *kahu* must go," he declared, "or by and by the foreigners will think that I myself am guilty."

The *haoles* applauded such measures. Here was a Commandment they liked to see enforced.

Then there was the Commandment, forbidding murder in a few short words. Once, if a native killed in sudden anger, it was proper for the victim's relatives to avenge the deed, unless the murderer took shelter in a place of refuge. If the guilty man were of equal rank with the victim's avenger, there might be an appeal to the king or the governor or to the chief of the district. The aggrieved one and the accused would then sit cross-legged in the judge's yard and each would eloquently argue his case till the magistrate made his decision.

But these customs failed when Honolulu swarmed with hotheaded sailors, and brown and white alike drank rum and got *huhu*. Again, as with theft, the traders wanted stern laws, strictly enforced, so that the riffraff of all nations would think twice before bashing their fellows on the head. They told the chiefs to build a lofty engine of death which would string up a murderer by the neck and leave him hanging limp from a rope's end—a potent reminder to the living to restrain themselves.

When it came to the Fourth Commandment—the one about Sabbath-keeping—the Hawaiians found it easy to obey the missionaries' God, who in six days had made Hawaii, Maui, Molokai, Lanai, Oahu, Kauai, the sea, the trees and everything, but on the seventh day had not worked at all. They need not beat their *tapa* on the Sabbath; there were plenty of other days to do that. *Taro* could go untended one day out of seven without being choked with weeds. As for cooking, they had always done enough at one time to last a while; they preferred their fowl and fish and sweet potatoes cold.

So the earth ovens no longer steamed all day on Sunday, baking hog or dog, yams or *taro*. Saturday, the people saw, was the time to make preparation—to heat the stones of the *imu* with fire, to rake out the coals, put in the leaf-wrapped food, dash in the water and cover the whole with stones and earth. By dark all would be ready—the meat tender and succulent, the potatoes brown-skinned and mealy, the *taro* mashed dry and bound up in *ti* leaves or mixed with water into a soft, bluish custard that filled the calabashes. Then, their toil over, the people could rest, just as God had rested when he had finished creating the world.

And in the morning, when the sun lay bright on the plain and on the sparkling sea, they could respond to the church bell. Their work done or laid aside, they could gather at "meeting," where the powerful Kalanimoku, the once haughty Kaahumanu, and Kauikeaouli, heir to all the Islands, sat as meek and humble as the blind and ragged Puaaiki.

But that was not all. In the village, too, the chiefs decreed the same decorum that, they were told, marked the Lord's day in

New England. Did a whaler or an Indiaman send half a crew ashore on Sunday, spoiling for fun? Let the men go to church. Or if in the long afternoon they sought the grogshops and the billiard tables, then, said the chiefs, let them be quiet about their pleasures. But fiddlers, hurdy-gurdies, native girls dancing, bawdy songs and hornpipes—all these that made the rum flow and the profits mount—were now outlawed on the Sabbath. It was bad enough to have such goings-on for the rest of the week, the chiefs declared.

When these laws were proclaimed, the foreigners grumbled and cursed. The Fourth Commandment was not good, the *haoles* said—not for Honolulu.

Then there was gambling. Binamu, when he preached on the *Kanawai,* named it as one form of covetousness, the sin so wordily condemned in the tenth law. To gain possessions by work—that was good. To take without giving anything in exchange merely because a ball rolled here or there, because this horse outran that or one cock finally killed another in a *hoohakamoa* match—that was wrong. It broke down thrift and led to fraud and stealing. So said Binamu.

The chiefs weighed the problem. The natives loved the old betting games; horse races and billiards were the white man's favorite pastimes. It would be almost impossible to stop gambling without forbidding the sports. Yet to ban the sports—except those that were cruel—seemed overharsh. They made no law against betting, therefore, but they condemned it severely. One who gambled might now expect scowls and reproaches from his peers, but he would not be punished.

"Thou shalt not commit adultery . . ."

When the chiefs learned the Seventh Commandment, they saw that they must put an end to two of their ancient love games. So they closed the *hale ume* and stopped those outdoor gatherings where the people sat in a circle by a leaping bonfire waiting the touch of the *ume* stick. From ancient times they had held these revels—*ume* for commoners, *kilu* for nobles—in which two who were not husband and wife enjoyed each other for a night. It was thought very lax in the old days to keep changing mates; like any other sort of shifty vagabondage, such fickleness was considered *hewa*. But for a man to choose a partner for a night's pleasure by skittering a cocoanut bowl toward a wooden pob or directing the flick of a long feather-tufted wand seemed fitting and amusing. All was done properly: the leader kept order, the chants were ribald but not rowdy, there were no spiteful altercations. According to the rules, unless a pair stayed together past daybreak, there was no cause for a spouse to be jealous. But it was clear why, early in their groping toward reform, the chiefs outlawed these games.

The Longnecks explained, of course, that the Seventh Commandment did not merely forbid adultery; it implied much that was positive, and to the Hawaiians new: chastity before marriage, monogamy, the affectionate rearing of all one's children. Slowly the serious-minded chiefs began to live by these strange concepts. After Keopuolani's death Hoapili chose only Kalakua—though five women of rank stood ready to join his household—marrying her in a public ceremony performed by William Richards. To signify her change of heart, Kalakua cast off her old name and became Hoapiliwahine. Namahana, too, kept only Laanui as husband, and Kaahumanu did not replace Kaumualii. Kalanimoku, once proud of his six wives, lived a lone widower until he found a young *alii* woman who pleased him. Then he was married to her by Binamu.

Some thought that Liholiho, in taking to England only one wife, his best-loved Kamamalu, proposed to break with polygamy. All agreed that the brother and sister Kauikeaouli and Nahienaena must no longer live as man and wife—though where to find consorts of suitable age and rank for these high-born children was perplexing, and it still seemed clear to their *alii* guardians that any offspring of the son and daughter of Kamehameha and Keopoulani would be a wonderful chief indeed.

Such changes caused no stir in commercial Honolulu. It mattered little to the white traders how many wives a chief allowed himself or whether the prince and princess lived in incest. But if the chiefs' zeal ever came between a *haole* and his native mistress or hindered the girls from visiting the ships, there would be a showdown. This the chiefs knew and were cautious—all but Kaahumanu.

Early in 1825 Kaahumanu began to talk of crushing what she now saw as a great wickedness. If a foreigner wanted to settle down and live with a Hawaiian woman all his days, as John Young, Oliver Holmes, Alexander Adams and Don Marin had done, very well, said Kaahumanu, let him take his chosen one to Binamu and be married to her. But if he had a wife in America or England and sought another for a little while in Hawaii, then was he not breaking the *Kanawai*? Should he not be denied? Should not the girls be taught that they were doing wrong, selling for trinkets or a snatch of pleasure their chances of heaven and eternal happiness?

Though she could not immediately win the others to her view, Kaahumanu, iron-willed as if she had been reared in Park Street parish, began to restrain the women of her household and those who lived on her lands. Single-handed she strove against evil.

MOMENT OF GRIEF

WHEN the news reached Kalanimoku in his stone house that the king and queen were dead in England, he wrote on a piece of paper: "My love to you, Binamu. Come to me, that I may talk with you about this thing that has happened. The king, Liholiho, and the queen, Kamamalu, are dead."

The word had come by the Nantucket whaler *Almira* that a frigate now on its way from England would presently bring home the living members of the royal party and the bodies of Liholiho and Kamamula, dead these many months of measles.

"Now must we pray to Jehovah," the premier said, when Hiram Bingham had come to him. Then, touching the shoulder of the ten-year-old boy who stood beside him, Kalanimoku continued, "Here now is our king."

Kauikeaouli burst suddenly into tears and, shrinking from *haole* sympathy, hid his face in the folds of the old man's dressing gown.

"If the king was prepared to die," said Kalanimoku, "it is well. If he was not—" Then after a moment he added, "What God has done—that is the thing which is right."

Word went about among the chiefs, and soon they began to assemble in the grass church. Some were wide-eyed and frightened. "Now comes the war," they whispered. Others asked, "Has the king gone to heaven?" So far, the news had not reached the commoners.

"For twelve days," said Kalanimoku, rising at the close of Hiram Bingham's sermon, "let us pray the prayer of contrition, that Jehovah may pardon and save this nation. Aside from that, let us go on with our business as before this sorrow came to us. Let the *pala-pala* be held each day, for we have now more need to learn what is right and true than ever before."

No criers went abroad. Instead, the news spread quietly through the village and out into the districts as one person told it to another. Everywhere there was gentle weeping, but of the old heathenish wails scarcely a sound. *Poi* pestle and *tapa* beater thumped on, and the drone of the *palapala* continued throughout the land.

Almost two months later the British frigate *Blonde,* her flags at half-mast, appeared off Diamond Hill. At the entrance to the harbor she dropped anchor and fired a salute of fourteen guns, answered straightway from the lower fort and from Punchbowl. Presently barges came ashore, bearing the returning travelers to the quay from which they had embarked in the autumn of 1823. The *alii* stood near the landing and hundreds of commoners, held in check by an armed guard, filled the surrounding plain. The men of the Mission had been escorted to the inner circle among the chiefs; they alone of all the foreigners shared this solemn moment of grief with the Hawaiians.

Boki, the first to land, lifted his hands and eyes toward heaven and wept. The others began to follow him off the barge in orderly procession, but as they reached the waiting crowd, they broke ranks and mingled with it, embracing and rubbing noses. The common people lifted their voices in a roar that almost drowned the booming minute-guns; many fell on their faces in the dust and kissed the feet of the *alii.*

"Where is my brother Kalanimoku?" Boki wanted to know. They told him Kalanimoku was too ill to leave his house.

"Where shall we pray?" asked Boki presently. They answered: in the grass chapel near the Mission houses. As the company set out for the church, Boki hurried ahead to stop at his brother's fine new house, and Kalanimoku, though infirm, crossed over with him to join in the service.

There were a hymn, a reading from scripture and a prayer—all in Hawaiian—but no sermon. Instead Boki rose to make his report on religion in Britain: "The king of Beretania said to me, 'Give good attention to the missionaries at your islands, for they were sent to enlighten you and do you good.'"

Five days later, the chiefs from the windward having been summoned, the bodies of the king and queen—each in its triple coffin of lead, oak and mahogany—were brought ashore and conveyed in spectacular procession to Kalanimoku's yard. There a thatched house, now abandoned as a residence, had been lined with black *tapa* as a temporary mausoleum.

THE MORNING AFTER the *Blonde*'s arrival, her commander, Lord Byron, cousin and successor to the poet, had come on shore with his officers and proceeded to Kalanimoku's stone house for a meeting with the chiefs. Part of the business was the delivery of gifts sent by the English king—to Kalanimoku a small wax figure of Liholiho and a gold hunting watch; to Kaahumanu a silver teapot, engraved with her name and the arms of Britain; to the little king, Kauikeaouli, a royal Windsor uniform of rich cloth, with sword, epaulets and a military hat.

Some of the chiefs had expected a full code of laws from England. Had not Liholiho gone abroad to see how King George ruled his people and to judge what part of Britain's practices could be used in his island kingdom? To many it seemed natural to suppose that either Boki or Lord Byron would now say, "This is what you must do to belong among the civilized nations."

But no. In council, after the succession had been fixed on Kauikeaouli and Kaahumanu's regency continued, Lord Byron spoke only of a few "hints" written on paper—hints which the Hawaiians might look over at leisure and adopt if they were pleased with them. These were not, Byron said, the dictates of the British government, for the chiefs would know best what suited their people.

Long afterward it became known that Lord Byron had secret instructions from his government to look closely into the state of the Islands, since by discovery and by voluntary cession in the time of Vancouver, Great Britain "might claim over them a right of sovereignty." But he was not to advance this claim unless another foreign power had attempted to establish "any Sovereignty or possession." As he looked about him and talked with the leader of the American Mission, the British lord saw no such attempt in the making. He and Hiram Bingham agreed that whatever laws the Hawaiians were to live under must be enacted and enforced by their own rulers. They discussed this and other problems with mutual understanding and respect.

But the British consul, Richard Charlton, saw things differently. Having cruised in the Pacific, Charlton had returned in 1823 to London and there had told his story of opportunity in the South Seas so well that a group of business men had fitted him out again to foster trade between the islands and the British manufacturers. The foreign office, too, had taken favorable notice of Charlton and commissioned him consul for the Sandwich, Society and Friendly Islands. He had arrived at Honolulu in April, 1825, a month before the *Blonde,* seeking above all British ascendancy in the Islands and fearing most the American influence over the chiefs. He must have been disappointed at Lord Byron's restraint.

NEW HEARTS

KAAHUMANU *hou*—the new Kaahumanu—the people called her nowadays, for she who had once been proud and imperious appeared to them meek and amiable.

Even though the house she had lately built was far up Manoa valley, she seldom rode to the Mission in her coach; usually she came on foot, stopping along the way to visit a school, to comfort a farmer whose hog had died, or to leave a little present of food or cloth for a new infant, that its mother might be encouraged to rear and cherish it.

Inside the Mission house, too, she was different. Once she had stood stiffly erect while the Longnecks prayed. Now if she happened in at the hour of family worship, she bent her plump knees to the floor, crossed her huge arms on the settle and humbly bowed her head while the brethren addressed themselves to heaven.

She and Kealiiahonui, with Kalanimoku, Namahana, Laanui, Kapiolani and Naihe, stood as candidates for baptism and church membership—still on probation, but encouraged to hope and strive.

Again and again Hiram Bingham explained what was required. It was good, he told them, to make laws for the nation against drunkenness, murder, adultery, incest and gambling. It was good to do away with idols and to go regularly to church and to give attention to learning. But all that was not enough. Their own hearts must be utterly pure and loyal, their own lives sincere and above reproach.

Kaahumanu and Kealiiahonui looked at each other with questioning eyes. They knew well that in the Christian code theirs was

237

not a proper alliance. In due course, Binamu had said, he would perform marriages to unite Kapiolani to Naihe, and Namahana to Laanui, even though in "the time of dark hearts" they had all had other mates. But there could be no Christian ceremony for Kealiiahonui and Kaahumanu, because the Word of God forbade a man to have his father's wife.

A fortnight after the funeral of the king and queen, Kaahumanu and her young husband called at the frame house. They had come, they said, from talking with Kalanimoku about the good of the nation.

"It will be many years," Kaahumanu said, "before the king can rule, for he is only a boy. Therefore, we must do two things: We must have Kauikeaouli instructed by the missionaries, and we must make the nation strong for that time when he is a man."

"That is well said," Hiram agreed.

"It is our thought," the regent went on, "that we two must separate. I shall live at Manoa, and Kealiiahonui will stay at the little frame house near the harbor. It is the wish of us both that we shall be baptized and become God's people, and this we know we cannot do if we remain together."

Kealiiahonui stood like an embarrassed school boy, twisting his American hat, rubbing the toe of his American boot against the door sill. When Kaahumanu had finished, he looked hard at Hiram Bingham. "Are we now able to be baptized?" he asked.

"Soon," said Hiram. "In about six months—if you are faithful."

HANNAH HOLMES HAD COME back to the Mission. For months after John Coffin Jones sailed away from the Islands, she had continued to avoid the Longnecks; then one day she quietly returned to their schoolroom and took her place among the scholars. The next Sunday she was in church.

Hannah found much that was new since 1820—the printing press in its little stone house, where Lumiki with native assistance made books in Hawaiian; a wealth of translated hymns and many long Bible passages; a special class for those advanced enough to teach others; ceremonial examinations in which hundreds of voices cantil-lated the magnificent words from scripture. But for all the changes, Hannah slipped easily into her old ways and gave herself up to the *pala* and the *pule*. Her friends at the Mission noted in their journals that she was "under serious impression" and shared that joy over the repentant that so nearly eclipses heaven's pride in the faithful. They had no fear that she would return to John Coffin Jones if he should come out again or yield to any other man unless he would marry her, for her views of right and wrong were now firm and clear.

Though she had listened to anti-Mission talk for four years, it had not turned her against the teachers. Nothing she heard now at her father's house or from her sisters' white companions deterred her when the conch shell sounded for classes or the bell rang for church.

She was often sad, though. Pa Homa and its master were both falling into ruin. The houses in the inclosure had grown shabby, the thorn bushes ran wild, the embankments had caved in, the ditches were dry and grass grew in the *taro* beds. Most of the tenants had gone off to new landlords. Only the Holmes daughters were fair and winsome.

Some at the Mission called these girls hussies, but not when Hannah was about. After all, as Oliver Holmes had pointed out long ago, their only future was with the white men who came and stayed a while; and if the men did not stay forever—well, that could not be helped. The girls merely snatched what they could in a precarious situation.

But to go a voyage just for some captain's convenience—that was a thing no Holmes daughter would now do. As a child of fourteen Polly had given way, weeping, to her father's insistence. As a young woman close to twenty, with Hannah to stand by her, she refused. When a British captain came to Pa Homa intending to carry her off by force, she fled to Kalanimoku's house and found protection. Turned from the prime minister's door, the captain stormed over to Mr. Bingham's. But he knew little of Hiram Bingham if he thought loud talk and cane-pounding would move him.

The Honolulu *haoles* could have laughed at the captain's discomfiture if they had not so hated Mr. Bingham. "Better try somewhere else," they advised. "Try at the Jacksons'." But Sally Jackson was stubborn, too. Eight hundred dollars did not tempt her. "Do you think we will sell our daughter like a hog?" she asked scornfully. The captain, sailing without a companion, cursed the missionaries roundly.

Not long afterward Oliver Holmes collapsed and died. The Yankee friends to whom he had always been a genial host arranged his funeral. They called on Mr. Stewart, who chanced to be at the Honolulu station, for a prayer; but they would not, even for Hannah's sake, ask Mr. Bingham to preach.

All the self-styled "gentlemen of Honolulu" marched in the funeral procession from Pa Homa to the foreigners' burying ground. Arm-in-arm with their mistresses, were they less concerned with honoring the deceased than with flouting the Mission, past whose yard they paraded? Some of the brethren thought so.

TABU

TEN-YEAR-OLD Kauikeaouli, son of Kamehameha and Keopuolani, young brother of the lamented Liholiho, was king of all Hawaii; but the power was in the hands of Kaahumanu, the regent, and Kalanimoku, the prime minister, and these two were Christians. Again and again in their councils they exhorted the other chiefs to forbid the ways and customs of the "time of dark hearts" and to enact stricter and holier laws for the realm. They thought of little else but their responsibility to enlighten their people and restrain them from evil-doing.

They dismissed casually the papers signed in 1820 and '21, promising incalculable piculs of sandalwood in payment for vessels and cargoes. Who was to say that the price had been fair at the time, even if the goods had been of the best quality? And why should sober and benevolent chiefs drive their subjects to the hills to pay the debts Liholiho had contracted when he was drunk on the foreigners' wine and brandy?

In the traders' houses in Honolulu exasperation and anger prevailed. "When the king returns—" the agents had once told themselves and their principals in America. And now that Liholiho was dead and hope from that quarter ended, they found themselves driven again. Things, they saw, would not get better; they would grow worse. The "liberal party" must bestir itself, must win some influential chiefs to its views. It must wean the young king away from the missionaries, and it must get that long-promised United States war vessel into Honolulu harbor.

They began to flatter weak-willed Boki and bend him to their purposes. Because he had been in England, had talked with King George and traveled over the oceans as the honored comrade of Lord Byron, he had a glamor and prestige in Honolulu that his brother and Kaahumanu could not touch. When white men reminded him that, having seen the world, he ought not to let the Longnecks fool him, he warmed and cozened to the flatterers and spoke their line at the *alii* councils.

Meanwhile, in the late summer of 1825 Kaahumanu's will prevailed. She persuaded the other high chiefs to extend to all of Oahu and Maui the tabu that kept girls from going out to the ships—a ban she had earlier imposed on her own people. The traders did not understand the criers who shouted this word up and down the village, but they saw the guards lurking at night near the landings to turn back the willful, and they learned from seamen who stormed ashore that there was a maddening dearth of women in cabins and forecastles.

One evening a girl, swimming off toward a whaler, was pursued, captured and put in irons. "Now," said the chiefs, "let the females see what it is worth to break the *Kanawai*." They had her shorn and fettered and displayed in all the villages. In Pearl River, in Waikiki, in Honolulu, in all the leeward districts of Oahu, a wave of reform followed. Girls who had long lived with foreigners presented ultimatums to their men: we marry or we part. More than twenty turned from their lovers to the Mission schools, where they were put to studying needlework, the alphabet and the story of Mary Magdalene.

Foreign Honolulu boiled over. This was too much. Twenty men from English whalers waited noisily on Hiram Bingham. Why, they wanted to know, was this new prohibition made? Hiram referred them to the chiefs, and they got their answer from Kaahumanu. The old practices were wicked, she said; they would never be allowed again. If the seamen did not go away quietly, she would inform their officers and get them properly punished for breaking the peace. The seamen snorted. Their officers, they said, had egged them on. Their officers did not like the new law either. But they straggled off boisterously.

At William French's store a British captain and the American Stephen Reynolds turned abusive tongues on Hiram Bingham. Since he had come to Honolulu, they said, the chiefs—once so virtuous—had become thieves, liars, whore-mongers. The nation was going backwards; Hawaii would never again attain to that degree of civilization it had had in the days of Kamehameha. Its people were neglecting their lands; they would starve. The Islands would never recover from the baneful work of the missionaries.

A native took melons and yams alongside the *Aurora* for barter. "Get us women," the sailors shouted.

"No," said the native, "I am on God's side."

"Oh-ho!" cried the Aurorans. "A Bingham follower!" With that they seized his canoe, broke its outrigger, crushed its ribs and threw the vendor and his wares into the water. Later Kalanimoku got the fellow ten dollars in damages.

For the first time an American captain, departing for home, refused to carry letters and journals for the Mission.

"Now THAT we are members of the church," Kalanimoku said, rising at the close of the service, "it is right that we should lift our united voices in favor of the whole of Jehovah's law. Let us, therefore, assemble—the chiefs and the king and our teachers—in my yard tomorrow morning to talk about this thing."

His voice was full of vigor, yet all who heard him knew that he could not live much longer. He was swollen with dropsy and almost blind. Whenever he went out of his house, one of his young chiefs must walk beside him to support him and guide his steps. But yesterday Dr. Blatchley had tapped him, and today he had taken the communion. Thus refreshed in body and spirit, he felt strong to do battle for the Lord.

In the village, the rumor circulated that the pious chiefs, now baptized and admitted to the church, were about to enact ten terrible laws, with death as the penalty and Kaahumanu alone as the judge. Two foreigners, who stand nameless in the record, spent the whole of that Sunday afternoon rounding up their white fellows, organizing them to oppose "with their united influence the adoption of *any* laws." Boki's name was widely used. Boki wants us to come and support his views against Kaahumanu, they said. Boki invites—no, urges—all liberals to be present.

It is doubtful that Boki was the first to think of summoning the *haoles* to the meeting. Nor was Boki, in all likelihood, the first to say that no drastic changes should be made while the British consul, Mr. Charlton, was away at Tahiti. But if Boki did not see these fine points of diplomacy for himself, he was quick to grasp them when they were pointed out to him by a foreign finger. Caution, great caution, deliberateness and moderation—these were the watchwords of the liberals. And for these policies Boki was to stand in the Monday morning council, backed solidly by "the gentlemen of Honolulu."

In Kalanimoku's yard the trade winds played on the cocoanut trees and the bright *kahilis* on the morning of December 12. The prime minister moved about painfully, greeting his fellow-chiefs, peering out of his dim eyes at Kaahumanu, Kealiiahonui, Namahana, Laanui, Kahalaia, Boki and the young king, as if to discover how each stood on the solemn matter that had brought them together. Boki was pert and brash, knowing himself cast as the leading actor in the morning's drama. Little Kauikeaouli looked worried, sullen, unhappy. It was not good that his elders wrangled.

Somewhat before the appointed hour thirty-odd foreigners—residents and visiting captains—arrived in a body with a great tramping of boots. A few sat down, native style, on the mats; but many stood, their hats in their hands, as if this were not a place where they chose to stay longer than necessary. Astonishment and displeasure showed in Kaahumanu's round face; she knew these men for her enemies. Kalanimoku, too ill to go among them, sent a young chief to bid them a guarded welcome.

Then, precisely on the hour, Hiram Bingham, Levi Chamberlain and Elisha Loomis arrived in six-year-old Sunday coats with ruffled shirts and white stocks as stiff as their moral codes.

"We are here to oppose you," said John Ebbets; and though he had done the Mission many a kindness through the years, there was now neither friendship nor humor in his tone. The missionaries protested that, so far as they were concerned, there was nothing to oppose. They had no project; they had come as observers and invited guests—and so, no doubt, had the Honolulu gentlemen.

Kalanimoku began to speak. He pled for good laws and stout hearts to enforce those laws against all evil-doers. Kaahumanu followed. She was not the orator the prime minister was, but she was downright and dogged. The listening *haoles,* though they understood few of her words, could see that she was calling for stern measures.

Boki came next with his "Let us be cautious." It was his desire, too, he said suavely, to have the laws of God binding on all people, but until Mr. Charlton came from Tahiti—

The moment Boki sat down, the white men began to voice their support of his position. Captain Meek, not long from Tahiti himself; Captain Cooper, one-time mate of the *Thaddeus;* British Captain Lawson; Harbormaster Alexander Adams; and Storekeeper Stephen Reynolds all had their say. Others would have followed had not Mr. Gowing, the interpreter, growing exuberant, slipped in a few words of his own. *"You* are the rulers of this land," he told the chiefs. *"You* have a right to make laws. We have no objection to that, but we object to the missionaries having anything to do with it."

"That is right," Hiram Bingham interposed in a flash. "The missionaries do not wish to interfere. Let the chiefs do as they like." Then turning to the natives he told them in Hawaiian that the thing Mr. Gowing had said was good—that the chiefs should make whatever laws they wished; that *no one* ought to interfere.

Captain Ebbets, silent till now, saw the liberal forces in trouble, and tried to change tactics. The chiefs, he said, were not yet wise enough in the ways of civilization, commerce and diplomacy to make laws. Today's proposals were not the chiefs' own; they were, despite Mr. Bingham's denials, the wish and dictates of the missionaries. That was why the foreigners opposed them.

Then every man who held a grudge against the Mission tried to voice it; a dozen were at it at once. To make themselves heard they shouted and coarsened their talk. Billingsgate epithets flew thick and fast. Mr. Gowing could not have translated such language if he had wanted to.

"What is it?" "What do they say?" the chiefs asked, distracted. The meeting seemed on the point of breaking up; but presently Boki began to reiterate his views, and at last the liberals were willing to be quiet.

When Boki had finished, in spite of all that had been said against the plan, the Christian chiefs still believed they should make a strong declaration for righteousness. Kealiiahonui, who had parted from Kaahumanu that they might be baptized, stood staunchly with his former wife on the issue. Rising, he began to say something about King David and his resolution to serve the Lord—

"Who?" asked Boki impudently.

Kealiiahonui was hurt and showed it. He had been warming up for a good long speech. Why should Boki, who had held forth twice already, interrupt him? But Boki was of high rank; therefore Kealiiahonui answered courteously, "David."

"Was you there?" Boki asked—in English, to insure a good laugh from his partisans.

"No," said Kealiiahonui patiently, "but in the Bible it is stated—"

Boki signaled him to silence and began his third oration of the morning. But he had scarcely uttered three words when his brother, Kalanimoku, who outranked him as he outranked Kealiihonui, abruptly motioned him down. Then Kalanimoku turned to the boy king. "You see," he said, "that we do not agree among ourselves about this thing. The *kuhina nui* has the right to say, for she is the regent and my brother Boki is not. But Kaahumanu and I, speaking together just now, have agreed that it is best for you, the king, to decide. Shall we, then, raise the united voice of the *alii* for that which God commands? Or shall we not?"

The little king knit his brow. Earlier, in the midst of the babel,

Boki had said to him, "If you give your consent to the Commandments, I will not support you in the government." Kauikeaouli saw his chiefs split into factions, with shrewd and powerful white men backing one party, the beloved missionaries standing with the other. He was afraid.

"I think we should say no more today," he decided. "I wish the meeting to be at an end."

One month later the *Dolphin* came to port.

1826

MAN-OF-WAR

IT was not all the American traders had hoped for—this little eighty-eight-foot, twelve-gun schooner, *Dolphin*. They had expected the flagship of the Pacific Squadron. But Commodore Hull, busy on the Coast, had dispatched his first lieutenant, John Percival, to the Mulgrave Islands to pick up mutineers, and thence to Honolulu to serve his countrymen in the matter of the debts.

The *Dolphin* towed into the harbor on a Saturday, the stars and stripes fluttering at her masthead, and Percival sent word by the pilot that the next day he would be ready to exchange salutes. Boki consulted his brother and reported: "Our gunners do not work on the Lord's day. Therefore, let the salutes be fired on Monday." When the guns of the *Dolphin* boomed on Sunday regardless of the Lord, there was no answer from the shore. Then, presently, the insistent church bell rang out across the plain. Jack Percival was nettled. Even a proper salute, fired tardily on Monday, did not appease him. From that moment trouble was brewing.

He had courage and skill—this forty-seven-year-old officer—and a temper like tinder. He was known as one whose "iron will the devil himself could not shake," one whom his crew fairly worshiped—"notwithstanding his very severe and often harsh conduct"—because they knew he never gave an order that he could not perform himself.

He had gone to sea as a cabin boy, with "only nine months' schooling and a clean shirt." Five years later, when he had risen to second mate, he had his first brush with the British. A press gang seized him at Lisbon and sent him aboard HMS *Victory*. Twice shifted from vessel to vessel, he finally led a group of Americans in a bold break for liberty. Grasping "the boozy shipmaster by the throat with one hand"—so the story went—he "pointed a pistol at the fellow's heart and muttered, 'Silence or Death.'" Thus the Americans escaped to a Yankee merchantman.

By 1813 he had been in and out of the Navy and was in once more, this time commissioned a midshipman. He had visited Santa Cruz, San Cristobal, Rio, Pernambuco and a score of other ports; he had again been taken a British prisoner and again escaped; he had "conducted himself with perseverance and zeal and sobriety as a good and faithful officer"; and, with a heavily armed fishing smack disguised by a load of vegetables, had lured a British tender to spectacular capture off New York.

The early 1820's found him chasing pirates in the West Indies; then in '23 he joined the Pacific Exploring Squadron as first lieutenant on its flagship, the *United States*. He was a good choice for the hazardous mission to the Mulgraves to bring off the *Globe*'s mutineers. For persuading the Hawaiian chiefs to settle their debts, he was hardly the man. But the two assignments lay in the same direction, and so "Mad Jack" came to Honolulu.

The *Dolphin* was immediately laid up for repairs. Most of the seamen were quartered in "the Hulk," a broken-down vessel moored off the shipyard. The officers went ashore to find lodgings.

"When the chief Lord Byron came from Great Britain as a friend," Kaahumanu remembered afterward, "we offered him a house, which he occupied as our guest . . . When this man Percival came we offered him a house, but he refused it and joined himself to our enemies." For a day or two the lieutenant stayed at the Wooden House, the tavern that William Warren now ran for Marshall & Wildes. Then he took a grass house that afforded him more privacy at night, but he continued to dine at the tavern.

Boki promptly called on the lieutenant to sound out his views on certain matters. Did the missionaries, he asked Percival, have authority from the American government to make laws for the people in Hawaii?

Percival's answer, reported later under oath by Dixey Wildes, was that he "did not know of any authority which the missionaries had to interfere with the government." He said the United States was "very cautious in that respect," that it "did not interfere with the internal concerns of any government."

Boki had another question. Was there a law in America that forbade women to go to the ships?

No, Percival said, there was not—not unless the women were riotous.

Then the lieutenant countered with a question of his own: *Had* the missionaries interfered in the Hawaiian government?

Well, yes, Boki answered cautiously. The missionaries had wanted the chiefs to make the Ten Commandments into a law.

So Percival heard, on his second day ashore, that the American teachers were meddling. It was a first impression that sank deep; indeed, he never forgot it.

Even before the interview with Boki, Percival must have known of the tabu on women. Though the council of December 12 had failed to make new laws, the earlier proclamation against prostitution remained in effect. Guards still watched along the harbor, and females swimming off to the ships were still pursued, captured and punished. Ashore, good girls packed up their fish and *poi* on a Sunday and fled to the hills rather than fall into the hands of the newly arrived sailors. To the *Dolphin*'s officers as well as her crew, all this was irksome. And whenever in the village Percival asked who was responsible, he heard the same answer: It is Kaahumanu—and Bingham.

Afterward when a Navy court of inquiry tried to get at the facts, it was hard to tell whether in January, 1826, many women were evading the law, or only a few. Some persons who were then aboard ships in the harbor testified that the girls came off freely and openly, never more so; others told of their sneaking out under cover of darkness or dressed in seamen's clothes. One remembered asking why the women did not come and being told that it was because the sailors did not pay them. Another thought that "every man forward that wanted a wife had one." Levi Chamberlain, passing among the vessels in port, was "gratified to see them free from women." At no former season, he added, had "such a pleasure been granted." Multitudes, he believed, were prevented from going on board.

On the whole, it appears that, though the guard may have been somewhat relaxed after the chiefs' meeting of December 12, the prohibition was effective enough to annoy the *Dolphin*'s crew during her first days in port.

A FORTNIGHT after his arrival, Lieutenant Percival paid the Mission a call. He regaled the family with a sketch of his career, remarked freely and unfavorably on the character of the Hawaiians and rebuked the brethren for supposing there were any true converts among those who flocked to their meetings. Their whole system was wrong, he told them. They ought to be teaching children, not adults. If they would devote themselves to the young ones, he would commend them and support their efforts. But as it was—

While he talked, Kaahumanu entered, quietly and without knocking, as she was wont to do. She sat near him and, though she did not understand his words, she studied his ruddy face and emphatic gestures.

"I hate the sight of that woman!" Percival exclaimed to the family, knowing Kaahumanu could not take his meaning. She had sent spies to watch him at Pearl River, he complained. And then he told the whole story.

On Sunday, a week after he had fired his first salute, Percival had joined a group of foreigners on a junket to Pearl River. Whether they went to explore, to enjoy the scenery, to fish or to escape a Puritan Sabbath, the lieutenant did not say. But Kaahumanu had had her own idea of their purpose. Her messengers had sped to Ewa, warning the women to keep out of sight, the attendants at the ponds to allow no fish to be drawn out on the Lord's day, and all the people, if called on for food, to serve it cold from Saturday's baking. This was the law of God and the chiefs, Kaahumanu had reminded her people. The gentlemen from Honolulu had had a dreary time of it.

Percival then told Hiram Bingham that he intended the next day to say "something unpleasant" to the chiefs. What, he asked, did one do about interpreters? Could you trust any of them?

Hiram advised that the communications be put in writing. Then the interpreters could not so easily mistake the meaning or mislead anyone. But Percival said fretfully that "the foreigners objected to doing business in that roundabout way."

There was another thing, Percival added. If tomorrow the chiefs should send for any of the missionaries to join in the conference, he "desired them not to come." He did not "wish to know the missionaries as connected with government."

"Very good," said Hiram.

But the conference did not take place next day. Late the same afternoon word came that the *London* of New York, China-bound for teas, was breaking up on the rocks at Lanai and that her $100,000 cargo, chiefly specie and bullion, was in danger.

Since the *Dolphin* was dismantled, Percival chartered the Marshall brig *Convoy* and hastened with fifty of his men to the *London*'s relief. In his absence, life at Honolulu flowed on with only a store robbery and a windstorm to break its surface calm. At the Mission, Elisha finished printing and binding four thousand copies of Tract No. 4, *Ke Kanawai o Iehova, The Commandments of the Lord*. The people read it avidly.

BY THE TIME he came back from Lanai and found his own vessel fit again, Jack Percival had come to consider the long-standing debts of the chiefs a trivial matter compared with the tabu on women. At the tavern, where Boki came and went, he would sometimes tease the governor by asking, "Boki, why do you have a tabu on women; why do you keep the women to yourselves?" And Boki, to clear his own skirts, would answer that it was "the old queen."

Sometimes Percival would grow deadly serious, arguing that, while it might be well to teach the women about chastity, it was wrong to punish those who fell into sin. Then Boki would say in grogshop English, "Damn missionary done it."

Often the lieutenant's anger flared, and he himself berated the missionaries—for selling slates and pencils instead of giving them away, for exceeding their instructions, for meddling in what was not their business. Percival's invectives were always bright with profanity; "blasphemous" and "obscene" they seemed to the Mission brethren; only good, strong sea talk to the traders.

Boki, for all he sided with the traders, hastened to tell Kaahumanu whatever Percival said. The Christian chiefs—misunderstanding, exaggerating, taking literally every excited syllable—began to fear for their teachers. All the talk about shooting, pulling down houses, burning the village with fire from the little man-of-war sent them rushing to Binamu to ask what they should do.

Hiram Bingham told them not to be afraid. The man-of-war captain, he said, would not attack his fellow-Americans, whom it was his duty, rather, to protect.

"You are our teachers," cried a petty chief. "If you are killed, we are left in the dark!"

"We are not going to be killed," Hiram told them again. "Only be strong and show that you are renewed in heart. Show the man-of-war captain he is wrong when he says you are not on God's side."

So the chiefs passed out the newly printed copies of the *Kanawai,* stiffened the harbor guard and sometimes went themselves among the ships looking for girls.

"This," Percival told Boki, "is a very shameful thing with your chiefs."

As Percival's stand on the tabu became known, men came to him with their tales. Some residents said that Kaahumanu had imprisoned girls with whom they had lived for years, "wives" with whom they had had children. Two men from the *Dolphin,* claiming to speak for the whole forecastle, complained bitterly at the dearth of women. Percival promised to "talk to the missionaries."

His long-delayed conference with the chiefs about "something unpleasant" was set at last for February 21. Boki came to Kaahumanu with the summons. The man-of-war chief had asked the Hawaiians to gather in the early evening in Kalanimoku's yard. They knew what demands he would make.

Kaahumanu had two thoughts—that Binamu should be present and that all statements should be put into writing, lest in the heat and flurry of discussion the chiefs should promise what they did not intend. While Boki sought Percival to lay these proposals before him, Kaahumanu went to Mr. Bingham's house. There an agitated Boki returned to say, "The American chief will not write. He will come and talk. If Binamu comes to the council, he will shoot him. He is angry and ready to fight. His vessel is small, but it is just like fire."

Boki, it was clear, was in a funk, ready to yield anything to keep the peace. "We must meet the man-of-war captain," he said again, "and if we still restrain the women, we must fight."

Kaahumanu said, "Let us be firm on the side of the Lord."

"But what will come of it?" Boki asked.

"You are a servant of God," said Kaahumanu, referring to the high stand he had taken when first he came from England, "and you must maintain His cause." Then they both wept, because it seemed that whichever way they turned, great evil would come to their people.

At length Kaahumanu showed Boki what she had put down on paper—her thoughts concerning the tabu. She had written that she had the right to control her own people; that she had not sought money through prostitutes; that in apprehending and punishing them she had done no injustice to foreigners. Her orders, the statement said, applied, not to strangers, but to her own subjects, whose good she sought by attempting to withdraw them from vice. The man-of-war captain well knew, the paper concluded, that if a person went from one country to another he was bound to conform to the laws of that country while he remained there.

Hiram Bingham, who had already refused to attend the council unless the communications of both sides were written, had helped Kaahumanu to word her document and had translated it into English for her. But the sentiments were hers; of that there was no doubt. She told Boki to show the paper to the captain of the man-of-war, not to withhold or conceal it.

Said Boki, "It will make him very angry; he will be *huhu loa.*"

A THUNDER STORM prevented the council that evening. The next day at noon the chiefs came together in the prime minister's yard and waited with sober faces for the American lieutenant. When he came, he was not *huhu,* as they had expected. He was smiling and friendly and spoke without threats or abuse. Sometimes, as the conference went on, his face flushed and his eyes snapped until the *alii* thought he was angry again. But the words that the interpreter conveyed to them were conciliatory.

"Who is the king of the country?" he asked.

Kaahumanu pointed out Kauikeaouli.

"Who is his guardian?"

"I," said Kaahumanu.

"Who has charge of his country?"

"I and my 'brother' Kalanimoku, he being under me."

"You, then," said Percival pleasantly, "are 'king.' I also am a chief. You and I are alike; you are the person for me to talk with. By whom are the women tabued?"

Kaahumanu replied, "It is by me."

"Who has told you that women must be tabu by the law?"

"It was God," said Kaahumanu.

Percival laughed. "It was Bingham," he said flatly.

"It was by Mr. Bingham," Kaahumanu admitted, "that the word of God was made known to us."

Well, then, Percival said, looking around the company, he would give them some advice. They had better go slow, lest going fast they tumble down. The very strict tabu was not good. It would be well to do as other lands did. In England and America prostitution was not punished. In those countries some women were tabu and some not; ungodly women were not tabu. It was well to let such women go their own way and have their own thoughts. Let them take the money and the cloth of foreigners and live however they would. Let a line be drawn between those that were pious and those that were not.

Here some of the chiefs broke in. They did not wish to draw any lines, they said. They wished all their people to turn from wickedness. If prostitution was allowed in America, one said, then let Americans get their prostitutes there and not seek for them in Hawaii. If the lieutenant had brought *haole* women in his ship, the chiefs would have laid no tabu on them.

It was not for himself that he was looking out, Percival answered. He was old and did not care about a mistress. It was for his boys. They wanted women; and if that was not good, it was no concern of his. If it was wrong, they alone were to blame. Indeed, the boys were growing so restive that he could not tell what they would do when they came ashore on a Sunday.

Then he spoke of how in olden times—in the days of Kamehameha—the nation had "attended properly" to the ships, both English and American. Those, he said, were the good ways that had made no trouble for the people.

"In former times, before the word of God had arrived here," Kaahumanu scornfully retorted, "we were dark-minded, lewd and murderers. Now we are seeking a better way."

Percival did not argue the point. Bidding them an urbane and courteous farewell, he left them to mull over his advice before letting him know what they had decided about the women.

Those at the Mission house, when they learned the course of the meeting, felt let down. If Percival had been fierce and threatening as on the day before, they knew that the Hawaiians—even irresolute Boki—would have stood firm as Diamond Hill. But now who could tell? The teaching of almost six years might crumble away because Percival had smiled and counseled compromise.

After two days Percival sent again to Kaahumanu. Had the chiefs considered the matters lately put before them? If so, let them, as a sign of good will, set free the women they had confined for whoring. Let them do this before Sunday, and the boys could then have their "wives" when they came ashore on liberty. He awaited her answer, for she was the regent.

"What shall we do?" Kaahumanu asked the Longneck teachers.

They answered: "It is not for us to make laws, or to say who should be punished and who go free; but we say, as did St. Paul, 'Therefore, be ye steadfast, unmovable. . . .'"

So Kaahumanu did not release the women. And fearing the sailors might force their way into the light stockade at Waikiki, she ordered the prisoners to be brought on Saturday to the fort and put under closer guard.

Night settled down on an uneasy Honolulu.

COMPLETED BUSINESS

S UNDAY was fair, but in the afternoon a fine rain fell, preventing the usual outdoor preaching. Inside Kalanimoku's
house a few natives had gathered. Boki was there, and Namahana and her husband; other chiefs were arriving. Hiram Bingham
had just come in with his umbrella. All at once four noisy seamen—
three white and one black—burst from the veranda, shouting as
they swung their clubs, "Where are the women?" They were the
vanguard, it turned out, of a hundred or more from the *Dolphin*
and the whaleships, who, having laid their plans in the village, now
straggled angrily toward the neighborhood of the Mission.

"You go home," Boki told Binamu, full of concern. Hiram,
thinking of his wife and child in the stone cottage across the way,
moved to leave the hall. Knots of men jostled him as he came down
the steps. Above, he heard the tinkle of breaking glass as Kalanimoku's tall windows shattered under the seamen's clubs. The yard
below had filled with surly sailors. Hiram eluded one who would
have stopped him and stood in a sheltered spot, watching. Some
chiefs had come down into the melee, but they made no move to
save the premier's property or to turn back the menacing intruders.
As Christians they thought it wrong to fight unless life were in
danger. Then, too, their teachers had told them, "The man-of-war
is from the American government. Its sailors will not harm us; it
is their business to protect." Therefore the chiefs stood astonished
as the hostile crowd waved clubs and smashed windows. They did
not know what they ought to do.

In trying, after a moment, to cross to his own house, Hiram

Bingham fell into the hands of the mob. Men cornered him with their sticks, shouting threats, taunts and demands. One said, leering, "It's damned funny we can't have our wives on board." Another whipped out a knife. When a third swung at Hiram's head, Namahana, moving quickly, deflected the blow with her massive arm, so that Hiram could parry it with his umbrella.

In an instant the Hawaiians went into action, and soon the sailors began to get the worst of it. No one can say how many heads would have been bloodied and how many men left dead in Kalanimoku's trampled yard if Levi Chamberlain and Elisha, running down from the Mission, had not joined with Hiram and the head chiefs in calling for restraint.

"*Kapu*," they shouted. "Thou shalt not kill! Only hold them fast."

"You are vile!" retorted a native, tasting battle. "How can we bind those who use knives against us?" And quite forgetting his Christian scruples, he hurled a huge stone at a fallen seaman.

Now Mad Jack Percival hurried from the harbor with some of his midshipmen and began to lay about with his whalebone cane and to seize and tie ringleaders. A tardy trio of sailors, scuttling up from the village, dodged in at the Bingham house, broke down the gate, dashed in a window and beat upon the door. Then, crazily, one of them turned on another and knocked him senseless.

An hour later, when Percival had his men back on board the *Dolphin,* he came again to Kalanimoku's house to talk with the chiefs and the missionaries. Kalanimoku, who had listened in pain and distress to the shouts and the scuffling, lay with his eyes closed, only half hearing the words. Through his interpreters, Marin and Sumner, the lieutenant was promising to repair the property damage (charging the cost to the rascally seamen) and to punish the mob's leaders with the lash. Turning to the Americans, he asked that Dr. Blatchley come aboard in the morning to attend the wounded and that Mr. Bingham point out those who had menaced him with knife and club.

Then he launched into a violent protest against the tabu. He called it an insult to the American flag. He threatened that he would "never leave the islands until it was repealed." He spoke so long and so loud that Kaahumanu knew herself defeated. She did not tell Kalanimoku what she felt; but as she came from his bedside, she consulted with Boki and they prepared to relax the ban.

In the morning the regent yielded to the "angry captain" with this proclamation: "Come with us, you who wish to go in the right way; and those who will not go in the right way with us, let them go their own way."

So the frail sisters went free from the fort and swam openly off to the vessels, where they "were received with shouts and exclamations of joy." The ships' boats plied by daylight and loaded female passengers in plain view of the village. Women went out by the scores; they danced on the deck of the *Dolphin;* they sang and laughed as they scrambled aboard the whalers. Honolulu was again a port in paradise. And it was said that the pay from the sailors, more generous than ever before, was now all a girl's to keep. The chiefs no longer collected a tax on sin.

When Kalanimoku heard what went forward, he sent for Boki and Kaahumanu and asked them, "Who has done this great evil?"

They said timorously that they had given in only to prevent another riot, only because the man-of-war chief had vowed he would never leave while the tabu remained, only from fear of the guns on the little schooner. Kalanimoku's rebuke was scathing. But when *poi* has been spilled, you cannot put it again into the calabash.

JACK PERCIVAL was now, more than ever, the hero of the gobs and the deckhands, of the midshipmen and the mates. But the traders and agents were a little irked. The business for which he had "touched" at the Islands—to prod the natives into the payment of their five-year-old debts—was still to be done, and the chiefs were in no mood to discuss sandalwood. Aggrieved and resentful, they talked among themselves and sometimes to their teachers, of protesting to Commodore Hull or even to Great Britain against Percival's interference with their laws. One measure had been relaxed under pressure. Who could tell when the next demand would come? Every day they heard fresh tales, most of them hysterical and false, of how the man-of-war captain had encouraged his sailors to "knock off the tabu"; of how the plan for a concerted raid, after dark, had miscarried only because a few impatient ones had jumped the gun; of how another attempt was in the making to "pull down Mr. Bingham's house."

Native soldiers patrolled the streets all night. In a circular letter Lieutenant Percival advised the whaleship captains, in view of "the excitement of the seamen towards Mr. Bingham," to let only a small portion of their crews go ashore on Sunday. Boki reported that "Captain Percival had made application to him to take away the missionaries," but that he had answered, "No, we wish them to stay and instruct us." So it was a time of unrest and foreboding, a time of uncertainty and distrust. It was not a time to talk of unpaid notes for vessels that had long since bilged and rotted.

Perhaps there was no need for haste. The *Dolphin* was not leaving yet. A whaleship captain had started a petition and obtained a long list of officers' signatures, attesting that the presence of the United States schooner at Honolulu was indispensable. With Percival there, they said, their men would not desert. They could count on Percival to send out an extra anchor in case of storm or to support a Yankee in an altercation with a Britisher.

There were many reasons why the whaling fleet, so largely American, should have a government vessel at hand. The captains did not mention the tabu, but they undoubtedly feared it would be reimposed if the *Dolphin* left.

At length, toward the end of March, Percival met the chiefs in council to thrash out the matter of the debts. This much the *alii* acknowledged: though Liholiho and Kaumualii were dead, their pledges must still be paid—paid by those who survived, by the government, by the whole Hawaiian people. But when or how, the chiefs declined to say; and they reminded the lieutenant bitterly that an American firm had owed a vast sum to the Hawaiians since the days of Kamehameha. If the debt of Liholiho became the debt of his successors, they asked, why didn't the claim of Kamehameha become the claim of the present government against the Winships?

Weeks later, on the day before his sailing, Percival presented a paper for signature. Boki signed; and Kalanimoku, though feeble and suffering, went to the village to subscribe to the agreement and get a copy. The thing was in English, and the premier, satisfied with a vague notion of what it was all about, did not ask for a translation. He could get one at the Mission.

"Do you know what is in the papers that you handed me?" Hiram Bingham inquired that evening.

"No," Kalanimoku admitted sheepishly.

"Does the king know?"

"No."

"Does Kaahumanu know?"

"No," said Kalanimoku, more and more embarrassed. "It was a measure of the foreigners altogether. They wished me to sign it. Boki had signed. Perhaps my brother knows what it is."

The papers authorized William Sturgis of Boston to act as "Commercial Agent for the Sandwich Islands in the United States." In the hope of pressing their old claim against the Winship firm, the Hawaiians had named as their representative in America one of the traders to whom they owed much sandalwood. The men of the Mission felt that Percival had tricked the chiefs and feared that Sturgis' appointment might afford "some facilities to the enemies of this nation." But they need not have worried, for William Sturgis, when notified, declined to serve and the newly created post was not filled.

One after another the whaleships left for their cruising grounds, until the *Dolphin* was almost alone in the harbor. Then on the morning of May 11 she weighed anchor and departed. "The mischief-making-man-of-war has left us!" cried the chiefs in glee. And some, making a joke of it, wailed as they had done in former times at a death. "*Auwe! Auwe!* The man-of-war has gone from us. Alas! Alas for the prostitutes!"

THE GOOD WAY OF LIFE

THAT spring the sickness came to Honolulu. Suddenly in mid-April hundreds lay abed with chills and fever. In one day Dr. Blatchley treated fifty patients. The Sunday congregations fell from thousands to hundreds. Nearly all the chiefs were stricken, and at the Mission many were ill.

Death began to walk through the village. Kahalaia went so quickly that the chiefs at Lahaina could not be summoned in time to watch at his bedside. Someone whispered that he had been poisoned; and his mother would not come to Oahu lest she also should die. But the malady caught her at Lahaina, and she followed her son to the grave. Pauahi went too. And then it was Tamoree.

George, the son of Kaumualii, had so quietly nursed his woes since the failure of the Kauai rebellion that few in Honolulu had given him a thought. For months he had scarcely noticed his wife, Betty, or his little daughter. He only drank, pitied himself, hated others, and drank again. Now came the fever and the stabbing pains, and he knew that he would die. But he did not want to be reminded of God and heaven and hell, nor of mercy freely offered to the repentant—any more than he had relished that gospel as the jesting, self-confident prince of Cornwall and *Thaddeus* days.

Elisha spoke conventional phrases of warning and comfort. Was George prepared to die? Would he like a prayer to be said?

Slowly Tamoree turned his burning eyes. "No prayer," he murmured. There was a flash of the old defiance in him. "Too wicked."

At dark the next day there was a turn for the worse. As a native attendant put it, "The devil entered into him." He thought people were coming to kill him with swords. Then he thought the chiefs had poisoned him. Then the Old Fellow had seized him to take him to hell. He leaped up and ran, shrieking for help.

When Elisha saw him the next morning, dressed for burial, his handsome features were composed and he looked the prince once more. Kealiiahonui said sadly, "My brother found not the good way of life."

ONE GREAT TRUTH Kaahumanu had learned from her humiliation by the American man-of-war chief: laws alone could not reform her people. The people must be taught and persuaded; one by one each must receive a new heart.

So she planned a tour of Oahu. With Binamu, Namahana, Laanui and a large company of native teachers she circled the island, speaking her thoughts about the word of God. She provided horses, two wagons and two canoes to convey any who grew footsore; but nearly three hundred of the band walked all the way. Those who had books took them, and many carried slates and pencils. Each day the native teachers taught the *pi-a-pa* and the catechism; and wherever they stopped, Binamu read from the scriptures.

So far, there was only one translation of the gospel according to St. Matthew. Hiram Bingham had labored twenty months on it, comparing the Latin, the English and the Tahitian versions with the original Greek, that the Hawaiian words might say with clarity and precision all that the original narrator had set down, all that King James' translators had preserved and intensified. Now, seeing how eagerly the crowds of *maloed* natives listened as he read from his manuscript, Hiram knew that his work was good.

But not good enough for the press. At Lahaina William Richards, with Taua, the Tahitian, and Malo, the Hawaiian, had done another translation; and on Hawaii Asa Thurston and Artemas Bishop had made a third version with Governor Kuakini to help them. There were many hours of meticulous comparison and revision to come. *Matthew,* the first book of the scriptures in Hawaiian, would not be ready for printing for another year at least.

Meanwhile, Hiram carried the Word to all the back districts—to Kaneohe, to Koolauloa, to Waianae, and to Ewa—and, standing under the trees, read of the noble ancestry and humble birth of Jesus, of His strange power and goodly ministry, of men who were cured of dreadful diseases, of a young girl raised up from death, of devils cast out, of multitudes fed with fish and bread, of little children blessed by His hands. He read the stories that made things clear to simple minds, of plantings that flourished and those that withered; of wild, thorny growth that choked untended crops; of a pearl precious beyond others; cf good masters and evil; of servants who were faithful and those who were not; of a little ferment that spreads through the whole calabash of *poi;* of lamps that were destitute of oil; of a *luau* prepared for the highborn who would not come, and of the common folk who ate the roast meats in their stead. And then at last he read of the arrest and trial and sad death of the Teacher, and of how He came alive out of His burial vault and secretly met His followers in the mountains to give them the commandment: "Go ye, therefore, and teach all nations."

While Binamu, in his long black coat, read and interpreted the gospel, Kaahumanu sat nearby in the Chinese chair that they had hauled in one of their carts, her affectionate gaze running through the ranks of her subjects. When Hiram had finished, she rose and, standing barefoot in a white cotton dress, spoke to the gathering, not as a regent, but as a mother or sister.

The ancient tabus, she reminded her people, had been broken, the false gods thrown down and the false priests set at naught. But the people must not think that peace and order could be had in the land without laws, or eternal happiness without self-denial. Listen, she exhorted, to the teachings that the Longnecks have brought. Give "prompt and cheerful obedience" to the commands of the true God and be not astonished if the rulers make them binding on all the Islands, forbidding murder, adultery, incest, sorcery and theft. Above all, Kaahumanu pled, let each one seek a knowledge of the truth for himself through the *palapala*.

At Waianae, where the women came together to pray, Kaahumanu knelt down in their midst and led their petition. To many it was a nine days' wonder.

Elisha, at his type case in Honolulu, could remember every inlet, stream, ridge and bay, every cluster of huts and canoe landing, all the hungry-eyed men and eager, timorous women that he and William Beals had visited in 1821. That the *palapala* might reach them at last, he drove himself despite the pain in his side and the dizzy faintness that clouded his vision. He turned out 22,000 spellers in the month the company was on tour, besides six thousand more *Kanawai* tracts. This he managed only because his native helpers were now able to do the press work once the form was locked and the paper moistened and spread. But the boys bore constant watching.

The books went out as fast as they were dry and folded. At the frame house the scholars waited with their gifts, for it was not considered proper nowadays to take a book without making some little return. Those who had nothing to offer sometimes begged for work that they might earn their spelling-books. Once supplied, they walked away, their eyes glued to the strange black characters, their tongues struggling with vowels and consonants.

But ALL THIS did not harvest any sandalwood. Despite the grudging acknowledgments and sulky promises Percival had wrung from the chiefs, no bands had gone to the hills to bring out the wood already cut; and no new trees had fallen but those to build a church Kuakini had ordered at Kailua. Storehouses were bare, and the patience of the traders had worn thin.

In April John Coffin Jones had arrived in the Marshall & Wildes schooner *Tally-ho* ("The best vessel that ever floated on the ocean"), full of exuberance and optimism. Percival, he thought, had done "essential service" to the American concerns—and at a time when Captain Wildes, in Canton, predicted prices of $13 a picul or higher!

In three weeks, though, Jones was writing Marshall, "I can give you no possible hope or encouragement that we shall be paid . . . nothing but the sound of the church-going bell is heard from the rising to the setting sun, and religion is crammed down the throats of these poor simple mortals whilst certain famine and destruction are staring them in the face . . ." So violent is the remainder of this letter, that it suggests a personal grievance against the Mission. John Coffin Jones had one. For Hannah Holmes would not return to him.

Hannah was now with the Longnecks every day in the school-room and many times a week at meetings. Her sisters might stroll arm-in-arm in the public path, laughing and chattering with white men; but she moved only between Pa Homa and the Mission, walking modestly in her long dress and straw bonnet with her hymnal or her speller. She had become fast friends with Kaahumanu and had pledged herself to follow the *Kanawai* to the last "thou shalt." That meant she would give herself to no man who would not marry her.

But perhaps Hannah had not thought *this* man would come out again. Had she started guiltily to overhear them say one day at the Mission, "Jones is here. He came yesterday in the *Tally-ho*"? Or had she learned the news from Polly or Jennie or Charlotte, who were often at the village? Or had Jones, turning abruptly from the company of his fellow-merchants, hurried to Pa Homa and stood suddenly, wind-blown and handsome in his sea togs, with arms open to the woman he had left two years ago—only to hear her say *no*?

However it was, Hannah's ordeal had begun anew. Though she loved the Mission and all that it stood for, she loved John Coffin Jones, too. That much was clear even to the Longnecks. "We have every reason to suppose Jones is desperately in love with Hannah," one of them admitted, "and she in turn has a real affection for him . . . Her trials are peculiar."

So John Coffin Jones, in private anguish, wrote home that "religion the most absurd and unreasonable stalks throughout this land, spreading desolation & dismay." He spoke of a creed that was "a libel on the goodness of God," and of the "hypocritical emissaries sent here from the workshop of their sect." He called the conduct of the missionaries "infamous, degrading, revolting . . ." and was "mute with astonishment that God in his justice should permit such a pestilence to cumber the earth."

Hannah's New England conscience told her to be firm, to go away from Honolulu if she must, but not to live again as the brown wife of the American consul. The Longnecks did not need to admonish her. She knew what she had to do. A native vessel, the *Pakukai*, was sailing for Lahaina, carrying William Richards and his family after an absence of some months from their station. Hannah asked to go with them and live in their household. There, where the young princess Nahienaena had grown pious and Hoapili governed inflexibly in the name of the Lord, she would escape from temptation and from the torture of a love she must deny. Mr. Richards told her she would be most welcome. But she did not go. She was not that much of a Puritan.

At Pa Homa, where the thatched dwellings had fallen into disrepair, Jones presently built a house for Hannah, a coral villa with high basement and broad steps leading up to a wide veranda. Though he had resumed possession of his old inclosure in the village, he would need, he said, to get away sometimes from the worry of business and come to her. If she would not accept him as a lover, then he must be content just to look at her. Surely no one could deny him that small comfort.

KAUIKEAOULI

O N the Big Island, in 1826, the people were building a church. In February, while the *Dolphin*'s bluecoats had Honolulu in hubbub, Governor Kuakini had taken his subjects into the forest to cut and draw down stout timbers for a frame 180 feet by seventy-eight. All summer they worked, erecting and thatching the house and ornamenting the corner pieces. When they had done, it towered, bright and handsome, over dingy Kailua, large enough for nearly five thousand worshipers. By September it was ready to be dedicated.

Kuakini summoned all the Christian chiefs from the leeward and all the Longneck teachers to come and rejoice with his people over the new *hale pule*. The missionaries, scattered now at five stations, took the opportunity to call their "general meeting" in Kailua. On their return trip, both chiefs and teachers, so the plan went, would pause at Lahaina to see eight persons of rank, including the princess, received into the church.

The Honolulu *haoles* rejoiced that Hiram Bingham would be gone from their village. Just to have him out of sight would be bliss, they thought—however things went on at Oahu in his absence. They were glad to part with Kaahumanu, too. But when the rumor rose that King Kauikeaouli would go to the windward, they were acutely vexed.

By 1826 the strife between the "liberal" party and the Mission had become, above all, a contest for the allegiance of Kauikeaouli. Though Boki often played the traders' game, he did not fully satisfy them as an ally. He hedged and vacillated. And, besides, he was inferior in rank and power to the Christian Kaahumanu and Kalanimoku. The liberal gentlemen, therefore, sought to wean the eleven-year-old king from his teachers and persuade him to assert his will in government. In these efforts Richard Charlton, British consul, back now after six months in Tahiti, shared conspicuously.

Charlton cannot have cared a rap whether the Yankee traders collected their sandalwood debts. But if there was anything on foot against the missionaries, he was hand-in-glove with the Boston crowd. He had great influence over Boki, who had tended to be pro-British ever since his voyage. It was Charlton's design to extend his sway over Kauikeaouli too.

As Kalanimoku ailed and suffered, the boy king kept more and more to his own train of *alii* comrades and retainers. Every morning he had a lesson from one of the Longnecks, sometimes from Binamu, sometimes from Lumiki, sometimes from Mr. Chamberlain or from one of the others temporarily at Honolulu. But later in the day he rode horseback with Charlton and Boki or played billiards (Boki now had a table of his own) or went with a jolly *haole* company to the races and afterward to the tavern.

It is not strange that an eleven-year-old preferred these jaunts to study and prayer, nor that he liked to hear again and again from these companions of the afternoon that he was old enough and wise enough to make laws and manage the nation's affairs. In a little while, his liberal friends reminded him, Kalanimoku would be dead. Then if he chose to stand with Boki against tyrannical Kaahumanu and scheming Bingham and to call his kingdom his own, he would probably find foreign residents to back him to the hilt.

Still, the young king loved his "father" Kalanimoku; and, when he sat by the premier's couch and heard that the Longnecks were good and that they sought the welfare of all the Island people, then Kauikeaouli wanted with his whole heart to be like the Iron Cable of Hawaii and win the approbation of Binamu.

Early one morning the traders came in a body to Kalanimoku to protest the king's trip to Hawaii and Maui. "Suppose a ship of war should come to Honolulu and the king not be here!"

Kalanimoku said mildly, "If the king wishes to go, he shall go."

Thus rebuffed, the foreigners hurried off to warn Kauikeaouli that if he went now to the Big Island, he might never return. Kahalaia, they reminded him, had been poisoned by jealous rivals—or so some had said. Was that not sufficient warning that the king should stay close to his proven friends?

It was the hour of the daily lesson, but the presence of a missionary tutor did not check Richard Charlton's tongue. The proposed journey, he blustered, was a plot of Mr. Bingham's to get the king away from Honolulu and perhaps to hold him prisoner at the windward while seizing all his Islands. This "vagabond, liar, hypocrite" —the epithets flowed freely—this schemer whose "cloven foot showed all too plainly under the garb of religion" must be removed from the Mission before he matured his evil designs. Meanwhile, Charlton shouted, he would himself follow the king and protect him wherever he went. "Where the king is," he declared, "there is my home; where he stays I stay; in the house he stops, I stop—if Mr. Bingham is nigh."

Kauikeaouli hardly knew what to make of this. It was the chiefs, not Mr. Bingham who had urged him to go to Hawaii Island. They had told him he could set the people to cutting sandalwood as well as see Kuakini's church. He had thought that would please the *haoles*. But no, it seemed that nothing worse could have been proposed. Were all the Longnecks wicked men? the young king asked.

No, Charlton said. Only Mr. Bingham. But the others were blind. They did not see how their leader was maneuvering to become a dictator.

Kauikeaouli looked from one to another. Then he said he would ask his "father" Kalanimoku what was right, and that he would do.

By eleven o'clock that morning fifteen hundred chiefs and people had been assembled in council in Kalanimoku's yard. At the last moment the premier sent across the way to summon the men of the Mission. Then he spoke long and earnestly. He recited the kingdom's history since Kamehameha had died, reviewed what Liholiho had said before he sailed for England, spoke lovingly of Kauikeaouli. "We acknowledge him king," he said, "but we wish him to follow the counsel of experience." He defended the Longnecks with vigor. Neither Binamu nor any other of the teachers had done anything wrong during all the time they had been there, Kalanimoku asserted.

Beads of sweat gathered on the premier's wrinkled forehead. He who had once talked with such ease labored now in his illness, drained his little strength to the lees. The people listened intently, bending to catch every syllable.

When Kalanimoku sat down, Kaahumanu and Boki in turn spoke briefly in support of what had been said. Let us be united, they urged. Even Boki said, "Let us stand together against the interfering foreigners."

Then the king came in, humble before his elders, but cocky too, knowing himself the center of much concern. He sat between the premier and the *kuhina nui*. Kalanimoku made another speech, short this time, for he was very tired. At the end he turned to the king. It was the united desire of the chiefs, he told the lad, that he should go to Kailua. Kaahumanu, who was to sail immediately, had promised to send the vessel back in a few days. Would Kauikeaouli go then? "Yes," the boy king said. "I will go."

In the harbor a native vessel waited for Kaahumanu and her train. Because she would be gone for many weeks she had gathered all the women of her estates and addressed them lovingly, exhorting them to be strong in the right and to hold themselves from the adulterous foreigners. Hannah Holmes had come and listened, and later she had spoken privately with Kaahumanu about a passage to Lahaina. Hannah said she had not yielded to her American lover, but that she could not forever refuse him if she stayed in Honolulu. No, she must get away to Lahaina and live there as a good woman. In the afternoon she had sent on board a trunk of clothing and had promised to be at the landing when Kaahumanu was ready to depart.

But again Hannah did not go away. Two days later she told one of the Mission that she had been "forcibly detained." And when she thought it over, she said, she saw that it was her duty to stay a little longer. Mr. Jones was sick. He had a swelling in his feet; he needed someone to carry his meals to him. When he was well, Hannah said, she would go to Lahaina. Perhaps when the *Pakukai* came again to fetch the king, she would go. Yes, that would be the time to make her escape from temptation.

By the time the *Pakukai* came back to Honolulu to carry Kauikeaouli to the windward, the boy had changed his mind. For six days the liberal foreigners had applied themselves to his entertainment. Thirty or more of them had ridden with him to Manoa to see sugar made and to partake of a *haole luau*. At dark the cavalcade returned, somewhat noisily, to the village grogshops, proposing to add a night to the hilarious day just ended. Kauikeaouli, remembering perhaps how early his Longneck teacher called each morning to hear him read and spell, stoutly refused to drink more than a glass. But as his comrades grew mellower with every round, the boy could see what wit and banter, what surcease from worry, what light-hearted fraternity he would forego if he joined himself irrevocably to the Christians.

His host at the Manoa plantation had been the British John Wilkinson, once a West Indies planter, who had come out in the *Blonde* under Boki's patronage to introduce sugar-culture in Hawaii. The chiefs granted him some fertile acres up the valley beyond Kaahumanu's estates and the Mission's garden plot, that this new crop might flourish in their land. Wilkinson burned off the rank grass and broke ground with the ox team and plow the Mission lent him. While his plants burgeoned, he built a rude mill for crushing the cane. But the heavy rains of early 1826 washed out his dam and flooded his fields, and sickness decimated the labor force Boki had recruited for him.

The officers of the *Dolphin* had found him likable and had had "frequent and friendly intercourse" with him. One of them had predicted that his experiments would do more toward the civilization of the natives than all the other works of the white man among them. But the fact that rum, as well as sugar and molasses, could be made from the cane had already, in 1826, set the warnings for a storm that was to shake Honolulu through the rest of the decade.

The day after Kauikeaouli rode with the foreigners to Wilkinson's, Boki came in agitation to the Mission. It was medicine he wanted, for the planter. He feared the Englishman was near his end. Elisha, the only man then at the station besides the doctor, sent also a written note of spiritual admonition. But Wilkinson, unconscious when Boki reached him, was soon exploring firsthand the "awful subject of eternity."

The planter's death did little to dim the spirits of those who had made *luau* with him on his last day on earth. They were as ready as ever to propose escapades that might divert the boy king from leaving Honolulu. But better than a dozen jaunts and revels, better even than trumped-up charges against Mr. Bingham, was the card fate dealt them just before the regent's vessel returned. For that night murder was done in Honolulu.

Five or six natives, coveting the new clothes of a Spanish sailor, had followed him as he went to bathe. Drunk and hotheaded, they had not waited till he removed his finery. Near the pond they struck him down with a skull-crushing blow, stripped him and threw his body into the water, covering it with grass. As it turned out, the murderers had been observed in the act, pursued and three of them taken.

The village foreigners, led by Richard Charlton, cried out for prompt and thorough justice. "Let the fellows be gibbeted tomorrow," they said. "They are guilty; two of them have confessed, and these have sworn that the other was with them. Unless you act promptly," the *haoles* warned the chiefs, "we shall know that you are unfit to govern Hawaii as a civilized nation."

Boki quickly acquiesced. He ordered the gallows set up on the plain, where the whole village might see that he was firm with evildoers. But Kalanimoku said, "Let us go slowly. Hanging is a new thing here. Before it is adopted, let us send for the principal chiefs of all the islands and confer on the subject; and if they approve, then let us put these men to death."

So the execution was delayed. The foreigners were displeased. Some of those who the year before had spoken for caution in law-making now called loudly for strict codes and drastic enforcement—to protect the lives and property of foreigners.

On one point Boki and his brother agreed. They said Kaui-keaouli must now stay in Honolulu, for if he went to the windward, and Boki with him as had been planned, the people on Oahu might commit more mischief.

The *Pakukai,* therefore, departed without the king. And without Hannah Holmes, too, though at first her friends at the Mission understood that she had sailed, resisting, as they joyfully expressed it, "the solicitation of one, with whom she is really in love, who loves her and is kind to her, tho he cannot be prevailed upon to marry her." But she had not gone, and whether John Coffin Jones held her this time by physical force or persuasion was never clear.

After that Hannah came no more to the Mission, and the family hardly ever saw her. Once Levi Chamberlain met her sauntering along near the frame house as if she had hoped to encounter some of her old friends. Was she as happy now as formerly? Levi asked her. Hannah took a long time to answer. She kept looking up the path to the door of the house, at the shade trees—transplanted from the mountains and now grown sturdy here—at the Mission chickens feeding contentedly in the yard. "Yes," she said, with a tremulous smile that faded under Levi's stern scrutiny. The next instant she was tearful. "I cry a great deal," she admitted. "I cry every day." Levi had thought as much.

KUAKINI, GOVERNOR OF the island of Hawaii, thought he had earned a seat in heaven. In the third year of the Mission, when there was no teacher on his island, he had built a *hale pule* for the white man's God. And now that that little chapel had become too strait for Mr. Thurston's congregations, the governor had raised the noble church that was about to be dedicated. He had roused his people to the effort, the strong-armed to get the timbers and *pili* grass, and the skilled ones to thatch and decorate. He himself had swung the ax on the mountain side.

More than that, he had given good laws to his people and fostered the schools. In his frame house at the head of the village he had lived with American dignity, dressed in American clothes. He served tea and coffee; he always asked a blessing at table; he had read his English Bible from Genesis to Revelation and had helped with the translation of Matthew.

But when Kuakini asked to be the first one baptized on his island, he was refused. For all his good works the missionaries said he was not ready for the kingdom. He was not humble and contrite. He had not admitted himself a "lost man" and thrown himself on God's mercy. There were some in his district of far lower rank who had outstripped him in the race for the heavenly prize.

He had sent his ultimatum to Oahu. He would be baptized now, he said, or never. He had thought this was a great blow for his cause, that the Longnecks would not be so foolish as to dispense forever with his aid and influence.

But they did not alter their decision; and when they came for the dedication of *his* church, the chosen ones gathered together and closed the door on him. He beat on the wooden panels; and when they did not open to him, he sat down on the threshold and raged mightily. Through the thatch he could hear the voices in prayer and song, those of his sisters among them. But it was not because they were descended from the ancient kings of Maui that Kaahumanu and Namahana sat with the elect, nor because they had been the queens of the Conqueror. They sang, "Kindred in Christ, for His dear sake a hearty welcome here receive."

Kaukini lifted his big muscular body off the doorstep and stomped home. Behind the green blinds of his little house he wrestled with himself. All night he read his English Bible. "Verily,

verily, I say unto thee," he read, "except a man be born again he cannot see the kingdom of God."

In the morning he sought Binamu. "I am nothing," he said. "Teach me how I shall find a new heart and become one of God's people."

That day Kuakini began the long probation that would lead eventually to his baptism.

PRODIGAL SON

ELISHA, struggling alone with the work of the Honolulu station, had no time to be ill. Every morning at the "palace" he heard Kauikeaouli in his lessons; every Sunday he addressed the natives who thronged Kalanimoku's yard, and sometimes in the afternoon those that gathered at Waikiki. On Friday evenings, while Maria advised the female converts, he met for conference with the men. On Saturday when the men and women came together "to make their hearts joyful" for the Sabbath, he was there to give them the blessing of the Mission. On the first Monday in October there was the "monthly concert," when the faithful the world over joined in praying for missions. Three hundred natives passed up a horse race to attend and hear Lumiki speak.

There was correspondence. There were visits to the sick and the wayward. Kalanimoku, unable to rise from his couch, expected a daily call from his Little Teacher. There was farm work to be done on the plot in Manoa.

The printing was in abeyance, and that was good. For the weariness and the grim ache in his side receded so long as Elisha did not swing the lever of the press. If he did, even a time or two, the pain flared, hot and fierce, and all his strength oozed, until he reeled and staggered. Dr. Blatchley, who had pronounced both himself and Elisha too ill to stay another season in the islands, said it was the climate. Enervating the doctor called it. Bad for the liver. A sea voyage and the return to a temperate zone should, he thought, put them both back on their feet. Had it not done so for Daniel

Chamberlain?

Elisha wondered. If a cooler climate was all he needed, surely he could find one nearer at hand. In the uplands of Hawaii, above Hilo or Kailua, couldn't he rest a while and breathe bracing air without deserting the Mission and going back to America? Matthew was almost ready for the press, and the other gospels in the early stages of translation. Thousands of copies must be struck off, folded and bound. But nothing would change the doctor's opinion that Brother Loomis ought to go home.

There was another problem about the printing. If Elisha did not crack under the strain of it, the tired little press, it seemed, would. It shook now and chattered like an old man stumbling toward his grave. Someone had proposed that Brother Loomis return to America and print Matthew there. Afterward, his strength renewed, he could come out again with a new press to print the other gospels. At the general meeting in Kailua the brethren were considering all this. They would send word when they had settled the matter.

On a Sunday—one of Honolulu's hottest—Elisha told the story of the Prodigal Son to two thousand listeners. "And he arose and came to his father. But when he was yet a great way off, his father saw him . . . and ran and fell on his neck and kissed him." So went the story of one who returned to his father's house from a far country. As he set forth the scene for the natives in their own tongue, Elisha could see himself walking down the long hill past Doc Harkness', across the bridge at John Hobert's and on through the village to his father's farm. Yes, in Rushville they would fall on his neck and kiss him, no doubt. Though he had not wasted his substance in riotous living, he would return as a prodigal who had nonetheless squandered his youth and his strength. Looks, if not words, would remind him how they had warned in 1819 that this going to the heathen was a foolish, unprofitable thing.

But could he not go home, attend to the publishing, carry a first-hand report from the Mission to the Board and the Christian public, set straight in America the record so many seemed determined to skew, put his children in good schools and then, having breathed enough northern air to invigorate him for a decade or two, come back, bringing a new press and a good font of type with plenty of *k*'s?

The pain and the dizziness told him that, if he went, he would not come back.

Levi Chamberlain and the Ruggles family were the first to arrive from Kailua, bringing the minutes of the general meeting. Elisha read what he had expected to find: he was to return to America "for the double purpose of improving his health and of superintending the printing of publications in the Hawaiian language."

It was the season of departures. He began immediately to seek a passage home.

THE KIND-EYED CHIEF

AT mid-afternoon on October 11 the United States sloop of war *Peacock* was off the bar at Honolulu, signaling for a pilot. Less than an hour later she was moored in the inner harbor. For the first time in many months a vessel had crossed the bar under full sail without ever having anchored outside. It was a good sign for any who sought omens.

The *Peacock*'s commander, Thomas ap Catesby Jones, a thirty-six-year-old Virginian, could boast a Navy career even more distinguished, if slightly less melodramatic, than John Percival's. Seven youthful years spent at New Orleans suppressing smuggling and piracy, had, unlike Percival's early exploits, given him a respect for law and government. And the War of 1812 had found him as ready and shrewd, as gallant and bold as ever Mad Jack had been. Battling LaFitte's Baratarian pirates or a British fleet in Lake Borgne—becalmed, outnumbered, wounded, his ship in flames or his crew decimated—he had fought so brilliantly that afterward he had been awarded "high praise" by a court of inquiry and honored with a sword by his native state.

After five years as inspector of ordnance at the Washington Navy Yard Lieutenant Jones had been dispatched to the Pacific under Commodore Hull. Now, because all reports, even Percival's, cast doubt on the success of the *Dolphin*'s visit to the Islands, Hull had sent the poised and affable southerner to complete the job.

Jones expected no paradise at the Islands. He had heard that the country lay barren and the people starved; that commerce languished, theft and murder were rampant, and American property

284

insecure; that the inept native rulers were misled and hoodwinked by self-seeking preachers. He had heard, too, that British influence, fostered by Consul Charlton, threatened American enterprise and prestige. But he was no man to accept what he heard without question. He had always been disposed to have a look for himself.

From the deck of the *Peacock* he saw the terraced foothills green with flourishing *taro* patches. He came ashore to be welcomed as urbanely by Boki and Kauikeaouli as by John Coffin Jones and John Ebbets. Kaahumanu was still at the windward and Kalani-moku confined to his house, but in the name of all the chiefs the young king insisted that he would supply the *Peacock*'s crew of 180 with free provisions as long as the vessel remained in port.

"You are not to pay for anything," he said, smiling boyishly among his uniformed body guardsmen. "You are our welcome guests. No, you shall not pay for anything at all."

Though Jones was pleased, he did not accept the offer. He found, despite the rumors of famine, that his purser could buy in the Honolulu market "an abundance of fine Hogs, Goats, Poultry and Fish; also sweet potatoes, Taro, Yams, and fine cabbages and Pumpkins, some Irish potatoes, onions . . . with many other culinary productions—the supply always keeping pace with the demand, and that too without enhancing the prices."

The lieutenant did accept a residence on shore—Kaahumanu's two-story wooden house—with such apparent pleasure and gener-ous thanks that the natives named him "the kind-eyed chief." If he found the town of Honolulu a bit boisterous, he was not at a loss to name the cause. "What might we not expect of sailors," he asked in one of his earliest reports, "when those who convey them there and who ought to set a better example declare that 'there is no Law round Cape Horn' . . . and . . . that the Rulers of the Islands have no authority to punish foreigners who transgress their Laws?"

Glad as he was to talk at length with his countrymen about their problems, Lieutenant Jones proposed that a message be sent at once to Kaahumanu on Hawaii, requesting her return. Both the American consul and his British colleague shook their heads at this. Kaa-humanu, they said, had been so disturbed by Percival's visit that nothing would now persuade her to come to Honolulu while an American war vessel was in port. Jones took the statement as a sour commentary on his predecessor's relations with the Hawaiian government and waited, quietly studying the people with whom he had important business to transact. Not until he had been a full month in port did he meet the chiefs in council. By that time he had observed a good deal.

For one thing, he had read the Mission's circular, issued at the general meeting at Kailua and sent to Honolulu to be printed and distributed.

Goaded by the whisperings and hints—and indeed, by the out-spoken accusations of the British consul—that their leader schemed for political control of the Islands, the brethren at Kailua had voted to publish a new statement of their goals and a defense of their policies. Hiram, assigned the task of composition, took up his pen with alacrity. He had lately borne in silence so much sneering, backbiting and reproach—heard himself so often called King Bingham and his gospel pronounced bigotry and sham—that he was at the bursting point. In Honolulu he had always kept a rein on his tongue; there was at best too much loud, loose talk, and anything he said could be distorted, garbled and turned against him and the Mission. But now, appointed by his fellows to fight back—though with dignity, of course, and restraint—he sprang to his task like a brig taking the "trades."

Addressing himself to the "Friends of Civilization and Christianity," he quoted again those words that had rung in the ears of the pioneer band as they left their homeland: "You are to aim at covering these islands with fruitful fields and pleasant dwellings, and schools and churches, and raising up the whole people to an elevated state of Christian civilization." In the light of this commission he went on to justify the course they had pursued for six and a half years. He acknowledged the difficulties and claimed for himself and his colleagues only a modicum of success, but he defended the methods and utterly denied the self-seeking.

"We have sought," he wrote, "to inculcate on the people that they must render to all their dues . . . being not slothful in business but fervent in spirit, serving the Lord . . . We have to all, both chiefs and people, insisted not only on a belief of the doctrine, but also obedience to the precepts of the Bible, including justice, honesty, integrity, punctuality, truth . . ." This was aimed at the foreigners who day after day blamed the Mission for the chiefs' "dishonesty" in the matter of the debts.

You could see Hiram warming to his assignment as the paragraphs rolled on, see him growing confident and almost gleeful. "Is it nothing," he asked, "that the vices of the drunkard and the gambler, with which the land was formerly almost overrun, should now be limited to a comparatively small number?—that schools should be established in every part of the islands, and be attended by 25,000 scholars? . . . If all this is nothing, then we confess that our labors have been in vain. If we . . . have mistaken the grand principles of reformation, or if we have taken a wrong step, we will be grateful to any man who in a friendly manner will inform us of it."

Then came the challenge. "From those gentlemen who reside or occasionally touch at these islands, we ask an investigation of our conduct. We do more—we challenge it."

Below the eight signatures was the notation: "By the General Meeting of the Sandwich Island Mission, at Kailua; signed by all the members present from the five stations."

When the script reached him in Honolulu, Elisha tore the dustcover from his type case, estimating that the piece, in double column, would run to more than three pages of folded demy. He set the date line, reached into the upper case for the heading, cut in a capital *W* for the opening "Whereas." Since the days at Bemis' he had liked cogent, resounding words that came alive in his ears as he set them in his composing stick. These did.

He had not expected to use the press again. His native helpers were dispersed. But the text was tonic for him. Three hundred times he swung the lever that there might be an abundance of copies; and if he ached and grew faint, he said nothing of it.

"This morning," he wrote on October 26, "I carried copies of the circular letter to the village and distributed them among the foreigners. I have since heard that they have made quite a ferment."

A CALABASH OF SOUR POI

FROM the first the Mission had set its face against gambling. It was bad enough, the American teachers thought, that the Hawaiian sports were invariably the occasion for betting. It was far worse, they held, when the gambling was done in billiard halls or dramshops, where drink whetted avarice, and losses whetted thirst. They were distressed to see that Kauikeaouli went often now to Boki's place to stake his dollars or his silver plate or his uncut sandalwood on the roll of a ball.

There were always plenty of native talebearers to report the details—how Mr. Charlton had praised the king for his manly independence. "That's right," he had said to the lad about his gaming. "That's like King George. That's very good."

But it was not good, the Longnecks warned the young king. "There is no harm in play," they told him, leading the daily lessons from spelling to conduct, "if it is not carried to excess. But gambling is wicked. It is forbidden in the word of God." Kauikeaouli did not like being scolded. He preferred to hear Richard Charlton or John Coffin Jones say that he should make all the laws, that nothing should be forbidden in Hawaii by Kaahumanu or Bingham or God, but only by himself, the twelve-year-old king.

One Sunday in "meeting," Levi Chamberlain came out boldly on the subject. "Theft and gambling," he said, "are two great sins that grow out of covetousness. They are of equal magnitude. No member of God's kingdom can countenance either."

Boki listened respectfully, for he found it easy to lead a double life—on Saturday to drink and gamble with the liberal party and join them in cursing out the missionaries; on Sunday in his best

European suit, to pray and sing with the Longnecks and sit stolid through the sermon. None of the others, he could see, preached as stirringly as Binamu; but what they said amounted to the same thing—no fun on earth, every delight forbidden. That was all very well for Sunday. Monday he could go to the Britannia or the Jolly Tar or the Good Woman (for the Honolulu taverns were beginning to adopt names and hang out signs) and make merry again.

But the *haoles* in the village badgered him. How did he like being classed with the thief who stole the missionaries' bread knife? someone would ask, grinning, as Boki picked up his cue. Hadn't he had enough of being insulted by the Longnecks? Boki thought it over and decided that he had.

Sunday came again; and upwards of three thousand dusky listeners squatted thigh to thigh in Kalanimoku's yard, respectfully attending to a young convert's sermon on "Ephraim is a cake not turned." As the native preacher closed, Boki rose in the midst of the congregation and in strident tones proclaimed that he had a thing to say.

"I have been charged," he began in Hawaiian, as all eyes turned toward him, "with being a thief. Yet I have done nothing wrong— nothing. King George in England told me that I, Boki, should watch over the king. This I have tried to do, but the foreign teachers—they have held it against me. They do not like what I do, and they call me *thief!*"

Astounded, Elisha and Levi Chamberlain saw the congregation turn their way as Boki thrust out his long arm and pointed.

"Where is my fault?" he shouted. "What have I done?"

Boki folded his arms. There was a moment of silence before he hurled his ultimatum. "From this time we shall attend this meeting no more—the king and I. We shall have our own minister and our own place." He stalked toward the gate.

Elisha sprang up to intercept him. "Governor Boki." He spoke low in Hawaiian as the chief came up. "You are mistaken—you have been misinformed."

Boki glared down at the little Longneck. "I have not," he said sharply. "I know."

He left the yard, but the rest of the congregation sat still in their places, for the meeting was not over. They looked down their noses, shamed that a great chief had behaved so indecorously. At dismissal they pressed around Levi and Elisha, offering their *aloha* in the manner they had learned from the Longnecks, by grasping the hand and shaking it hard. It was long before the two men, half-suffocated and limp of arm, were allowed to cross over to the Mission house. Even then fifty or sixty followed them home.

"What did Boki mean?" Elisha asked a petty chief.

"We do not know," cried a dozen in chorus. "But we love you, our teachers. You are not bad, as Boki said. You are *maikai*. We love you." Some of the people wept.

When Elisha and Levi were admitted to Boki's house next morning, they found him seated on the floor, wearing only his *malo* and counting his pearls. In his left hand he held a great heap of lustrous stones; with the right he plucked them out, one at a time, and placed them with others of like size on the mat in front of him. He did not look up.

"Boki," said Elisha, "we want to have some conversation with you."

"What conversation?"

"About what you said of us in meeting yesterday. Which of us has done you wrong?"

"Him." Sullenly Boki pointed to Levi.

"When, pray tell?" cried Levi.

"On Sabbath-day-week."

Elisha and Levi looked at each other.

"Boki," said Levi, "I did nothing of the kind. I spoke against gambling and said it was a great sin—as great as theft. I did not say *you* stole, or even that *you* gambled."

"I heard."

"Now, see here, Boki," said Elisha. "If you heard that a week ago yesterday, why weren't you angry then? You have been pleased ever since, until yesterday. What happened yesterday?"

Boki counted his pearls in silence. He had emptied his hand and begun to rearrange the piles. Then impatiently he tossed all the stones into one heap.

"Gambling is not wrong," he said. "King George gambles. So does his minister, Mr. Canning. I will gamble, and the king will gamble. You wish to prohibit everything we delight in."

"*We* prohibit nothing," Elisha protested. "The chiefs—"

It was not their business either, Boki asserted. It was Kauikea-ouli's alone. The king should make laws and not the chiefs. This, Elisha recognized as the liberal party's line. "We have nothing to say on that point," he declared with finality.

On the surface the affair was as trivial as the tantrum of a naughty child. Yet it could cause real trouble for the Mission. "We had better talk with Kalanimoku," Elisha said.

The old chief lay on his mat, breathing heavily with pain, but when Elisha and Levi entered, he opened his eyes and spoke a warm *aloha*. He had heard, he said, how his brother Boki had accused certain Longnecks. But he wished that Lumiki would tell it all again, just as it happened. He closed his eyes and listened to the recital. Elisha thought the premier had fallen asleep and did not hear; but when he broke off and motioned Levi to retire with him, Kalanimoku called, "Stay."

Elisha went close then and sat down beside the low bed.

"You have committed no fault," Kalanimoku said. "Boki is to blame; he is mistaken. He has done wrong. You have my confidence. I love you. Boki is wrong. We all know he is a gambler."

"He stands alone," said Laanui, the husband of Namahana, speaking of Boki later that day. "It is only one who has become an enemy."

Namahana said, "Boki is but a calabash of sour *poi* that swells till it runs over the sides."

On Tuesday Kalanimoku sent the Mission eight fine mullet. Manuia sent five. And to outdo them in showing favor, the king on Wednesday sent forty assorted fish from the royal ponds.

WRITTEN WORDS

AMONG the proposals that Lieutenant Thomas ap Catesby Jones wished to lay before the Hawaiian government were some additions to the port regulations, some "articles of arrangement" about the trade and a new tax law, looking toward the speedy liquidation of old debts. Unlike Percival, he wished to put everything into writing, that matters might be well studied and fully understood before the formal exchange of promises. For this, he must have a translator—someone who knew the written language and could turn out a document worthy of official signature.

At the Mission he had expected to find such a person, one who had done page after page of scripture in Hawaiian and knew the overtones of the words and the shadows they cast in the minds of those who read with uncertainty and wariness. But the translators were in Kailua, conferring over Matthew. At Honolulu were only Dr. Blatchley, Samuel Ruggles, Levi Chamberlain and Elisha Loomis. And because he had dealt with the written word far more than the others, Elisha became the translator of the lieutenant's crucial papers.

Other matters crowded the days. Only in the warm, sweet nights was there time for the exacting task. Such phrases as "ad valorem" and "most favored nation" were almost as new to Elisha as their Polynesian equivalents would be to the chiefs. Sometimes he wondered whether he could do the thing he had undertaken. But he had to do it. For here, in these formal, pompous papers, the American government was saying in effect, "You, the chiefs of Hawaii, are the rulers of a sovereign people, advanced so far in learning and diplomacy that difficult matters may be settled by reasonable discussion, and mutual decisions recorded for the guidance of both our nations in days to come."

The traders had always talked of coercion: "Let the United States gunboat come, and we shall get our debts fast enough." Now the gunboat had come; and its commander proposed, not to frighten or punish recalcitrant savages, but to *negotiate a treaty*. Elisha shut himself up in the printing office and burned the Mission's tallow candles recklessly as he wrote, struck out, revised, challenged, despaired and with fresh courage wrote again.

On TUESDAY, November 14, though Kaahumanu had not yet come from the windward, Lieutenant Jones called the chiefs into conference to hear the first of the words his government had sent him to speak. Certain foreigners had told him he was foolish to wait for "the old woman." Boki, as governor of Oahu, and the king, fast approaching years of discretion, they said, had power enough. And if not, the ailing Kalanimoku would confirm whatever those two sanctioned. Whether or not he trusted this advice, Jones thought it time to make a beginning. He knew the negotiations must be slow if they were to be successful.

"The Sandwich Islanders, as legislators," he reported afterward, "are a cautious, grave, deliberate people, extremely jealous of their rights as a nation and are slow to enter into any treaty or compact with foreigners." Elsewhere he wrote of "their abhorrence at impetuosity in any person with whom they have to transact business" . . . "I made it an invariable rule, therefore," he said, "never to press a point when I could discover the slightest disinclination on their part to discuss the subject, but by giving them their own time to canvass and consult together, I found no difficulty in carrying every measure I proposed."

In all, Thomas ap Catesby Jones stayed eighty-seven days in Honolulu. He gave elegant *luaus* and costly gifts, far exceeding his expense allowance and flattening his private purse. But, as he told Congress almost twenty years later in justifying his course, it would otherwise have been impossible to accomplish a single object of his mission "without resorting to harsh and coercive measures."

A month after his arrival, then, Lieutenant Jones presented his credentials, proposed his port regulations and gently directed the minds of the rulers toward his treaty. He did not mention the debts until later; but about this time, with the sanction of the chiefs, he began rounding up the American deserters for deportation. No matter how long a fellow had skulked in the Islands, if he could not show his discharge papers, he was arrested. Percival had taken a few of the more recent and readily found; Thomas ap Catesby Jones was more thorough. He summoned all and examined the right of each to remain. Even some who had come legally were ordered away because they had no visible means of livelihood or "did not support a good character."

Thirty vagabonds were divided among the whalers to be carried home. The rest were signed on the *Peacock*'s crew. It was a great house-cleaning. An unaccustomed quiet fell on the port. ". . . for the last several weeks of our sojourn there," Jones wrote to his superior, "the town was equal to the best regulated city in the United States."

Rumor born of hope or malice had it that Lieutenant Jones would take away the two missionaries who had angered Boki. Native busybodies ran to the frame house to report and deplore. They found Lumiki gone to teach the king and Mr. Chamberlain opening hogsheads. Nobody, not even the Longneck women, had time to hear their tale.

THE TRIAL

TWELVE "friends of civilization and Christianity"—among them Meek, Reynolds, Ebbets, Wildes, Grimes, John Coffin Jones and Richard Charlton—replied in writing to the Mission's circular. They would be glad to accept the challenge it posed, and they thought the presence in port of Lieutenant Jones and his officers gave opportunity for a fair hearing.

Elisha sent the word to the Big Island. From peaceful, scholarly deliberation on Greek roots and Hawaiian homonyms, he summoned the translators to dubious battle in Honolulu. They wrapped up their foolscap pages, gathered their wives and children and sailed, arriving at midnight, December 2. Leaving the others on board, Hiram Bingham took Sybil and their two children into the boat and rowing by the tall ships and the guardboat of the *Peacock,* came unhailed and unchallenged in the quiet of the night to the shore he had left amidst commotion more than four months before.

Elisha told the Mission's leader all he had done in that four months—the good and the bad, the wise and the blundering, the fortunate and the ill-starred. The opposing forces, he said, were more clearly defined than ever before: on the one hand the "liberal" foreigners, Boki and his household, and to some extent the king; on the other the Mission, a multitude of the common people and most of the chiefs. And if anyone doubted how the high chiefs felt, there were their letters—from Kuakini, Naihe, Kapiolani, Nahienaena, Hoapili, Hoapiliwahine (once called Kalakua), Kaikioewa, Kinau, Kapule, Kaahumanu, Kalanimoku and John Young. As soon as he had distributed the circular, Elisha had begun to gather these testimonials.

John Young wrote from his retirement at Kawaihae, "During the forty years that I have resided here, I have . . . seen this large island, once filled with inhabitants, dwindle down to its present few in numbers through wars and disease, and I am persuaded that nothing but Christianity can preserve them from total extinction. I rejoice . . . that a code of Christian laws is about to take the place of tyranny and oppression. These things are what I have longed for, but have never seen till now . . ." Elisha, refolding that letter, remembered the gray-haired seaman-chief sitting beside him in the grass house at Kawaihae, recounting in his deep, drawling voice what he had seen at Kawaihae, at Kailua, in Nuuanu valley.

Kalanimoku had roused himself to put down on paper what his constant neighborliness and generosity and his consistent Christian conduct had long attested. ". . . I know of no faults in you," he had written to his teachers. "If I knew of any I would mention them to you. No, ye are upright . . . Be not agitated; it is on our own account you are blamed; it is not yourselves . . . Examine ye, Mr. Bingham and company, my sentiments, that ye may know; and if ye desire it, transmit my communication to the United States, to our chief. It is with yourselves to do it . . . Karaimoku."

Boki, in no mood to compose a letter of his own, had agreed to sign his brother's. But, reminded by his liberal friends that he had recently given a foreign visitor a screed of complaint against the American teachers (of which the Honolulu gentlemen doubtless had a copy), he saw that he could not now endorse the Mission's work. Some thought his petulant outburst in the midst of a Sunday meeting was an attempt to excuse himself, on grounds of recent injury by the Longnecks, from sharing in Kalanimoku's words of praise. At any rate, he did not sign.

TWELVE OF THE Honolulu *haoles* had joined in answering the Mission's circular; some forty of them came to Boki's house for the public hearing on December 8. But when the two factions were face to face, it was clear that the issue had not really been joined.

"From those gentlemen who reside or occasionally touch at these islands," the circular had said, "we ask an investigation of our conduct. We do more—we challenge it."

And the twelve had promptly responded: "The persons whose names are subscribed desire to express their readiness of mind to comply with the invitation, and to accept the challenge. . . ."

Yet on the eve of the meeting, when the place and hour were under discussion, they had somewhat changed their tune. Then they "had no wish or intention of arraying themselves as . . . accusers, or appearing as . . . judges." They had, they insisted, "expressed no readiness to make an investigation . . ."

So the meeting started badly—without chairman or agenda, without well defined issues or accepted burden of proof. Through William Richards, whom it had named its spokesman, the Mission took its stand squarely on the now-famous circular. "If there is no one who appears to point out . . . any mistake in our grand principles," they maintained, "or anything wrong in the steps we have taken, then we leave it to the friends of civilization to judge whether the ground we have taken is not feasible, and our circular to be approved."

Richard Charlton, protesting that he was not an accuser, began presently to spin a thread of complaint about the schools. "Very, very much dissatisfied," he said he was. When men were obliged to quit their work and repair to their books several times a day, so much mischief was done, so many fertile fields went to waste, such ruinous consequences threatened the country, such a dearth of supplies confronted visiting ships . . . He broke off to return to the iniquity of the schools. In one of them he had seen with his own eyes, he said, four couples committing fornication during prayers.

Let these charges be made specific, William Richards countered for the Mission. What fields had gone to waste? On what island were they? What ruin threatened whom? What vessels had been unable to buy vegetables? Where, precisely, was the scandalous school Mr. Charlton had visited? Who were the fornicators? Let these things be written down. Let Mr. Charlton call his witnesses.

Other liberals chimed in. If there were ever so many witnesses, they grumbled, not one would dare testify against the Mission. Two chiefs, not named, had said day before yesterday, "If we should tell the truth, our heads would not remain on us one month." Captain Ebbets flung out irrelevantly, "Who supports you? Who gives you your bread? Who gives you your meat? Answer me that?" And when he did not get an answer, he added, "If any of you ever go to America I'll prosecute you."

"What have you called us here for? What have you called us here for?" another captain put in sharply.

The quiet words of Lieutenant Thomas ap Catesby Jones were like a dash of water on rising flames. "I propose that the circular be read, entire." Some persons, he said, had obviously misunderstood it from looking at it in detached parts. Let them hear it all again.

Here and there among the traders you could see impatience and resentment as William Richards lent his deep voice and pastoral manner to Hiram Bingham's scholarly rhetoric. But the lieutenant listened like a judge, weighing every line of it. When he rose again, he summed up the circular's purport almost as if he had written it himself. "Now," he said, "as I see it, it is the business of those gentlemen who replied to this circular to direct the attention of the missionaries to some special charge and bring their evidence in support of it; otherwise nothing can be done. For surely no one expects the missionaries to arraign, try and condemn themselves." For his intrusion, if such it was, he begged the company's pardon.

The American consul moved adjournment. If his country's ranking representative felt that way, what was there for the rest of them to do?

The lieutenant saw that perhaps he had gone a bit too far. He sprang up again to add that he did not appear as the champion of the missionaries, that he knew the missionaries might err as well as other men. Where he thought they could improve he was ready to express it to them. But this he did believe: that if, as all would allow, many and great evils existed in the land, there were other reasons to account for them besides the presence of a Christian mission.

Stephen Reynolds repeated the motion to adjourn. The "trial" was over.

At Namahana's house Kaahumanu waited for a report of the meeting. "The Lord turned their counsels into foolishness!" she exclaimed when she heard, and added, "I told Boki if the missionaries were found bad and sent off the islands, I should go with them."

ONCE FOR ALL Lieutenant Thomas ap Catesby Jones had decided in favor of the Mission. In his official statement on the "trial," he declared it "the most perfect, full, complete and triumphant victory for the missionaries that could have been asked by their most devoted friends." In the month he remained at Honolulu after the meeting in Boki's house he was as assiduous in showing good will toward the Longnecks as in negotiating with the chiefs.

He entertained the whole Mission company, examined the letters of approbation from the chiefs (which, because of the farcical nature of the meeting had not been presented there) and sought the views of the brethren on the delicate matters he was commissioned to settle. He invited Hiram Bingham to preach aboard the *Peacock* every Sunday so long as the sloop was in port. When he called a conference on the debts he invited not only the principal chiefs and Consul John Coffin Jones, but, as advisers and interpreters, all of the men at the Honolulu station.

Thus, by action as well as by official pronouncement, he let it be known that he found the charges against Hiram Bingham groundless and the work of the Mission worthy of encouragement. John Coffin Jones, whatever his private grievance, could not as an officer of the American government defy its accredited emissary; nor as a business man seeking an adjustment of the debts could he challenge or hinder the steps the lieutenant took with the chiefs. So for a month there was peace among Americans; and Richard Charlton, the Englishman, must retire to ponder his next maneuver.

THE TREATY

FOR the signing of the American treaty the chiefs put on their European clothes. Kalanimoku, whose house had been chosen for the ceremony, lay, heavy and bloated, on a crimson couch to receive his guests—the chiefs in purple broadcloth or dove-colored satin; the chiefesses in brocaded silk, ivory fans in their hands and tortoise-shell combs in their hair; the officers of the *Peacock* in navy blue with gold braid and brass buttons; and the men from the Mission in their Sunday worsteds.

It was the season when the benign "trades" fail and the southerly "sick" winds blast the island with their briny breath. Kalanimoku's hall, for all its spaciousness, was stuffy. Flies swarmed everywhere; *kahilis* were more than decoration.

There was little reason for any to ask here what the treaty provided. Days ago a copy of Elisha's translation, with English and Hawaiian in parallel columns, had been given every chief, each section written out large and clear by hand, because even the most schooled felt more at home with script than with printed words. They had met once with Lieutenant Jones to discuss the items and had gone away to think them over in their own houses.

This was a great and exciting moment for the nation—the making of its first treaty with a foreign power. It was not so much what was promised between the two peoples—perpetual peace and friendship; protection of United States ships, their cargoes, crews, and officers "so long as they shall behave themselves peacefully and not infringe the established laws of the land"; salvage of wrecked vessels; the right to sue for and recover claims; the surrender of runaway seamen; and an equitable system of port fees—it was not so much these separate items that seemed momentous as the assumption of a written obligation to play the game of commerce according to the rules of the civilized world. The young king, though he would not be a signer, looked on proudly.

There was another document, drawn up with Lieutenant Jones' advice. It provided a plan for working off the galling foreign debt built up by the purchases of 1820 and '21. Every man, "unless infirm or of too advanced an age" must go to the mountains annually for sandalwood; "every woman of the age of thirteen years or upwards" must pay a mat or *tapa* or the sum of one Spanish dollar. All moneys collected were to be deposited in "a chest secured by iron hoops and firmly nailed," to be placed under the charge of "some trusty person" and on no account opened without giving notice to the creditors. Payment was to be made every three months, the assets on hand being delivered to the creditors in proportion to their claims.

"It is good," said one chief to another as the meeting began, "that we become honest toward the Americans; but it is bad that we cannot now build the stone house of worship for our own people."

"Yet," said Hoapili, "God will dwell with us, whether we sit within stone walls or under the thatch or even under the sky."

"It is my thought," Kaahumanu said, "that we should pray."

"That is a good thought," said the American lieutenant. He looked at Hiram Bingham. So there was prayer while the *kahilis* waved.

Now, Kalanimoku said, after a little more consultation, they were ready for the signing. But Richard Charlton, like a wedding guest who speaks at the crucial moment rather than forever afterward hold his peace, called out brusquely, "Stop. This thing can not be done!" These islanders, he said, as all eyes turned toward him, were "mere tenants at will, subjects of Great Britain, without power to treat with any other State or Prince." If they entered into this treaty with the United States, England would "assert her right which his King and Country had never relinquished."

Then there was consternation in Kalanimoku's hall, and native murmured to native, "What does this mean?" Had not King George said to Boki, "I will watch over your country. *I will not take possession of it for mine"?*

Lieutenant Jones spoke calmly, measuring his words. What, he asked the Britisher, was the nature of his commission from the English king?

"Consul General to the Sandwich Islands," Charlton replied, not seeing the trap.

"What are your duties or functions?" Jones pressed him, smooth as butter.

Charlton said they were "in accordance with the acknowledged international understanding of the office." He was beginning to sound impatient, annoyed with the inquisition.

Was it, then, customary, Jones asked, "for a Prince or Potentate to send Consuls, Consuls General or Commercial Agents to any part or place *within his own dominions"?*

Nothing now could save the dumbfounded Consul General from his own words. He had given himself the lie. He stood silent, his face dark with rage. Anxiously the Hawaiians turned to the Longnecks for the meaning of this pass between the chiefs from England and America. They did not want anything to go wrong with their great international venture. Kalanimoku, raising himself on his couch, insisted on hearing again all that had been said. At last the whole company was satisfied. Charlton had sunk into the shadows. The signing of the treaty could go forward.

The regent took the quill and wrote, large and clear, Elizabeta Kaahumanu. The premier must be next. Lieutenant Jones had two officers carry the page and the writing materials to him. He signed and sanded. Then Boki signed, and Hoapili, and Lidia Namahana, and last of all Thos. ap Catesby Jones for the United States of America.

A WEEK LATER Lieutenant Jones gave a "splendid dinner." His fifty guests included the American residents, the *Peacock*'s officers, masters of the few vessels left in port, the king, Boki and many other chiefs. But the gaiety was flawed by thoughts of Kalanimoku. Two doctors—the Mission's and the *Peacock*'s—had said he could live but a few more days. It was not the way of the chiefs to feast and make merry when one of their number lay dying. Still, the "kind-eyed" American was their friend, and soon now he would be going back to his own country. So they went to his feast, and then, before twilight had quite left the sky, they hastened again to Kalanimoku's house. The men of the Mission left early too. Though they did not watch at his bedside, they felt very close to their premier-neighbor.

Boki, however, stayed on. And when, hours later, the party was over, he went with his *haole* comrades to make a night of it. Perhaps he had not wanted to be seen leaving with the Longnecks. Perhaps he had meant to go soon afterward and join the watchers at his brother's house. Whatever his intention, morning found him in the village, still carousing.

Kalanimoku had said, "We all know that Boki is a gambler." But when a young chief told him, "Boki has been drinking all night, and even now he drinks," the dying man cried out against the unwelcome news and did not want to believe it. In the days of dark hearts, yes. But not now, when they all knew so well the woes and follies of "the wine when it is red." Anger gave the premier strength. He stood up and called his *kanakas*.

It was noon. The devoted *alii* watchers had gone to their dinner below. In the room were only the back-scratchers, the fan-wielders and those who had brought Kalanimoku his *poi*. He ordered these servants to get his handcart ready, to help him to the veranda and down the steps, to pull him speedily to Boki's house. And there, indeed, was Boki, maudlin, blear-eyed and still tippling.

Kalanimoku stood a while, supported by his *kanakas,* and looked upon his brother. Boki was too stupefied to find any meaning in the visit till Kalanimoku spoke in terrible scorn. "I have heard . . . I have . . . come to see . . . and I now see and know."

Boki began to whimper. "I have sinned," he said. "I am wrong."

But he protested that all was the fault of his *haole* friends.

Kalanimoku did not hear him out. "It is done," he said. "I shall leave you."

At his own door he fainted. The house was in turmoil. The distracted watchers got him to bed; some ran for help to the Mission. When they saw Hiram Bingham take up the medicine kit, they told him Kalanimoku must surely be dead before they could return to him. But they were wrong. The chief rallied and after a few days was so much better that he resolved to go to the island of Hawaii, to the scenes of his young manhood, and there end his days.

1827

ALOHA

IT was the season's end. All but one of the whalers had left Honolulu. The *Parthian* lingered, loading such wretched parcels of sandalwood as could somehow be got down from the mountains. She would sail early in January for Canton. The *Peacock,* Lieutenant Jones announced, would go soon to rendezvous with its squadron off California. Captain Grimes prepared to take the brig *Convoy* to Valparaiso, there to sell her if he could get as much as $8,000. The *Tally-ho* was destined for Norfolk Sound, to be sold to the Russian governor. The *Owhyhee* made ready for one last try at trade on the Northwest Coast. In another fortnight Honolulu harbor would be empty of foreign vessels.

There was a final wave of activity ashore. "Settling bills with various persons," wrote a village merchant; "so many going off makes us over head and ears."

The Loomises were to sail on the *Convoy,* hoping at Valparaiso to find passage round the Horn. Neither Elisha's health, it was agreed at the Mission, nor the printing of Matthew could brook a season's delay.

When they heard that one part of the Bible had been fully brought into Hawaiian and would be printed into books in America, many chiefs came to place their orders. They wanted their copies richly bound like books they had seen at the Mission, in leather ornamented with gold. They would pay at once, that there should be no doubt of their getting the scriptures. Elisha, noting down the deposits, promised that each should have his name in gilt on the red cover.

But the chiefs could not think only of fine books. Every dollar they handed to Lumiki reminded them that now without delay they must begin to make themselves honest toward the *haole* merchants.

In the cocoanut grove below the fort, therefore, they called together the people on the morning of January 2, saying:

"As a nation we have a great debt to the men of America. It is owing since the days of dark hearts, when the king and the other chiefs bought from the foreigners and did not promptly pay them. Fifteen thousand piculs of sandalwood we must bring now from the forests and deliver to these men, or we must give them payment in money or in woven mats or fine *tapa*.

"So before the first day of September every man is to deliver to the governor of his district half a picul of sandalwood; or if he does not wish to do that, let him pay four Spanish dollars or any property worth that same sum. And every woman of the age of thirteen years or upwards is to pay a mat twelve feet long and six wide or *tapa* of equal value or the sum of one Spanish dollar."

This seemed to some a hard thing, until they heard the rest of it—that for the first time in Hawaii the man who cut or carried down the wood should have some for himself. "Every man who shall proceed to the mountains for sandalwood," the new law said, "shall be at liberty to cut one picul and on delivering half a picul to the person appointed to receive it, shall be entitled to sell the other half, on his own account, to whomsoever he may think it proper."

A half the proceeds of a man's work would now be his to keep! Why should any sluggard linger in his house? A Honolulu merchant wrote of this day, "Some came to buy axes before night."

ELISHA RODE alone up the valley Palolo, which no member of the Mission had yet explored. Its utter stillness and its wild, tangled beauty calmed his torn and restless spirit. He had thought no one dwelt in Palolo, but far up the glen he came upon a score of houses in a cluster and found, in one of them, a little school kept by one who had got his letters from a native teacher at Honolulu. From a single tattered, unbound primer they read by turns or learned sentences by rote. Even those who did not know the alphabet could say all the words glibly. Elisha gave them brotherly greetings and wished them well; he had not the heart to say that he was the maker of books and that he was going away.

He came down, then, to Waikiki, where he had conducted worship on many a recent Sabbath; and here word had spread that Lumiki the Longneck was leaving the Islands. So the people crowded around, reaching up their hands to shake his in *aloha.* There had been about forty, he judged, as he rode on at last toward Honolulu. All at once a *kanaka* was running after him, shouting, holding something wrapped in *ti* leaves. Two large fish, the fellow said, from a petty chief who loved the missionaries and was sorry one of them must go to America. Perhaps he would come again?

If God wills, Elisha told him.

ELISHA HAD often watched from the shore as the natives towed a ship beyond the reef. Now from the deck of the *Convoy* he saw them at this task for the last time. They were his friends; they called him Lumiki; they had listened to his sermons, brought presents to his children, hauled coral blocks for his printing office and studied his books. Yet with every stroke they carried him irrevocably from Hawaii, where he had wanted to live out his days.

On shore the brethren and sisters of the Mission had said cheerful and meaningless words: ". . . a well-deserved rest . . . a sea-voyage to make you fit . . . the bracing effect of a temperate climate . . . a return with the next reinforcement . . ."

But Elisha knew in his heart it was farewell.

Below the mist-wrapped peaks the mountain ridges were green in the morning sun, and the valleys between them cool and black. As the brig moved outward, the palm-tufted plain seemed to narrow and the foreign houses and grass huts to huddle together along the edge of the harbor. Off toward Waikiki Elisha could see the Mission buildings—empty and quiet for the moment. Those who had locked the doors and fastened the gates to come to the landing with him had not yet returned and opened up. But in a little while they would be at it again—all the bustle of family life, all the noisy coming and going of natives. Tomorrow the church bell and the singing of Old Hundredth, and on Monday the clatter of the well-worn press as the boys he had trained swung the lever under the direction of Hiram Bingham, who could turn his hand to anything.

If Elisha thought of Moses on Pisgah, he deemed him a fortunate man. For the Lord showed Moses Canaan and said, "Thou shalt not go over thither . . ." and he laid down his task at the brink of Jordan. But Elisha had dwelt for a season in Hawaii and done the Lord's work as well as he knew how and now had been called to go back. That was hard indeed.

He looked toward Maria. She, too, was gazing shoreward, the baby in her arms. She was not pretty any more. Her skin was wind-burned, and there were fine, crisscross wrinkles around her eyes. Downward lines at the corners of her mouth had canceled out its sauciness. Her hair, once curling bright around her face, looked dull and straight and wispy. But her eyes were as blue as ever, and they could still twinkle. Elisha would yet lean on her quiet courage.

The *Peacock,* which had come out ahead of the *Convoy,* was saluting. Locked in her captain's strong-box to be carried to the United States was the treaty—a written document, negotiated, signed and sealed by people who knew what they promised and were glad to do what was just and right. And in a very special sense it was Elisha's treaty. For had he not rendered its legal English phrases into words the chiefs could clearly understand, that a commoner, if he availed himself of the *palapala,* could read in the public posters?

Elisha knew that he would soon be dust, as would Charlton and Bingham, Percival and Jones, Boki and Kaahumanu. New voices would take up the exhortation, the detraction, the defense—and who could say with what outcome? But always, through the wonderful, quiet efficacy of printed words, there would stand the record of what true, peace-loving men, white and brown, had agreed together on a day in 1826, that the "life of the land" might endure in righteousness.

Perhaps that was enough.

APPENDICES

PERSONAGES

HIRAM BINGHAM, 1789–1869, and SYBIL MOSELEY BINGHAM, 1792–1848

How Hiram Bingham, son of Calvin and Lydia Bingham of Bennington, Vermont, became a preacher, found a wife and sailed for Hawaii as the head of the American Board's Mission is told in *Grapes of Canaan*. Something is told, too, of his service to the Mission in its first years—of his preaching, writing, building, doctoring and translating, of how the natives grew to love him and the men of commerce to hate him.

For another fourteen years after 1827—uncompromising, tireless, though often ailing—Hiram Bingham (Binamu to the chiefs, Brother Bingham to his colleagues) continued his leadership. In 1840 because of Sybil's serious illness the Mission "reluctantly, yet on the whole cheerfully" recommended that the Binghams visit the United States.

In America Hiram compiled from his notes and journals a ponderous history of the Mission, *A Residence of Twenty-One Years in the Sandwich Islands,* and solicited from door to door the subscriptions that made its publication possible.

Hiram offered to go out again to Hawaii after Sybil's death in 1848, but the board did not send him back. Times had changed, and the younger missionaries differed with their former chief on many points. Thus the man who for years had symbolized the Mission to both friends and enemies now became, for want of other occupation, the pastor of an African church in New Haven.

In 1854 at the age of sixty-five Hiram was married a second time, to Miss Naomi Emma Morse. Nine years later some of his friends gave him a small annuity, which supplied his needs as long as he lived. His death came in 1869, almost exactly fifty years after the sailing of the *Thaddeus*. Plans in the making to have Brother Bingham return to the Islands for the golden jubilee of the Mission—in April, 1870—had to be given up.

317

Hiram Bingham's most enduring work, perhaps, was his translation. To the Hawaiian scriptures he contributed Luke, Colossians, Hebrews, Leviticus, Psalms 1 to 75 and Ezekiel, besides collaborating on several other books.

ELISHA LOOMIS, 1799–1836, and MARIA SARTWELL LOOMIS, 1796–1862

Elisha, son of Nathan and Dorcas Loomis of Middlesex Township, Ontario County, New York, was the seventh child in a family of eleven. Half a mile from the village that later took the name of Rushville, he spent his first sixteen years like any frontier boy born at the turn of the nineteenth century. He learned to ride, to plow and plant, to build and—though school terms were brief and teaching often inept—to read, write and cipher with assurance.

At sixteen, when J. D. Bemis of Canandaigua advertised for an apprentice, Elisha persuaded his father to bind him out to learn the printer's trade. The indentures promised that for five years—until he was twenty-one—he would "faithfully serve" his master, "his secrets keep, and his lawful commands everywhere obey." He would not "go to taverns or any other places of resort or otherwise absent himself day or night from his master's service without his leave."

Elisha, however, did not serve out his articles. With his master's permission and encouragement (for J. D. Bemis was a man of good will) Elisha offered himself as missionary printer in the spring of 1819 and soon afterward departed to attend the summer term at the Foreign Mission School.

In September, when he was returning from Connecticut to say his farewells in Rushville, he stopped over in Utica to avoid traveling on Sunday. And in Utica he met Maria Sartwell. Maria was twenty-three, well educated for a girl of that day, attractive, skilled in the household arts—particularly in the weaving of linen. She had taught school, but in 1819 her occupation was the folding of books for the publishing house of Seward and Williams.

Somehow the boyish printer destined for the Sandwich Islands and the young woman who had "long been wishing to engage in a Mission" were introduced. On September 16 Elisha wrote to Samuel Worcester of the American Board: "I have now spent several days with her—could not be more pleased with a person . . . I cannot but regard what has taken place as a particular interposition of Divine Providence." Elisha and Maria were married in the vestry of the Presbyterian Church, September 27, and had "a sort of reception" at the home of Publisher Seward.

When, in 1827, the Hawaiian adventure was over and Elisha brought Maria and their three children back to Rushville to his father's house, he grasped at whatever offered a livelihood. There was an opening with the *Rochester Observer,* a religious weekly in the raw community on the Genesee River. In the two years that followed he not only spent hours at his own type case and press but pushed forward, in the face of harassing delays and blunders, the printing elsewhere of 125,000 tracts and thousands of pages of the gospel according to Matthew, Mark and John. In that period he talked almost incessantly for the cause of the Hawaiian Mission, visiting missionary societies and church meetings in scores of upstate villages. He wrote, tóo, answering some of the hostile articles that appeared in the quarterlies and weeklies.

By the fall of 1830 Elisha's health would no longer permit him to work as a printer. He closed up his business (with assets "about eighty dollars in money and some household furniture") and left Rochester. By canal packet and lake schooner he made his way to Mackinac Island, where at the American Board's Indian mission he taught young Ojibways their letters, edited a spelling-book and tried to rid himself of the illness which he sometimes thought was a liver complaint, sometimes called a disease of the spine and finally diagnosed as consumption. Increasingly he longed for Hawaii and wrote of returning there some day. But the Board had seen the folly of sending any but the most rugged into the foreign field.

In 1832 Elisha was again in Rushville, where he opened a "select" school in the upper story of the dilapidated district schoolhouse. To shelter his family, which now consisted of Maria and five children, he built himself a small frame house, which stood among apple trees on a two-acre lot he had "bought" from his father. Before the new venture was two years old, however, he was forced to suspend his school. His disease now had the best of him.

For two years more, Elisha, ill and without regular income, strove to provide for his family. But despite economy and resourcefulness the ends would not meet. He wrote to the American Board. What could the Board do for a disabled missionary? Rufus Anderson, the new corresponding secretary, was kind but cautious. The Board, as always, had more claims on its funds than it could meet.

About three hundred dollars in all was eventually granted, the last hundred dollars to enable Elisha to spend the winter of '35–'36 in Florida in quest of health. It was June when he got home to Rushville, "greatly fatigued." In New York he had caught a severe cold. For the next two months he was much of the time in bed, taking morphine to quiet his racking cough. He died on August 27, 1836.

SAMUEL WHITNEY, 1793–1845, and MERCY PARTRIDGE WHITNEY, 1795–1872

"There is in this college a young man, belonging to the Sophomore Class, named Samuel Whitney," wrote Chauncy A. Goodrich, a Yale tutor, in August, 1819, addressing Samuel Worcester of the ABCFM. "Being considerably advanced in life," Mr. Goodrich continued, "he looks forward to five more years of preparatory study with great reluctance." Whitney, therefore, the letter states, had applied "for liberty to offer himself" to the Hawaiian Mission "as a Schoolmaster—or Instructor in common literature and the first elements of religion."

Goodrich thought the young man, a native of Branford, Connecticut, was well qualified for the post he sought, not only because of his "attainments in Latin and Greek" and his "habitual kindness and patience" but also because of his "sound constitution" and "large and athletic frame."

A few days later Samuel Whitney wrote about himself, confessing to some boyish wildness before the age of eighteen but picturing himself since that time as circumspect and pious. He had been apprenticed to learn the shoemaker's trade, but on hearing of the "deplorable condition" of the heathen had resolved to follow the long course that would make him a preacher and a missionary.

Accepted for the Mission, he looked about for a wife, and with the aid of friends found one in Mercy Partridge of Pittsfield, Massachusetts.

Three days before the *Thaddeus* made Hawaii Samuel Whitney had a narrow escape, and the tale of that near-drowning is still told wherever there are descendants of the pioneer company. Whitney, full of energy and seeking exercise was overside on a temporary scaffold, helping to paint the vessel. A rope gave way, and Samuel was plunged into the sea. An able swimmer, he kept himself afloat until he gained a bench one of his brethren had thrown from the deck. The helm was put to and a boat let down; in a few minutes Samuel Whitney was safely on board again. The bench, too, seems to have been rescued, for the Whitneys kept and used it in their home at Waimea, Kauai, for many years.

At the Islands Samuel Whitney continued his studies and in due time was examined and ordained by his brethren Bingham and Thurston. Only two couples of the *Thaddeus* company ended their days in Hawaii —the Thurstons and the Whitneys. As Hiram Bingham put it: "Mr.

Whitney drawn, like Moses, from the flood in March, 1820, . . . used and laid down his silver trumpet at Waimea, and, Dec. 15, 1845, ascended from the mount of Lahaina-luna" on Maui, where he had gone seeking to renew his health.

ASA THURSTON, 1787-1868, and LUCY GOODALE THURSTON, 1795-1876

When Asa Thurston, a Yale graduate and a senior at Andover, was accepted by the American Board, he did not know any young woman whom he could ask to share his missionary service. But a fellow-student had a cousin, Deacon Goodale's daughter, who taught school a few miles from her home in Marlboro, Massachusetts. It was not hard to arrange a meeting nor to win Lucy Goodale's consent to a life partnership with this earnest and stalwart missionary, eight years her senior. The wedding was on October 12, 1819, less than two weeks before the *Thaddeus* sailed from Boston.

Most of their years in the Islands the Thurstons spent at Kailua on Hawaii. They had five children, and because Lucy refused to send little ones back to America as the other Mission families did, the young Thurstons were educated by their parents until they reached their late teens.

Twice when it was time to place grown children in college or seminary, Lucy traveled to America, leaving Asa at his post. She doubled Cape Horn five times and traveled more than ninety thousand miles by sea; Asa never went back, even for a visit, but lived out his fourscore years in the Islands, dying in 1868.

When, in 1870, the Mission celebrated its golden jubilee, only Lucy Thurston and Mercy Whitney were there to represent the pioneer company. For an hour and a half "without faltering and in a clear voice" Lucy told a churchful of listeners about the early days on the Mission.

Two years later she undertook to write the story of her life. "First driven, then drawn" to the task of rereading, editing and arranging her journals and letters, she completed the work in November, 1875, and wrote this dedication:

"To the American Board of Commissioners for Foreign Missions, who have been the guide and life of my riper years, and the nourisher of my old age. Lucy G. Thurston."

SAMUEL RUGGLES, 1795-1871, and NANCY WELLES RUGGLES, 1791-1873

As early as June, 1817—almost two years before anything was said to

Hiram Bingham about the Mission—Samuel Ruggles was writing to Samuel Worcester of the ABCFM, "I am told . . . that I have been made mention of . . . as one . . . to be qualified to return with the natives of Owhyhee to their Country to preach the Gospel.'

Ruggles liked the idea, but as all his twenty-two years had been spent in poverty, he hastened to inquire: "What can be done for my support?"

Youngest in a family of nine, he had been an orphan from an early age. An older brother had helped him, and friends had taught him to read and write. At sixteen he had resolved to get a liberal education and if possible to become a preacher, but the going had been exceedingly difficult. By 1817, though he had got through Vergil and had just commenced the Greek testament, he thought he would have to give up his studies and "get into business somewhere."

"I have one consolation," he wrote to Dr. Worcester, "that if God has anything for me to do he will bring it to pass."

Apparently God and the ABCFM saved Samuel Ruggles from going into business. Even before the Foreign Mission School was opened at Cornwall, he entered the employ of the Board as teacher and agent. Some of his time he spent soliciting funds for the school and some of it instructing the Hawaiian boys. He alone of all the missionaries knew Obookiah.

When the time came to look for a wife, Samuel found Nancy Welles of East Windsor, Connecticut, was willing. They were married shortly before the *Thaddeus* sailed.

Stationed first at Waimea on Kauai with Samuel and Mercy Whitney, the Ruggleses were afterward assigned to Hilo and still later to Kaawaloa, where the chiefess Kapiolani was their generous patron. But Samuel had never been robust and by 1833 he was ordered home to America. The change seems to have given him new strength, for he lived—first in his native town of Brookfield, Connecticut, and later in Fort Atkinson, Wisconsin—to be seventy-six. Nancy survived him two years.

THOMAS HOLMAN, 1791–1826, and LUCIA RUGGLES HOLMAN, 1793–1886

The story of Thomas and Lucia Holman—all that is known of it—is told in the main narrative of *Grapes of Canaan* up to that day in October, 1821, when they sailed away from Honolulu in the ship *Mentor,* bound for the United States.

The *Mentor* reached America in March, 1822. The Holmans went to Bridgeport, Connecticut, and there the doctor undertook to establish himself and build at home the career he had missed abroad. But in Connecticut in 1822 many good people were horrified at the thought of excommunication. Whatever the doctor's side of the story, they were inclined to distrust a man who had fallen under the church's displeasure.

In vain Dr. Holman struggled to do in Bridgeport what he had so readily accomplished in the foreign quarter of Honolulu—to justify himself and throw the onus on others. In vain he begged the American Board for a statement of vindication. Broken in spirit, he declined in health. In 1826, four years after his return, he died—the first of the pioneer Mission group to go. And by a curious edict of fate, Lucia was the last. She moved back to Brookfield, her native town, and presently became the wife of Esquire Daniel Tomlinson, a man of prominence in Brookfield. After his death in 1863 she went to live at New Milford with the daughter that had been born in the Islands. "Forgotten among mankind" she outlived even Lucy Thurston by a decade, dying in 1886 in her ninety-third year.

DANIEL CHAMBERLAIN, JERUSHA CHAMBERLAIN, and their five children: DEXTER, NATHAN, MARY, DANIEL AND NANCY

On a day in March, 1819, Daniel Chamberlain, substantial farmer of Brookfield, Massachusetts, presented himself at the Charlestown home of Rev. Jedidiah Morse and said that he would like to be considered for the Sandwich Island Mission. Dr. Morse, a member of the American Board, looking the candidate up and down, saw that he was in his middle thirties and had a strong, lean face and friendly blue eyes. Then the preacher opened the letters of recommendation Daniel had brought with him from neighbors in Brookfield.

"He is a man of decent talents and education," one had written, "well informed and skilled in husbandry, none more so, a man of energy and perseverance in what he attempts, of economy and judicious arrangements, who has been prosperous in all that he has put his hand to . . ."

Daniel's pastor, Rev. Eliakim Phelps, had written, "Captain Chamberlain (the title came from Daniel's rank in the militia) is a man of respectability in this place . . . and so far as we can judge a real lover of the cause of religion . . . I can conceive of nothing that should induce him to leave his present situation but a desire to do good . . ."

To this mild testimony Daniel added his own sincerity and earnestness. He said he had a wife and five children, a comfortable home, a productive farm and many friends in Brookfield, but was willing to sell his farm, dispose of his furniture and uproot his family in order to have a share in the work of evangelizing the heathen.

The men of the Board were taken with him and apparently saw no obstacle in the size of his family. By April 15 they had notified him of his acceptance "as an assistant in the contemplated mission to the Sandwich Islands."

Daniel decided at once to send his older sons to the Foreign Mission School at Cornwall for the summer term, paying their board and tuition so that they would not be an expense to the institution. Thus Dexter and Nathan had received a good grounding in missionary theory and had made friends with the native boys before the *Thaddeus* sailed.

On the voyage Daniel had charge of the cabin stores. It was his eye that measured the shrinking sugar supply, his hammer that ripped open a new cask of beef, his nose that detected spoilage in the lime-watered eggs, his say-so that disposed of moldy cheese and rotten potatoes. He needed no female help in planning the daily menus; he served what he had. "Our provision is good," he observed, "and no one ought to complain of it." Some did, apparently, but Daniel refused to be upset about it.

All through the 18,000-mile trip and through the first hard years in Hawaii Daniel and Jerusha were Father and Mother not only to their own brood but to the whole inexperienced band. In their quiet, comfortable way they ministered to the Mission as truly as did those who preached on Sunday. They were the salt of the earth.

Of their life after their return to America in 1823, the Mission annals tell almost nothing. The family settled in Westboro, Massachusetts. Elisha Loomis, who called on them in July, 1827, wrote back to the Islands, "Mr. Chamberlain's family are doing well, boys grown up— Dexter living at Pawtucket."

And there the record ceases.

THE SECOND COMPANY (the first reinforcement)

The Reverend Artemas Bishop and Mrs. Elizabeth Edwards Bishop
Abraham Blatchley, M.D., and Mrs. Jemima Marvin Blatchley
Levi Chamberlain, secular agent

PERSONAGES

The Reverend James Ely and Mrs. Louisa Everest Ely
The Reverend Joseph Goodrich and Mrs. Martha Goodrich
The Reverend William Richards and Mrs. Clarissa Lyman Richards
The Reverend Charles S. Stewart and Mrs. Harriet B. Tiffany Stewart
Betsy Stockton, a Negro, who accompanied the Stewarts

The Native Youths Who Came to America from the Sandwich Islands

OBOOKIAH, the careless New England pronunciation of
OPUKAHAIA (Oh'poo kah heye'ah) "Ripped belly"

Born about 1792, orphaned at twelve in tribal warfare, schooled by a priest-uncle in the rites of paganism, Obookiah ran away to sea at fifteen and came eventually to the attention of students and teachers at Yale University. He was educated in various New England parsonages and became a church member and an enthusiastic Christian, taking the baptismal name of Henry. He was known for his good-natured mimicry as well as for his piety and industry. "Who dis?" he would ask his American friends, then imitate the manner of someone they readily recognized.

His death from typhus came in February, 1818, at the Foreign Mission School in Cornwall, Connecticut, where he was in training to return as a teacher to his own people.

HOPU (Hoh'poo) "Catch"

Hopu, whose Christian name was Thomas, left his home in Kohala to go as cabin boy on the same ship that carried Obookiah from the Islands. The two boys became fast friends as they voyaged to China and around Good Hope to New York and New Haven. There they attracted the interest of the Yale students and received some instruction in English. While Obookiah continued his studies, Hopu chose the life of a sailor, and served in several privateers during the War of 1812. Later he hired out as a coachman, but in 1815, unemployed and destitute, he was ready to take passage back to Hawaii if one offered. His old friends in New Haven persuaded him to accept their help and to resume study. He became a member of the Foreign Mission School when it was opened, sailed with the pioneer company in 1819 and served the Mission faithfully for many years in the Islands.

HONOLII (Hoh noh lee′ ee)

Honolii, whose Christian name was John, arrived at Boston in 1815 in a ship belonging to Ropes & Company, merchants. He had been taken aboard at the Islands to supply the place of a sailor who had died. When benevolent New Englanders offered to see him educated, Ropes & Company "cheerfully released" him and gave $100 toward his expenses. He was then about nineteen years old. Eventually joining the other Hawaiian boys at the Foreign Mission School, he was commended by the principal for his "considerable vigor of intellect" and his "discreet and stately deportment." Though he did not speak English with the ease and clearness of the boys who had been longer in America, he proved especially helpful to the missionaries in the study of the Hawaiian tongue, because he retained "his native language in a high degree." He sailed on the *Thaddeus* and served, both at Honolulu and at the Kauai station, as interpreter and assistant during the early years of the Mission. Somewhat frail in health, he dropped from the scene in a relatively short time.

KANUI (spelled Tenooe in the earliest records; Kah noo′ ee)

William Kanui came to Boston about 1809 with Captain William Heath Davis. A boy of twelve, he hired out as servant in a "respectable family." Like Hopu he served on privateer cruises during the war. Afterward he worked in several public houses and at length went to New Haven to learn the barber's trade. When he was discovered by some Yale students who offered to pay up his debts, he consented to "go to studying" under their direction. Presently he joined Obookiah and Hopu at Goshen, where they were being tutored prior to the opening of the Foreign Mission School.

Though Kanui was reported as "unexceptionable in his conduct" as long as he remained in America, he caused the Mission much concern almost from the day the *Thaddeus* sailed. Stationed at Kailua in 1820, he proved so recalcitrant and wayward that the Mission soon excommunicated him. For twenty years he remained outside the church, though much of that time he was somewhat friendly to the Mission. At last, about 1840, he was received again into good standing.

TAMOREE (Tah moh ree′ ee)

Tamoree, as the prince of Kauai was called in New England, is a quick, slipshod pronunciation of the name borne by his father, Kaumualii. The boy's American friends spoke of him as George P. (for Prince) Tamoree, but on Kauai after his return he was known as Hume-

hume (Hoo' meh hoo'meh). Tamoree's mother was apparently a woman of the common people. Since rank in Hawaii was inherited through the distaff side, this placed Tamoree, though he was older, below his half-brother Kealiiahonui. For a time Kaumualii seemed disposed to consider Tamoree as heir apparent, but after the events of 1821 and 1824 had wiped out the last vestige of Kauai's independence, the question ceased to be important.

Tamoree's story from his arrival in America about 1807 to his death in Honolulu in 1826 is told in the main narrative of *Grapes of Canaan*.

THE OTHER HAWAIIANS

BOKI (Boh' kee) "Boat" or "Boss"
A younger brother of Kalanimoku, Boki was governor of Oahu most of the time between 1819 and 1829. He went with Liholiho to England, returning on the frigate *Blonde* when Lord Byron brought home the dead king and queen. After that, Boki led the opposition to Kaahumanu and Kalanimoku, bringing the Islands to the verge of civil war. Encouraged by foreigners, he engaged in several business ventures and ran deeply into debt. In 1829 in hope of retrieving his fortunes he organized an expedition to seek sandalwood in the New Hebrides. From this undertaking he never returned; his vessel and all aboard her mysteriously disappeared in the South Pacific.

HOAPILI (Hoh ah pee' lee) "Joint partner"
This chief, a young counselor in the days of Kamehameha I, took Keopuolani to wife after the Conqueror's death. He thus became guardian of her children, the prince and princess. Though later Prince Kauikeaouli returned to Honolulu and came under the guidance of Kalanimoku, Hoapili continued to have charge of Nahienaena. When Keopuolani died, Hoapili chose the dowager Kalakua and was married to her in a Christian ceremony. In 1824 Kaahumanu appointed him governor of Maui, an office he "sustained with dignity" until his death in 1840.

KAAHUMANU (Kah ah hoo mah' noo) "Feathered"
Oldest daughter of Keeaumoku, one of Kamehameha's loyal chiefs, and Namahana, one-time queen of Maui, Kaahumanu became the best-loved wife of Kamehameha I and, by his dying wish, *kuhina nui,* or guardian of the realm. Liholiho named her regent in December, 1823,

when he left for England. She continued in this post when the boy Kauikeaouli succeeded his brother as king. Ruling with a firm hand, she was opposed much of the time by foreigners and by a native party led by Boki. She died in 1832.

KAHALAIA (Kah hah' lah ee' ah)
A nephew of Kalanimoku, this young chief governed Kauai between the abduction of Kaumualii and the rebellion of 1824. He died in the epidemic of 1826.

KAIKIOEWA (Kah ee' kee oh eh' vah)
Father of Likelike, and staunch friend of his son-in-law, Kalanimoku, this high-ranking chief, was made governor of Kauai after the rebellion of 1824 and held the post as long as he lived, using his influence to advance Christianity in the Islands. His death was in 1839.

KALAKUA (Kah lah koo' ah)
A younger sister of Kaahumanu, Kalakua was one of the wives of Kamehameha I and the mother of two of Liholiho's queens, Kamamalu and Kinau. After she married Hoapili, she took the modest name of Hoapiliwahine.

KALANIMOKU (Kah lah ne moh' koo) "Rent heaven"
Sometimes this chief's name appears as Kalaimoku, which means prime counselor. Foreigners, paying tribute to his statesmanship, called him Billy Pitt after England's Sir William. Because of his courage and energy, the chief's countrymen hailed him in his later years as "The Iron Cable of Hawaii." He was friend and adviser to Kamehameha I, led Liholiho's army to victory in the civil war of 1819 and served as prime minister until his death in 1827.

KAMAMALU (Kah mah mah'loo) "The shade"
Liholiho's favorite wife Kamamalu was the daughter of Kamehameha I and Kalakua and therefore a half-sister of her husband. She was one of the foremost in the new learning brought by the Mission. She died in London on July 8, 1824.

KAMEHAMEHA I (Kah may hah may' hah) "The Lonely One"
Born (probably) in 1758 while the night skies were lighted by a "fiery star" with a flaming tail, Kamehameha the Great united the Islands by

conquest, then ruled them in firmness and wisdom. He died in Kona, Hawaii, May 7, 1819. "Only the stars of the heavens know the resting place of Kamehameha."

KAPIOLANI (Kah pee' oh lah' nee)

Descended from the ancient kings of Hawaii and holding great tracts of land on that island, Kapiolani and her husband Naihe became converts about 1824 and thereafter did much to help the missionaries. Kapiolani died in 1831.

KAPULE (Kah poo' leh) "Prayer"

When the missionaries first visited Kauai, Kapule was Kaumualii's queen, though she was not the mother of either George Tamoree or Kealiiahonui. At first when her husband was carried off to Honolulu and made consort to Kaahumanu, Kapule remained on Kauai, but eventually she moved to Oahu and found a new partner in a chief named Kaiu. In baptism she took the name of Deborah and Kaiu took that of Simeon. Their child was christened Josiah Kaumualii, after "a good man in scripture and a good man (lately dead) in Hawaii."

KAUIKEAOULI (Cow ee' kay oh oo' le) "Hang on the dark sky"

This brother of Liholiho, born 1814 to Kamehameha I and Keopuolani, became king in 1825 when the news of his predecessor's death reached the Islands. He did not assume full power, however, until after Kaahumanu's death in 1832. In 1840 he gave the Hawaiians their first written constitution, a document which showed strong American influence. It created a representative body, chosen by the people, and thus for the first time granted the commoners a share in government. He was known for "mildness of character, amiability of disposition and soundness of judgment." He died on December 15, 1854.

KAUMUALII (Cow moo ah lee' ee)

Kaumualii is the correct Hawaiian form of what New Englanders called Tamoree. Both the father, king of Kauai, and the son, George, actually bore the name, but in this form it almost always refers to the father, who for years ruled the leeward islands. In 1810 Kaumualii, yielding to Kamehameha's threats and the Yankee traders' persuasion, voluntarily ceded his kingdom to the Conqueror and became a tribute-paying vassal. Abducted from his home island in 1821, he lived on Oahu until his death in 1824. He was said to be always mild and gracious in manner.

KEALIIAHONUI (Kay ah lee′ ee ah hoh noo′ ee) "The King Whose Strength Is Attained through Patience"

Royal son and heir-apparent of Kaumualii, Kealiiahonui received this name in 1810 when his father and Kamehameha I made their peace. In 1821 he, as well as his father, was compelled to unite with Kaahumanu, that there might be no attempt to reestablish the old regime on Kauai. After Kaumualii's death, Kealiiahonui and Kaahumanu desired a Christian marriage, but were denied on grounds that scripture forbids a man to have his father's wife. Both were afterward baptized and received into the church. Kealiiahonui eventually married another woman.

KEEAUMOKU (Kay ay ow moh′ koo)

This brother of Kaahumanu was named for his father, a chief close to Kamehameha I. White men called him Cox. He governed Maui from 1820 until his death in 1824.

KEOPUOLANI (Kay oh poo oh lah′ nee)

She was the "high tabu chiefess," the sacred wife of Kamehameha I, mother of Liholiho, Kauikeaouli and Nahienaena. The first chief to be baptized, she died at Lahaina in 1823 and was given Christian burial there.

KIAIMAKANI (Kee eye mah kah′ nee)

This was the chief who fomented rebellion on Kauai in 1824.

KINAU (Kee′ now)

Kinau, a daughter of Kamehameha I and Kalakua, was one of Liholiho's five wives. Though she gave him no heirs, she later, as the wife of Kekuanaoa bore two sons who became kings—Alexander Liholiho, who reigned as Kamehameha IV, and Lot Kamehameha, who was Kamehameha V. She succeeded Kaahumanu as *kuhina nui* and for that reason was often referred to as Kaahumanu II. Kinau died in 1839.

KUAKINI (Koo ah kee′ nee)

A young brother of Kaahumanu, Kuakini (by foreigners called John Adams) was governor of Hawaii Island from 1820 to 1845. A part of this time he governed Oahu as well. After his conversion he stood for a rigid enforcement of all laws on natives and foreigners alike.

LAANUI (Lah ah noo′ ee)

A chief of the third rank, he became the husband of Namahana and abetted her in her good works.

330

LIHOLIHO (Lee ho lee′ hoh)

Liholiho (Kamehameha II) was born in 1797, son of Kamehameha the Great and his "sacred wife," Keopuolani. In his fifth year Liholiho was made heir to the throne and caretaker of temples and gods. From that time on, he was trained in the rites of the old religion. Civil war broke out in 1819 when, after his father's death, he defied the tabus, but his army triumphed and the rebel leader, a cousin of his, was slain. Liholiho ruled the Hawaiian kingdom until his departure for England in late 1823. He died in London on July 14, 1824. He had five wives—Kamamalu, Kekauluohi, Kekauonohi, Pauahi and Kinau—but no children. He was, therefore, succeeded by his younger brother Kauikeaouli.

LIKELIKE (Lee keh lee′ keh)

Daughter of Kaikioewa and favorite wife of Kalanimoku, this chiefess died in childbirth in 1821.

LILIHA (Lee lee′ hah) "Disgust"

Boki's wife, the daughter of Hoapili, succeeded to the governorship of Oahu when Boki left the Islands in 1829. Because of her laxity in enforcing the laws, she soon fell under the displeasure of the older chiefs, especially Kaahumanu. She was removed from office in 1831 and replaced by Kaukini, who for a time governed both Hawaii and Oahu. When Kauikeaouli came of age and assumed full authority, many expected him to appoint Liliha *kuhina nui,* but he named Kinau instead.

NAHIENAENA (Nah hee eh′ na eh′ na) "Raging fires"

Daughter of Kamehameha I and Keopuolani, sister of Liholiho and Kauikeaouli, this lovable princess, born 1815, lived only until her twenty-first year. Once a faithful church member and teacher, Nahienaena had turned away from the Mission before her "wasting sickness" came upon her.

NAMAHANA (Nah mah hah′ nah)

Named for her mother, the queen of Maui, Namahana was a sister of Kaahumanu and Kalakua. She was extremely fat and good-natured, and the commoners, who loved her, called her by her pet name Piia. In 1824 she became governor of Oahu while Boki was in England. Her consort at that time was the minor chief Laanui. When Namahana was baptized, she chose Lydia as her Christian name.

PAUAHI (Pow ah′ hee) "Fire-destroyed"

This queen of Liholiho derived her name from the fact that as an infant she narrowly escaped death by fire. She died in 1826.

GLOSSARY OF HAWAIIAN WORDS

AE (ah' ay) : yes (in full assent)

AIKANE (eye kah' neh) : friend

AKUA (ah koo' ah) : god

ALII (ah lee' ee) : chief, king, the nobles

ALOHA (ah loh' hah) : love, affection, greeting

AUWE (ou way') : oh! alas!

AWA (ah' vah) : bitter, fermented drink brewed by old-time Hawaiians, not intoxicating

BERETANIA (Ber eh tah' nee ah) : Great Britain

ENUHE (eh noo' heh) : caterpillar

HALE (hah' leh) : house

HALE PULE (hah' leh poo' leh) : house of prayer, church

HALE UME (hah' leh oo' may) : house where the common people played at adultery

HALEMAUMAU (hah' leh mow' mow') : house of fire, fire pit of the volcano Kilauea

HAOLE (hah' oh leh) : foreign to Hawaii, a foreigner; hence, a white man

HAPAHAOLE (hah' pah hah' oh leh) : part foreign; hence, part white

HEIAU (hay' ou) : large place of worship, temple

HEWA (heh'vah) : fault, error, sin

HOLOKU (hoh loh koo') : woman's dress in "Mother Hubbard" style

HOOHAKAMOA (hoo' hah kah moh' ah) : cockfighting

HOO-ILO : Fall and winter; according to David Malo, "the season when the sun declined towards the south, when the nights lengthened, when days and nights were cool, when herbage died away."

HUHU (hoo hoo') : angry

HUHU LOA (hoo hoo' loh' ah) : very angry

HULA (hoo'lah) or HULAHULA (hoo'lah hoo'lah) : dance and song

IMU (ee' moo) : ground oven

332

KAHILI (kah hee' lee): fly-brush, feather-tipped staff used as a royal standard

KAHU (kah' hoo): guardian

KAHUNA (kah' hoo' nah): an expert, sometimes a sorcerer

KAHUNA PULE (kah' hoo' nah poo' leh): priest

KANAKA (kah nah' kah): man, human being

KANAWAI (kah nah' weye): law

KAPU (kah' poo): forbidden, Hawaiian form of *tabu*

KILU (kee' loo): adulterous game played by the chiefs

KOA (koh' ah): forest tree

KOU (koo): kind of tree

KOELE (koh ay' leh): field cultivated by the common people for their landlords

KONA (koh' nah): the south or southwest

KONA-KU (koh' nah koo'): south wind

KONA-MAE (koh' nah mah' ay): withering wind from the south

KUHINA NUI (koo hee' nah noo' ee): great regent, guardian of the realm

KUKINI (koo kee' nee): foot racing

KUKUI (koo koo' ee): candle-nut tree

KULA (koo' lah): dry land, land back from the sea

KULEANA (koo' leh ah' nah): very small land claim

LANAI (lah neye'): porch, shed, booth

LANI (lah' ne): sky, Heaven

LAUHALA (l-ow, to rhyme with cow, hah' lah): pandanus leaf used for weaving mats

LUAU (loo' ow'): feast

MAIKAI (m eye' k eye'): good, excellent

MALO (mah' loh): loin cloth

MELE (may' leh): song

MOI (moh' ee): sovereign, king

MOO: small field, part of a chief's estate

OHELO (oh hay' loh): edible red berries

OLI (oh' lee): chant

OPAKAPAKA (oh pah' kah pah' kah): kind of fish, delicious eating

PALAPALA (pah' lah pah' lah): writing, the new learning

PALI (pah' lee): precipice, cliff; precipitous pass in the Koolau range at the head of Nuuanu valley

PAPA (pah' pah): according to tradition, the original female ancestor of the Hawaiians

PAU (pah' oo) : woman's skirt

PAUKU (pah oo' kah) : garden patch, part of a *moo*

PI-A-PA (pee ah pah') : primer, spelling-book

PIKO (pee' koh) : navel

PILI (pee' lee) : coarse grass

POI (poy) : paste or pudding made of *taro;* for the Hawaiian "the staff of life."

PUHENEHENE (poo heh' neh heh' neh) : guessing game played by concealing pebbles under bits of *tapa*

PULE (poo' leh) : to pray, prayer, worship

UKULELE (oo' koo lay' leh) : lice, fleas, a small guitar

UME (oo' meh) : adulterous game played by the common people

WAIKIKI (w eye' kee' kee') : spurting water; in the direction of Waikiki

WAHINE (wah hee' neh) : woman

WAKEA (wah kay' ah) : according to tradition, the original male ancestor of the Hawaiians

OTHER STRANGE WORDS

PICUL (pik' ul—Javanese and Malay, from pikul, to carry on the back, a man's burden) varying Oriental commercial weight; in Hawaii, China, etc. $133\frac{1}{3}$ lbs.

TABU (tah'boo'—Tongan; akin to Samoan and Tahitian) : set apart or sacred by religious custom, forbidden by tradition or social usage; to place under tabu

TAPA (tah' pah—Native name in Marquesas Islands) : barkcloth made from a kind of mulberry tree

TARO (tah' roh—Tahitian) : plant grown throughout the tropics for its edible starchy roots

TI (tee—Samoan) : any of several species of Asiatic and Polynesian trees and shrubs